FORLORN SUNSET

also by Michael Sadleir

Novels

FANNY BY GASLIGHT

THESE FOOLISH THINGS

DESOLATE SPLENDOUR

PRIVILEGE

Non-Fiction

TROLLOPE

BLESSINGTON D'ORSAY

BULWER AND HIS WIFE

THINGS PAST

MICHAEL SADLEIR

FORLORN SUNSET

Where forlorn sunsets flare and fade
   On desolate sea and lonely sand,
Out of the silence and the shade
   What is the voice of strange command
Calling you still, as friend calls friend
   With love that cannot brook delay,
To rise and follow the ways that wend
   Over the hills and far away?

Out of the sound of the ebb-and-flow,
   Out of the sight of lamp and star,
It calls you where the good winds blow,
   And the unchanging meadows are:
From faded hopes and hopes agleam,
   It calls you, calls you night and day
Beyond the dark into the dream
   Over the hills and far away.

WILLIAM ERNEST HENLEY

CONSTABLE · LONDON

LONDON

PUBLISHED BY

Constable and Company Ltd.

10-12 ORANGE STREET, W.C. 2

·

INDIA

Longmans, Green and Company Ltd.

BOMBAY   CALCUTTA   MADRAS

·

CANADA

Longmans, Green and Company Ltd.

TORONTO

·

AUSTRALIA

Dymocks Book Arcade Ltd.

SYDNEY

First Published 1947

*The frontispiece and jacket
are drawn by John Piper*

*The verses quoted on the title page
are printed by kind permission of
Mrs Maud Henley and Messrs
Macmillan & Co. Ltd.*

Printed in Great Britain
by T. and A. CONSTABLE LTD., Hopetoun Street,
Printers to the University of Edinburgh

for

BRUCE MARSHALL

"There are in London localities as little known to the majority of the denizens of the 'great Wen' as the icebergs of the northern seas or the scorching sun-fires of the tropics. . . . Into the recesses of some dark metropolitan obscurities the mind is never led, even by books, maps or charts.

Descend with me to the level of the Thames. We will penetrate the black labyrinths of sloth, of crime, of idleness, of poverty. Stacks of wretched houses, the dwellings of the wicked, the unfortunate, the furtive, the blighted and the damned are huddled together in mean design, one unblushing hotbed of mental and physical decomposition.

These warrens are called back streets, and the back streets of the Waterloo Road are perhaps farther back in the world of morals and the Bill of Health than any other back streets in the suburbs of the metropolis.

Dirty, slipshod, improvident wives of improvident mechanics loiter and gossip in gin-shop doorways with females in figured finery whose occupation is betokened by evidence of stale carmine and a shameless arrangement of dress. Children—squalid, in-kneed, bandy and bow-legged—fester in the fetid air, crying whoop at nightfall and, by day, wayward, wanton and neglected, playing pitch and toss in nooks, corners and bye-places away from the scrutiny of passer and police."

Dombey and Daughter by Renton Nicholson (*circ.* 1850).

"We say quite frankly that all those who are squeamish, and all those who are prudish, and all those who prefer to live in a fool's paradise of imaginary innocence and purity, selfishly oblivious of the horrible realities which torment those whose lives are passed in the London inferno, *will do well not to read* THE PALL MALL GAZETTE *of Monday and the three following days.* The story of an actual pilgrimage into a real hell is not pleasant reading, and is not meant to be."

The Pall Mall Gazette (Saturday, July 4 1885).

* Preliminary to the publication of *The Maiden Tribute of Modern Babylon.*

CONTENTS

CONTENTS

BOOK V: NINE YEARS RUIN AND REND (1869-1878)

BOOK VI: FORLORN SUNSET

Fanny by Gaslight was concerned with the amusements (predominantly vicious) of rich people in London during the seventies of last century. *Forlorn Sunset* is a story of the same period, but presents the evil folk who pandered to those amusements, and the miseries (and therefrom arising vices) of their poor and helpless victims. Inevitably it lacks the glamour of its predecessor, and the characters encountered are for the most part disreputable. These qualities may be regrettable; but they are inherent in the book's theme if it is to be truthfully and consistently developed, and I believe the underworld of the time to have been very much as here portrayed.

MEN, WOMEN AND LONDON

A

1 : EARLY LIFE AND MISFORTUNES
OF PAUL GLADWIN

HIS FATHER had been a pawnbroker who became a money-lender and a rich man, dying, ultimately, a violent death—not at his son's hand, but through his son's fault. This was one of the things that unhappy creature could never forget.

Starting in a small way in a street off Norton Folgate with a young wife and a baby boy, John Gladwin, by grinding toil and by closing his heart to pity, steadily improved his standing and profits. From Hogg Lane he moved to the corner of Brunswick Place and City Road; thence south-west into Clerkenwell; and by the late 'forties was established in handsome premises in Farringdon Street.

The pawnshop proper gave on to this important thorough-fare, with the three balls in gold on the glass panels of the swing-doors and the words MONEY LENT above and below them. Up a lane alongside the building was a second door, always closed and bearing a small brass-plate lettered GLADWIN. To this door came those clients who desired to keep their business especially private. They rang the bell, were discreetly admitted, and in due course shown out again to the tune of several hundred per cent.

John Gladwin was a hard man and a close one. Traffic in misery was to him so much £. s. d., and to the gathering of £. s. d. he gave every hour of his life. Indeed if, as was certain, he did not spare his victims, neither did he spare himself. His wife and only child were now installed in an ornate villa in Highbury, where they enjoyed every comfort except (if comfort it were) the company of husband and parent. Every morning, Sundays included, the master drove down

3

to his place of business and there remained, interviewing clients or poring over his ledgers, until late in the evening. At certain times of year and despite his wife's protests, he even stayed in his office all night, counting his gains, weighing the advantages to himself of leniency here or of sudden foreclosure there, preparing his campaigns for the coming months. On these occasions he was quite alone and pooh-poohed any idea of danger. "Who ever heard of a pawnshop being cracked?" he would demand. "Burglars don't risk their necks over the sort of junk my place is full of." He always treated his money-lending activities as a very minor branch of his business and was careful that no one should suspect the true scale of his dealings.

Yet he had one further ambition beside the piling up of money—to make his son into a gentleman. While the boy was still small and business prospects critical, he determined that Paul should have the best schooling within his reach. He managed during his years of struggle to get a nomination to Christ's Hospital, and made up his mind by hook or by crook to find the money needed for the modest fees. Actually, by the time the lad reached school age, the father's business was well on its feet; and during the years when Paul was a Bluecoat boy his parents and their way of life were becoming rapidly more prosperous and comfortable.

This, as it turned out, was the lad's first misfortune. John Gladwin did not understand that a schoolboy—and particularly a member of such a school as Christ's Hospital then was—must, if he is to make friends and become an integral part of the school-community, conform to the general standards of pocket-money and home-background, and that these must remain constant throughout his time. As his wealth increased, the father advertised the fact by elaborating the son's private life, with the result that his school-fellows held back in embarrassment at their companion's greater resources, and he gradually found himself belonging to no particular group because he was considered too grand for the generality. This slowly intensifying loneliness was the harder to bear because Paul had none of his father's delight in riches, and suffered agonies of shame at each fresh outbreak of ostentatious generosity. He longed to be one of a crowd, to be indistinguishable from his kind, to be driven to the same shifts of economy and to enjoy the same simple pleasures as the huge majority of his fellows. But when he tried in his shy way to dissuade his father from driving him into gilded solitude, he was merely told roughly not to be a fool, and that if only success had come to the business earlier he would now be at Eton or Harrow.

The father was determined not to repeat the mistake of planning his son's life on lines less expensive than he could afford. The next stage of Paul's education must begin as it would go on. Through the agency of a man of good family who was deeply in Gladwin's debt, and in return for a further post-dating of a bill already overdue, the promise was secured of a set of rooms at an exclusive Oxford college, and in due course the schoolboy was packed off to make his début as an undergraduate.

Although he was full of forebodings, and much dispirited by his father's triumphant exhortations to hold up his head with the best of them, Paul welcomed escape from the embarrassment of school. But a term or two at Oxford were sufficient to show the unlucky young man that he was now worse off than ever. Thanks to a large allowance and an equivocal background, he found himself at once courted and isolated. It would have been hard enough, even with parental collaboration, to have concealed the existence of Gladwins of Farringdon Street. Seeing that Gladwin Senior took every opportunity of boasting of his boy at Oxford who was in with all the nobs, and paid him a highly unwelcome visit at a populous moment in the University year, the connection between them was as notorious as though it were placarded about the High. The consequences were inevitable. The College aristocrats treated poor Paul with aloof contempt, but a small group of rather dubious rowdies made a dead set at him. These men were delighted to drink his wine and ride his horses, admitting him in return to the advantages of their boon-companionship. At first he tried to stand out against them. His instincts were orderly and studious; if he could have made two or three friends among the quiet decent under-graduates he would have been happy, and a credit to the college and to himself. But the sort of men he would have liked and who (had they made the experiment) would have liked him, avoided him even more carefully than the real "bloods". Not only were they frightened of his money, but they not unnaturally mistook the persistent attentions of the fast set as proof that this was the milieu he preferred.

So at last, weary of rebuffs from right and left, and because he was essentially the diffident type who depends on some sort of social intercourse for self-expression, Paul accepted the friendships offered him, no others being available. Soon enough he was too deeply involved in his new circle ever to hope to escape from it. He did not really enjoy their mono-tonous and noisy drinking-parties, their ceaseless gambling, the silly practical jokes they played on humble townees. It distressed rather than excited him to double down a lane and scramble over a high wall to escape the Proctor and his bull-dogs. But, as happens in most cases of the kind, he found an easy way to blunt his sensitivity and build up a spurious courage. He began to drink; and as his friends were always glad to drink with him, experiment soon became a habit.

At the beginning of his third year a particularly discreditable escapade, involving the daughter of a tradesman and the wanton destruction of property at an inn in Wallingford, brought him into final conflict with authority. On several occasions already he had been up before the College Dean and before the Proctors, who were at first forbearing and then progressively more strict. Both University and college authorities were now aware of Paul Gladwin as an undesirable specimen, whose rowdiness and extravagance and self-indulgence and drunkenness were something more than mere youthful high spirits. He had in their view forfeited the right to be regarded as "wild", and henceforward was labelled "vicious". So, when the Wallingford episode de-livered him into their hands, they seized their opportunity and sent him down for good.

His reception at home can be imagined. The father, on

6

whom responsibility for his son's downfall really lay, was savage with wounded pride. The mother begged for leniency; but John Gladwin, even if he had not forgotten years ago how to show mercy, was now too angry to think of anything but his own humiliation. He declared that he no longer had a son, and turned the boy out of his house with a hundred pounds in his pocket and these parting words:

"That's all you'll ever have from me, you drunken wastrel; so I advise you to put your fine schooling to some practical use while you can still buy yourself bread and butter."

Bread and butter! Paul hardly knew such food existed, nor did he really believe that his father meant what he said. He took rooms in the West End and, getting into touch with the two or three friends who had been rusticated at the same time as himself, proceeded to make hay as though the sun would never stop shining.

And for a while a sort of spurious sunshine persisted. He won heavily at cards, pulled off a lucky double, and became a familiar figure on the Rifle Grounds at the Primrose in Chalk Farm and to the driver of the last and noisiest Sunday bus from Cremorne to the Haymarket. But after good luck came bad, and prospects were suddenly critical. The average son of a well-to-do father, even though the two were not on terms, would have found means to raise the wind with the help of a bill-discounting attorney or an accommodating Hebrew in Cliffords Inn. But Paul, fortunately for himself, was too nearly related to the professional activities of these gentlemen to dare apply to them. To boast to one usurer of reversionary prospects from another is the worst policy imaginable. So he was driven to do what he told himself he would never do—appeal privately to his mother.

She squeezed what she could out of her housekeeping money, and sent with it a short but terrible letter. She told him that his father was implacable; that his name might never be mentioned. In a final tear-stained sentence, she said with heartrending simplicity that her life was broken to pieces.

Paul fell suddenly into a deep pit of remorse. For several days he refused to see any of his friends, drank nothing and even wrote to his father imploring forgiveness. When he had no reply, he summoned all his pluck and rang the bell at the side-door off Farringdon Street. As luck would have it, the door was opened by his only friend on John Gladwin's staff—a genial honest fellow called Toby Langrish. This man, although he hated the trade his master followed, was too loyal a soul to desert one who treated him with grim justice. He stayed on, therefore, taking such small opportunities as offered of helping the humble clients of the pawn-shop. With the large-scale money-lending side of the business he had no concern, and it was the merest chance that this morning he was on duty at the side-door. He knew nothing of the breach between father and son, and greeted Paul with cheerful heartiness.

"Walk up, Mr Gladwin; walk straight up. The boss is alone."

Paul took a firm hold of himself, mounted the stairs and, lest courage desert him during the seconds it would take to knock and be told to come in, walked straight into his father's room. It was perhaps the third time in his life that he had been there. John Gladwin was at his table, with ledgers open before him and to one side a huge cash-box with raised lid. The box was crammed with notes. The door of a wall-safe, whose very existence Paul had not previously suspected, hung open, showing pigeon-holes stuffed with papers.

For one moment the usurer stared at his son, then with a low roar jumped to his feet.

"How the devil—" he shouted. "Get out of here, d'you hear me? Get out, you blackguard!"

Seizing a stout walking-stick which stood by the fireplace, he rushed forward and struck Paul across the face. The young man turned and fled. He had a fleeting sight of Langrish open-mouthed at the foot of the stairs, and, as he escaped into the lane, heard his father bellowing for the doorman to come up immediately.

With an angry bruise on his cheek and bitter fury in his heart, Paul strode rapidly along Farringdon Street. He was hardly conscious of his direction; and only realised that he had turned north instead of towards the river, when a lump of filth missed his head by an inch and, with raucous cries more like those of animals than human beings, two small bundles of rags shot scuffling between his legs. He looked about him, and his absorption gradually fell away. Though he had never been there before, he knew where he was. He had penetrated one of the most shameful spots in central London—the desolate waste known as the Farringdon Street Extension.

A few years earlier it had been decided to drive a thoroughfare through the tangle of evil slums which lay between Holborn Hill and Clerkenwell Green. Work had been started from the northern end of Farringdon Street and several blocks as far as Chick Lane had been demolished. Then, for reasons never divulged but not unconnected with the interests of a noble landlord, the undertaking had been abandoned. There remained an open space of trodden earth, weeds, rubble, garbage and shallow ponds, with the low ruins of what had been Field Lane and Union Court like stumps of decayed teeth along its western edge. Wooden erections ran out at irregular intervals into this wilderness. They resembled groins on a sea beach, and had been intended to fix the level of the new street and bank it well above the flood-level of the Fleet Ditch, part of which—dark, swift and smelly—still lay open to the sky.

Over and around these groins, in and out of the fetid puddles, swarmed as hideous a crowd of stunted and miserable creatures as could be imagined. These were the rising generation of what was called "Jack Ketch's Warren"—Turnmill Street, Frying Pan Alley, Broad Yard and a whole maze of courts off Saffron Hill. Out in the open boys and girls from six to sixteen fought and gambled and pelted one another and passers-by with stones and mud and rotting cats. In the wrecked houses of Field Lane they clustered in corners, relieving nature, drinking gin, fumbling themselves and one another, sometimes launching yet another unwanted baby into savagery and destitution.

This abominable no-man's-land—the involuntary product,

but still the product, of a callous indifference to suffering for the sake of the rights of property—suddenly loomed over Paul, in his mood of vindictive desperation, as one aspect of his father's livelihood. Miles away in the country was a wealthy lord, whose stewards could invoke the law to preserve this evil wilderness; just down the street was Gladwin's pawnshop, thriving on the misery of slum-dwellers. More than that. The very locality of the Extension made it a symbol of John Gladwin's rise to prosperity; for, like a bridge built of human degradation, it lay between his earlier and humbler spout in St John Street, Clerkenwell, and the spacious premises near Ludgate Circus. There at this moment he sat in his upstairs room, with a safe full of bank-notes and sovereigns, hush-money extorted from the follies or wrong-doing of the rich. There, at street level, wretched women (maybe among them the mothers of these dreadful children) crept in to pledge one of their few possessions for the means to buy a meal or a few hours' oblivion.

Paul's anger flared again. Turning his back on the Extension, he hurried up Holborn Hill and made his way to a tavern in the Haymarket where he was likely to find some of his friends. They were there, and welcomed him vociferously. In half an hour's time they were starting for a race-meeting at Hampton Court. Some jolly girls were going with them, and of course old Paul must join the party. Anything to forget that awful moment in his father's room; anything to dull the pain in his face, and the mingled terror and rage which still possessed him; anything to shut out from his mind's eye the squalid horror of the Extension and the howling outcasts who surged over it. By the time the uproarious coachful had reached the race-course he was irrepressibly drunk, and describing the visit to his father with alternating shouts of laughter and dark threats of vengeance.

It was a low-class race-meeting, and the crowd was hardly even a mixed one. Every kind of shady character had congregated; and the few innocents who had rashly ventured to attend seemed unlikely to get away unscathed. Paul and his friends were neither shady nor innocent. They were out for enjoyment, but were fly to all the tricks of the fraternity. Toward the end of the afternoon, therefore, they had chummed up with a motley group of bookies, tipsters and hangers-on, with whom they adjourned to a convenient public-house to top off the day with a boozing party. One of the girls, sitting on Paul's knee, ran her fingers softly over the great bruise on his cheek.

"Poor lovey" she crooned hazily. "Poor little lovey . . . was it beaten by its nasty brute of a papa?"

With the novelty of something temporarily forgotten, the scene of the morning flashed back into Paul's memory. Too fuddled to recollect that he had already told the story several times, he launched into a long and detailed account of the whole incident, from the moment of his ringing the bell to that of his re-emergence in Farringdon Street. His own behaviour was now presented as considerably more valiant than when he had related it before (and even then it had been well edited). It appeared that he had wrenched the stick from his father's hand, broken it across his knee, laid the pieces on the corner of the table, and with cold dignity retired. To some of those, however, who now heard it for the first time, this part of the story was less interesting than that describing the interior of the money-lender's room. To one or two offhand questions Paul replied with painstaking solemnity. Clearly he regarded them as a tribute to his narrative, and wished to reward his hearers by removing any possible obscurities. Then he ordered another bottle, kissed the girl sitting on his knee, and began to tell the story all over again. It was difficult to get him to stop talking and accompany the party back to town.

That night—or, rather, early the following morning—Gladwins of Farringdon Street was broken into. It happened to be a night round-about Quarter-day, and the money-lender, having worked very late, had decided not to go home. He was taking a nap on a couch in a small room opening out of his office and was suddenly awakened by a noise next door. Hurrying to investigate he found two masked men in his room. The thieves, who had forced the safe and were on the point of departure with the swag, were no less taken aback than John Gladwin to find anyone but themselves on the premises. Seized with panic, one of them struck him violently on the head with a life-preserver. They then made their escape.

When the office-cleaner arrived a few hours later, she found her employer dead on the floor.

*   *   *   *   *

The Gladwin murder caused only moderate excitement. The 'fifties were poorly off for sensational periodicals with woodcuts of crime and disaster; further, to the world at large, the victim was only a pawnbroker, and pawnbrokers inevitably had dealings with shady customers and must take the risks of their trade along with the profits. Finally, Gladwin personally was as little known, even to the poor folk who came regularly to pledge their treasures in Farringdon Street, as was his main money-lending activity outside the individuals who were entangled in it. These were the last people in the world to advertise their connection with the murdered man, especially as those still in his debt had good reason to hope that the calamity to the usurer would mean release for themselves.

The police, therefore, were allowed to track down the criminals more or less undisturbed by amateur advice and staring crowds, and this, thanks to the naïveté of one of the two, they soon succeeded in doing. At the end of a fortnight a man was apprehended, passing a ten-pound note which bore a number recorded in a bank-note register found in the dead man's safe. The fellow confessed he had been one of the cracksmen, but swore that the blow had been struck by his companion. To save his own skin he turned King's Evidence as to the whereabouts of the still missing man, who was promptly jailed. He was found to be a member of a well-known race-course gang, with previous convictions for violent brawling. Public interest now faded rapidly. The affair had clearly been a regulation burglary, transformed by evil chance into assault with fatal consequences. Long before the men came to trial, the volatile attention of crime-lovers had turned elsewhere.

There was no such easy forgetfulness for the dead man's son. In addition to the pangs of conscience he suffered continual terror of being publicly involved. Suppose that either of the ruffians chose to denounce him? Such agonies did this fear cause him, that when after the first arrest nothing happened, he almost prayed that the second criminal would not be found. But he was found; and Paul passed more days in torment. In fact (though he never knew it) the very thing he dreaded had occurred. The man who had been betrayed by his comrade, moved by a wish to live in order to take revenge on the traitor and without any personal ill-will to Paul, declared that the robbery had been instigated by the son of the pawnbroker, who had quarrelled with his father and hired two mercenaries to crack the old man's safe. The police made private enquiries. Paul's alibi during the night was unchallengeable. Two at least of the party present after the race-meeting declared on oath that, though young Gladwin was all-to-hell-scammered, he had never seen either of the men before, never hinted in the presence of the others that they should burgle his father's place, and, as the crowd were together the whole time, had no words with them in private. Finally, the prisoner's record was so bad that anything he said required some confirmation at least before it could be credited. So, with traditional shrewdness, the police left Paul Gladwin alone. They did not wish to stir more mud than was necessary, and they had plenty of mud to go on with.

By degrees Paul's fears of public exposure were stilled, but private worries took their place. He had rejoined his mother in Highbury. She was prostrated by what had happened, and lay in a bewildered coma which her doctor declared might prove to be temporary—or might not. A will was found among the dead man's papers—correctly drawn, witnessed and signed—which post-dated the disinheriting of his son, but had not been altered since Paul's intrusion into Farringdon Street the day before the murder. It was a will at once characteristic and fantastic. It had a certain justice, more than sufficient brutality and a climax almost unbelievable. It settled a modest jointure on the widow, terminable with her death "because I have reason to fear that she will show indulgence to undesirable outsiders if my whole fortune is in her control"; it gave handsome legacies to certain "faithful members of my Farringdon Street staff" (including Toby Langrish); it bequeathed the residue as a personal legacy to the Chairman of a Missionary Society called "The Torchbearers", which described itself as "A Band of Pioneers, vowed to carry God's Word into the Dark Places of our Great Metropolis". To this bequest one condition was attached—that the testator's son Paul should be offered employment by the Society, in any capacity which seemed good to the Committee, at a salary of two pounds per week and no more. This salary was dependent on the recipient doing regularly whatsoever duties were assigned to him. If he neglected his work or proved insubordinate, it was to cease. Mrs Gladwin's jointure fell into the residue at her death, and would in consequence sooner or later increase the benefaction to the Torchbearers.

The prospect which now opened before Paul Gladwin was, to say the least of it, a bleak one. He had no money at all beyond the few pounds in his pocket. While his mother lived, he would have board and lodging; if and when she died, he would have neither, nor means to pay for them apart from the weekly pittance due from the Torchbearers. To earn this he must do their bidding; and it was unlikely, in view of the cruel and contemptuous stipulation which tied him to them like a tin can to a dog's tail, that they would regard him as other than a troublesome incubus and treat him accordingly.

Who were the Torchbearers? Why did old Gladwin select them as principal legatees? How richly did they profit from this abrupt, macabre and wholly unexpected philanthropy?

The Torchbearers were, as they themselves declared, a Society for disseminating Christian doctrines among the London poor. Founded by a devout old lady during the 'thirties, they constituted a small-scale missionary institution

14

of the narrowest evangelical kind. They were not interested in housing-improvement or slum-demolition; they had no educational aspirations; they made no propaganda in favour of open spaces or better sanitation; they did not clamour for control of slaughter-houses or garbage-dumps or over-crowding. Their representatives were taught that humanity's only need was the Word of God as recorded in the pages of Holy Writ; that the unfortunate and the downtrodden and the starving and the diseased would find comfort and plenty and health, if not in this world at any rate in the next, pro-vided they read the Bible or had it read to them. The Society, to the modest limit of its resources, employed missionaries both male and female, who distributed Bibles and tracts in poor quarters of the town, who held meetings in open spaces or in sour little halls or murky sheds, who penetrated the most noisome alleys in obedience to the call of duty. These men and women had the fearlessness of their complete and unimaginative sincerity. They hardly regarded as human beings the wretched people on whose salvation they were bent. Had they done so, their courage must sometimes have faltered. Had they related the shocking scenes of misery and degradation through which they moved to the actual lives of adults and children, there must have been moments when they would have asked themselves who was to blame, on whom might suddenly and savagely the blame be laid. But they never did; and because they were poor grim creatures themselves and betrayed no sign of sympathy or of con-sciousness that the life of the slums was other than ordained, they came and went unmolested, giving their dreary readings and intoning their melancholy prayers, while the population of the hidden streets either ignored them utterly or stood and listened in brutish silence.

That this obscure and rather pitiful little body of harmless fanatics should ever have come under the notice of old Gladwin, and, having come under his notice, should have been selected as his residuary legatees, was due to a queer and ironic coincidence. He had been a regular reader of *The Pawnbrokers' Gazette*, a weekly paper dealing with matters of interest to the trade, which occasionally enlivened its technical and statistical contents with quotations from other papers or from books referring to pawnshops and their activities. In the number which reached him the day after he had given his son a hundred pounds and turned him out of the house, there appeared an extract from the Chairman's address at the Torchbearers' Annual Meeting, credited to him by name. The extract was printed under the heading "As Others See Us"—a feature of the *Pawnbrokers' Gazette* which appeared every few weeks and, with undeniable humour, picked derogatory or derisive comments on pawnbroking from any kind or source, both bygone and contemporary. "God's Word alone" Mr Crocker had declaimed "can bring Light into the Darkness of Sin and Ignorance and Sorrow. Darkness is everywhere. The flaring Gin Palace; the Golden Lure of the Pawn Shop; the Glitter and Spangles of the Theatre or Music Hall are Darkness more profound for their seeming brightness and comfort." "This being so" (commented the irreverent compiler of "As Others See Us") "our confrères may safely reduce their expenses by burning less gas and oil after dark, and doing business by the Light of the Word."

In his mood of raw resentment against everything, John Gladwin read these paragraphs with bitter relish, sent for his lawyer and made his new will, then and there.

"We will see how this Holy Joseph resists the golden lure when it is offered to him" he remarked—"or rather we won't, either of us, but some people will."

The lawyer chuckled.

"I always wondered" he said "why the French say 'mountain of piety'."

He was a cultivated man, who read Paul de Kock in the original.

* * * * *

As matters turned out, this lawyer not only survived to witness the reaction of Mr Crocker and the Torchbearers to the legacy but had a very front seat indeed, for in due course it fell to him to acquaint the Committee of the Mission with their Chairman's good fortune.

A delegation of three called on him by invitation. It consisted of this Chairman, Gervase Wilbraham Crocker Esq. of Lashwater Park in the County of Surrey; the Rev. Aubrey Timms, an elderly but still menacing cleric with small private means, who no longer held a living because he considered the work of the Society to be higher and nobler than that of any parson; and the Secretary-Treasurer, Mr Malcolm Sneade, a darting quick-eyed rather foxy man, who was in the Torch-bearers for what he could get out of them—which up till now had been hardly anything at all.

The trio listened solemnly while the lawyer, having read the clause in the will appointing Crocker as residuary legatee, gave a rough indication of the property involved. Its extent was more than respectable. In cash it was not likely to amount to more than a couple of thousand pounds; but there was house-property in addition—in particular a considerable patch in south London, the value of which, though difficult to estimate, was, to judge from the income which it had yielded in the past, very considerable. Further, as he had that morning received the news of Mrs Gladwin's death, her jointure fell into the residue.

After a short silence Mr Crocker cleared his throat and thanked the lawyer for his clear statement.

"Very gratifying indeed" he added. "Most gratifying. Our work will benefit immeasurably."

"The Lord must have spoken directly to our dear-departed brother" boomed Mr Timms. "Blessed be the name of the Lord."

Mr Sneade's contribution was more practical.

"When does Mr Crocker inherit?" he asked. "How is the estate to be administered? And what about this young man who has to be employed by the Society?"

"I am the sole executor" the lawyer replied. "The debts are trifling; the legacies present no difficulties that I can see. Once the will is proved, there should be no great delay in transferring the balance to your Chairman's control.

"As for the administration of the estate, once it is in his possession, the will contains no instructions. But the testator said to me personally, at the time the document was being drafted, that he relied—and with every confidence—on Mr Crocker's devoting the proceeds of the legacy to the purposes of the Society, even though they were legally his private property. I hope I make myself clear?"

Timms and the secretary half-raised a hand and muttered agreement. Crocker bowed solemnly.

"Good. I will then proceed as expeditiously as possible. It is only fair to warn you that real estate sometimes presents complications in the matter of inheritance; and that although no unnecessary time will be lost . . . Anyway we shall see, gentlemen. . . .

"As for the testator's son, the condition attached to the legacy was admittedly a curious one, but was not specified in any greater detail than has already been stated.

"In this matter also" said the lawyer "I am clear that the Committee are free to make any arrangement they choose."

The delegation then withdrew, assured that they would receive in due course a schedule of their inheritance and that application to the Prerogative Court would be made without delay.

Nevertheless it was not until a twelve-month later that Sneade, Secretary to the Torchbearers, summoned Paul Gladwin to the office in Victoria Street and asked him whether he proposed to accept the situation secured for him by his father's will. He did not invite his caller to sit down; and the young man stood, listless and lonely, with five feet of mahogany between himself and the secretarial arm-chair.

"I have no option" he said with a slight shrug. "What is it you wish me to do?"

"You will pardon my saying so, Mr Gladwin" returned the Secretary—you could almost hear his teeth snap behind his foxy muzzle—"but that is hardly the spirit in which to enrol as a Soldier of the Cross. Even the humblest of God's warriors—and admittedly your position cannot in the nature of things be other than humble—is a Crusader in a Sacred Cause and—"

Gladwin interrupted him. "I apologise for any disrespect. What is it you wish me to do?"

Sneade flashed a vindictive look, seemed about to launch another oration, changed his mind, tightened his lips and picked a sheet of paper from his desk.

"The Committee decided at yesterday's meeting that you be instructed to report on some of the properties which have passed to the Society under the will of the late Mr Gladwin. Here are particulars of the first of them. You will visit it as accredited representative of the new owners, and let me have a written report on the general character of the district, the state of repair of the buildings, and whether the prospects—from the point of view of the Society's income—are favourable or otherwise and, if the latter, how they can be improved. You will find on this paper the name and address of the firm who acted for the late Mr Gladwin as agents and rent-collectors, and you will naturally interview them after you have formed your first impressions of the property itself. Here is a formal letter of authorisation in case you are challenged.

"And now good morning. We are today—let me see, Wednesday, isn't it? Wednesday. Very well. I will expect you in this room next Monday at noon with your report."

He picked up his pen, took some letter-paper from a drawer, and began writing busily. The interview was clearly at an end.

*   *   *   *   *

Gladwin, in the mild afternoon sunshine, sought a bench in St James's Park and unfolded his paper of instructions. The first entry read as follows:

"Angle of Waterloo Road and Lower Marsh, from Granby Street off Waterloo Road to James Street off Lower Marsh. The property (area about five acres) comprises the streets, courts and tenements between these frontages and the ter-

minus of the South Western Railway. Agents: Pershore &
Spelter, 12A Wellington Street, Strand."

Paul's eyes widened. He read the short paragraph over
again, very slowly. Then half aloud "God in heaven!" He
sat staring at nothing, while his brain fumbled after clarity.
"It *can't* be. But it *must* be. Angle of Waterloo Road and
Lower Marsh. . . . Belonged to the guvnor . . . and now
to those Bible-bangers. Well, I *am* jiggered!"

He put the paper back in his pocket and walked slowly
toward Whitehall. He had little stomach for his errand.
Indeed it scared him badly. And no wonder.

20

LONDON IN THE early 'sixties was still three parts jungle.
Except for the residential and shopping areas of the West
End and Belgravia, the Strand and Holborn converging on
St Paul's, the main arteries of Westminster and the City
proper, hardly a district was really "public" in the sense that
ordinary folk went to and fro, heedless of the route they took
so that it led them where they wished to go. There was no
knowing what kind of a queer patch you might strike, in
what blind alley you might find yourself, to what embarrassment, insult or even molestation you might be exposed. So
the conventional middle-class kept to the big thoroughfares,
conscious that just behind the house-fronts to either side
murmured a million hidden lives, but incurious as to their
kind, and hardly aware that those who lived them were also
London citizens.

Behind the house-fronts. . . . The very phrase has the
romance of menace! If you are not susceptible to the lure of
the back streets, to the thrill of turning out of a busy main
road in a great city and turning again and finding yourself in
quite a different world not twenty yards from the traffic and
bustle you have just left, you will think it nonsense even to
speak of menace and romance. Maybe it is: but it is very
real nonsense to its votaries. Even in the London of between
wars—with its increasing and tawdry uniformity, its standard-
ised lighting, its network of communications, its innumerable
by-laws, its police and street cleaners—there were some odd
patches left, where still lingered an irrational stillness, or a
forlorn desolation, or a ruined grandeur, or the picturesque
homeliness of vanished village life. But less than eighty
years earlier the town was like a beggar's coat, with more
patches than fabric; and dark, sinister and dangerous, while

they lasted, many of those patches were. There were waste-lands like the Farringdon Street Extension. There were Alsatias like the "Holy Land" (as they called the district of St Giles), like the Potteries in Notting Dale, like the crazy settlement known as Agar Town (which, by the middle 'sixties, was neatly obliterated under the sheds and sidings of the Midland Railway), like the "Old Nichol" behind Shoreditch church. There were pits of misery and filth—hopeless, help-less slums where human beings starved like starving pigs—from Marylebone to Westminster, from Clerkenwell to South-wark, and almost anywhere to anywhere east of Aldgate Pump. *And there was Granby Street*—which with its adjacent alleys had passed from the possession of a murdered pawn-broker into that of a band of missionaries.

The history of Granby Street is full of lessons for the student of the hidden aspects of Victorian London. Over and over again, when plotting the black areas of the town at this date or the other, one asks oneself "Why should this street or group of streets have gone under, when other neigh-bouring (and apparently similar) streets have not?" In the case of slum districts the answer is simple. The majority of the terrible poverty areas of the mid-nineteenth century were of old construction, and had fallen so badly into disrepair that only the unhappy creatures who could command no better living-space were constrained to dwell in them. The problem is more complex when it concerns the genuine black patches—the pockets of vice and crime. These tend to adjoin populous or fashionable areas (the vultures must have their carrion handy) and, being by no means haunts of the destitute, are no more ruinous than their inhabitants care to make them. Why, then, should a pocket be here rather than there? So far as Granby Street is concerned, this is why.

Waterloo (originally "The Strand") Bridge, designed by Rennie for a public profit-seeking company, was opened to the public on June 18, 1817, the second anniversary of the Battle of Waterloo. It was a toll-bridge, and the promoters looked to the toll receipts to provide dividends on the million pounds and over which they had spent. At the same time as the bridge was planned, a new roadway was designed to carry traffic from the southern shore of the river to a junction with Blackfriars Road at the Obelisk in St George's Circus. Terraces of good houses were built on either side of this new roadway, from the bridge-head toward the intersection of Lower Marsh and the New Cut. The hinterland of these terraces was marshy and open, and beyond them (where now is Waterloo Station) were small dwelling-houses with gardens, mostly occupied by persons dependent in one way or another on Lambeth Palace.

Until the early 'forties the residential status of the northern stretch of Waterloo Road remained good. The houses were tall and well-proportioned; the neighbourhood, though no longer rural, was still airy and pleasant, and access was easy to the Strand and thence to the City or West End. But lower down the hill building was going on too rapidly, and by 1845 an infiltration of rough characters from the Borough into the areas beyond the New Cut had already begun to flutter the comfortable bourgeois who occupied the respectable terraces. Nothing was said or admitted; but here and there a family moved out and no other took its place. The restlessness was so spasmodic and casual that at first the bulk of the residents were quite unaware that the neighbourhood was slipping. But then something occurred which turned a northward trickle into a mass-migration.

The South Western Railway had completed its first line of tracks and opened its London terminus at Nine Elms in 1838. Suddenly, late in 1845, it became known that the line was coming further into London, that there was to be a temporary terminus on the western side of Waterloo Road just below the terraces, and that plans were in existence for carrying the railway on a viaduct towards Blackfriars and then over the river to a permanent terminus in the City. During 1846 and 1847 it was learnt that the Railways were buying property; had already acquired the area in the angle of York and Waterloo Roads as far south as Charlotte Street, and even, for their projected final extension, patches behind Stamford Street.

The scheme was a joint-undertaking by the South Western and South Eastern Companies; and the linking-up from Waterloo to the City was designed to make London Bridge a "through station" and so provide direct access to the West End for the crowds travelling by the Greenwich line from Deptford, Woolwich and Blackheath.

Building on the part of the South Western started in earnest. A mile and three-quarters of arches were constructed at a cost of £900,000 to carry the line from Nine Elms to the new Waterloo Station which was opened (though still unfinished) in 1848. By this time the terraces were already half-deserted and the houses stood empty and forlorn, while anxious landlords considered their next move. Then a second blow fell. 1848 was a year of financial crisis and saw the collapse of the railway boom. Sound schemes were overwhelmed in the ruin caused by crazy speculation; and, among them, the sensible project for a South Western-South Eastern Junction Railway from Waterloo to London Bridge was abandoned for lack of funds. The immediate result was that the station near York Road, instead of being a mere temporary terminus, became an official and an established one.

The ruin of Waterloo Road as a street of residential decency was now complete. No nice family could have a home in the immediate neighbourhood of a big railway station. Think of the noise and crowds and smuts and general vexatiousness! But if the staid middle-class disliked a station at their doors, there were plenty of folk of other kinds who liked one very much. The landlords of the terraces were apprised that if they agreed to put their houses to a somewhat different use— to permit shops and eating-houses on the ground floors and above them small hotels and offices for business men of an unobtrusive sort, they would have tenants and to spare. They agreed.

The position of London landlords in the nineteenth century is not always clearly understood. Huge areas of the town, built-over during the century, formed part of certain great estates and were labelled in people's minds with the name of some noble family or with the dignitaries of the Established Church. These eminent persons were the ground-landlords and were only in a position to control the development of their property up to a certain point. 'Usually the great land-owners' men of business had a say in the lay-out of an area scheduled for building (hence the wide streets not uncommon in districts which subsequently sank into slumdom) and, having thus secured a standard of structure, tried, when choosing a building-lessee, to secure a standard of mainten-ance also. But in this direction their powers were fatally limited. They could insist that any assignment of a lease by the original holder should be registered with the ground-landlord; but they could not refuse an assignee as individually undesirable. Consequently, although they could select a respectable builder as original grantee, they could not prevent him from assigning leases (together with responsibility for ground-rent, which went naturally with ownership of a lease, seeing that the property was the security for the rent) to whomsoever should buy the houses he had erected. And such buyers could then re-sell or sub-let, and so on *ad infinitum*.

Clearly, therefore, London property was liable to become a mosaic and a palimpsest of ownerships and occupiers, and in certain cases every kind of division and sub-division took place. Layer upon layer of lessees, sub-lessees and resident tenants were superimposed on the original sale to a building lessee; and to fix responsibility for jerry-building or for mal-administration or for neglect to keep in repair or for toleration of undesirable elements was virtually impossible. It must, however, be added that the law was persistently on the side of the landlord. It functioned steadily in the favour of each one, from his High Mightiness the ground-landlord to the last but one in the descending scale, who still had someone weaker than himself and therefore exploitable.

If all these complications could arise over property origin-ally belonging to one of the half dozen great London estates, they were worse still in areas whose basic ownership was in several hands. Such an area was that around Granby Street. The west side of Waterloo Road, up to and including the

site of the original Waterloo Station, belonged to the Archbishop of Canterbury. They were the Archbishop's representatives who assigned the building-lease to the builder of
the terraces (this man obtained a similar lease from the owner
of the east side and built his two rows of houses according to
a balanced plan), and they were the Archbishop's representatives who, about thirty years later, granted to the South
Western Railway a building-lease on the ground required for
their new station. But southward from what became Charlotte
Street was not the property of the Archbishop, and the small
area which filled the angle of Waterloo Road and Lower
Marsh had at least three separate owners. The ground lay
low, was damp and soggy, and by the middle 'forties was
only partially developed.

The news that the railway was coming brought speculators
to the district even more quickly than it drove away the
respectable occupants of the terraces. Between 1842 and 1847
on both sides of lower Waterloo Road and half-way to the
Obelisk, vacant areas were in fierce demand. Building-
leases were competed for; streets of houses were run up at
breakneck speed; shops, warehouses, taverns and tenements
were sold and re-sold, let and sub-let. The three ground-
landlords of the corner territory south of the Archbishop—
no one of them a rich man and each aware of his property
only as an unprofitable patch of marsh—fell easy victims to
the gamblers in real estate. They sold out lock, stock and
barrel, to buyers ostensibly independent but in fact members
of a syndicate, which syndicate now became actual owner of
the ground and, under yet another name, building-lessee.
By the end of 1847 the Granby Street area was built to the
last yard, and began a career of brazen and crapulous infamy
without parallel in the history of nineteenth-century London.

It was a career of no more than thirty years. Between
1874 and 1877 the five notorious acres became the property
of the South Western Railway, who by 1879 had demolished
most of the houses, built the original South Station on half
the area and replanned and renamed the remaining streets.
In 1886 further demolition and railway extension took place;

and in the present century, when the existing South Station with its traffic approaches was built, every indication that the terrain had once carried streets and courts and houses vanished for ever.

*　　　*　　　*　　　*　　　*

As a London phenomenon Granby Street and its tributary alleys were unique. It is not enough to describe them as a red-light district, although this they certainly were. They were a debauch-market, with a peculiar shamelessness all its own. The walls of the houses served neither to screen nor to confine the traffic of the area. The rooms in which women and boys and even little children plied their trade lay as open to the street as though they were booths in an oriental city, and on gala nights the carnival surged up and down the roadways and in and out the gaping doors, without attempt or inclination toward privacy.

There were, of course, quieter periods. But no matter the day or the time of day, business went on. Granby Street was always "at home", and stayed there. Its inhabitants were not street-walkers beyond the limits of their own colony; and the gay dogs of clerks and shop-assistants who dawdled about the Strand with odd shillings in their pockets, had only to cross the river and walk a few hundred yards, to find what they were looking for and sometimes a broken head into the bargain.

Customers were also plentiful among sailors and soldiers, who at almost any hour of the day or night were hanging about the gateway to Portsmouth and, from the mid-'fifties onward, to Aldershott. A railway terminus always lowers the status of adjoining property. It attracts every kind of undesirable, whether he wishes to prey upon bewildered strangers, or to offer diversion to travellers with time on their hands, or to pick pockets in a crowd. The same descent from bourgeois respectability to dubiety as befell Waterloo Road also occurred round Paddington and Victoria and (at a comparatively recent date) round Marylebone. But no one of these produced a Granby Street—partly because the history of the neighbourhood, the nature of the ground and the conditions of original ownership were less favourable, mainly because the Granby Street location had three advantages peculiar to itself.

Of the London termini in the 'fifties no other stood, as conveniently as did Waterloo, within reach of a crowded pleasure district (Charing Cross Station was not built until the early 'sixties). The Strand, one of Victorian London's two main arteries of amusement-after-dark, was close at hand. But not too close. Granby Street lay suitably withdrawn, with a toll-bridge restricting all but pedestrian traffic between it and unwanted publicity.

In the second place, it had this pull over the stews of Drury Lane (which might have rivalled it on grounds of accessibility)—that no long-standing tradition of squalid poverty was attached to it. It was indeed something worse than a slum; but it was not a huddle of crumbling rookeries nor was the placard "slum district" hung about its neck.

In the third place, and conversely, it had a local tradition of its own, and one well suited to its needs—being, in fact, an extension of an old-established "vice area". Certainly Stamford Street—already, when Granby Street was built, a place of equivocal lodgings—looked down its nose at the shameless depravity of the new settlement, for Stamford Street stood fairly high in the social register of harlotry, its ladies belonging to the aristocracy of the Strand theatres and night-houses. But one had only to go east along the New Cut and Union Street to find oneself in the Southwark "Mint" —as evil a patch of villainous courts and thieves' kitchens as the south side could boast. This quarter owed its nickname to the fact that it occupied the site of a one-time royal Mint, which became an asylum for debtors in the mid-eighteenth century, and thereafter an expanding colony of bad characters of every kind. There was, therefore, a sympathetic hinterland to Granby Street; and the bosses of the "Mint" were closely concerned with the organisation and profits of what, in effect, was their shop-window.

28

PAUL GLADWIN, as he dawdled reluctantly past Hungerford Market, felt a faint curiosity as to what he would find in Granby Street blend with a nervous dread of going to find it. During his brief career as a gay young spark he had heard often enough of the notorious area. He had been told of the drunken women who leaned from every window or lurched from house-doors to catch at a passer-by, of the wild orgies on Saturday nights when the gin-palaces flared (the district had half a dozen of its own) and soldiers and roughs and tipsy sailors and bullies and half-naked screaming harlots danced round hurdy-gurdys in the streets, while other women and their clients pelted them from upstairs rooms, shouted obscenities and copulated on the very window-sills. From hearsay he knew of all this, but, acting mainly from disgust and partly from prudence, had given the district itself the widest possible berth. Its reputation was sinister as well as lurid, and no youth with any pretension to gentility would have dreamt of going near it, save in drunken recklessness or as a sort of sight-seeing expedition with a party of companions. Gladwin in drink had never been reckless; merely confiding, spendthrift and very, very talkative. As for deliberate descents into the underworld, they were not to his taste. Like most young men, he preferred sport and gambling and Caves of Harmony and noisy jollifications in the company of his kind.

But now he was going to Granby Street, and going alone. The idea became more and more distasteful, and he turned on impulse into Adam Street where his friend Matt Merton had rooms. Matt by good fortune was at home, lying full length on a sofa, smoking a long cheroot and twanging at a mandoline. He was a heavily-built genial person, a few

years Paul's senior, and the only acquaintance of the latter's
ill-starred months as man-upon-town, with whom a friendship
had developed.

Matt stared open-mouthed when his visitor, concealing the
real reason for the expedition, pretended to a sudden fancy to
have a look at this of all places.

"Upon my soul, Gladwin, you must be off the hooks
altogether to want to go trapesing about Whoreterloo"
(such in current slang was the district's name) "in the middle
of the afternoon! Surely dusk would give a little tone to the
jaunt, wouldn't it? I mean we shall look like Inspectors of
Nuisances or men from the Vestry. And anyway I've been
there, and once is plenty."

"Inspectors of Nuisances are precisely what we shall be,
old chap, except that at this time there is not likely to be
much doing in the nuisance line. No. I just want to have a
look at it. That's all. Come along, there's a good fellow;
get your hat and stick."

Matt grumbled and shrugged but did as he was bid, and
the pair of them set out along the Strand and over the bridge
to the south side.

You went under an archway into Granby Street, which led
at right angles off Waterloo Road. It was a single archway
about two-foot thick, and joined the houses on either side at
first-floor level. The houses in Granby Street were of
uniform two-storey design, built of the usual browny-yellow
London bricks, and with a flat parapet sheer with the house-
fronts, which rose high enough to hide the slates and gulleys
of the roofs. Looking down it, therefore, one saw a perspective
of flat walls, regularly pierced with windows and doors, and
topped by a level and shallow cornice of stone. About fifty
yards along, at the intersection of Henry Place, four public-
houses stood at the four street corners. Another hundred
yards and the street plunged into a low tunnel, which led
under the South Western station, emerged at the other side
as Griffin Street, and ultimately debouched into York Road.

When Paul and Matt stopped on the pavement of Waterloo

Road and looked through the archway, Granby Street was empty. In the sunshine it looked dingy and sour; but the roadway was clear of garbage and the doorways were not blackened with the grease of lounging backs. The two looked at one another, raised their eyebrows, nodded, and with an uncomfortable sense of adventure passed beneath the arch.

Outside in the main road the noise of wheels and hoofs and the raucous cries of street-arabs and hawkers had been incessant. Here in Granby Street was silence. It was an uneasy silence—the silence which in any large city is characteristic of a bad area. No children played or screamed; no slatternly women shouted at one another through lines of drying-clothes; no cheerful errand-boy whistled along the street. Paul had been right in guessing that three o'clock in the afternoon would be slackwater in Bettyland; but he had hardly expected this sinister tranquillity, which was not the tranquillity of emptiness, still less that of serenity, but rather of a menace temporarily off-duty and—behind the house-fronts—either slumbering or relaxed.

They had gone about twenty yards when a man turned the corner of Henry Place and came towards them. He was a small pale man, with a broken nose and the eyes of a rat, and as he approached he gave them a keen look from under the peak of his cap. As they came abreast, he stopped, touched his forelock and muttered in the ingratiating undertone of the professional tout :

"Beg pardon, gents, but there's nice fresh greens far end of Grove Place. Last door but one on left. Ask for Daisy. Not many of 'em workin this time o' day, but Daisy's the ticket. Tell 'er Slippy sent ye, and I wager ye won't regret it."

The visitors smiled amiably and Paul put a shilling into a very convenient hand. The man had pointed the way to Grove Place, so they turned left at the nearest of the four public-houses. Matt glanced back as they reached the corner. The little pimp was standing where they had left him, looking after them. He looked more rat-like than ever, with his head thrown back and moving slightly from side to side as though sniffing the atmosphere for profit or for danger. There was

31

a low sound of voices behind the closed bar-door of the tavern.

"Keep your eyes skinned, Gladwin. There are more folk about than one can see."

Grove Lane was an exact replica of Granby Street but had a shade more animation. Two doors beyond the public-house, a fat girl sitting at an open window caught at Paul's arm as he passed. She was dirty, uncombed, and rather drunk, and appeared to be wearing nothing but a chemise.

"Cub od, dearie" she said. "Cub ud 'ave a bulls-vorth of tick-tack."

"Sorry, honeypot" Paul replied with some presence of mind. "Promised to Daisy. Another day if you're free."

The woman grinned tipsily, and waved an unsteady fare-well. From the other side of the street a female voice burst into a shrill rendering of "Cupid's Battering Ram". There was the sound of a blow and the song ended abruptly.

Another intersection. St Andrew's Terrace led up from Waterloo Road, and opposite to it was the cul-de-sac called Grove Place. Here were more definite marks of slumdom than any the explorers had hitherto observed. In the roadway was a pile of rubbish and rotting vegetables; there were broken windows stuffed with rag and paper.

"Daisy may be slap-up to the minute at her job, but I don't like her neighbourhood" said Matt. "Haven't we seen about enough?"

"Quite enough" Paul replied. "Let's pad the hoof."

But, as they moved away, a shrill scream of terror or pain came from one of the houses in the cul-de-sac. The next moment a small girl dashed out of a doorway, and with a flying leap over the pile of garbage, reached the two young men. Throwing her arms round Matt's knees, she got behind him, blubbering:

"Don't let er get me! For Gawd's sake, keep er away."

A scrawny virago now appeared from the same doorway. She was brandishing a crop and shouting filthy abuse. When she saw the strangers she stopped short, and in that moment of respite Matt made up his mind.

32

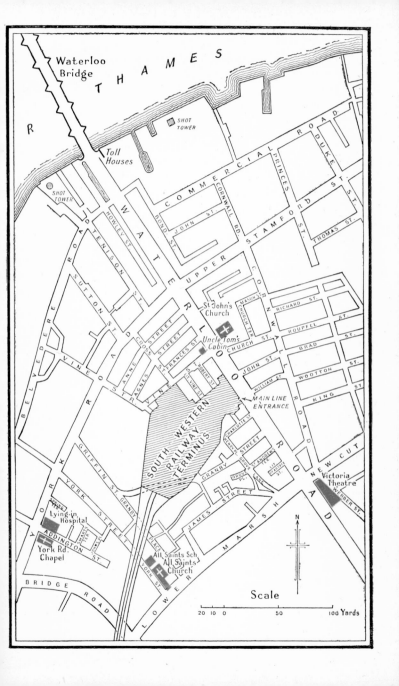

THAMES

R.

Waterloo Bridge

SHOT TOWER

Toll Houses

SHOT TOWER

WATERLOO ROAD

COMMERCIAL ROAD

PRINCES ROAD

DUKE ST.

HOWLEY ST.

TENISON ST.

SUTTON ST.

BOND ST.

JOHN ST.

CORNWALL RD.

STAMFORD

ST.

THOMAS ST.

BELVEDERE ROAD

VINE ST.

ADD LE STREET

COSSER STREET

S. ANNE STR.

FRANCES ST.

STRAGGLES ST.

VINE ST.

St John's Church

Uncle Tom's Cabin

MASON ST.

CHURCH TER.

CHURCH ST.

RICHARD ST.

ROUPELL ST.

BRAD ST.

JOHN ST.

WILLIAM ST.

WOOTTON ST.

KING ST.

MAIN LINE ENTRANCE

YORK ROAD

GRIFFIN ST.

YORK STREET

GRANBY ST.

ROBERT ST.

S. VINCT ST.

SOUTH WESTERN RAILWAY TERMINUS

CHARLOTTE ST.

GRANBY STREET

UPPER PL.

S. ANDREW ST.

LITTLE CHARLES ST.

JAMES STREET

WATERLOO ROAD

NEW CUT

Victoria Theatre

WEBBER ST.

Lying-in Hospital

York Rd. Chapel

ADDINGTON

MARSH TER.

ST. JOHN ST.

All Saints Sch

All Saints Church

YORK STREET

PLACE

LOWER MARSH

BRIDGE ROAD

Scale

20 10 0   50   100 Yards

N

"Quick! Take the kid and cut along like hell. Don't follow this straight street; take the curving lane on the right into James Street and then straight down into Lower Marsh. I'll keep the rear."

Paul seized the child by the hand and noticed for the first time that her tattered frock was torn and blood-stained all down the back. Almost dragging the little girl off the ground, he ran down the short curving alley into the broader James Street. In very few minutes they were among the rag-tag and bobtail who at all hours thronged about the stalls and shops of Lower Marsh. Meanwhile Matt Merton, keeping to the middle of the road, was backing slowly in the same direction. The woman with the crop emerged from the cul-de-sac and began yelling for help. A few women put their heads out of windows and yelled back to know the cause of the disturbance. Matt kept looking over his shoulder to see if his line of retreat were threatened. All was well. It seemed that such bullies of the district as were on the spot were congregated in the taverns at the cross-roads or fast asleep. Suddenly, however, when he was half-way to the outlet into James Street and the curve of the houses in Grove Lane blocked his view of the Granby Street cross-roads, he became unpleasantly aware of the sound of heavy boots, running in his direction from where the woman was still screaming. At that moment there was a slight sound at his back, and he swung round just in time to avoid a man in a dirty vest and still dirtier trousers, who had crept up behind and was about to put the hug on him. He hit the man hard in the face, jabbed him in the stomach with his stout walking-stick and ran for it.

Now the inside section of James Street (which, as the map shows, formed three sides of a rough square with Lower Marsh for its fourth side) together with the courts leading off it and the narrow alley joining it to Granby Street, was a recognised part of the Bad Lands. But the short stretch from the corner of Grove Lane to Lower Marsh was more or less neutral ground between the Alsatia of Whoreterloo and the ordinary rough and tumble of a poor quarter of London.

B   33

Matt, therefore, reached the crowded market street without
further molestation, plunged into the mass of shoppers and,
dodging in and out of stalls and loitering groups of people,
slipped into a convenient entry and leant against the wall to
get his breath. In a minute or two he peered cautiously out,
turned up his jacket-collar, altered the tilt of his hat and
strolled back as unobtrusively as possible toward the scene of
his escape. Keeping well to the south side of Lower Marsh
he gave a quick glance up James Street. It showed no
suspicious characters. His pursuers, whoever they had been,
had withdrawn to their own territory. He now considered
where to find Paul and the child. To risk a chance encounter
in this turmoil of a street market would be foolish; and
Matt argued that they would be waiting for him in some
place away from the danger zone, yet sufficiently individual
to be a likely rendezvous. He also guessed that Waterloo
Road, with its traffic and occasional police, would seem to
Gladwin to offer a safer way of escape than a deeper plunge
into the poor quarters around Westminster Bridge Road,
even though the former would take the fugitives along the
southern and eastern boundaries of the danger zone. So he
continued on his way, almost crouching against the house-
fronts, until Waterloo Road was reached.

He crossed quickly to the Victoria Theatre; but there
was no sign of Paul. Feeling sure that his friend would go
toward rather than away from the river, he turned northward and walked rapidly up the slope. Mean houses; mean
shops; a chapel; more shops and eating-places; the big
Wesleyan settlement with its forecourt; William Street, with
a pub at each corner. Then the stone mass of St John's
Church standing back in its little square, with the sunshine bland and primrose yellow on its massive portico and
pediment. Behind the church stood the vicarage with the
school-house next door. Matt was hesitating at the corner
of the square when his friend appeared at the other end
of it.

"I've taken the poor kid to the vicar" he said when they
met. "Couldn't think of anything better. He seems a fine

34

chap. His housekeeper has taken her in charge. Come and see him."

Quarter of an hour later they were taking their leave. The Rev. Alfred Meadows, Vicar of St John's, Waterloo Road, was a short rather stout man, with a heavy dark moustache and bright pugnacious eyes. He stood on the doorstep of his vicarage.

"You have done a good deed, young gentlemen" he said "and at considerable risk. That tragic patch of wickedness over there is not in my parish, and I can seldom fight directly against those responsible for its vile condition. To see that this poor child is tended to health, and then got safely away to where she can grow up to decent usefulness may seem too small an undertaking to matter. But every blow struck against the Devil is a blow for righteousness, and a good deed in the sight of God. 'Are not two sparrows sold for a farthing. . . .?' You shall hear how your half-farthingsworth progresses. And do not be afraid. I do not think they will find her here, and I shall do my best to get her away to safety as soon as possible."

In three days' time a letter from Mr Meadows was delivered at Matt Merton's lodgings. The little girl was already much better. She would have been cruelly beaten, had not the two young men by a miracle been near at hand; but the flogging had only just begun and, though she was cut and bruised, no serious harm was done. She was not very coherent as to how she had come to Granby Street or whence. "I am afraid" wrote the clergyman "it was one of those cases of kidnapping by connivance—on the one hand a getting-rid of an unwanted child, on the other a willingness to get hold of her for evil purposes. Her name, so far as I can understand her, is Lottie Heape."

4 : MESSRS PERSHORE AND SPELTER

ON THE DAY following the Granby Street adventure, and before
any word about the child had been received from Mr Meadows,
Paul Gladwin paid a visit to Messrs Pershore and Spelter,
Estate Agents and Rent Collectors of 12A Wellington Street.
The excitement of the rescue once over, he reverted to his
original purpose in making the expedition to Waterloo and
during the evening considered the implications of the whole
uncomfortable affair. This little Hell of narrow streets had
belonged to his father. In what sense "belonged"? Had he
been merely a ground-landlord, enjoying a modest but steady
income from a patch of property of which he knew nothing;
or had he been involved in the business activities of the
locality, sharing in their profits and therefore in the responsibility for their existence?

The question must be answered. The old man was dead;
and his wealth, however gained, had passed to foxy Sneade
and his absurd Society. But it was not on their account that
Paul was curious. Indeed he had almost forgotten that a
report on the district was due from him in four days' time.
What possessed him was a sort of bitter exultation at thus
stumbling on one of the hidden compartments of his father's
life. Not only that. He had made the discovery under
direct instructions from his father's heirs, the men who, by
becoming his father's heirs, had supplanted him. He—the
outcast son, the disinherited ne'er-do-well—was to be paid
for prying into the secrets of the parent who had ruined him,
and by the very people who had profited by his ruin. Hoping
for the worst, yet well aware that even the worst could bring
nothing but a sense of posthumous revenge, he made his way
to Wellington Street.

Now Wellington Street, as every Londoner knows, is the

36

approach to Waterloo Bridge and stands high above what is now the Embankment. In 1860 there was access by stairway from the Toll House on the eastern corner of the bridge, to Waterloo Pier which stood out into the river in front of Somerset House. But the western side of Wellington Street was a single terrace of high houses, which ran from the Strand to within a hundred yards of the bridge and then gave place to a narrow strip of land still called "The Necropolis". At the far end stood the office of the Woking Cemetery Company, under whose auspices the mortuary function of the site had already been transferred to rural surroundings in Surrey, leaving the ex-cemetery a forlorn and untidy waste. At no point on this side of the street was descent to river-level possible, nor indeed did any roadway exist at that level nearer to the bridge than the foot of the easterly branch of Savoy Street.

Arrived before Number 12, Gladwin could not for a moment see any sign of 12A. Then he discerned, on a narrow and grimy door squeezed between Numbers 12 and 13, the almost obliterated cypher for which he sought. There was no bell or knocker and the door was ajar. He pushed it open, and saw a long dark passage with at the end another door, half-glass, through which shone a murky daylight. When he reached this second door he found that painted on the glass were the names of Pershore and Spelter and the word ENTER!

The adjuration was a shade grandiloquent, for the door gave on to a lobby so small and box-like that any visitor tempted to enter with a flourish would most certainly bump his nose on the partition immediately in front of him. There appeared to be no exit from this lobby for anything larger than a cat, the only break in the three walls being a small square opening or "judas", closed with a wooden shutter and marked "Enquiries". The opening of the half-glass door had set a bell ringing, and the clang had hardly ceased before the shutter was swung back from inside and a broad pinkish face, framed in the opening, said "Well-what-is-it?" in a flatly hyphenated but truculent manner.

Although hardly prepared for quite this degree of in-

37

accessibility, Gladwin, having previously thought out his opening words, proceeded to say them.

"I am instructed to see one of your principals about some property belonging to Mr Crocker, Chairman of the Torchbearers' Society. Here is my authority" and he thrust Sneade's letter in the direction of the pinkish face, which withdrew, became a stubby-fingered hand with a good deal of reddish hair on the back, and accepted the letter.

"I'll-see-wait-a-minute" said the now invisible and somewhat muffled face, withdrawing its hand and slamming the shutter to.

Shortly afterward the caller became aware of a sound behind the partition to his right. A lock clicked back, and a portion of the plain boarding became an open door.

"Straight through" said the face's voice; and as Paul walked obediently forward he heard the partition-door closed and locked behind him. He was now on the threshold of a room full of daylight, simply yet adequately furnished as an office. While he hesitated a moment and looked about him, a short stocky figure, topped by the broad pinkish face and very little hair, slipped past him into a chair behind a desk near the door, and rattled off:

"Good-afternoon-Mr-Gladwin-please-sit-down-my-name-is-Spelter."

Although somewhat bewildered by the strangeness of his reception, Paul was aware that his host's tone had changed. He still ran his words into a jabber; but they had now a certain light and shade, and under their scurry were almost hearty. Also the broad rosy face, with its tufts of chestnut hair above the ears, was shrewdly genial. Mr Spelter might conduct his office with unusual precaution; but he himself at any rate was not an ogre.

The agent was holding the letter of authority in his hand, and now glanced over it at his visitor with a twinkle in his small bright eyes.

"Gladwin, eh? Torchbearers—Light-of-the-Word—Victoria Street—engraved-letter-head-superfine-bank. Pon-my-word-it's the rummiest go-ever—quite the rummiest!"

He paused a moment; then, seeming to realise that he had been thinking aloud and staring at the young man all the time, became suddenly businesslike. He laid down the letter, put his elbows on the desk and assumed an expression of polite attention.

"Ahem-yes, Mr Gladwin. 'Some property-belonging-to-the-er—the Torchbearers?' I think you said. What-property-precisely-would-that-be?"

"Granby Street" Paul replied curtly.

"Ah! Granby Street . . . Let-me-see-now, Waterloo-Road-corner-of-Lower-Marsh, I think. *Quite* a valuable-little-property, Mr Gladwin. Any help I can give you . . . delighted-I-am-sure. What-exactly-do-you-want-to-know about Granby Street?"

"Just this, Mr Spelter" Paul spoke slowly, choosing his words. "The property passed to this Mr Crocker under the will of my late father, John Gladwin of Farringdon Street. You may recall the tragic ending of his life a year or more ago—"

"Shocking—shocking!" murmured the agent, moving his head in a circular manner designed to indicate that he was both nodding an affirmative and shaking it in deep concern, yet fixing the other steadily with his gleaming eye.

"My instructions from the Society" continued Paul "are to visit the property, and then call on the accredited agents to discuss in what terms I shall report to the Secretary, and whether any recommendations in the Society's interest should be made as to the management or improvement of . . ."

The sentence petered out in uncertainty. Spelter waited politely for a moment and then asked gently:

"And have you visited-the-property, Mr Gladwin?"

Paul nodded.

"Ah! Have you any recommendations-in-mind?"

Paul pulled himself together.

"I have not yet attempted to consider any, Mr Spelter. What I want to ask you is precisely the nature of my father's ownership, as presumably the new owner will stand in the same relation to the property as he did."

There was a brief silence. Spelter dropped his eyes and

picked thoughtfully with a finger-nail at the corner of the blotting-paper which lay in front of him. At last, without looking up:

"You will forgive what-may-seem-undue-curiosity" he said "but how do you, the son-of-the-former-owner, come to be employed—for-I-gather-from this-letter-that you-are-in-these-people's employment—as an inspector of house-property?"

Paul had to think quickly. He did not intend to tell this perfect stranger any more of his private affairs than was necessary. He judged from his reception that the man had no previous knowledge of the terms of old Gladwin's will, may even at first have regarded his caller as the actual inheritor. But a re-reading of the Torchbearers' letter had corrected this impression, and now Spelter was uncertain how he stood.

The young man improvised.

"The position is a little complicated" he said "and a little embarrassing to explain. My father never spoke to me of any London property except the shop in Farringdon Street, nor did I know that he planned a legacy of any kind to a Missionary enthusiast. He left a wish, however, that I should be in some way concerned with what was *not* left to me, as well as with my own inheritance; and as I was naturally curious as to property of his of which I knew nothing, it was arranged that I should act ostensibly as—shall I say 'surveyor'?—on the Society's behalf."

This extempore and, even to Paul's ears, unconvincing statement concluded, he glanced a little anxiously at the agent to see how much had been believed. Spelter, who was still watching his own forefinger rib the edge of the blotting-paper, nodded thoughtfully:

"I see" he said slowly. "Thank you for answering what I fear was an impertinent question. I admire your choice-of-words. 'Surveyor' I-think-you-said? Yes—'surveyor' is excellent."

Suddenly he threw back his head and laughed aloud:

"Lawkamussy, Mr Gladwin, you'll be the death of me! It's a corker, that's what it is—an *ab-so-lute* corker! Look here, my dear sir, I'll be as frank with you as you have been with me. Your father was a very-shrewd-man, a very-shrewd-man indeed. When after the crash of 'forty-eight the railway scheme over there was dropped, options on more than one patch of property thereabouts were going cheap. He stepped in and bought the best of the lot."

"He became ground-landlord then?"

"Ground—building-lessee—tenant—the whole bag of tricks except resident sub-tenant. They were all merged in one in that particular locality—at least really in one though under different names."

"Then he profited directly from the—er—the activities of the area?"

Spelter's astonishment at this naïveté was clearly genuine.

"Profited? O' course he did! What do you think he-bought-it-for? Profited? Lumme, I like that!" He settled into his chair and gave a prolonged chuckle. As this died away, he added:

"Fly, that's-what-he-was-your-old-guvnor, *fly*!"

The man was becoming almost roguish, and his language as well as his manner grew more familiar. Leaning forward he prodded the air in Paul's direction with a short square-ended forefinger.

"What kind of property pays best? Short-term agreements, easy sub-lets and no questions asked. What drains a land-lord's pocket? Repairs, houses standing empty, complaints about this and that. Well, you've seen the place. The tenants pay high and get a hoick to the rent at every renewal 'cos they can't suit themselves so easy elsewhere even if any-where else would take 'em, which it won't; they ask for no repairs 'cos they prefer to do 'em themselves; the houses divide easy 'cos every room serves a purpose and sometimes more than one; there ain't no complaints 'cos there's no one to complain to; finally it's come-an-go, come-an-go all the time, and as you well know, Mr Gladwin, six tenants per house at an average of two or three months a tenant pays a damn sight better than your seven-fourteen-twenty-one-year affairs, with the tradesmen calling for orders and piano-lessons for the young ladies."

Listening to this harangue, Paul felt revulsion rising within him like a physical sickness. To steady his stomach and get a hold of his nerves, he got up from his chair and walked to the wide-open window, where he stood a moment looking out, his back to the agent. The latter began again:

"Of-course-it's-not-my-business, but I can't-help-wondering how this owl—whatsisname? Cooker? Crocker?—will fancy his little windfall. Still, that's his affair. For my part I'd be glad to pay over. Your dad's lawyer told me to sit on the swag till further notice, and that I've done. But I don't care for money piling up which ain't mine. Misleads you somehow."

Without turning round Paul asked:

"Do your firm actually collect the rents?"

Instinctively he felt that the question was unwelcome. After a moment's pause he heard Spelter say, a little abruptly "We have sub-agents", and then, with a return to the civil geniality of the earlier part of the interview, continue: "Well, Mr Gladwin, if there is any-further-information. . . . When-did-you-say you were to report?"

Knowing that he had said nothing on the subject, Paul was about to prevaricate, when his attention was suddenly arrested by what he saw through the window.

Spelter's room was on the ground-floor level of the terrace in Wellington Street. It gave the impression of having been built out at the back of the terrace, possibly on the site of a small yard, for one looked sheerly down from the window on to the house-roofs of the Savoy, huddled beneath in picturesque squalor. To the left, between banks of mud littered with refuse and decaying matter of all kinds, flowed the river, oily and secret even in the sunshine of afternoon. You could look across the bend to Westminster Bridge and see, beyond and to the right, the huge mass of the new Houses of Parliament, with the recently completed Victoria Tower soaring toward the brassy sky. To the extreme right, facing on to the Strand, the Globe Theatre turned a smoke-grimed back, which rose like a cliff above the slither of buildings lining the parallelogram of narrow thoroughfares called "Savoy Street". Only the bunched greenery of trees marking the whereabouts of the Savoy Chapel and the stolid cupola of the Lutheran Church stood out as individualities in the sloping welter of tiles and chimney-pots.

A dozen or fifteen feet below the window at which he stood (and this is what caught Paul's eye and held it) a house taller than its neighbours was joined to the embankment along which ran Wellington Street by a small space of flat roof. A narrow dormer door, set in the back-slope of the house-roof proper, gave access to these leads, and from this door, Paul saw a man emerge. The man was Slippy. Paul recognised him immediately, partly by the glimpse he had of the face with its broken nose, partly by the cap and jacket, most certainly of all by the swift movement of the head to left and right as he paused a second before scurrying across the open space to beneath Spelter's window. Hardly was he no longer visible from above, than there came the sound of feet mounting an iron staircase, and Paul knew, as surely as though he had been told, that there was an alternative entrance to Spelter's office and that for Spelter's office Slippy was bound. He swung round watch in hand.

"I had no idea it was so late, Mr Spelter. Forgive me if I break off this interesting talk. I should like to call again, if I may, and ask you to check the terms of my report. There is no real urgency for me to hand it in."

As he was speaking he moved quickly toward the door and into the passage. He thought he caught the sound of a gentle knocking in the corner of the room he had just left; and the readiness with which the agent hurried after him and undid the door on to the lobby seemed to confirm the suspicion. The parting was cordial, but on both sides oddly urgent. As Paul came out into Wellington Street, there sounded in his ears, in Spelter's dry embarrassed voice, the words: "We have sub-agents."

*　　*　　*　　*　　*

Wednesday afternoon, Granby Street. Thursday afternoon, Pershore and Spelter. Saturday morning, the reassuring note from Mr Meadows about the rescued child. By the time

Paul and Matt Merton had met and considered this note, the former had decided to take his friend fully into his confidence. He told him everything—about the Torchbearers, and why he had insisted on going to Granby Street, and what happened at Spelter's, culminating in the narrow escape from being seen by Slippy.

Matt was enchanted. By nature a docile and indolent person, who earned enough to live the bohemian life he fancied by writing accounts of prize-fights and short biographies of famous pugilists for *Sporting Life*, he was nevertheless always ready to use his powerful physique and considerable knowledge of boxing in any likely rough-and-tumble. Such a thing occurred only too rarely; and he now saw himself relentlessly on the track of Sneade, Spelter, Slippy and half a dozen other desperate ruffians.

"Gladwin, my boy" he said impressively "we must make a plan."

"What about?" asked Paul.

"What *about*! About everything. About that cove with the busted boco. About your bloody old Torchbearers. About the whole boiling of 'em. And to start with—whatever you say—we will rope in Toby."

Paul recoiled and muttered a vague protest. Toby Langrish, you will remember, had been employed by John Gladwin in Farringdon Street, had been a friend of the young master's and had chanced to be on duty at the money-lending entrance to the establishment when Paul paid his fatal call on his father. He was, in short, the nearest thing which existed to an eye-witness of that terrible encounter, and Paul had gradually come to avoid seeing him altogether. In the days immediately following the murder he had clung to Toby as being one of the few fragments of the past from whom he had nothing to fear, and the same impulse had driven him to bring Matt Merton and Toby Langrish together. But when the latter established himself as a publican within a stone's-throw of the site of the pawnshop, hatred of the neighbourhood overcame Paul's fondness for Toby, and he visited him no more.

Matt, on the other hand, to whom an agreeable tavern near Fleet Street had attractions apart from the personality of its owner, became a regular customer at the Marigold (as the little pub was called which Toby had bought with John Gladwin's legacy), and had several times suggested to Paul that they look the good fellow up.

Paul managed to evade the issue and, without saying why, to keep away. He was still frightened of everything connected with the tragedy of his father's death. Even after he was certain that he would not be personally involved, he felt himself a marked man. Where a youth of a stubborn and resilient temperament would have thrown off depression and sense of guilt and once more looked the world in the eye, Paul slipped into a permanent state of timorous remorse. Naturally a drifter, and with the edges of a quite respectable intelligence already a little blurred by liquor, he was incapable of fighting back; worse still, not merely did he capitulate to his own defeatism, he realised that he had done so, was bitterly ashamed and shrank more fearfully than ever from the humiliation of chance encounters. He walked the streets with downcast eyes, lest he happen to meet someone who might recognise him; and the persons he wished most desperately to avoid were the few in any way implicated in the quarrel between father and son.

But a moment had now come when the problem of seeing Toby or not seeing him could no longer be burked. As stated, he began to protest. But Matt shouted him down.

"Don't be a fat-head, man! Toby wants to see you again badly. It hurts him to get the go-by from an old pal, and he's the A 1 ticket in the rough-and-tumble this job is going to be. Not another word. You're coming to the Marigold here and now."

As afraid to say "no" as formerly he had been to say "yes" Paul yielded, and was soon following in his friend's energetic wake. They pushed their way down the crowded Strand, along Fleet Street and towards Ludgate Circus. Matt, a pace or two ahead of his reluctant companion, threw over his shoulder an occasional word of encouragement. Just before reaching the Circus he swung left into the narrow chasm of Black Horse Court, pulling up a hundred yards along at a small tavern whose weathered sign proclaimed it THE MARIGOLD. Nothing less like that garish but cheerful flower could be imagined than the cramped and dingy exterior of this side-street "public"; but, once inside, you realised that here was yet another of those startling contradictions between outward appearance and inward fact for which London has always been famous.

The bar-parlour was quite small. Under a heavy black marble mantel a coal fire blazed merrily. Two Windsor chairs stood on either side of the grate, and benches upholstered in red plush ran along two of the other walls. The fourth wall was mainly occupied by a shining mahogany bar, on which were ranged shining glasses and pewter mugs, and behind which stood a plump man with pink cheeks and a shining bald head. Everything in the Marigold shone so gleamingly that the whole place must have been polished daily within an inch of its life; and it was a problem of some interest whether, when Toby Langrish had brought the rest of his establishment to the highest pitch of coruscation, he set to work on his own head, or whether that crowning brilliancy was achieved by someone else and, if so, by whom. For Toby was a widower who lived alone over his tavern, and was known to be assisted during waking hours only by a very old woman who cooked and did for him, and by a very small boy who swept the floor and ran errands and minded as much of the bar as he could reach while the landlord went down to the cellar to replenish his supplies. As half this limited staff was too old and the other half too small to make a job of the master's head, you were forced to conclude that he did it himself and to give him credit accordingly.

When the two young men entered, the Marigold was empty. At this time the former employé of the late John Gladwin had only been landlord for about twelve months. His legacy had covered the cost of the goodwill and refitting of the little tavern; but as the goodwill had previously been rather bad, he was still making up lee-way and his bar was seldom crowded.

At the sight of Paul, Toby gave a shout of delight and leaning across the bar stretched out a large red hand, while his face shone like a human sunrise.

"Why Mr Gladwin, sir" he cried. "Often and often I've wondered what had become of you and asked our friend here how I could find you. Why have you not been near me? You've got to forget all that trouble, y'know, and get to business. Well, well! It does me good to see you."

Paul hung his head in embarrassment, but returned the handshake with convulsive gratitude. To give him time to recover his wits, Matt broke in.

"Give us a drink all round, Toby, and I'll tell you a story. Gladwin's got to business, all right. That's what we've come about. You've got to help us."

The bar-keeper listened in silence to Matt's colourful account of Paul's predicament and their recent adventure and, when the tale had been told, remarked bluntly:

"The only problem at the moment is what should Mr Gladwin do?"

"That's no problem, my good Toby" cried Matt. "He tells 'em to go to the devil."

"Tells who?"

"Why, old Sneade of course and the rest of the riff-raff."

Toby shook his head with a smile, and began to polish the zinc counter as he always did when about to speak seriously.

"Steady on, Mr Merton, steady on. I hate to do you out of a free-for-all, but the job's not quite so simple. To begin with, Mr Gladwin is dead broke apart from what these people pay him. Two, we don't know yet whether this codger Sneade is already wise to the sort of place Granby Street is. Three, Whoreterloo's only one of several bits of property— that right, Mr Gladwin?—and may be the only queer crib in the whole boiling—sort of got in by mistake y'know."

"Oh, but Toby" Paul interrupted "Spelter was quite definite that the guvnor knew the kind of place it is."

"I dessay he was, Mr Gladwin; but he sounds to me a

chouser, that bloke. I can see more than one reason why it might pay him to tie up your guvnor's memory with a jungle of molly-shops now that he's got a bunch of holies to deal with. Those chaps may preach their heads off; but they are nuts on the offertory. They won't be content, as the old man was, with a regular return on their money; they'll not only want to squeeze the orange, but also to stick their noses into the peel to see what's left. And then, when the shout goes up, Mr Kiss-me-arse Spelter will only have obeyed instructions and would some other investment be more acceptable?

"No, no, Mr Gladwin. Your dad had his faults and he was a hard man. But he was no sort of a fool; and only a fool, with the connections he had among the nobs, would risk being shown up in *that* kind of game. As he *would* have been shown up. D'you fancy those monkeys in the Mint, if they had a really warm man like old Mr Gladwin in the bag, wouldn't sooner or later have put the screw on him? O'course they would. Mind you, I don't say he asked too many questions about his house-property anywhere. A steady investment to him was a steady investment, and that was enough. But that he was personally mixed up in running that particular fish market (and the word goes round, seeing that all but a few in this town are in the hands of one bunch of crooks) is Hell and Tommy."

"My eye, Toby! You'll need another pint after that" said Matt, blowing noisily. "I'm dry with listening, so slap us another all round."

When the three of them came to the surface, Paul returned to the matter in hand.

"So just what do I do?" he asked.

"Well, sir" replied Toby "if I were you, I'd show up on Monday and make a brief businesslike report to the effect that the property is of a kind which the Lord High Torchbearer would probably prefer not to own (say it's gone downhill or something), and suggest he sell his interest and buy something else. It will be jam for Spelter, I know; but we've got to consider *you*; and until something turns up you must hold that job."

"Damme" Matt said "where do I come in?"

"You'll come in sooner or later, Mr Merton, if this baby-flashtail you pinched from them is worth anything. I doubt your having got to the Rev. Meadows without someone noticing; and they don't like a fox among the chickens. Meantime can you get our friend Gladwin something healthier to do?"

Matt shrugged.

"I'll try. It's not easy. You don't know anything about cricket, I suppose, Paul? The old man wants another Ned Rub."

"Sorry, Matt. I know nothing about anything except how to spend money I haven't got and where the drinks are good. That's the result of being turned into a gent."

"Bosh! You can string sentences together like a good 'un. We'll find something, never fear, and old Sneade can torch himself for a change."

*　　*　　*　　*　　*

Wednesday, Granby Street. Thursday, Wellington Street. Saturday, the Marigold with Matt and Toby. And in prospect Monday (only two days away) and a "brief businesslike report" . . . Paul felt a hollow in the pit of his stomach, and spent a solitary evening filling it up with gin.

Maybe he was lucky not to know that on the Friday Spelter had called at the Torchbearer offices, sent in his name to the Secretary as "the late John Gladwin's man of business, in connection with certain South side real estate", and secured an interview with Sneade. He brought with him a considerable sum of money in cash, and left it behind against the Society's formal receipt for about three-quarters of the amount. He found the Secretary an intelligent and unprejudiced man, with whom it was easy and pleasant to come to an understanding.

As he took his leave he said:

"I hope I have not exceeded my duty in warning you that young Gladwin-may-be-troublesome? I admit that I assumed he would be more of a chip-of-old-block, and was for a

49

moment more—er—communicative-than-is-my-habit. Now that we have discussed the matter . . . quite all right . . . would be a pity if he were to go spouting-all-over-the place. . . ."

"Yes, yes, Mr Spelter. You have acted very correctly. We need not anticipate anything untoward. *Good* morning."

* * * * *

Paul entered the Secretary's room at the appointed hour on Monday with three variants of the opening sentence of his statement jostling one another in his far from well-ordered head. He was very nervous; and the attempt, continued during Sunday, to make good the gap in his stomach had only made him still more jittery. His worry was unnecessary. When he had closed the door and was standing facing Sneade across the fine mahogany desk, the latter began to speak.

"I can understand, Mr Gladwin, your feeling a certain chagrin at the terms of your excellent parent's will; but I confess I was not prepared for a deliberate and malicious attempt to destroy the prestige of a body which I suppose you regard as having usurped your rightful inheritance."

What in the world was the man talking about?

"I—I—I—" began Paul.

"Allow me" Sneade raised a commanding hand. "I shall make myself perfectly clear. Last week you were instructed to visit a small area of house-property and, having made yourself familiar with the locality, to call on the reputable firm of estate agents who acted for your late father in connection with this property in order to obtain from them information and advice. You were then to report to me. You do not dispute my statements so far, I take it?"

"N—n—no" stammered the bewildered young man. "But—"

"I have not finished. What in fact did you do? You gained admittance to the private room of one of the principals of the estate agency, and proceeded to accuse him and the Society of which I have the honour to be Secretary of permitting the property in question to be put to the vilest uses.

You charged him, our Chairman, the Torchbearers and therefore my own self—*and therefore my own self, Mr Gladwin*—of complicity and profit-sharing in organised bestiality."

This was raving madness, nothing less. Slightly stimulated at the thought of dealing with a lunatic, Paul found his tongue.

"What in God's name is all this nonsense?" he cried.

Sneade rose to his feet and, leaning across the desk, snarled: "I think we will leave the Supreme Being out of this painful conversation. Further, I will not be shouted at by a subordinate or be told that what I say is nonsense. Fortunately you will not have to keep up your pose of puzzled indignation much longer, as I have very little more to say. Just this. You are no longer employed by the Society, and only the respect in which we hold your father's memory and the fact that he wished us, *so long as we could see our way*, to give his worthless son enough to keep body and soul together, restrain us from taking suitable and drastic measures against an abominable slanderer. You may go, Mr Gladwin, and I hope that we shall never meet again."

He struck downward with the palm of his hand on the button of a desk-bell. A lugubrious individual in threadbare black shuffled into the room.

"Conduct this person to the street door, Crowler, and make certain that he leaves the premises."

* * * * *

In this way did Paul Gladwin lose even the tiny share which might have been his of his father's wealth, and the only permanent employment which his father ever helped him to get.

THE REV. ALFRED MEADOWS had accepted the living of St John the Evangelist, Waterloo Road, some five years prior to his appearance in this story. He came from a senior curacy in Rotherhithe. He had fearlessness, bull-dog pertinacity and an inability to condescend toward even the most disreputable poverty—qualities which parish work in the wilds of Victorian London could not fail to develop in a man honest and courageous enough to absorb them.

The church of St John, designed on classical lines by Bedford in 1824, was a forceful and in an aggressive way a dignified building, but one little enough appreciated in the 'fifties and 'sixties, when parsonical gothic, however ill-assorted with its surroundings, was considered the only style worthy of the Establishment. But Mr Meadows—who, when he stood square on his short thick legs and thrust forward the firm line of his jaw overhung by heavy dark moustachios, was not unlike the pillared portico of his church —was indifferent to the beauty, either external or ceremonial, of the place of worship in his charge. His duty, as he conceived it, was with the bodies and souls of men; and although it would be too much to say that he regarded his church services and his sermons as a minor element in his activity, it is certain that the work in which his heart really lay was carried on in the streets and alleys of his parish rather than within the precincts of God's House.

This parish was bounded on west and north by the curving bank of the Thames and was cut more or less in half by the straight line of Waterloo Road.[1] South and west of this, it extended about two-thirds of the way to Westminster Bridge Road and inland as far as the South Western station, at the

[1] See map, p. 32.

main entrance to which it rejoined Waterloo Road. To the east of this thoroughfare the parish comprised the whole area from the river to the New Cut, as far as Broad Wall. This meant that it included the dustmen's and refuse-pickers' colony on Thames-side below Commercial Road, that portion of "Grand Tartery" known as Upper Stamford Street, and a network of dubious slums branching eastward off Cornwall Road. The Granby Street area, however, was not (as Mr Meadows told Merton and Gladwin) within his territory. It belonged to the small L-shaped parish of All Saints, Lower Marsh, one arm of which ran along Westminster Bridge Road to the river (thus taking in the southerly third of York Road and marching with St John's), the other consisting of the strip of residential alleys between Lower Marsh and the railway, the most easterly corner of which formed the Granby Street Alsatia.

Now in these days—during, that is, the sixties of last century—there began to stir in the minds of rich people in Belgravia a realisation that "over there", in the easterly and southerly wilderness of London (which no one of them had ever visited) were poverty and misery. Uneasily conscious of the contrast between their own lives and those of the slum-dwellers, a group of wealthy individuals would select a vicar in some poor district, make a pet of him and provide him with funds—often very large funds—for the alleviation of distress. Alternatively a well-to-do West End parish would adopt a slum parish in the East End, and finance it annually to the amount (maybe) of many hundreds of pounds.

The benefactors seldom dreamed of going to see the district they planned to help, or considered that anything further was required of them once they had paid their money. The "adopted" clergymen, therefore, were left to their own devices in spending the charitable subsidies, and in a few cases used the money with more parade than discrimination. In effect, they bought for their Church a superficial reverence, because they could not (or would not) trouble, by example and toilsome service, to inspire a genuine piety. When a vicarage becomes a Mecca for vagabonds and a vicar a dole-distributor, the rot of pauperisation has set in. So much for attendance at Sunday service, tickets for coal, free meals, cash paid out to all and sundry who came whining with distress stories—such prodigalities as these, however Christianly meant, will reduce any parish to moral chaos. The deserving poor suffer in silence for their self-respect; the unscrupulous parasites thrive on the heedless scattering of unadministered charity.

Of the handful of parishes who thus purchased what should have been won by Christian endeavour, that of All Saints, Lower Marsh, was a notorious example, and a sore trial to its neighbours. Its reputation for bread, circuses and ceremonial invited exploitation by wastrels from miles around, infuriated the Nonconformists, and caused distress and difficulty to poor Mr Meadows, striving next door to pit humanity and common sense against the demoralising glitter of sacerdotal bribery.

Not, one may be sure, that Mr Meadows envied his neighbouring vicar the responsibility for Granby Street. He had troubles in plenty of his own. Indeed, just because they were not, like Granby Street, utterly irreclaimable, the dark patches under his care were the more troublesome and heart-breaking. They were not the people themselves who drove him to despair. He might deplore their degradation, their turbulence and their squalor; he might observe with a heavy heart, as he passed through Tenison Street or along his section of York Road, the perpetual in-and-out traffic, with drunken men in tow, of painted slatterns of all ages who kept an open door or hired six feet of flock on broken springs, somewhere upstairs behind the grimy frontages.

But he did not condemn. What chance had these folk to be other than squalid and vicious?

Nobody cared for them or helped them. From babyhood boys and girls were turned into the streets, to learn such lessons as the streets could teach and thereafter to feed themselves as best they might. These and other shifts forced on its victims by grinding poverty were obstacles enough in the path of goodwill. But there were worse enemies than they—

agencies actively at work to drive the boys to loafing, sneak-thievery or pimping and the girls to sell the only labour they could offer. It was with these agencies that Mr Meadows was doggedly at war. His ceaseless—at times it seemed his hopeless—battle was against the small landlords who profited by debauching their property; against the Vestry, who in part consisted of such landlords; and against the Overseers, whose duty it was to support him but too often found it to their interest to do the opposite.[1]

In connection with this campaign he made the acquaintance of Gervase Wilbraham Crocker, and the encounter came about in the following way.

A hair tonic had enriched the first recorded Crocker, and

[1] Prior to the establishment of the L.C.C. in 1888, London Local Government—in so far as were concerned administration of the Poor Laws, relief of distress, rate-collection and general supervision of housing conditions and public decency—was on a parochial basis. The whole body of rate-payers of each parish were supposed to meet and elect parish officers—Churchwardens, " Overseers " (or " Directors " or " Guardians ") of the Poor, Rate-collectors, etc.—and these officers constituted the Vestry, and became the governing body of their particular parish. A few central authorities existed before the creation of the L.C.C. and, after that date, Vestries still survived in certain parishes, but in the main with powers greatly curtailed.

At the date of this story government by Vestry was still more or less universal. It is easy to imagine, on the one hand the confusion and jealousies likely to arise between a host of semi-independent and narrowly localised administrative bodies, on the other the possibilities of corruption inherent in a system which presumed active participation of the great majority of rate-payers, but in fact —owing to the apathy of some and the private preoccupations of others— fell into the hands of cliques of local bosses and was exploited in their private interest.

Two incidents which actually occurred during the seventies of last century in South London parishes will demonstrate the sort of thing which went on, and the type of person in authority with whom Mr Meadows had to contend in his battle on behalf of poverty and slumdom.

A contract for constructional work of some kind was open for tender. With the figures before them, the Vestry decided to give the contract to the man asking the highest price. The vicar of the parish, who sat on the board, protested. " It is all very well for Mr —— to talk " said a fellow-member in full committee. " He has no relations in the trade."

The other incident concerned Outdoor Relief, which at that date amounted to the sum of half a crown a week plus a loaf of bread. The aged poor had to attend the offices of the Vestry to collect their relief, and on the board of one particular parish was a man who owned a group of small tenement houses let to recipients of this Outdoor Dole. This man stood in the road outside the offices on pay-day ; and as each of the tenants came out with his or her half-crown, he levied the amount of rent due to him.

had converted the second into a country gentleman. This product was manufactured in Southwark; and the incumbent of St Michael's, Lant Street, over supper with Mr Meadows one evening, was discussing his own difficulties in a parish far more incorrigible than that of his host.

"In quite half my district" he said "there is literally nothing I can do. Here and there in the north-eastern section we make a little progress, here and there the people will at least listen and believe we mean them well. But from my very vicarage up to Union Street and beyond lies an area we just cannot reach. God knows I have tried; and I am glad to be able to say that I have never been actually molested. But they mock at the Church and insult her ministers; and for all the results obtained, we might none of us ever have penetrated that horrible maze of courts. The only missionaries who seem to come and go are a few queer Bible-Readers. I doubt their having any influence. Poor souls, they look as dreary as the streets they visit. This, however, is curious. There is a man called Crocker who owns works in my parish, and he is said to be connected with this funny sect. He's a rich man and has a taste for philanthropy. Unfortunately, although I have met him and thought him genuine in his charitable impulses, I am so baulked by the desperate conditions all around, that I have no practical suggestions to make to him as to how money could be spent to advantage. Of course I could take his money and waste it, like our friends just over there; but—well, you understand. . . ."

Mr Meadows nodded sympathetically, and for a few moments the two men ate in silence. Then the visitor suddenly looked up and gestured with his fork.

"Gracious me!—this only just occurs to me—I wonder whether Crocker could be induced to help you? Admittedly your case against the Overseers is not altogether the sort of thing which appeals to him. He loves committees and agenda and solemn resolutions and public demonstrations on behalf of religion and virtue; and of course, short of conferences with counsel, there won't be much of any of them in which he can appear in person. But it might be worth trying. If you *are* really going to court, you will need funds—"

"I shall indeed" replied Mr Meadows "and plenty of them. Your philanthropist will be a Godsend. How do we tackle him?"

* * * * *

A fortnight later Mr Meadows was introduced to Mr Crocker in the study at St Michael's vicarage. He saw a large, globular individual, who although not yet forty-five looked ten years older, with a smooth pale face, a bald head, and a general resemblance to a hairless seal. The man was dressed entirely in black and had a heavy chin and a protruding lower lip. His manner was unctuous, and his voice more caressing and oily than the clergyman could have wished. But, as they talked, Mr Meadows came gradually to share his colleague's belief that this strange and unprepossessing individual was genuine. He appeared to have a passion for charitable endeavour; and that the enthusiasm should be combined with a desire to be connected with as many governing bodies, councils and committees as possible, did not make it any less concrete.

Mr Crocker listened in solemn silence while the clergyman described the crusade on which he had recently embarked. He had formed a committee of respectable local tradesmen to whom the steady deterioration of the neighbourhood was a serious matter. Two ex-policemen had been engaged by this committee to watch, over a period of some weeks, a particular pair of houses in Cross Street, off York Road, and to make a careful hour-by-hour record of the couples going in and out. This record Mr Meadows had then presented to the Overseers as a formal complaint by inhabitants of the parish who (in the words of the Act of George II which still governed the method of dealing with brothels and brothel-keepers) "bore lot and paid Scot", and demanded that action be taken. The Overseers were at first abusive, then sullen, and finally, though outwardly acquiescent, deliberately obstructive. The vicar now wished to force the issue and sue these unjust stewards in the High Court, but neither he nor the local committee could afford to risk losing their case. Would Mr Crocker help?

The big man stood for a few moments as though bowed in prayer, his hands lightly clasped in front of him. Then he slowly raised his head and gazed at the clergyman with small, surprisingly bright eyes.

"You may count on me, Mr Meadows" he said (his voice was like black velvet). "You may count on me. With your permission I will instruct my solicitors to retain my friend Tremlett Q.C., and give myself the pleasure of calling upon you tomorrow to obtain a copy of the painful record of these houses of sin, as well as any other particulars which our legal advisers may require."

The strange creature was as good as his word. The case was won; the houses in Cross Street and several more were prosecuted by the exasperated but frightened Vestry, and those in charge were fined. The Overseer chiefly responsible for baulking prosecution in the past was so severely censured in court, that the Vestry had no option but to dismiss him immediately the case was over. Meadows was justifiably proud of his victory; and felt toward his benefactor such gratitude and respect, that he ceased to notice the eccentricity and sanctimony which appeared to be as inherent a part of the man as were his zeal and generosity on behalf of righteousness.

He racked his brains for some means of repaying, by counter-service, what he owed to Mr Crocker. It seemed hopeless. How should a humble priest of a poor parish find a way to benefit a rich man he hardly knew, and one whose path might never again cross his? In despair he gave up wondering; but he did not forget.

*   *   *   *   *

Crocker, no less than Meadows, was much gratified at his successful intervention in the affairs of St John's parish. But, as the vicar of St Michael's had foreseen, it had not been possible for his share in the Cross Street purge to be publicly advertised. No offer of a vice-presidency was attached to it; no fund, which might have borne his name, was to be established. The case was a straight fight between a crusading parson and a venal Vestry, and such glory as emerged from the battle attached to Meadows and his brilliant counsel, whose pitiless handling of the defendants was warmly applauded.

Crocker felt no jealousy on this account. He was not a jealous man. But he loved to think that his good deeds so shone before the world that others emulated them, and that his name would come to be enshrined in the hearts of generations of God-fearing folk as that of a Great Exemplar. He had, therefore, no hesitation in talking freely of the part he had played behind the scenes in the High Court affair; and it was soon fairly widely known that, but for Crocker's support, the Rev. Alfred Meadows would not only not have won his case, but might have been unable to bring it at all.

*   *   *   *   *

There now occurred one of those coincidences which are so much commoner in real life than in fiction that novelists are advised to avoid them, lest their stories lose the glamour of impossibility and read as drably as fact.

Mr Meadows had occasion to attend a diocesan meeting in Dean's Yard, Westminster. When the meeting was over, he remembered that he required some new slides for the magic-lantern with which he sometimes sought to enliven the boys-club and girls-club evenings in his Parish Room. These slides were obtainable at a shop in Victoria Street, and as it was a fine afternoon and the shop near at hand, he decided to go there and choose his slides forthwith. He crossed the open space in front of the Abbey and, turning left, began strolling along the south side of the handsome new thoroughfare, which a few years earlier had been driven through the slums around Tothill Fields. Suddenly he was aware of three men coming towards him on the opposite pavement. They were walking abreast and apparently engaged in earnest discussion. Perhaps it would be more correct to say that two of them seemed to be earnestly pleading with, or trying to convince, the third, who moved along between them with the smooth majesty of a ship under full sail and, though doubtless listening to the adjurations or reasoning of his companions, permitted no indication of approval or otherwise to disturb his large pale face.

This man was Mr Crocker.

On his right, nearest to the gutter, frisked a small lean individual with darting eyes, who gestured sharply as he talked and might have been on wires, so restless and varied were his movements. Meadows, however, wasted little time on a being unknown to him. His attention was fully engaged by the figure on Crocker's left, a square figure with short legs and the high complexion which goes with red or sandy hair. This was no stranger; and as, in a fraction of the time it takes to tell, the vicar took in the personalities of the approaching trio, he realised that he himself must not be seen. Swinging about, he ran up the steps of the house nearest at hand and into the vestibule where the names of office-holders were placarded. The vestibule was empty, so that Meadows was able, immediately the three had crossed his line of vision, to watch them from behind as they went slowly up the street.

At the corner of Tothill Street, they paused. The talkative pair were driving home their argument. Crocker stood solemnly between them, clasping an umbrella to his stomach. Then he bowed with unsmiling condescension and hailed a passing cab. The other two, hat in hand, stood looking after him; then they conversed for a few moments, their heads close together. When they parted, the quick-moving unknown retraced his steps along Victoria Street and the man with the red face disappeared in the direction of the Park. The vicar emerged from his hiding-place and made his way thoughtfully home.

The next day two things happened. In the morning Mr Meadows wrote to Mr Crocker to ask whether he might call on him at the Southwark factory at any convenient date and hour. In the afternoon a frightened little girl of nine was brought to St John's vicarage by two strange young men, with a sensational but manifestly true story of her rescue at their hands from a flogging forthwith and worse to come, in the stews near Waterloo Station. The clergyman handed the child over to his devoted housekeeper. In a couple of days he was able to report to her deliverers that she was on the mend and that the injuries, though shocking enough, were surface-wounds only.

His reply from Mr Crocker came promptly. In its portentous way it was almost cordial, and Meadows soon found himself in a solemn mahogany office on the premises of Crocker's Delilah Hair Tonic, facing the lugubrious but formidable figure of the Chairman himself. He had prepared his opening words and wasted no time over small-talk.

"Mr Crocker" he said "I have come on what may seem at first sight an impertinent mission. You know, however, how much I owe to your kindness and can guess that I should wish above all things to do you some service in return. I ask you, therefore, to believe me when I say that I have felt it my duty to seek this interview."

Crocker acknowledged this prelude with a gentle nod of the head. He was sitting back in his chair, looking down at the blotting-paper on the desk in front of him, his hands lightly folded across his midriff. When he spoke he did not raise his eyes or make any movement save with his lips.

"Between man and man, Mr Meadows, in a spirit of loving kindness, there can be no impertinence. Besides your cloth entitles you to say whatsoever our Father bids you. Proceed."

"Thank you" replied the clergyman. "Then I will speak my mind. About a week ago I chanced to see you in Victoria Street, walking with two other—er—gentlemen. One of them was a perfect stranger to me; but the other was not, and I conceive it only right that I should tell you that man is a scoundrel. I refer to an individual by the name of Spelter."

Crocker slowly lifted his heavy eyelids and glanced at the speaker across the desk. Characteristically he made no reference to the identity of his companions in Victoria Street.

"How is it you are familiar with so disreputable a person?" he asked.

"His business premises are within quarter of a mile of my church—in Wellington Street just across the bridge. They bear a double name: Pershore and Spelter; but Pershore, if he ever existed at all, is no longer active. Spelter is the firm. His business, which describes itself as that of a Surveyor, Estate Agent, Rent Collector and General Factor, is intimately connected with the exploitation of slum property—and worse than slum property—in the most miserable and abandoned areas of Lambeth, Southwark and the Borough. Quite early in my incumbency I came across his traces in my own parish which, incidentally, although very poor, is (apart from a few black spots such as that which you enabled me to erase) reputable, in comparison with its neighbours. I determined to identify the man and see what he looked like. I now get frequent glimpses of him, because my vicarage almost overlooks his quickest route from Wellington Street to more than one of his theatres of operation. I could not mistake him. The person on your left in Victoria Street, Mr Crocker, was Spelter; and now that I have told you what I know of him, I hope I may have done something to put you on your guard in the event of his wishing to enter into any business relation with you." He rose and held out his hand. "I will take no more of your time. Thank you for receiving me and listening so patiently. Good morning."

"Good morning, Mr Meadows." Crocker remained seated, but leant heavily forward to touch the clergyman's hand. "I am obliged to you for communicating to me your opinion of this man. Should I happen to come across him, I shall bear your words in mind."

He sank back into his chair, and did not move for some minutes after the door had closed behind his visitor.

GERVASE WILBRAHAM CROCKER was not a stupid man; but for a man of his age, means and varied activities he was abnormally simple. Lethargic by temperament and incurious about the affairs of his fellow-men, he attributed to others some degree of his own self-sufficiency, and relied on his native caution (which, except when it came to blazoning abroad his own benefactions, was very strong) to keep the inquisitive minority at arm's length. This blend of indifference to others and belief in his own capacity for secretiveness made him a poor judge of character. However interested one might be in the affairs of Mr Crocker, it was only necessary to conceal the fact to be safe from suspicion.

Undoubtedly he would long ago have been catastrophically fooled, had he been more venturesome in his dealings with life. But his ambitions were restricted, and hitherto, although he was laughed at behind his back for his mania for sitting on committees and seeing his name as patron of this and that, he had come to no other harm. As he was wholly unable to see himself as a figure of fun, even this mild punishment at the world's hands caused him no distress.

That he should have received Mr Meadows at the headquarters of the Delilah Hair Tonic Manufacturing Company Limited did not indicate that he took an active part in its commercial proceedings. He had inherited from his father a profitable and well-run business, and his only duty was to appear as Chairman at the Annual Meeting and deliver a well-rounded and complacent address about the year's working and the Nobility of Service to the Community. It pleased him, however, to keep a private office in the Southwark factory, and, on his frequent visits to London, to drive thither from his club in a hired brougham, receive from his confidential clerk a report on the various missions, charities, bazaars and what not in which he was interested, and then drive back again to St James's Street. The majority of his appointments were made at his club; but the clergyman had asked to come to Southwark and Crocker, being a considerate person, had suited his plans to meet the other's convenience.

He now sat perfectly still and with closed eyes, brooding in his slow and careful way over what Meadows had said.

Until Sneade had introduced him to Spelter in the Torch-bearers' offices some days earlier, he had never seen or heard of the man. He had not liked Spelter, but neither had he particularly disliked him. He was seldom sufficiently inter-ested in other people to be for or against them. As for the proposal which he had been asked to consider, he had taken in its terms (which meant nothing to him beyond what they said) and according to his usual practice refused to commit himself. He now summoned these terms from the recesses of his memory.

Spelter, who described himself as an estate agent with special knowledge of properties in the south-eastern district of the city, had stated that he had for some while acted on behalf of the late John Gladwin in respect of a small group of streets off Waterloo Road which had now passed into Crocker's possession. As soon as he had been apprised of the new ownership, he had realised that property suitable enough to a private and absentee landlord-speculator was not necessarily suitable as part of the endowment of a Society with the exalted ideals of the one over which Mr Crocker presided. Further, he had reason to think that the value of this particular property would rapidly decline, so that good taste and com-mercial prudence combined to recommend a change of investment. To the Chairman's enquiry as to the nature of the property and why it was likely to lose value, Spelter had replied, first that it was small-house property in dilapidated condition, which might call at any time for a heavy outlay in repairs; and second, that it was threatened by railway extensions, for which Statutory Powers would be obtained and, maybe, a forced sale imposed.

He ventured to suggest, therefore, that Crocker empower him to sell this particular property and buy another or others in its place. He had reason to believe that he could at the present moment obtain x thousand pounds for it, from a party less well informed than himself about the condition of the buildings and the prospects of the area. He held himself at the disposal of the Society to recommend substitute properties, if it was decided to reinvest in real estate. Sneade had warmly supported Spelter's proposal.

Crocker had received two impressions only from this exposé—that he owned some bad property which might involve him in heavy expenditure, and that this property might be forcibly taken from him at an arbitrator's price on behalf of a Railway Company. He disliked the idea of heavy expenditure, and he knew, as between private ownership and the requirements of powerful bodies like railway companies, to whose side arbitration would lean. Certainly he refused to commit himself; but these were the considerations which possessed him as he drove away from the corner of Tothill Street. It did not occur to him to question Spelter's description of the property; and his ignorance of that part of London (despite the location of the Delilah works and the fact that trains from his Surrey home ran into Waterloo) was so complete, that even Lower Marsh —casually mentioned by Spelter and the only precise indication given of the whereabouts of the area under discussion—was but a name to him. He left all that sort of detail to Sneade; and Sneade seemed to think this property should be disposed of. He felt that after a further day or two of reflection he would probably agree.

That had been his mood prior to the clergyman's visit. Suddenly, however, a new element had been introduced into the problem. Crocker had learnt to admire the Rev. Alfred Meadows during their association over the Cross Street affair. He still did not know precisely where Cross Street was, nor did he wish to do so. Still less had he any inclination to go and look at it. But he had been impressed by the sincerity and forcefulness of the vicar of St John's, both during the preliminaries to the case and before the High Court. And now this man, whom he respected and trusted, roundly declared that Spelter was a scoundrel, and warned his kind benefactor against having any dealings with him.

If Spelter were indeed a scoundrel (and as Mr Meadows said he was, he was) his proposal to the Torchbearers must be in some way a dishonest one. Very characteristically, Crocker did not at the moment bestir himself to speculate on the nature of the dishonesty. It was sufficient to him that he—Gervase Wilbraham Crocker—might be the victim of a plot. He decided that he must proceed with the utmost caution until he felt himself impregnable against any kind of conspiracy. He rang for his brougham and started for Victoria Street to try a preliminary skirmish with Sneade.

The carriage had only gone a few hundred yards when, with an impulsiveness very foreign to his nature (and in itself proof of his high regard for Meadows), he determined to call at St John's vicarage and thank the vicar for what had chanced to be a most opportune piece of advice. The short detour was made, and in a few minutes he was greeting Meadows in his bleak and untidy study.

"You are no doubt surprised to see me again so soon" he said, "but since you left me I have carefully weighed your words. I will not attempt to conceal that the man in my company the other day was this man Spelter, nor that he had a business proposal to make concerning the welfare of the Missionary Society of which, as you know, I have the honour to be Chairman. My growing inclination had been to accept his proposal; but now, in view of what you said to me, I shall investigate the matter further, and not commit myself one way or the other. I have called to thank you for —possibly—having saved me from a hasty decision I might have come to regret."

"My dear sir" rejoined Meadows "nothing could please me more than in some slight degree to have repaid your kindness to me."

"More than repaid, Mr Meadows; more than repaid. I

regard myself now as in your debt, and beg you to call upon me at any time for any help I can render you."

An idea flashed into the vicar's mind. He hesitated a moment, and then said tentatively:

"You embarrass me with your goodwill, Mr Crocker. I seem to cancel one obligation only to pile up another! But inasmuch as we parsons are inveterate beggars on behalf of others, I will take you at your word and ask if you can help me to find a temporary refuge for an unfortunate waif of the slums."

He proceeded to give a rapid account of the rescue of Lottie Heape and her lodgment in his care.

"It is essential" he concluded "that I find some worthy soul out of London—or at any rate this part of London— who will take in the little girl and care for her until she can be put in the way of earning an honest living. It is dangerous for her to remain here. The sewer rats, from whom she was providentially saved, will shrink from nothing, once they know where she is, to get her back again.

"Why should they want her back?"

Meadows stared for a moment in sheer astonishment at the man who asked this singular question. But there was no trace of irony or cynicism in Crocker's voice or expression, and he realised the enquiry to have been made in genuine ignorance. Instinctively he began a stumbling, evasive explanation, such as one would give to a schoolboy or a young lady.

"Well"—he began, "well, you see, sir, that—er—girl-children are valuable to the ruffians who—er—that is to say to the persons who profit from what we call—er—the Social Evil. They buy the children or kidnap them, sometimes in babyhood, with the deliberate purpose of launching them at the earliest possible age into a life of sin, and themselves enjoying the wages of the poor creatures' degradation. . . ."

Crocker gazed owlishly at the Vicar.

"You shock me immeasurably" he said after a moment of silence. "I have heard tell, of course, of miserable outcasts selling themselves in the streets of our cities. But I have always assumed these women had entered upon an evil life from sheer wantonness. Now you tell me that they have been forced into it to the profit of others! Dreadful, dreadful —I had no idea . . . no idea at all. . . ." Again he fell silent, and stood with bowed head, pulling at his lower lip. With a deep sigh he added: "And this little girl at present under your care was destined to this fate, and may yet suffer it if she be not removed to safety?"

"I fear there can be no doubt of it."

Once more Crocker appeared to fade into laborious reverie. His unwieldy figure in dead black, topped by a large oval face and bald head, fungus-pale in contrast, was oddly pathetic. More to himself than to Meadows he murmured:

"Whosoever shall offend one of these little ones, it is better for him that a millstone were hanged about his neck and he were cast into the sea."

He seemed to pull himself together and be turning to go when, as though suddenly aware of the clergyman standing at his elbow, he said in his normal voice:

"The young men who saved this child did a brave deed. Who were they?"

"I only know their names and that one of them writes for the newspapers. He is called Merton and the other Gladwin."

"The other—did you say Gladwin?"

The vicar nodded, and observed with some embarrassment that Crocker was again gazing at him with ruminative solemnity. At last

"Is Gladwin a common name?" asked Crocker.

"I don't think it is, very. I cannot recollect having known anyone so called."

"Nor I, Mr Meadows, nor I."

Sneade stood up as the Chairman of the Torchbearers entered the room.

"Good day, sir. Pray be seated."

"Thank you, Mr Sneade. I wanted to have a few words with you in regard to the matter we were discussing the other

68

day—the proposal made by Mr—er—Spelter. I have not yet come to any conclusion, because I am not sure whether I quite understand my present position *vis-à-vis* this property. Is Mr Spelter formally recognised as my agent, as apparently he was the agent for our benefactor?"

"Not formally, sir, no. He has carried on during the interregnum and, as I reported the other day, paid over to me recently an accumulation of income which he had been holding on your behalf. I am sure, however, that if you decide to keep the property he will be glad to serve the Society in the future as he served the late Mr Gladwin in the past."

"This money derives from rents?"

"Yes, sir, from rents."

"And Mr Spelter collects them?"

"Possibly not in person, but he is responsible for the collection."

Crocker sat without speaking while he digested this information.

"As I recall the sum paid over to you" he said at last "it was a considerable one for small house-property in bad repair. Assuming we accept the x thousand pounds which it is suggested the property would fetch, I doubt our finding an investment with an equivalent yield."

"You must remember, sir, that the money is an accumulation. Also that heavy expenditure on repairs must be envisaged." To himself Sneade wondered whether it would not have been wiser to dock the Society of more than a quarter of the total sum. What was the old man getting at?

"Have you visited the property, Mr Sneade?"

"I, sir? Oh, no. I am no judge of streets and buildings as real estate. I have always been more of a country than a town mouse." He showed his sharp teeth in a tight mirthless smile, and Crocker, who had seen that smile often and often, wondered fleetingly and for the first time whether "mouse" were not a misnomer. "*Experto crede* is my motto, sir, and there can be no doubt that Spelter knows his job in that area."

The Chairman nodded.

"Whereabouts exactly did Mr Spelter say this property is?"

Sneade darted an uneasy glance at the impassive face.

"I—I really hardly recall—somewhere in the neighbour-hood of Waterloo Station, I believe."

"You have the schedule of the Gladwin bequest?"

"It is lodged at the bank, sir."

"This money received the other day—I presume, as you gave the receipt, it appears in our books. May I see the entry?"

Sneade rose, and going to a safe in the corner took out a ledger. He was disturbed by this interview, and anxiously tried to recall the wording of the entry registering Spelter's payment. He found the page in the ledger, and his fears were confirmed. Discretion as to whereabouts had not then seemed so essential as adjustment of the sum received. There the entry was: "Granby Street, etc. rents." What an idiotic mistake to have made! More than idiotic. Perhaps calami-tous. Hardly daring to breathe, he held the ledger open while Crocker peered over his shoulder.

"Granby Street" muttered the Chairman. "Granby Street. I never heard of it."

He wandered back to where his hat stood on the corner of the desk, picked it up, looked inside it, and then said, in a manner which for him was almost nonchalant:

"By the way, what about young Gladwin?"

This sudden challenge had the effect of rallying Sneade. There was at least no danger in this topic.

"What about him, sir? I do not quite understand."

"I seem to recall that we were to employ him in some capacity. I fear it slipped my memory, but this other matter has brought the Gladwin bequest back into my mind, and the young man with it."

"I am afraid" replied Sneade with gentle melancholy "that he must be written off as hopeless. I devised an occupation for him, as I was bidden, and wrote asking him to call here and see me. But he never turned up and I have heard nothing more of him. You will remember, sir, that his father was compelled virtually to disinherit him, and—" he shrugged his shoulders—"well, you cannot make a silk purse out of a sow's ear."

70

Crocker listened in silence and slowly shook his head. "Dear, dear" he said. "Is that so? A great pity." Without another word he lumbered from the room.

Crocker weighed carefully the incidents of his conversation with the Secretary of the Torchbearers. The man had seemed nervous and a little evasive. It really looked as though something were in the wind.

At his club a few days later he found himself next to a prominent solicitor with whom he was acquainted.

"May I ask you a question, Lorimer? Not a professional question, but one which as a Londoner and a man of the world—neither of which I can myself claim to be—you may be able to answer?" As the other nodded, he went on: "Are you familiar with a locality near Waterloo Station called Granby Street?"

Lorimer thought a moment, then shook his head.

"No. I am afraid not. But no doubt I can find out for you. You want to know. . . .?"

"Oh, just the sort of district it is, you know" said Crocker vaguely. "Shops or decent working-class houses or very poor or—well, any general information."

The next time he saw Lorimer, the lawyer drew him into a corner.

"Granby Street" he said. He leant forward and spoke in a rapid undertone. When he had finished, Crocker thanked him gravely for his trouble and moved out of the room. His expression had remained unchanged during the lawyer's résumé of what Granby Street stood for, and his voice, when he spoke, was dull to indifference. Lorimer looked after him with a puzzled frown. "Well" he said to himself "he's a queer customer and no mistake! What did he expect?" And with the slight resentment of one whose funny or sensational story has fallen flat, he buried himself in a newspaper.

Actually Lorimer's story had not fallen flat at all. Very much the reverse. Crocker was both shocked and perturbed, and the supine stolidity with which he had received the

71

startling information was his natural protective colouring. He drove to his Southwark office and sat down to consider his position.

It was an awkward one. A major proportion of the income bequeathed, and now legally transferred to him for the benefit of the Torchbearers, derived from a district which no decent man—let alone a Missionary Society—could conceivably tolerate. The money produced by his ownership of this district came through the agency of a man reliably stated to be a man of bad character. It was now obvious that he must be so; no one but a bad character would be in a position to collect rents from such a source. Therefore, to quarrel with Spelter was equivalent to losing the money. That was remediable; the Society's income could be made up out of Crocker's own pocket. But his individual ownership of Granby Street would remain. How could it be liquidated? The only way to be rid of it was by sale. Yet was he— a man of substance, a J.P. and a member of any number of public committees—to appear before strangers as vendor of this unsavoury property? Impossible. Equally impossible was it for him to act through a third party without taking this third party into his confidence. He would never be able to bring himself to confess to a friend that he had been landed in such a discreditable predicament.

There remained the fact that Spelter, who was in the secret already, had offered to negotiate a sale. No doubt this meant that a sale would be to Spelter's advantage. But it was now evident that to let Spelter arrange a sale would be a way of shaking off this detestable legacy, and would keep his own connection with it from the ears of outsiders. As he brooded on the matter, it struck him what a queer kind of legacy it was, to such a Society as theirs! For the first time it occurred to Crocker that John Gladwin might have made his Will, not as a tribute to the work of the Torchbearers, but out of malice.

With a heavy heart, and after a broken night of vain reflection, Crocker sent word to Sneade that he felt he ought to act on Spelter's suggestion, and that the latter should be asked to submit the best offer obtainable for "the south side property we were discussing a few days ago."

Meantime, and despite this harassing preoccupation, he did not forget Mr Meadows' anxiety over the rescued child. Before very long the clergyman received a letter from Lashwater Park.

"I have found a refuge for your little girl. Among my outside staff are a childless couple who will be glad to take her in. They live in one of my lodges which can accommodate a newcomer. The child will be cared for and happy, and in due course we will see what can be done to find her respectable and useful employment. There is, of course, no question of payment. It is a privilege to assist in snatching one little brand from the burning. The enclosed draft will buy her the necessary minimum of clothing and a railway ticket."

There followed instructions to send the child by a certain train, which would be met at the other end. A postscript read:

"Should you happen to know of a suitable young man to prepare my elder son for the Entrance Examination to Westminster School, may I be favoured with a word? The boy is now ten and will require a year of special tuition, if he is to succeed."

BOOK TWO
LASHWATER

LASHWATER IN THE 'sixties was still a pleasant little country town, with a mellow High Street and Assembly Rooms in the massive, unpretentious, yet well-mannered style of the very early 'thirties.

Of course it was damp, being situate on the very banks of the Thames at one of the places where the river valley is at its widest and shallowest. Flat meadows surrounded the town. In winter or after heavy rain these were regularly flooded; in autumn they lay for weeks on end under a drenching mist. But since in those days the meadows were not built over, and since Lashwater itself stood just above flood-level, the towns-people took flood and fog for granted, and forgot winter and autumn in the joys of spring and summer. Then indeed the meadows made amends. Garish with marsh-marigolds, starred with meadow-sweet and gilly-flower, their soggy dykes alight with yellow mimulus, they sang a song of colour from dawn to dusk, and the sober little town smiled back at them from its slight eminence, and preened itself to hear in harmony the glowing voices of the meadowlands and the whisper of the gentle river.

Why Lashwater existed where it did is easily explained. Since the mid-eighteenth century a fine brick bridge with stone facings had carried over the Thames a turnpike from London to the west. With the bridge had come a posting-inn; the area had become accessible from London; shops had sprung up among the scattered hovels of the earlier hamlet; and in the place of the tiny chapel-of-ease had been built an imposing church (also of brick with stone facings) in the tantalising style of the mid-seventeen hundreds, which sought to lighten classicism with gothic jimps but achieved only a solemn frolic.

77

From that time onward Lashwater was a town, and, everyone agreed, had excellent reason for being one.

Some time during the final decade of the eighteenth century a somewhat mysterious gentleman appeared in Lashwater. It transpired that he had purchased a considerable area of land along the river, including a low mound on which stood a mean and partially derelict house and fragmentary ruins of a one-time monastery with, growing around them, several fine cedar-trees. The newcomer demolished all of the house and most of the ruins, incorporated what remained in a new house, fenced in the mound, laid out gardens, and christened the place Mount Felix.

This gentleman's name was Hilary St Maur. He came of an old Catholic family, was evidently well-to-do, and showed himself highly cultivated in directions unfamiliar to the robust, genial, but (it must be confessed) limited occupants of the few country-houses in the neighbourhood. His very appearance made them uneasy; for he was a thin, graceful man, with liquid eyes and a Van Dyke beard framing a mouth unusually dainty for an English squire. He wore long cloaks with coloured silk linings and a wide-brimmed hat. His house was no less unconventional, being elaborately neo-gothic and plastered all over to a deep cream, which admittedly gleamed prettily through the dark spread of the cedars, but so emphasised the cusps and pinnacles and blind tracery of the façade as to have an effect unduly fanciful for the neighbouring gentry's taste.

All manner of rumours as to the past of the St Maurs and their reasons for coming to Lashwater circulated in the town and neighbourhood, but of these rumours the truth fell sadly short. The family had lived in Italy. Their circle had been passionately interested in sculpture and painting; and the St Maurs would have asked nothing better than to spend a lifetime of cultured lotus-eating in the beautiful villa near Florence. But the children were growing up, and the parents felt they should be given an opportunity to sample the adult world of their own country and decide for themselves whether to settle there or not. Friendly co-religionists were asked to find a suitable site for a house, giving preference to an area of greenery and running water, for both of which the Italianate St Maurs, much as they loved their exile, had nostalgia. In this manner they came finally to Lashwater. The wealth of the family derived from sugar plantations in the Indies.

The usual exchange of civilities took place between the leading persons of the district and rich newcomers who, however disconcerting, were evidently gentlefolk. But little progress toward intimacy was made from either side, for the St Maurs and Lashwater bored one another. Gradually the former so far withdrew into the elaborate seclusion of Mount Felix, that in time they saw hardly anyone save occasional visitors from London.

Thus a traditional isolation became attached to the house on the mound, which persisted after the death of the first Hilary and throughout the lifetime of the second. Indeed during this latter period it was intensified by the financial stringency which the abolition of slavery and the ruin of the sugar plantations brought upon the household. Whereas the previous generation had been able to indulge their sense of superiority to their neighbours in the grand manner and with every luxury, the ménage now found itself embarrassed; and consciousness of having fallen from a high estate combined with an absence of close local contacts to drive Mount Felix more than ever in upon itself.

With the accession of the third Hilary, however (whose name was in fact Hugh), conditions changed. Hugh St Maur was a sociable person with a gay and pretty wife. He had no false modesty about his comparative poverty; indeed he made a joke of it.

So friendly and unassuming were Hugh St Maur and his wife that they rapidly became popular in the town of Lashwater and its immediate vicinity. Further afield was beyond their orbit, for they kept no carriage, but only a couple of skewbald hackneys which were constantly to be seen in the High Street or in the neighbouring lanes and fields. There was a happiness about the St Maurs which charmed the well-disposed and was perfectly genuine. They *were* happy, having only this grief in common that they had but one child and she a girl. They would have dearly liked a son, not instead of Hester whom they adored, but in addition to her. That, however, might never be, for Hester's birth had been a difficult and dangerous one, and the mother was forbidden to have another baby.

*   *   *   *   *

In the year 1861 the eighth birthday of Hester St Maur was made an occasion for a children's party. It was summer, and the pleasant, rather neglected gardens of Mount Felix were loud with the cries of excited young. Two groups of adults—one of parents, chattering restrainedly, the other (less murmurous) of nursemaids and grooms—were gathered on opposite sides of the house. The cake had been cut and a large tea eaten and the shadows of the cedars were beginning to lengthen. One last game of hide-and-seek was in progress, and then the visitors must begin to go home.

One of the gothic extravagances committed by the first Mr St Maur had been an end-wall of a miniature and non-existent church. Complete with three traceried lancet-windows (the tracery suitably broken to register decay), with on each side a flying buttress (one ruined) and with irregular edges to its roofless gable (in the chinks of which grew grass and wild geranium), this two-dimensional erection was so placed that the moon, rising from behind the wooded slope beyond the river, would at a given moment of her course cast a gleaming line across the water, and shine through the shattered tracery in a highly rhapsodical and ghostly manner.

This picturesque frontage, viewed from the house, showed no trace of the side-walls of the building it purported to survive. The romantic ruin rose sheer to its inconsiderable height. But away from the house and toward the river some sort of prop had been essential; and the architect had provided rough stairways of plastered masonry, which climbed upward from their foundations and supported the windowed façade. Between these, and just below the level of the window ledge, ran a broad shelf on which a man could stand and look up across the sloping lawns to where Mount Felix shone pale behind the cedars. Access to the shelf was easy from one of the stairway-buttresses; but the other was cut off in its prime, having been hollowed out to make a small room, in which, while the place was building, the workmen had kept their tools and drunk their beer, and to which in later days the gentry could hasten for shelter, should they be so unfortunate as to be caught in a shower while inspecting the ruin.

In this small room on this summer afternoon of the year 1861 Hester St Maur, aged eight, and Mervyn Crocker, aged ten, were hiding from the pair of children chosen to be "he". They had been there several minutes, and shrieks from here and there about the grounds told of less skilful fugitives found and captured. Hester was a dark-haired little girl, with a skin of dusky cream, a faint colour in her cheeks and melting eyes like those of a spaniel. Her face narrowed below the ears, and a dimple at one corner of a lively little mouth, combined with a pointed chin, gave her an elfish look, so that the lower part of the face spoke of humour and mischief while the upper was all caressing wistfulness. She slipped a hot hand into that of her companion.

"I like you, Mervyn" she said gravely. "I shall marry you when I grow up."

The boy grinned. He had an engaging ugliness, with a wide mouth, eyes set far apart, and tow-coloured hair and eyebrows, the latter hardly visible among the freckles on his forehead.

"That will be prime" he said, looking down with kindly condescension at his small admirer. "Can you cook?"

Hester shook her head.

"Not yet" she replied, "but I suspect I will. I must ask mamma how. I'll go out calling though every afternoon. You can come with me sometimes."

"Who will we call on?"

"Silly! On whoever lives near, and as we don't know where we'll be we don't know who they'll be . . . Ssh!"

She tugged at his hand and pulled him toward the inner corner of their hiding-place.

"Someone coming" she whispered. "Not a sound!"

The footsteps of one of the seekers sounded on the loose stones below the wall. Then paused as their owner gazed about him. The crude stairway was very steep and the seeker already a little weary of his part. He decided against the climb and moved away.

Hester peeped out and began to jump up and down with delight.

"We'll win! We'll win! We've only to run for home. No one will come by here now."

Mervyn allowed himself to be dragged down the steps. Crouching and running through shrubs and under a sunk fence they reached "home" breathless but victorious.

"Touching this marriage" he began, when he had recovered his breath. "Have you decided when it shall be?"

The small girl considered this problem seriously.

"I *think*" she said at last "it will be when I am twenty-one and a half. That will be in November or perhaps early December, and give me time to get the Christmas tree ready and choose the crackers." She turned to him, her little face puckered with amusement. "Wouldn't it be awful if, just as we were preparing for the wedding and I was buying my clothes and you were telling all your friends at the Club how lucky you were, someone *pounced* on me and carried me off?"

"Goodness me, Hetty" he answered, playing up well and affecting great alarm. "That would be *terrible*! You must be *very* careful for months before and not stir outside the house without a great bulldog on a leash."

She clapped her hands.

"A brindled bulldog and his name will be Victor and he will pull so hard that I shall go *scootling* across the roads too quick for anyone to catch me or *pounce* on me."

At this moment the seekers appeared.

"What a shame" they cried. "We caught all the others."

The party dissolved into thanks and farewells. Mr and Mrs St Maur, with Hester between them, stood a few minutes on the terrace watching the children and their belongings straggle across the meadows toward the town. Then, with a final wave to the last of the departing guests, they turned into the house.

"Bed-time and past it, Hetty darling. Run along, and in ten minutes I'll come and tuck you up."

*   *   *   *   *

Among the last to leave were Mervyn Crocker and his younger brother John. Their route lay diagonally across the meadows and not in the direction of the town, for their home stood on high ground two miles inland from the river and could be reached across country by those who knew the tricks. The two boys were seized with the sudden energy which release from the restraints of even a jolly party is apt to provoke in their kind. They ran and shouted and took flying leaps over the dykes which crossed their way. Hester and her matrimonial plans were swept into oblivion, the pleasures of the party and the scrumptious spread for tea and the fight in the cedar-tree between two climbers who met like rival explorers many boughs up and each claimed the right to go higher on the ground that he had got there first— of none of these was a word spoken. Breath was required for purposes more important than retrospect. When at last the boys emerged from field and lane into the rising stretch of road which led to their home, they were hot and blown. Panting but happy, they plodded up the hill and, turning a corner, beheld just ahead of them the huge wrought-iron gates of Lashwater Park and the gable and chimney of the lodge which guarded them.

Lashwater Park, the seat of Gervase Wilbraham Crocker, although the most imposing private residence in the immediate vicinity of the little town, had not the prestige to which its magnificence would seem to entitle it. It was too recent, for one thing, having been completed as lately as 1845. For another, its owner's fortune derived from a hair tonic; and joyful acceptance of a hair-restoring magnate as one of themselves did not as yet come naturally to the conservative gentry of the town and district. For another, the name blandly adopted for his mansion by a wealthy newcomer was considerably resented, because it implied that here was the great house of the neighbourhood. There had been a Lashwater House (Colonel Charteris) since the seventeen-eighties; Mount Felix, prior to the destructive arrival of the St Maurs, had been known for its ruin's sake as Lashwater Abbey; even Lashwater Dene (the Misses Dugard) dated back to 1820. For a perfect stranger to buy St Monica's Hill (an unfenced and beautiful expanse of woodland, sand-pits and open heath, with a fertile little valley running upward to its centre from a fringe of meadows, which ever since Lashwater existed had been a favourite haunt of pedestrians, lovers, birds'-nesting boys and collectors of wild-flowers), to enclose it, to build himself a big house and to christen the whole abomination "Lashwater Park" was in the opinion of old residents intolerable presumption.

The vulgarity had not been committed by Mervyn Crocker's father, but by his grandfather. It was Grandfather John Crocker who had launched the hair tonic on its triumphant career. It was Grandfather John Crocker who in advanced middle-age—wealthy, brusquely unashamed of his origin and past and with as keen an eye for business as ever—hearing rumours to the effect that old Lord Mallenden wanted money, had gone straight to his lordship and offered a big price for St Monica's Hill. It was Grandfather John Crocker who, having startled the absentee landowner into selling, had erased St Monica from the map of Surrey and put Lashwater Park in her place. The old man had lived for ten years in his fine new house, ruling his family and servants like the despot he was, and died in 1855 at the age of eighty-two. The Park had passed to his only son Gervase, already a man in his late thirties with two sons and a daughter.

These boys they were who now, back from the party at Mount Felix and within a few yards of the gates of home, saw that, just inside and at the door of the lodge, stood a cab.

It was a recognisable station-cab and had evidently just arrived. The cabby was unroping a small tin trunk on the roof, while Frost, the second gardener who lived in the lodge, waited below to receive it. Mrs Frost and Marsham—the butler from the Park—stood by the open door, and between them was a female child. Mervyn and John, frankly curious, stopped and stared. The girl appeared pale and frightened. She was about Mervyn's height and wore a shabby black cloak and a plain black straw hat. Her eyes, like those of a trapped animal ready at the first opportunity to make a bolt for it, darted hither and thither in scared dismay. But Mrs Frost had her by the hand, and now the tin trunk was being carried into the cottage. Marsham was turning towards the cab when he saw the young masters.

They were still a little out of breath, their hair was tousled and their shirts were patched with sweat. The butler regarded them with great solemnity.

"There should be room for all of us" he said "unless your lordships prefer to run the last lap also."

The boys made a dive for the cab, which moved off in the direction of the big house.

"What's on, Marshy?" demanded Mervyn. "Who's the kid and where've you been?"

"Acting on instructions from your papa, I fetched from the station a child I have never seen before and deposited her with Mrs Frost for reasons of which I know nothing."

"Oh, cheese it! You might tell a chap!"

"Hardly my place, Master Mervyn, to tell even a chap what is not my business. Besides, beyond the fact that the child's name is Heape I have nothing to tell. No doubt your papa . . ."

At this moment John essayed a sudden lunge at his brother, designed to push an unsuspecting opponent on to the floor of the cab. The elder boy saved his balance and lunged back. The rough-and-tumble lasted for the rest of the short drive, and in the heat of battle Marsham and his secret were forgotten.

*　　*　　*　　*　　*

On the very day when the child from the Granby Street area arrived at Lashwater Park, the master of that establishment was going through the painful process of cutting the connection between himself and the very same district. A painful process indeed—mortifying, manifestly a piece of trickery, yet something which had to be endured lest worse befell.

Spelter, asked to submit an offer from the client of whom he had spoken, reported with great regret that the "prospect" had cooled off. Instead of the x thousand originally hinted at, he now talked of a mere fraction of that sum. Laughable, agreed Spelter, just laughable; but there it was. He was encouraged to try again. In a very short while he returned with a proposal of a different kind. Cash was tight. If Mr Crocker insisted on cash, he would get virtually nothing for a property which, whatever its shortcomings, at least paid a dividend. Might he adapt his original suggestion to the present difficult conditions and offer in exchange an alternative property—or rather a handsome allocation of Founder's Shares in an alternative property? Certainly the yield would not at first be so good. But a safe one and a half per cent was something in these days, and a starting dividend at this rate could be guaranteed. A Company was being formed to build and administer a chain of hotels in London, in one or two places on the south coast, in Paris, in Brussels, maybe in a town in Germany. Travellers would be able to rely on the same standard of comfort and the same general tariff in each one of the Company's hotels, and if the venture succeeded, quite a network of affiliated hostelries might be envisaged. The investment would carry with it the right to a seat on the Board of Directors and to appoint a nominee and a successor; this was a valuable right, not often available to an investor.

After Spelter had withdrawn, Mr Crocker decided to put an end to a position he was finding intolerable. He now saw clearly that he was at the mercy of the estate agent and of whomsoever might be behind him. If he refused to submit to what was in fact robbery, he would be threatened with exposure. If he accepted, he would in all probability be acquiring something worthless. Of the two, the latter was preferable.

He turned to Sneade and spoke with the emphasis of embarrassment.

"There is no point in discussing this matter further. I shall pay into the Society's funds a capital sum sufficient, after investment in some trustee security, to bring in more or less what this accursed property has been in the habit of producing. The amount can be calculated on the basis of the money paid in by Spelter over the period of accumulation. I will then personally surrender the property and receive in exchange the shares in this hotel venture. They are doubtless highly speculative, if not worse; but as a Founder-shareholder with the right to appoint a permanent director I shall be in a position to influence policy to some degree or, if I disapprove, to cut loose at any moment. I am sick of the whole matter, and ask nothing further than to be free of it. Tell Spelter to send in the particulars of the new Company."

The Secretary murmured appreciation of the Chairman's public spirit, and promised to carry out these instructions without delay.

DECEMBER 1868 and a white Christmas.

The third of three bitter winters has already clamped down on England. Already in the big towns misery is piling up. Lack of work, lack of food, lack of fuel—worse than the previous year, worse than the year before—are destined before the spring of 1869 to thrust thousands of children underground, thousands of parents into the violence of despair. But outside the towns, in favoured country districts, beautiful wintry weather calls the fortunate classes out of doors, to enjoy with rosy cheeks and bodies warmly clad, the sports which winter brings.

The meadows round Lashwater are parterres of snow-covered ice, patterned with a tracery of the low dykes which carry foot-paths across the marshes. Between Mount Felix and the town an exceptionally large sheet of ice has been cleared for skating, and in the pale wintry sunshine of early afternoon a throng of all ages is laughing and stumbling and forging dangerously ahead and cutting figures-of-eight and generally enjoying itself. Small boys are squealing and sliding recklessly between the legs of skaters expert and otherwise. Solicitous young men, gravely assisting pretty girls to acquire smoothness and balance, are constrained to hold them by both hands or even, in some cases, to steady them round the waist. Away on the far side, where the crowd is sparse, a haughty gentleman with a short brown beard and a round fur cap is performing miracles of grace and ingenuity. His arms are folded; his chin is well in the air, and he swoops forward and backward, and twirls and spirals now on this edge, now on that, with such an air of not being there at all that he is clearly conscious of the admiring glances thrown at him from every side. This is

Mr Alaric Concannen, Counsellor of Embassy in St Petersburg, home on leave for Christmas and showing the benighted English how the Russians do it.

A tall schoolboy, skating with a slight dark girl of fifteen, approaches the imaginary but unmistakable enclosure in which Mr Concannen is giving his exhibition.

"I wish I could skate like that" she says.

"I hope if you could you wouldn't be so cocky about it."

"Oh, I *should*; and so would you, like you used to be over climbing trees. You're jealous, that's what you are. Thank Heaven I'm not the jealous sort."

He laughs good-humouredly and they skate cheerfully away.

Mervyn Crocker at seventeen is a well-grown, clear-eyed boy with the ingenuous gaiety of childhood already maturing into frank manliness. He is an important person at Westminster now, with only two more terms before he goes to university; but there is nothing of the school "blood" about him nor any of the sullen loutishness which sometimes characterises boys of his age when home for the holidays.

"I think we've had enough, Hetty" he says. "You mustn't overtire yourself. Don't forget it's the dance tonight."

She sat on the dyke while he took off her boots and skates and put on the fur-topped substitutes in which she would walk home. She watched him with thoughtful tenderness, his fair head bent over his task, his rather prominent ears rosy with the cold air and exercise. No one could call Mervyn a beauty; but there was that about him which spoke of candour and simplicity. Hetty St Maur was still a child; but her instincts, even if she were not aware of them, told her this boy was a friend to be trusted and at the same time an innocent who might easily be hurt.

"Will there be lots of people?" she asked suddenly.

"There! Now her ladyship is shod for the road again. Lots of people? Tonight do you mean? Honestly, Hett, I don't know. About forty or fifty I should think. I shan't know any of them except you and those Cartwright girls and

89

some of mamma's elderly cronies. So you'll have to dance
with me all the evening."

"Really, Mr Crocker, you forget yourself. A girl has to
be very careful not to get talked about. Besides I'll have to
dance with Jack Golightly and Michael Charteris and Mr
Concannen so that he will take me skating tomorrow—and
oh, lots more."

"Listen, young Hester" he said severely "if I have any
more of your imperance you'll be desked and not come at
all. I shall go and tell your mother that this is to be a grown-up
dance not a children's party, and that you can come to the
Christmas tree on Boxing Day instead."

She laughed happily and squeezed his arm. They were
now approaching Mount Felix. "Dear Mervyn! I'll be
good, I promise; so don't start mamma off again, please!
I had a real howdy-do to act the young lady for this one
evening, and tomorrow it's back to pinnies again and those
nasty scales on the piano. Look, there she is!"

Mrs St Maur was standing at the gate of her garden, which
rose in a gentle white slope behind her toward the cedars and
the house. The branches of the cedars stretched out level
with snow, and the pale building behind them blended so
completely into the general whiteness that it was hardly
recognisable as a building at all.

"Well, children" she said as the two approached. "Have
you enjoyed yourselves? It is nearly tea-time. You'll stay
and have some tea, Mervyn, of course?"

"It's awfully kind of you—" he began.

"Ooh!" cried Hetty, the child in her suddenly taking
charge, "you aren't, I *hope*, going to start saying *awfully*.
Too *awfully* nice. *Awfully* sweet of you Mrs St Maur." She
took two mincing steps and back again.

"I'm always in trouble!" he laughed. "Apologies, made-
moiselle, and to you, Mrs St Maur. Begin again." (Speaking
very crisply with a pause between each word.) "It is extremely kind of you, but I fear I must return home to assist
in preparing for this evening's—er—for this evening's—
Rowdy-dow! There, Miss Particular!"

With a wave of the hand he swung away across the snow-covered flats. Mrs St Maur looked after him smiling. "Not quite grown up yet, thank goodness" she said.

"And me, mamma?"

"You, darling, are not grown up at all, even though you *are* going dancing. Run and wash your hands for tea."

* * * * *

When Mervyn came through from the stable-yard entrance into the main hall of Lashwater Park, the first thing he saw was a pair of steps, and on the top of them Paul Gladwin, fixing branches of evergreen along the cornice.

Seven years ago Paul had come to the Park in order to prepare the boy for his entrance exam. Eighteen months' work had surmounted the obstacle with credit, and he had stayed on to tutor the younger brother John. By the time John also had gone to Public School, Paul had become so established a member of the Crocker household that Mrs Crocker declared she could not get on without him, and that he must remain as general factotum and prop to her declining years.

And this whole sequence of events had arisen from the postscript, added by Mr Crocker all those years ago to the letter to the Rev. Alfred Meadows, offering asylum to the child Lottie Heape.

It had chanced that Matt Merton, hearing from Meadows that Lottie had gone to the country, paid the vicar an evening call and was asked, quite incidentally, whether he could suggest a tutor for a schoolboy. He instantly thought of his unlucky friend. Paul had had a good education, could be trusted to treat a pupil kindly and with patience, and desperately needed a job. Also, though this he did not say aloud, a removal from the depressing experience of a struggle for livelihood in London and from the ever-present temptation to drown his sorrows, might be the making of one who otherwise would surely unmake himself. So Matt ventured the recommendation, and in due course arrangements were made for Paul to meet Mr Crocker.

It was an odd encounter. Crocker, of course, knew who the young man was; Paul had no idea whatsoever that this solemn uncommunicative gentleman had any connection with the Society who had inherited his father's fortune. He had been told by Meadows merely that Mr Crocker had interested himself in the rescued child and would be glad, if prospects seemed favourable, to help one of her rescuers. The interview opened with the commonplace exchange of question and answer as between potential employer and candidate for a job.

Mr Crocker then sat in unembarrassed silence, presumably cogitating the qualifications of the young man at his side. They were in the smoking-room of Crocker's gloomy but impressive club. The huge dark paintings on the walls, the heavy curtains looped to either side of the tall windows, two somnolent old gentlemen at either end of the room, sunk in black leather arm-chairs and gently snoring, and now, before his eyes, the silent black-clad bulk of the man who held his future in his hands, combined to bring Paul to the edge of panic. He sat forward on a very small chair, clutching his hat fiercely to keep his hands from trembling, while his eyes wandered uneasily about the room.

Suddenly Crocker spoke.

"Mr Gladwin, why did you not keep the appointment given you some weeks ago by the Secretary of the Torch-bearers' Missionary Society?"

Paul's mouth fell open and he stared helplessly at the speaker. At last the sense of the actual question penetrated his mind and he made an effort to answer it, leaving aside the inexplicable fact that this man had asked it.

"I—I—did" he stammered. "I was sent to report on some property and when I came back to do so, I was dismissed on the spot."

"Why?"

"I do not know, sir. I assure you I do not know. The Secretary accused me of slandering the Society and himself and had me turned into the street. If you will let me tell you all about it—"

92

"No, thank you, Mr Gladwin. You have told me all I want to know. Well, then, we will consider as provisionally settled that you prepare my son for his examination. We will make a four weeks' trial. I shall expect you at Lashwater in a week's time. You will receive three pounds per month and, of course, board and lodging. Good day."

When Paul had gone, Crocker sat on, digesting what he had just learnt. As was his way, he had advanced one step and no further. This rate of progress was always sufficient to him, for he liked to consider every event concerning him or his affairs as it occurred, and not to confuse his judgment or endanger his caution by looking back for causes or forward for effects. He now knew that Sneade had lied; and the knowledge sufficiently convinced him that Sneade was in some way involved with Spelter and to personal advantage.

Probably the two men had been in alliance from the first over the question of the Granby Street property; and it brought Crocker as near to fury as his temperament permitted to realise how helpless he was, even now, to take adequate revenge on them. Against Spelter he could do nothing; the little he could do to punish Sneade should be done.

He interviewed an influential member of a powerful Society which maintained Rescue Homes and organised relief in poor quarters of several large cities. He convinced the Rev. Mr Timms that a concentration of the forces of righteousness would make for greater power against the Evil One. He then called a meeting of the Torchbearers and proposed that they accept a formal invitation from the —— Society to join forces. Prolonged discussion followed, with Mr Timms in favour and Mr Sneade against. It became necessary for the Chairman to give his casting vote. A month later the Torchbearers were merged in the larger organisation, and Mr Malcolm Sneade was unemployed.

* * * * *

"Hullo, Mr Gladwin" called Mervyn. "Why didn't you come skating? It was skee."

Paul climbed down from the steps and studied the effect of the latest portion of evergreen.

"My dear fellow" he said. "I can't go gallivanting off on a day like this. All the decorations to do and your poor mother in a stew over the refreshments and one of the maids gone down with colic and I dunno-what-all. Still I'm glad you had a good time, and if the frost holds I'll come out tomorrow."

"Golly!" cried Mervyn. "I'd not thought of the refreshments! I must slip along and have a peep at them."

Paul laughed. Seven years at Lashwater had transformed him. His skin was clear. There was colour in his cheeks, and he had so filled out that one would have said he had gone on growing. It was still a weak face, and at the back of his eyes lingered a faint shadow of unhappy memories; but whereas when he had been twenty-four he had looked thirty, now that he was past thirty he might well have been younger.

As Mervyn hurried off, Paul called after him:

"Only a peep, I don't think! But go easy. Mrs Crocker will never forgive me if we run short tonight."

The supper delicacies were being laid out in the large larder opposite the kitchen. When Mervyn arrived the place was empty, and he began prowling round, tasting a salted almond here, a preserved cherry there. He was just wondering whether, if he scooped a gobbet of whipped cream off that topping charlotte russe with his finger the mark would look like a natural swirl or as though the mice had been at it, when a girl in a print frock and apron came in carrying a heavy tray of jellies and aspic. She came in backwards, pushing the door open with her behind, and Mervyn was aware of her before she saw that there was anyone in the room. His awareness was of a special kind. He knew quite well who the girl was and, off and on, had seen her about the place for years. So much was ordinary recognition, but now (and not for the first time) something beyond recognition stirred him to uneasy excitement.

Late the preceding summer and already during those early

days of the Christmas holidays, he had been conscious of a queer pang of breathlessness each time he happened to catch sight of her. It was as though his heart had missed a beat, and the sensation was at once alarming and agreeable. This had happened perhaps half a dozen times in all, and on the occasion of such fleeting and casual encounters as normally occur between a son of the house and one of the maids. At first he thought to have imagined it; but when each time the pang recurred and seemed to gain in strength rather than to weaken, he was forced to recognise that the girl was the cause of it. The experience first puzzled and then worried him; but at the same time it tantalised.

Now, in the moment it took for the girl to turn about, he felt the mysterious stimulus more strongly than ever, and a blend of confusion and anticipation kept him standing there staring. As soon as she saw him, she murmured an apology:

"I beg your pardon, sir. I didn't know anyone was here."

With her eyes on her tray, she crossed the room to where there was still space on one of the broad slate shelves. Mervyn watched her as though bewitched. She was sixteen years of age and well grown. Her full tip-tilted breasts pushed up against the plain bodice of her print frock; she moved with an easy grace, and her small head, on a long lithe neck, had poise and finish. She wore her dark hair short, and the curls which framed her face and clustered along her forehead sat close as a bonnet. She was intriguing rather than beautiful. The eyes, brightly observant under their drooping lids, were a little too near together, and the space between eyes and mouth a shade too long. But the nose was finely modelled, the lips rich and challenging, and the colouring—from the delicate flush in the cheeks to the warm cream of the perfect throat and chin—vibrant with life. There was character in the face, and behind the mask of demure humility which was her professional wear, one was conscious of an intelligence wakeful and determined.

Mervyn came to with a jerk. The girl had almost reached

the shelf she sought and, as it was rather high, was gathering herself together for the effort of raising the tray.

"Oh, I say! Let me do it. It's too heavy."

He was at her side in a moment, took the tray from her, lodged it safely on the shelf and turned to find her looking straight at him.

"Thank you, sir" she said. The voice was low and respectful, but she did not drop her eyes. They continued to fix him with a steady gaze, which was neither friendly nor unfriendly, but partly appraising and partly questioning. He felt an acute embarrassment and looked uneasily away, so that he did not see the flicker of amusement provoked by his awkward movement and fiery blush. But with all his discomfort he had no inclination to escape, and racked his brains for something to say.

"Why are you here, carrying trays about" he demanded at last. "I thought the still-room was your lay."

"Yes, sir. But Sarah is taken queer and I am doing her work." After a moment's pause she added "I'm glad of it, *now*."

He glanced at her nervously. She was still watching him, with her head slightly tilted backwards and her eyelids drooping. He could not help saying it:

"Why 'now'?"

She smiled mischievously.

"Because I shall see something of the dance and all the ladies and gentlemen."

He was at once disappointed and relieved.

"Where will you see them from?"

"Well, I am to help Miss Straker with the ladies' cloaks, coming and going, and give a hand during supper and—I oughtn't to say this—there is a place on the big landing where you can climb through and look down into the hall."

"Oughtn't to say it!" he laughed, all at once a boy again. "Why, you silly, do you suppose I don't know that! I've scrambled all over this house as a kid. So that's where you'll be at off-times. All right, I'll pay you a visit. . . ."

"Oh, you won't be able to do that, sir, not while the dance is on. You'll be far too busy."

"And after the dance is finished, you won't be there."

"No—o. I suppose I shan't, so that's off. But it was kind of you to think of coming to see."

"Well, I must vamoose" he said. "Haven't had tea yet. So long! Don't carry too many heavy trays."

As he went down the passage, he heard her singing softly to herself. She was singing "Paddle your own Canoe".

*　　*　　*　　*　　*

About an hour later, Sarah's substitute was in the pantry carefully setting out small glass bowls on glass saucers in which, when the time came, the ice-cream would be served. The butler and footmen were upstairs arranging the supper-room; the kitchen was wilting under the lash of the cook's tongue; the general turmoil was so great that everyone seemed to be somewhere else and the pantry was deserted. Hearing a soft step in the doorway the girl looked round and saw Paul Gladwin. He smiled in a deprecating way and said nervously:

"I just came to see how you were getting on, Lottie. You must have a terrible lot to do."

She turned back to her work.

"Plenty, without standing about gossiping" she replied pertly.

He was disconcerted and moved uneasily from one foot to the other.

"If there's anything I can do" he began.

"You can leave me alone, Mr Gladwin, that's what you can do. It's not right for you to keep after me all the time. I don't like it, and I'll get into trouble."

"Oh, Lottie, don't be prickly with me! I only want to help you."

"When I want help, I'll ask for it" she snapped, but the next moment went on more pleasantly: "As a matter of fact, I've just thought of something you *can* do, if you will. I have to doss it tonight with one of the housemaids, for I'll

be up late and that Sarah is sick and mustn't be disturbed.
I'll never get anyone to listen to me now it's so late, and
I forgot earlier. Get me a couple of rugs from somewhere
and a pillow or two and leave them by the housemaid's cupboard. That *would* be kind. Will you try?"

"Rather!" he said eagerly, and, flushed with pleasure at
the smile she gave him, hurried off to do her bidding.

LOTTIE WAS THE child of a skilled plumber and glazier called Hannay, and Dora Heape, barmaid at the Wheatsheaf Tavern in Farnham. The man was employed on restorations to the Castle which in the autumn of 1849 were undertaken at the order of the Bishop of Winchester, and made the girl's acquaintance in her professional capacity. He was an up-standing rogue, with all the dashing charm of his Irish descent and a good deal also of its calculated irresponsibility. Dora was a blooming passionate girl, generous both by nature and in physique. The pair were soon infatuated with one another; and as both of them were good healthy animals, it was not long before a love-child was conceived. There can be little doubt that, had fate permitted, they would have married (though whether for better or for worse, who shall say?) ; but fate and the father's volatile ambition were against them. The contract for the Crystal Palace was signed in the spring of 1850, and Messrs Fox and Henderson, the contractors, broadcast offers of work at high wages to precisely the type of craftsmen to which Hannay belonged. He was too innately a vagrant to wish to stay long in any one spot, too adventurous to neglect an opportunity for fresh experience and good money, yet too soft-hearted to bring himself to tell his mistress to her face that he was off and away. He flitted to London one evening without a word, and Dora was left to face her pregnancy alone.

The girl was distressed by her lover's desertion, but only for a short while. She took life as it came, equably and without useless lament, and, as her time drew near, left Farnham and went to live with her grandmother in the still obscure and peaceful village of Aldershott three or four miles to the northward. There her girl-baby was born, and there the two of them remained until the child was three years old.

Dora was devoted to her baby, and in the absence of any sign of life from its father gradually forgot all about him. She had enjoyed their love-making; but the little girl was a more than adequate symbol of it, and Dora was not one to pine for the embrace of any particular man. There were lots of men, but there was only one Lottie of her very own.

At the same time she could not be content for very long with the solitary preoccupations of motherhood. She wanted to see people and to be seen, and chance favoured her as wholeheartedly as earlier it had been unkind.

During 1854 active preparations began for the big new Military Training Camp, which experience in the Crimea had taught the authorities was an essential feature of future army policy. The landlord of the quiet village pub, who had naturally become friendly with Dora thanks to her earlier employment behind a bar, was shrewd enough to foresee the effect the great Camp would have on the fortunes of Aldershott, and enterprising enough to act on his foresight. He bought a good-sized house on the outskirts of the village nearest to the Camp-boundary, altered it to meet the requirements of an up-to-date tavern, christened it THE SEBASTOPOL and invited Dora to resume her former activities. This, her little girl being happy, healthy and well-cared-for by the grandmother, she was very pleased to do. By the time the Camp was finished and in working order, she was established at the Sebastopol, which very quickly demonstrated how truly its proprietor had read the future.

The transformation of a sleepy country village into a raw, riotous jerry-built scatter of small houses and shops and shooting-galleries and billiard saloons and shacks and cock-pits and low-class boozing-kens came about with extra-ordinary rapidity. Among the squalid and flimsy buildings of the mushroom town the Sebastopol, thanks to its twelve-month start, stood out with something of the dignity of a public building. As indeed it was, in more senses than one.

The boss was a tolerant kindly man, who wanted people to enjoy themselves so long as they paid him for the privilege and held their liquor properly.

But he was also a disciplinarian, who knew that the personnel of any administration must remain apart from and in control of the clientele. Therefore he distinguished strictly between the girls in his employ and those who frequented the tavern with, or in search of, soldiers with money in their pockets. Dora and her colleagues were friendly and familiar, quick to give chaff for chaff or to put turbulence in its place; but they were "respectable" girls and were soon accepted as such and generally popular.

For three or more years all went well. Dora spent such time with her child as business hours, generously interpreted, allowed; Lottie was taught her letters and her numbers and how to be useful about her great-grandmother's cottage; the Sebastopol, with outward decorum, catered to all and sundry in the most complaisant manner imaginable. But when the little girl was nearly eight years old, two disasters befell.

Dora's grandmother died suddenly, and a General of unparalleled piety, whose only vice was that he had none, was given the Aldershott Command. This aggressive moralist was not unwilling to advertise his determination to stop everyone else from doing the things he did not himself wish to do; and, as the man responsible for the Camp and its occupants, he claimed the right to control the behaviour of local residents who, but for the Camp, wouldn't be there at all. There was a general clean-up of town and neighbourhood, and among the casualties was Dora's friendly employer. The General disapproved of the use to which the licensee of The Sebastopol put his first-floor rooms; the man was flung out neck and crop, and a sour puritanical successor reigned in his stead.

What was poor Dora to do with her child? Under the old régime, although technically she "lived in" at the Sebastopol, she had been permitted to sleep at her grandmother's and be with the little girl at least three nights a week. No doubt under the old régime, now that her grandmother was dead, she would have been free to bring Lottie to her own room for a few days while she found another refuge. But this was out of the question in the changed circumstances. Indeed, if the new boss realised that his unmarried barmaid had a child at all, he might even dismiss her. So the mother spent distracted hours desperately searching for somewhere to lodge her little girl. Aldershott town, still growing with dizzy rapidity, was by now a bustling place of considerable size, swarming with adventurers of every kind. But, as is the case with all upstart towns whose reason for existence is extraneous to themselves, its population in these early years was a restless and self-seeking one. There was no tradition of neighbourly spirit nor indeed had the majority of households any quality in common save a desire to get ahead of one another. An acquaintance of the grandmother offered to take the child in for a couple of nights while her own daughter was away; but she could do no more nor knew where else to recommend.

Dora's two days of respite were nearly up, and her much-curtailed leisure had been vainly spent wearily tramping in search of an asylum. She had retreated in despair to the house of the kindly neighbour and, at the end of her tether, was crying in a chair while Lottie played unconcernedly near by, when the woman of the house returned.

"Oh, there you are!" she cried cheerfully. "I've news for you and wondered how to find you. As you know I mentioned to one or two folk what you were looking for, and just after dinner a woman called here to say she thought she might be able to take the kid. Here's her address."

It was the other side of the town in one of the newest streets of hastily constructed cottages, but Dora set off at once, trudging doggedly along. The woman seemed a pleasant person, and the house, though flimsily and meanly built, looked clean. The terms were higher than Dora had hoped to pay, but she could not afford to quarrel with what seemed the only available solution of her problem. She paid a week in advance and, hiring a cab, transported Lottie and her few belongings to the new home. When, the next afternoon, she went round in her only free time to see her daughter, the house was shut up and no one answered her knocking. She grew frantic, and made such a noise beating on the door that a woman came out of the row opposite.

"There ain't no one there" she said. "The lady and a child went away this morning."

"Went away? Where to? Who is she?"

But the woman merely shrugged.

"Dunno" she said. "I've seen er before but never spoke to er or eard er name."

* * * * *

When Lottie and the strange lady reached London, they drove a long way in a cab. The child was excited by the journey and chattered ceaselessly to the woman with her, who said her name was Mrs Ryan and treated her charge with indulgent kindness. When at last the cab stopped, it was at the door of a very tall house, built on a curve and forming part of a circular ring of houses which surrounded an open space of untidy gravel and rough grass with a tall plane-tree in the centre. Mrs Ryan, holding Lottie by the hand, rang the bell, and when after a few moments the door opened six inches and a head appeared in the gap, said a few rapid words and thrust the child forward. The chain was taken off, the door swung back and Lottie felt herself drawn into the hallway, while the woman went back to the cab to collect the little bundle of clothes and pay the driver. She quickly returned, took the child's hand again, and led her into a small back room whither the man who had opened the door had preceded them.

He was a small fresh-faced man in his middle forties, who wore side-whiskers but no moustache or beard. His bird-like yet self-confident manner, his rather too-knowing eye and his unexpectedly neat dark clothes gave him something of the appearance of a valet in a pretentious but second-rate hotel. His name was William Slode.

He patted Lottie on the head, gave her a picture book

to look at, and, bidding Mrs Ryan to be seated, came to business.

"Looks all right" he said. "How much?"

The woman chuckled.

"T'other way round, Mr Slode. A week's keep in advance."

"Capital, capital! Your perk of course, as well as the usual. How did you manage it?"

"Fluke. Absolute fluke. The mother was clean stumped and I happened to get the tip. But I'll have to keep clear of that town for a while. The kid's ma apart, there's a new boss down there poke-nosing into every house in the place. That kind of thing plays hell with plants of this kind."

"Very well, you shall go to Edinburgh for a bit; and I'll send old Mother Tetley back to Aldershott. She can keep the place warm, till the weather improves."

Unlocking a drawer he handed over two bank-notes, and Mrs Ryan took her leave.

* * * * *

Larne Circle, in which stood William Slode's big house, was one of the oddest of the many oddities which in Victorian London still lurked alongside the high-roads, removed from sight and almost forgotten, sunk in the huge mystery of the most mysterious city in the world. Hardly one of them now survives—and it is only by assiduity and good fortune that the researcher of today can discover they ever existed.

Known locally as "Ganderton's Folly" (and except locally it was barely known at all, save to those who had special reasons for doing so) this macabre yet pathetic symbol of an unrealised ideal—an ideal ridiculous but lovable—mouldered into a degradation it did not deserve. Information about Ganderton is sparse. Indeed, except in a privately issued and rather incompetent monograph called *Oddities of Islington*, compiled by an old chap who kept a Pets' Bazaar in Upper Street during the early nineteen-hundreds, I have never found his name in print. According to this solitary authority, Ganderton was a speculator of ambitious and rococo tastes who, early in the 'forties, conceived the idea of laying out an ornate and romantic settlement along the north bank of the Canal, east of Lower Street (now Essex Road).

In 1840 this hinterland was virtually unbuilt beyond the beginnings of St Peter Street and Queen's Head Lane. Of course Lower Street was fringed with houses for its whole length, and there was a considerable patch of tenements on the right of it just south of the New North Road, which half a century later was to earn an evil repute as the "Popham Street Area". Kingsland Road was built up on the left to the Canal and as far west as Hoxton Town (later Hoxton High Street) and beyond, on the right as far east as the bend of Hackney Road. But the whole area from St Peter's Church to what became de Beauvoir Town was open country.

From the wedge of high ground, which carries at its point the Angel and on its widening back the breadth and traditions of Upper Street and the uncertain status of Lower Street, the ground to south-eastward falls gently away toward Hoxton and the pocket in which lies London City. Ganderton's scheme, having secured a few acres of land on the south-eastern crest of this slope (if crest it can be called), was somewhat to embank it along the edge of the Canal and then to erect, according to a careful ground plan, the sort of houses which appealed to his own imagination and, in his sanguine view, might set a standard to which other builders would aspire. It was obvious to him that the surrounding neighbourhood was set for development in the near future. What greater service to the community could an idealist perform than to set that standard high?

The central feature of Ganderton's design was Larne Circle, a ring of tall houses boldly conceived, façaded on a curve and pierced by entries at four opposite points. He was keenly conscious of the decorative value of wrought-iron balconies and plaster-mouldings, and did not stint his Circle of these embellishments. Of the four pierced entries, that on the south-east gave unexpected access to the Canal, which was reached by a stairway taking two elbow turns and debouching on to a miniature wharf.

Having planned his Circle and carried the houses to within

D*   105

reasonable distance of completion, Ganderton proceeded to create an outer ring of even more unconventional dwellings. This involved a semi-circular road enclosing the north-westerly curve of the Circle and, where at each end it abutted on the Canal, on a somewhat lower level. Access to the Circle from this road was given by short streets running to the three practicable entries. Two of these streets, from north-east and south-west, rose steeply uphill; that from the north-west sloped gently down.

Impossible to account for follies such as Larne Circle. Why was it built just there and just like that? Why was it sufficiently embanked to stand well above the cutting in which flows the Canal, yet insufficiently raised to permit level access from Lower Street? Why indeed was no adequate roadway driven to connect the area with that main thorough-fare? No one will ever know. Even the proprietor of the Pets' Bazaar did not know, but confined himself, in place of explanation, to the arch conjecture that Ganderton was a Goose.

It seems kinder to regard him as a visionary, with the courage to attempt to realise his visions and the ill-fortune to perish for them. Before the circular road was fully built up, Ganderton went bankrupt and died; the property was put up for forced sale by the creditors, and fell into hands very different from those foreseen by its luckless creator. It became, in brief, a divisional headquarters of an organisation comprising some of the worst men and women in London, and of this particular headquarters little William Slode, with his twinkling eyes, his cheerful giggle and his smooth pink cheeks, was in command.

Already by 1860 when Lottie Heape was brought there, Larne Circle and its outer ring carried the marks of premature decay. Never fresh and young because never finished, they soon began to crumble. Forlorn and uncared-for, the twisted ironwork, the plaster ornament, the ingenious brickwork of chimney and balustrade rusted and flaked and chipped.

Railings were uprooted or broken and not replaced. Shutters lost a hinge and flapped drearily on windy nights, but no one troubled to repair them. The place could not look quite a slum. Its original lines and orderly ground plan still imposed on it a tragic dignity. But its atmosphere was dangerous and had something of the potential lawlessness of a gipsy encampment. "Leave me alone" it seemed to say "and I will reciprocate. But meddle—and you will see what happens!" And indeed on other grounds also it bore a fundamental resemblance to a gipsy stronghold, for those in possession felt themselves to be outlaws and were proud of it.

There were originally eight houses in Larne Circle, two in each segment. Three of the segments were unchanged, and the six houses which composed them were outwardly as neglected and crumbling as the rest of the property. But the fourth segment (that backing on to the Canal) now constituted a single large house and was in excellent, if forbidding, repair. The windows were strongly shuttered and on the ground-floor barred. The main door did not stand open as did those of the other tenements, but was kept firmly shut. The cornice was not cracked and broken; the roof (if one had been in a position to inspect it) would have proved solidly tiled and leaded. This was Slode's house, and the house in which Lottie Heape was to spend the next few months of her life.

The Slode ménage consisted of a crushed and spiritless little woman dignified by the name of "Mrs Slode", who, assisted by two slaveys only one degree more wretched than herself, dragged out a miserable existence in the basement; of Evan Slode, a boy of sixteen; of two severe but well-conducted females of mature age; of an immense negro porter called Lollipop, and of a fluctuating collection of little girls.

These children were not ill-treated. True, they were house-bound, their only playgrounds being a flat space of roof, which lay at the back of the house and would have overlooked the Canal had not a wall shut out the view, and a yard in the very centre of the block, specially contrived

when the two houses were made into one. But they were
well fed, tended when sick and given every care which
physical well-being might require.

In the matter of moral training, however, things were very
different. They were lambs to be decked for a particular
sacrifice, and every means was adopted of dispelling ignorance
and of breaking down inhibitions and reserves and natural
modesty. No attempt was made to conceal from them the
life to which they were destined; indeed they were encouraged to understand why one of their number left suddenly,
and shortly afterward another and another. As for the most
part their heredity was bad, this abominable policy of deliberate
demoralisation was generally carried through without trouble;
but occasionally there were outbreaks of recalcitrance, and
then the culprit was handed over to Evan Slode, whose rôle
need not be particularised beyond saying that it was that of
"initiator".

In the ordinary way Evan was not permitted to mingle
with the girl-boarders (many of whom never saw him at all)
but was confined strictly to a different part of the house
with a side-entrance of its own. He was a heavily built,
rather fat boy, with a head of blue-black hair flamboyantly
waved, a pair of very red, wet lips, and gross podgy hands
whose backs were already thickly grown with hair. He
carried himself with a boorish swagger and assumed all the
airs of a swell mobsman. He was, however, very frightened
of his father.

*   *   *   *   *

Lottie cried for two days after her arrival in Larne Circle.
She was scared and lonely and wanted her mother. But she
was very young, had a full share of her father's insouciance
and of Dora's cheerful acquiescence in what each day might
bring, and for the first time in her life was experiencing the
companionship of other children. In a week she began to
feel at home; and after a month hardly recollected any other
kind of existence.

In their own section of the building the girls were allowed

to roam more or less where they wished (such rooms as were regarded as outside their province were kept carefully locked), and even the little office in which William Slode had received Mrs Ryan was open to them. Slode had always a kindly greeting for any child who peeped round his door and, if he passed one on the stairs, he would throw her a friendly word or pull a paper of sweets from his pocket or even, in his more expansive moments, chase her with growls along the corridor till the house rang with delighted shrieks.

One day Lottie, tired of playing with the dolls which were provided in the big upstairs play-room and wishing it were time for tea, wandered downstairs in idle search of entertainment. Lollipop was sweeping the hall and gave her a wide grin. Rolling his eyes he pretended to threaten her with the broom and, giggling with pleasure, she skipped into the first doorway that presented itself. She found herself in the office. William Slode was at his desk. On one side of him sat a massive woman, handsomely upholstered in black satin, with jet and bugles on bosom and shoulders which rustled crisply when she moved: on the other, dressed for the street, was one of the senior pensionnaires, a girl of fourteen or so, called Sylvia.

Abashed at the sight of the group, Lottie stopped short and was backing quietly away when Slode called to her:

"Come in, my dear, come in. This is Mrs Moresby, who is taking our dear little Sylvia to live with her for a while. It will be a nice change (won't it, Sylvia?) and perhaps kind Mrs Moresby may one day take a fancy to Lottie also."

"Come here, dearie" said Mrs Moresby. "You look a very happy little girl, I'm sure. But then you are all happy here, aren't you?"

She put her arm round the child who now stood at her side.

"You must come and see me some time; would you like that?"

Lottie hung her head and murmured "Yes, ma'am" at the same time nervously fingering the handsome reticule which lay on the lady's knee.

"Pretty" she said.

"Isn't it pretty? Look inside, my dear, but be careful not to harm it." She turned to Slode and went on:

"Well, Mr Slode, that is all in order. Sylvia shall remain in Bury Street till his lordship sends for her or comes himself. I could get considerably more from old Mannheim, but of course he isn't real class, and the other is a powerful friend."

Slode nodded.

"Certainly, certainly. And you can fob off something else on old money-bags. He'll be none the wiser."

Lollipop put his head round the door.

"De kerridge waitin', Marse Slode."

Mrs Moresby rose, kissed Lottie on the cheek, waved a hand to Slode and moved toward the door.

"Come along, Sylvia dear, we mustn't keep the poor horse waiting."

The door was closed behind them, leaving Slode and Lottie together.

"A nice lady, that" he said "knows her job too. Just help me get these pretty pictures in order, there's a good girl. They are numbered in the corner, do you see, and have got all mixed up."

But Lottie had not gone very far with the arranging before the clang of the outer door was heard and Slode shuffled the pictures together.

"Run upstairs now and have your tea. I did not think it was so late. We'll finish the pictures another time."

*   *   *   *   *

The months went by, and Lottie was subjected one after another to the corrupting influences available in Larne Circle. She absorbed very little of their significance; but inevitably came to take for granted aspects of life normally hidden from young people. Then came the terrible day when, quite by chance, she became involved in the struggle between Evan Slode and poor little Jennie. There is no need to describe the incident which, if Evan had obeyed orders and locked the door, she would never have witnessed. What mattered was that her passionate and impulsive temper suddenly mastered her, and that she flew at the bully and scored his cheek savagely with her nails. He turned on her in fury, knocked her flat with a brutal box of the ears and went to his father to complain. William Slode had no particular sympathy with his son, whose blundering stupidity had provoked this deplorable occurrence. But he insisted implacably on submissive behaviour from the helpless inmates of his house. Life there must run smoothly and pleasantly, amiability and a pretence of avuncular geniality being his cherished hypocrisies. It tickled his distorted sense of humour to practise them, and he found them commercially profitable. Invariably if one of the victims showed fight after Evan had finished with her, she was condemned to be tamed. How much more punishable was this deliberate attack from a little devil with whom Evan had had nothing to do! If this kind of thing were to be tolerated, he would have a collusive revolt on his hands, and that must not happen.

"She shall go to Long Meg for a bit" he told himself. "That'll knock the cockiness out of her."

He summoned one of the women in charge of the child-lodgers.

"Lottie Heape is to be sent to bed without supper for her naughty temper. Do not punish her otherwise. She is going to be properly disciplined elsewhere."

He also sent a note to Big Jimmy, his opposite number in the Southwark "Mint", telling him to expect the child and hand her over to Long Meg. For Meg lived in Jimmy's territory, and everything must be done in order.

Next day Lottie, her arms tied to her sides under her cloak and a handkerchief round her ankles, was removed in the special cab attached to the establishment and in due course was delivered at Grove Place, alongside Waterloo Station.

A week later Long Meg had just started to follow her instructions, and at the first sign of obstinacy or cockiness to wallop the little devil so she wouldn't forget it, when the child slipped through her hands, dashed out of the house, and was somehow snatched away from under the hag's very nose by two strange young men.

WITH SUCH PARENTAGE and (if one may use the word) such an upbringing, it was natural enough that Lottie should have become precocious. But precocity was not all of it. The unusual circumstances of her childhood had inverted the normal processes of education. The period between her kidnapping by Mrs Ryan and her despatch to Lashwater had forced her to witness, in a concentrated and exaggerated form, an aspect of life of which she could not possibly have any precise understanding. As things were, the facts communicated and the illustrations and cartoons put into her hands in Larne Circle, as well as the sights seen during her few days among the shameless visitors to Long Meg's pestiferous hovel, had impressed on her mind (with however little real comprehension) potentialities of human nature of which many women remain totally ignorant all their lives.

Then had followed seven sheltered years at Lashwater, initially as a mere child in the cottage home of Mr and Mrs Frost, later as an apprentice in the still-room and dairy at the Park under the humorous and energetic care of Mrs Crocker and her dairymaid. During these years Lottie's education had progressed beyond the three R's to the limits of such simple schooling as came the way of village children. Further she had been taught to sew, and had acquired an elementary knowledge of herbs and their uses, of preserves and jam, of pickles and chutneys, of mincemeat and lemon-curd, of cheese and butter-making. Also, in contact with her mistress, she had learnt to speak (as they used to say) in a manner above her station. In other words, during the second half of her short life she had passed through a stage which would ordinarily have begun about half-way through the first.

With the coming of puberty, this dislocation of childish

experience bore dangerous but perhaps inevitable fruit. Her father's engaging but artful volatility, her mother's readiness to surrender to the pleasures of the moment, provided her with an intuitive key to the dark riddle of sexuality. She realised by instinct that herein lay both profit and pleasure, and, seeing that all her responses derived from the same source of parental full-bloodedness and animalism, she was foredoomed to become at once an exploiter of the passions of others and the plaything of her own.

The development of these qualities had already progressed by the time Lottie was sixteen. Indeed their first manifestations had taken place two or three years earlier, and in connection with Paul Gladwin. He, when he had first arrived at Lashwater, had naturally sought out the child whose extrication from squalor and misery was the starting-point of his own new life. The gentle naïveté of his character inclined him toward children. They responded readily to his approaches; but, as they came to sense the vacillation and timidity which were inherent in him, tended to mock at him and, like schoolboys who will rag the best and kindliest teacher if he has not the knack of discipline, to play tricks they would not dare to play on someone of tougher fibre. Lottie soon reached this stage of amiable impertinence, which in her case did not express itself in terms of childish ragging, but inevitably spoke the language of flirtatiousness. Gradually she evolved a technique of seeming-reluctant advance and abrupt withdrawal which would have done credit to a coquette of experience.

No one could have fallen an easier victim to this elementary trick than poor Paul. The only incident in his life of which he could be at all proud was Lottie's deliverance from Granby Street. She stood, therefore, in his eyes as the only solid prop to his self-esteem, and rather than lose this prop, he would endure every trivial humiliation. No matter how she teased him, with what imperious little whims she imposed on his good nature, to what outbreaks of impudent temper she subjected him, he remained patient and forbearing. As time went by, and the growing child added to her repertoire of wiles primitive experiments in tantalisation, the man, for all that he was twice her age, fell more deeply into her toils. He wished for nothing save to make her happy, and for her happiness to show itself in a friendly greeting or a smile of welcome when they met. Sometimes it did so, and his heart sang; more often she was enigmatic or perfunctory; occasionally she was purposely cruel.

And now for several months she had been oftener cruel than kind. Naturally reckless, self-reliant, yet as eager to be mastered as to defy mastery, she found his submissiveness, his refusal to hit back, increasingly exasperating. It was an insult to a girl of her spirit that a man should express his devotion in terms of cringing resignation; and her reaction was to scorn and torment him the more, for the vengeful pleasure of seeing his distress.

On the particular afternoon of the dance her sudden determination to tempt and to subdue Mervyn Crocker had given a new, acrid twist to her readiness to wound Paul Gladwin. She knew perfectly well that he had never, even in the gentlest way, attempted to make love to her. She knew, also, that if he guessed her designs on Mervyn, he would oppose and thwart them. So, in order to hurt him grievously and drive him into miserable retirement while she tried out her plan, she would accuse him of what was furthest from his mind.

Another twist, this time toward malice. Not only should he be made to suffer and, while suffering, to keep his distance; he should also—and in all innocence—be made an accessory to a scheme he would abominate.

She read her victim aright. It came as a painful shock to Paul when in the empty pantry she taunted him with so pursuing her that it might get her into trouble. The suggestion that, in an adult sense, he was plaguing her with unwanted attentions took him unawares and horrified him. When immediately afterwards, with one of her lightning changes to amiability, she asked him to do her a small service, he had brightened, as always, and had temporarily forgotten the pain caused by her previous remark. But as the time wore on this pain returned, and the lights and music and pretty dresses and general gaiety of the evening lost their savour.

What could have induced her, he asked himself, to imagine such a thing? How could there be an element of that kind in such a relationship as theirs?

Characteristically he prepared to blame himself.

Was it his fault? Had he, in an unguarded moment, said or done something which had given her so false an idea of the quality of his affection? Uneasy and depressed in spirit he lurked on the fringe of the festivity.

Mrs Crocker discovered him leaning unhappily against the wall and watching the dancers with troubled eyes. She was a plump shortish woman, whose serene comfortable face had a demure twinkle behind its placidity and her way of speech a captivating suggestion of a stutter. She had all the humour her husband lacked; but being, like him, a person of strong religious principle and one brought up to regard frivolity as among the lures of the Devil, she kept her sense of fun so much under control that it only glimmered through the interstices of her homely conversation.

"Why are you not dancing, Paul? Or has someone deserted you?"

"No, no, Mrs Crocker" he replied, forcing a cheerful smile, for he was fond of this unpretending simple lady. "I am a little tired, that's all. I think being indoors all day has made me stuffy. How well the party is going! You must be pleased."

"As so much of it is thanks to you" she said, patting his hand "I declare freely that it is going excellently and that I *am* pleased. But I would like to see you enjoying the fun. There are some charming girls. Let me choose for you."

"You are very good, but I beg you to excuse me. Ah, there go Mervyn and little Hetty! She looks altogether the young lady. Remarkable with what ease a girl can grow up by wearing another gown and dressing her hair differently! A boy got up like a man merely looks a fool."

"Which is one of the things we women like about him" she rejoined "provided he only *looks* one."

Paul laughed.

"And how do you make sure of that?"

"Alas, it is sometimes very difficult" she sighed. Then added briskly: "Well, if you really won't dance, I won't plague you. But I shall find you a nice partner for supper. I insist on your having a share of all those good things you worked so hard over." With her wide consoling smile she left him.

A few moments later the master of the house himself came and stood by Paul's side. At home Mr Crocker was a different being from the solemn pietist prominent in London philanthropy. He was still a very serious man and physically as globular as ever; but he shed his ponderous righteousness along with his suits of sombre broad-cloth, and devoted his time to the management of his flower-garden and to his particular and over-riding hobby—the propagation of orchids. To see Mr Crocker, in pepper and salt tweeds and wearing a remarkable high-crowned hat of pale brown felt, moving sedately yet with tenderness along the gangways of his orchid-houses, was an experience not to be forgotten; nor was it one easily come by, for his natural secretiveness extended to his hobby, and he was reluctant to permit mere sightseers to intrude on his treasures' privacy.

Tonight, of course, he was in evening dress—evening dress of a peculiar kind, which suggested a compromise between the gloomy livery of charitable enterprise and the sans-gêne of home. He wore a low turned-down collar, which hardly showed above his black tail-coat, and a white tie in a loose bow with its ends tucked in on either side. So far the effect was evangelical, if not frankly methodist. The shirt front was normal, the studs plain and black. But Mr Crocker's considerable frontage was covered by a flowered waistcoat of brilliant and variegated colours, across which was slung an immense gold watch-chain. Sobriety was restored by regulation dress-trousers, only to be once more dispelled by a glimpse of scarlet silk socks between the trouser-ends and the low patent leather shoes.

"Well, my boy" he began "so you have ranged yourself with the older generation. I shall never cease to marvel at the zeal of women in preparing entertainments of this kind. If it were left to us to set them going. . ."

"Yes, sir. But then we are mostly introversive or, as the ladies prefer to call it, selfish. We like to give pleasure to the young, but they identify themselves with youth and share the pleasure as well as bestow it."

"A pretty sight, all the same" said Crocker "although flowers are as pretty and much quieter. By the way, you recall Mr Dominy's visit? Well, I believe I shall have a new hybrid to show him when he comes in the summer."

"Really, sir? That is great news."

"I say that I *believe* so. I am not yet sure. We have been experimenting with various ratios of temperature and lighting, and it looks as though we have hit on the right one." He looked round the crowded dance-floor and sighed. "I think I have been in evidence long enough. There is a catalogue from St Alban's . . . I must look over it again."

As he moved away, Paul asked

"Shall we see you at supper, sir?"

Crocker shook his head.

"No, Gladwin. My ball-supper days are over. I should be ill for a week. Good night."

Mervyn, in the opinion of Hetty St Maur, was not himself. There were times when he was the cheerful rattle she knew so well, giving joke for joke, building plan on plan to create a fantastic future, chattering about Westminster in the queer jargon peculiar to the school, treating her with the affectionate familiarity of a childhood friend. But there were intervals when he seemed suddenly distrait, and once, while they were sitting out by the big fireplace in the morning-room, she had caught him staring into the flames with the heightened colour of one marvelling at some roseate vision.

She said nothing, then or at any other time, for she felt rather than knew that over-solicitous females were a nuisance; but she wondered what could be on his mind and wished she could help him. When about midnight a message was brought that her mother's maid had called to take her home and that the cab was waiting, she was surprised that he should accompany her part of the way upstairs and only turn back at the foot of the short flight of steps which led to the bedroom where the ladies had left their cloaks. She would have liked to think it a special attention, paid in order to console her for having to leave before the dance was over; but something told her that he had acted almost involuntarily, and certainly he appeared to be hardly aware of what he was doing.

Yet, when they said good night, he was the old familiar Mervyn. Hetty kissed Mrs Crocker with excited thanks for a lovely evening, looked round for Mr Crocker (who had not been visible for a long while and in fact was now sipping seltzer water and eating biscuits in his study) and turned finally to Mervyn.

"I shall have to treat *you* as master of the house" she said "and drop my curtsey. It *has* been fun. I loved every minute of it."

"It would have been a poor show without you, Hett" he replied. "I drew some very odd lots from the general greeze while you were skipping about with all your fancy-blokes. By the way, any luck with the Tsar of Russia?"

She pouted.

"No! He treated me like a kid just out of leading-strings and asked me whether I read Miss Yonge."

"And do you?"

"Of course I do. She's sweet. But I told *him* I found her namby-pamby and preferred Miss Braddon."

"Bang-up! He'll go back to Petersburg with stories about the Girl of the Period which will give the Alexandrovnas fits!"

Both laughed merrily.

"I must go, Mervyn. Once more thank you all very very much."

He watched her whisk away beyond the outer hall, then turned and began thoughtfully walking back toward the ball-room. The big clock in the vestibule said nearly half-past twelve. How much longer would the dance go on? The floor had thinned out considerably. The few remaining chaperons were nodding in their chairs. Another half-hour?

He felt suddenly tired, and going to the refreshment buffet in the adjoining room drank a glass of champagne. He was joined by another youth, and they chatted in a desultory way of the topics of the day. They discussed the new weekly paper *Vanity Fair*, Mabel Gray's levée at the Holborn, the Schleswig-Holstein question and whether at last Cambridge would win the Boat Race. They filled their glasses and became distinctly more elderly. Dizzy was subjected to some severe criticism, and grave doubts were expressed as to whether Gladstone was really a Leader. Another glass, and General Grant's prospects in the White House were destructively canvassed.

What next would have come under the lens can never be known, for the sister of Mervyn's companion appeared at the door, ordered him tartly to get ready and come home, adding that if he didn't look slippy they would leave him to walk.

LASHWATER PARK, inspired no doubt by the Queen's example at Osborne, was an Italianate house with a Frenchified *porte-cochère*. On either side of the long central façade—with its two- or three-light, round-topped windows, its balustrades ornately bracketed and hiding shallow roofs of serpentine tiles—wings curved forward, like the claws of a crab clasping the vast sweep of gravel into which debouched the carriage-drive. One of these wings was an arcaded loggia, the other a Winter Garden reminiscent of that at Compiègne. Seeing that the latter was twice as high as the former, the mass of building, looked at face on, appeared (retaining the crab-simile) to have one claw badly swollen.

In one respect the Crocker architect had fallen short of his august model, in another outstripped it. He had provided only a single campanile (which rose from behind the central block and at one corner as though the crab had a back leg in the air), but in compensation had crowned the main hall with a dome, topped by a lantern in good Michael Angelesque style. Presumably he argued that St Peter's was Italian also, so why not take a hint from there? It could not be denied, however, that the effect of the mixture was a little odd.

The interior of this main hall—octagonal in shape and rising to the roof—was in harmony with the external design. The cupola was carried on Corinthian pilasters terminating in semi-circular arches, which curved inward to support the ribs of the dome. The landings giving access to the first and second floors of the house, and reached by a staircase purposely excluded from the central hall, ran behind the pilasters. That on the first floor had direct openings into the hall; but the one above—level with the inward spring of the arches, whose spandrels opened a few feet above its floor—was masked. All but one of these spandrels were filled in with masonry, but one had been left open so that the daylight from the lantern crowning the dome could filter through to a particularly dark spot on the landing. An active and not too bulky person could climb into this still accessible spandrel, crawl through the depth of the arch, and emerge on to a small balustrated balcony which clung, rather like the nest of a house-martin, to the base of the cupola. Similar, though unserviceable, balconies marked the lower points of the other arches, and from below gave the effect of a circlet of carved bosses.

When, after half-past one, the last of the guests had gone and sleepy servants were putting out lights, seeing fire-guards were in place and clearing the worst of the litter from the margins of the dance floor, Mervyn went to his room. He believed himself heavy with sleep; but when he got into bed the joint effects of fatigue and champagne kept him wakeful and restless. Also he was conscious of a feeling of tension. His nerves would not relax. They were expectant of something, yet afraid of it. He got up and drank some water and walked about the room; but the sense of excitation increased.

Hardly knowing he did so, he put on a dressing-gown and went softly into the corridor. His felt slippers were soundless on the thick carpet. He climbed the stairs to the second floor, and moved round the landing to where the spandrel opened at shoulder level. It was a bright moon-light night and, as powdered snow lay on the outer surface of the dome, a reflection nearly as bright as in day-time shone through the windows of the lantern and shimmered at the end of the short triangular tunnel leading to the balcony.

Against his will, driven by an impulse beyond his control, Mervyn swung himself up and worked his way slowly through the tunnel. He cursed himself silently. "Dolt! Idiot! Go back to bed! You're mad!" But he crept on. He reached the far end of the opening and looked cautiously out. She was there, on the floor of the little balcony a couple of feet below him. He saw her aureole of dusky curls, her eyes shining like dark pools in the uncertain light, and the slim body wrapped in a cloak, full-length on blankets and pillows. She raised a hand and beckoned to him.

When he awoke next morning, he lay rigid for a few moments, while his brain, stupefied with sleep, struggled slowly to activity. Then, as though struck down by a sudden virulent fever, he broke into a burning sweat of shame. From head to toe he tingled with a single gigantic blush, while his limbs shook and his teeth chattered. Brought up with extreme strictness by parents as pious as they were innocent, his natural simplicity had accepted without question the boundaries set to knowledge and experience. He had not resented, because he had hardly noticed, the restrictions placed on his reading, the absence of all discussion or explanation of a dozen aspects of existence which a more inquisitive boy would surely have remarked. At Westminster, of course, he had heard schoolboy smut of the usual kind; but it made little or no impression on him, because some of it bored him and the rest he neither understood nor wished to understand. And now *this* had happened to him—to *him*, Mervyn Crocker, of all people! How *could* he? What had possessed him? Shame seized him again, and with a shudder he hid his head under the clothes and lay there trembling. But gradually the pressure of remorse relaxed, and that of rapturous memory assailed him in its place. He now warmed to a different warmth; his limbs now quivered, muscles braced, with a thrill of excited recollection. How it all came flooding back!

Once more the scent of her hair was in his nostrils, her warm breath on his lips; once more her low urgent whisper sounded in his ears; once more he felt the smooth cool body caress his own. With a violent effort he threw back the bed-clothes and leapt to his feet. For the time being the spell was broken.

During the days which followed, bitter self-reproach, rudely

interrupted by fits of longing which left him more abased
than ever, kept him so silent and solitary that he was suspected of being ill. His brother John and his twelve-year-
old sister Georgina were dumbfounded when he refused to
skate with them, and, mumbling something about a holiday
task, shut himself in his room. There he remained for hours,
only appearing, sullen and listless, at the meals he could not
avoid.

More serious still was his refusal to take Communion on
Christmas Day. His parents, all dressed for early Service,
waited for him in the carriage. The minutes passed, but he
did not come. His mother hurried upstairs to his room and
found him in a dressing-gown reading the Bible. No; he
was not coming. She was at first too taken aback to do
more than utter sounds of astonishment; then she reprimanded him for treating such a subject with levity; then
pleaded for a reason why; then scolded. But he sat there,
his head bowed over the Bible, and merely repeated "No,
mamma, I am not coming today. I have to think something
out." Weeping, half with anger, half with fright, she gave
it up and, returning to her husband, squeezed his hand and
muttered that they must go alone.

There followed a period of acute unhappiness for the
whole family. Mr Crocker tried reasonable argument as
between man and man; Mrs Crocker beseeched her son to
take her into confidence and, if he were sick or in trouble,
to let her help him; the younger children were first irked by
the general malaise and then furious with Mervyn for causing
it. But he was obstinately reticent. "Please let me alone"
he said. "I shall be all right again soon", adding with a
pitiful attempt at gaiety "I think I am having some kind of a
brainstorm. It will blow itself out."

Only Paul Gladwin had an inkling of what was wrong.
Of the real facts he had not the smallest knowledge or
suspicion, but he could recognise remorse when he saw it
(few had a greater experience of it than himself) and he was
sure that Mervyn had done something of which he was
ashamed. That, and only that, could account for the hours

of solitude from which he emerged pale and haggard as after
some spiritual struggle; that, and only that, could explain the
denial of the Communion Table.

As for the steady refusal to give even a hint of what was
troubling him, Paul guessed that this was due as much to
sheer inability to confess as to unwillingness. He knew too
well that things can happen about which it is physically impossible to speak, even if one may wish to do so. He was,
therefore, careful to avoid making any remarks to Mervyn
which might seem to probe his secret wound, and felt that
in his inarticulate way the boy noticed the forbearance and
was grateful.

But in his own mind Paul could not refrain from pondering
what might have happened—not out of curiosity, but in
order that he might, if chance offered, help to dispel the
shadow which lay over his former pupil. He soon decided
that the mental suffering must have been caused by some
sexual experience. Even if Mervyn had had an opportunity
of committing (or becoming involved in) any of the recognised misdeeds which might have provoked so prolonged a
spiritual disturbance, it was not in his nature to have done so.
Expression of sex, however, is a part of Nature herself. It
cannot always be controlled, even by the strongest will.
Mervyn was not a weakling, but he was still a boy; and
further, as Paul knew well, he was ignorant to the point of
danger of the whole delicate and inscrutable subject. Some
sudden initiation into the workings of sex could not fail to
shock him profoundly, and that his nerves as well as his
conscience had been badly jarred was only too plain. So
Paul wondered and worried, but to no effect.

Mervyn's affliction could not escape the notice of the
St Maurs. When Hetty came in from skating on the afternoon following the dance she seemed preoccupied, and after
tea, challenged by her mother, admitted that she feared
Mervyn could not be well. He had not turned up with John
and Georgie, and when she asked after him, John had flushed
and said crossly that Mervyn was a beast and declared he had

work to do but that was all my eye and he'd promised to come with them and then wouldn't.

"You're sure he's not ill?"

"'Course he's not ill. He's either in love or some rot like that or he's gone loopy."

Hetty had said no more; but she remembered his queer alternations of absentmindedness and elation during the dance, and decided in her own mind that some secret excitement possessed him, from which even she was to be excluded. It sounded uncommonly like a love affair; and although she told herself it was none of her business, she found it impossible to think of anything else, and the words Who is it? Who can it be? beat ceaselessly against the wall of her brain.

To her mother she spoke purposely of possible illness. If she could not prevent Mervyn's private affairs tormenting her own mind, at least she could show her loyalty by putting others off the scent. Mrs St Maur said she was sorry to hear the news and would enquire on Christmas Day. When Christmas Day came, and she met the Crockers returning from church, the boy was not with them. Further, it was so evident that Mr and Mrs Crocker were seriously upset that she felt it kinder not to stop and speak to them. So she for her reasons and Hetty for hers kept silence, and—like Paul, but far more conjecturally—worried and wondered.

BY NEW YEAR'S EVE the cloud over Mervyn had begun to lift.
Youth and the passage of time had revived his drooping
spirits and dulled the edge of his self-torment. He was quite
cheerful in the afternoon, helped John with his ship's model
and at tea-time talked and laughed like his normal self. One
sign he gave, however, that although convalescent, he was
not yet wholly cured. He said he was not going to the big
New Year's Eve party at Colonel Charteris'. He didn't feel
like it. He would rather go to bed early.

They were too relieved to see him so nearly himself to risk
causing a relapse by protest or argument.

"Do as you like, dear" said his mother. "A rest will be
good for you. I will tell them to leave a tray in the library
and make up a good fire, and you can sit there quietly and
make tea and roast chestnuts and go up whenever you feel
like it."

"Thank you, mamma. You are an angel to me. I had
forgotten all the servants were going out too. Sure that's
not a bother?"

"Of course not, darling."

The party-goers left at half-past eight. They had nearly
reached Lashwater House when Paul, who was in the brougham
with Mr and Mrs Crocker and Georgie (John was ahead of
them, proud to be the only passenger in the covered gig),
suddenly beat his forehead.

"What a fool I am! Mrs Crocker, I am so sorry but I
clean forgot to make up the accounts for the Coal and
Blankets Club, and Watkins *must* have them tomorrow.
You'll have to excuse me coming to the party I'm afraid.
I must go back in the carriage and tackle them."

"Oh Paul, what a shame! Couldn't they wait a day or two?"

"I suppose they *could*; but I should never hold up my head. It's my own silly fault and I insist on paying for it."

So back he came to the Park alone in the brougham, let himself in by the side door of which he always carried a key, and went quietly upstairs to his room. The house was completely silent. The landings and corridors were dimly lit by a gas-jet here and there. In his room the fire had burnt very low, but he managed to revive it and hoped the few fragments of coal in the scuttle would keep it going, at any rate for long enough. Then he sat down to his work.

By half-past ten the room felt very cold. The fire had nearly burnt out and there was no more fuel. Paul looked ruefully at his paper-strewn table. Another hour yet, if not more. He decided he could not sit that length of time, growing colder and colder. He must go in search of coal. There was, he recalled, a full scuttle in the inner hall near the foot of the stairs, which would not be needed first thing the next day. Picking up his empty scuttle, he set out to make the exchange. He had reached the final turn of the stairway, only a few steps above the level of the hall floor, when the library door opened, and a shaft of light struck across the hall toward where he stood. Unwilling to disturb Mervyn's solitary evening by a long explanation of his presence, he drew back behind the solid newel post which, at the angle of the stairs, rose from the banisters to the under-slope of the flight above. From where he stood, it was possible to see into the library. The door was now wide open, yet no one came out. This was strange, and instinctively he looked into the lighted room.

*   *   *   *   *

They had been gone for over an hour, and Mervyn, lying back in the big chair, sighed with pleasure at the silence and the solitude. He had read for a while; then made himself some tea; and was now more than content to watch the little blue flames frisk over the surface of the coal or, in the heart of the fire, to imagine landscapes or animals or human faces which formed and dissolved as the glowing mass sank slowly in upon itself.

He was so lost in the dreamy delight of being once more at peace again, both in mind and body, that he did not hear a soft tapping at the door nor the slight noise of the turning handle. When a shadow moved across the hearth he came to with a start, and was aware of Lottie standing at his elbow.

"Oh, sir!" she said softly. "Do forgive my coming in like this, but I have longed to see you so!"

He sat up abruptly, his hands gripping the arms of the chair.

"Lottie! What in the world—Why aren't you gone out with the rest?"

"I wanted to see you" she answered simply, "so I stayed behind."

"You knew I was here?"

She nodded.

"They sent me in to do the fire and leave the tray, as mistress ordered."

He stared at her without speaking. At first he was dazed by her sudden appearance; but as he looked at the graceful little figure with hands quietly clasped in front and lips gently parted, he felt the fascination of her more-than-prettiness stealing over him. Was it the carriage of the head or the slim beauty of the legs or the flowing line of the body from shoulder to ankle as she stood relaxed before him, which quickened his pulses and set up a singing in his ears? Slowly yielding to the excitement, which had returned in double strength and soon victoriously possessed him, he devoured her with his eyes. She looked back at him without moving, a smile behind her steady gaze but none on her lips.

The last barrier went down before the onward sweep of his now triumphant craving. He jumped to his feet and took her in his arms:

"Lottie, Lottie!" he murmured, his face in her curls "You lovely, lovely thing—"

She clung to him fiercely, pressing herself against him.

"Sit down again" she whispered. "Sit down, lovey."

He stumbled back to the deep chair, and in a flash she was on his lap, cuddling into the hollow of his shoulder, her legs hooked tightly across his knees. Thus for a minute or two they remained. Mervyn's heart was knocking wildly, and she looked up with a tiny laugh.

"Your heart beating—I love to hear it. Come here, dear heart, and let me feel you beating."

She slipped her hand under his velvet smoking-jacket, between the buttons of the soft silk shirt, and laid it on his left breast. Then, with a soft purr of satisfaction, snuggled her head against his chin again.

The minutes slipped by. The fire sank slowly. Tiny crackles, hisses and whispers spoke of fragments of coal broken off or spurting into gas or gently settling into the central hollow. The boy and girl were lost in the enchantment of their game of love. They did not speak. Movement there was, and sighs, and the faint sound of long sweet kisses, but no words.

At last Lottie gave herself a little shake and returned to earth.

"Dearest, it is late. I must go or the others will come in. Shall we ever be alone again? We *must* be—*must*. Think of something quickly!"

He pulled himself together with an effort.

"The loft over the carpenter's shop" he said. "I have a key and will fit up something."

"When?"

She was on her feet now, straightening her dress, putting her hair to rights. Suddenly with a delighted laugh:

"Oh look! You naughty boy, you have torn my clothes to pieces."

The regulation black serge dress buttoned between the shoulder blades. It now gaped open, short of two buttons and torn almost to the waist. Beneath, a calico bodice had suffered more damage still, for it had been wrenched off the shoulder and split the whole length of the seam.

"A pin!" she demanded. "Any sort of a pin!"

E 129

He looked helplessly round; then from the centre of his broad black tie pulled out a gold pin with a pearl head.

"Take this for the moment. There isn't another."

"Do it for me. I can't reach. Only the dress; the other thing doesn't matter."

As he fumbled clumsily with the torn serge, she repeated her earlier question.

"When?—in the loft?"

He thought a moment and named a day and hour.

"There!" he said, fixing the pin. "That's the best I can do."

"That'll be all right. I'll run and change it. Kiss me good night, lovey."

She went to the door and, as it swung open, turned to look back at him. He was standing with ruffled hair looking after her with adoring eyes. She let go the handle of the door and ran back towards him.

"You do look so sweet! I must give you one more hug."

When Paul looked into the library, he saw Mervyn with Lottie in his arms, their mouths glued together. The pin in the girl's frock had come undone, and the material yawned loosely open, showing the crumpled bodice and a glimpse of ivory skin.

PAUL CARRIED A grievous burden of mental suffering during the rest of the school holidays. He must do something to save Mervyn from this wretched entanglement; but what was he to do? There was no thought of self in his anxious unhappiness. He was Lottie's slave, and though he loved her, he never dared to picture himself her lover. Inevitably, when the time came, she would prefer another; and resignedly he was prepared to further her happiness in his own despite. But that she should already have made a choice, and have singled out this straightforward ingenuous boy—these were the bitter truths which must, in one way or another, be hidden from the world.

Mervyn must be saved. There was no doubt in Paul's mind whose the initiative had been. He knew the boy too well, and at the same time (though this he left unsaid, even to himself) he had a definite and uneasy sense of the lines along which Lottie was developing. But how was Mervyn to be saved?

The effect on the parents of a realisation that their boy was making love to a servant, and a child of sixteen at that, was almost unimaginable. Their strict standard of moral conduct, their rigid plan of keeping their children from a knowledge of anything which seemed to them dangerous or disagreeable or harmful to the youthful mind, their sense of social propriety—all would be so deeply outraged as to provoke penalties of unwise severity.

No; the parents must be kept in ignorance. Should he speak to Mervyn? He shrank from the hateful task. To confess oneself an eavesdropper—even an involuntary one— is always a painful business; and to admit having seen what he had seen to a boy in the feverish grip of his first passion was an ordeal too grim for him to contemplate. In his heart of hearts Paul was afraid to confront Mervyn—not physically afraid, but terrified at the thought of what the boy would say, how he would look, what their relationship would become in the far-stretching future. He sought to deceive himself with the argument that, once Mervyn was back at school, he would forget the girl and no real harm would have been done. But he did not really believe this. The truth was that he would not speak to Mervyn because he dared not.

Lottie remained; and though he was almost equally frightened by the prospect of challenging her, he came gradually to the conclusion that he would have to do it. Accordingly, when Mervyn had returned to Westminster and John to his school, he summoned his courage and watched for an opportunity.

One was not easily found. Lottie was out of sight in the back premises most of the day, and even if Paul should happen to meet her in a passage or have occasion to visit still-room or dairy, he could not broach a matter of this kind by a passing remark or in the presence of others. However after a week or two fortune favoured him.

One afternoon he was pacing about the shrub garden, turning the miserable business over and over in his mind, when he realised that he had strayed into that part of the grounds which abutted on the kitchen quarters and was regarded as set aside for the use of the servants in their leisure hours. The long spell of wintry weather had temporarily broken, and the snow was rapidly melting. A damp mist hung low over the garden and even clung wraithlike to the branches of the taller shrubs. The leaves dripped steadily on to the sodden ground, which squelched and whispered under-foot. The air was filled with the plash and gurgle of water, so that the sound of a footstep was muted.

All of a sudden, as he was rounding the curve of a large arbutus, he saw her. She was wearing a cloak and bonnet and stood with her back to him some fifteen feet away. He stopped in his tracks and, in order to get himself well in hand, drew back a little so that the tree would hide him if she turned unexpectedly.

She was gliding to and fro in a slow rhythmic manner, as though trying the steps of some solo dance which she was improvising as she danced. Despite his preoccupation with the ordeal facing him, Paul could not but be struck with the beauty of her movements. Even wrapped in the ugly cloak she had the supple grace of a Naiad, and her limbs moved in perfect harmony.

"An enchantress in the making" he thought. "A Circe." There passed before his mind's eye the picture of Mervyn and Hetty dancing at the ball, and he added "Or perhaps a Lilith."

Then he stepped quickly forward and called her name.

She swung about, her eyes still shining with the intoxication of her strange ceremonial dance. But when she realised that interruption had come, and at whose hands, the radiance quickly died. She looked at him coldly, her mouth petulant.

"What are you doing here? This is the servants' garden!"

"I know it is, Lottie, but I want particularly to speak to you."

She shrugged her shoulders.

"Very well. Speak away, but look sharp about it. I have to go in a few minutes."

Time and again Paul had rehearsed what he would say when the moment came; but the girl's hostile and insolent manner (she stood half-turned away, in an attitude of in-attention and indifference) drove his prepared speech from his head and he began stammeringly to extemporise.

"Please believe" he began "that I would rather have any job to do than this." He paused, groping for words, and saw that she was scowling impatiently; then blurted out, "It's about you and Mervyn."

She whipped round like a flash.

"Say that again!"

"You see, I know about it, Lottie. I wish to Heaven I didn't, but I found out quite by chance and have worried ever since over what I ought to do."

"*Ought?* What business of yours is it? And how did you

find out? Sneaking round after me, I'll bet. And now I'm in for a pi-gas while you pat yourself on the back for having stopped a boy and girl from having fun. Keep your damned rescue work for those that want it and, for the last time, leave me be!"

Her voice rose as she spoke and became common and raucous. She was no longer the low-toned caressing little person whom Mervyn knew, but a shrill slattern involved in a street-corner quarrel.

Paul could face up to abuse more bravely than to pert contempt.

"Don't be an idiot, Lottie, and don't shout so. You wouldn't like the whole place to know what you've been up to, I imagine? As a matter of fact I'm not thinking of you at all; I'm thinking of him. There'll be the devil to pay if his father and mother get to hear of this nonsense, and it has got to stop. D'you hear me? *It has got to stop.*"

She seemed a little taken aback by his counter-attack, and for a moment looked at him in scared silence. Then her lips trembled, and she faltered out:

"Don't take him away from me, Mr Gladwin! I beseech you not to take him away. I shall die if I cannot see him sometimes. I—"

Her voice broke and she began to cry. "I love him so much" she mumbled through her tears "and I have no one else, no one in the world. . . ." With a gulp she mastered her sobs and went on, unsteadily but coherently: "I promise no one else shall have the least idea of it. I promise faithfully. And he is so happy with me. Don't you want him to be happy? *Please*, Mr Gladwin, leave us alone. We aren't doing any harm to anyone."

"You are in a fair way to do him mortal harm. If you love him as you say—for *himself* and not for the sport of love-making—you would understand as much. As for what will happen to *you*, if this thing goes on and is found out, —*as it is bound to be found out sooner or later*—well, it hardly bears thinking of. You'll be out of here neck and crop, and then what'll become of you?"

"I don't care a rap what becomes of me, if I cannot see Mervyn any more. Not a rap!" Her momentary collapse was over and her temper was rising again. "I can look after meself as well as most. And I *won't* give him up, so there! Do any damned thing you like, Mr Snitcher Gladwin; it won't fret my guts."

He shook his head sadly.

"I am sorry you are taking it like this. If you won't see that you are playing fast and loose with the boy's whole future, I can't make you. So I shall have to try some other method of keeping you apart, though it may turn out badly for you."

She changed tactics once more.

"Why are you telling *me* to give him up? Why not tell *him* to chuck me? I'll go quietly if he tells me to."

"Partly because he mustn't know I know. It would shame him into doing something rash. Mainly because the matter is in your hands, and you know it. You can stop it at once and you could start it again at once, if you wanted to."

She smirked complacently.

"Well, I won't contradict you on that."

Paul tried to reason with her.

"Lottie dear, think a little; please think for a moment how matters stand. He has two more terms at school. He takes his Oxford exam. in about a month and then has to work for the final examinations at school. It is important, the place he takes when he leaves. His mind will be distracted while this affair goes on—"

"And I suppose it won't be distracted when outsiders shove their oar in and upset everything?"

"For a little while, no doubt. But he'll soon get over it if you help him to do so."

"*Me* help him? I'll see you in hell first. Listen to me, you smeller, either you keep your nose to yourself and drop this botheration altogether, in which case you and me can still be friends, or you blow the gaff on your own and not try to get me to do your dirty work for you."

Paul turned away with a deep sigh.

"All right. I'm sorry to have plagued you."

He was moving off when she ran forward and caught him by the wrist. Her nails dug into his flesh.

"So you won't drop it?" she demanded, and her voice was suddenly dangerous.

"I will drop it here and now, if you do what I want."

"Which is?"

"First, that you give me your solemn promise that there shall be nothing further between you and him and that while he is at home you will avoid him absolutely, which you can easily do. Second, that you write him a letter—I will tell you what to say—putting a stop once and for all to this—this—dangerous nonsense."

She gave a harsh laugh.

"What do you take me for? I'll do neither."

With a hopeless little wave of his hands he began to walk away. "But that doesn't mean I shall do nothing" she called after him.

A WEEK LATER, as they were getting up from dinner, Mr Crocker said:

"I want a word with you, Gladwin. Come into the study."

Wondering what was in the wind and, without any reason, vaguely apprehensive, Paul followed his employer. He had thought both Mr and Mrs Crocker unusually silent over dinner, and tried to imagine what could have occurred to upset them.

Crocker waved him to a seat by the side of the writing-table and began to speak with even more deliberation than usual.

"I have an unpleasant duty to perform and I would ask you to let me say what I have to say without any interruption. The matter can be discussed when I have finished."

Paul's stomach felt suddenly hollow. Mervyn and Lottie had been found out. Perhaps the boy had written to her and the letter had been intercepted. He began desperately to think what defence he could put up, how he might soften the father's heart.

"Mrs Crocker's personal maid came to her today, saying she felt it her duty to report what had been told her by the dairymaid who, it appears, and in common with the rest of the staff, had the story from Sarah, one of the junior servants. According to Sarah, on New Year's Eve last, when all the servants returned from a party, she went up to the bedroom which she shares with Lottie Heape—the child in the still-room, you know—and saw one of Lottie's black dresses scrumpled up, half under her bed. She picked it up and put it in the girl's drawer, noticing that it had lost two buttons and was badly torn. When Lottie came up to bed (she had complained of not feeling very well and had stayed at home instead of going to the party, but had nevertheless remained down-stairs to hear an account of it from the others) Sarah was nearly asleep, and next morning had forgotten about the torn dress.

"It appears that nothing further transpired until a few days ago, when Sarah, going to the bedroom for some reason during the day-time, found this same dress, still unmended, lying on Lottie's bed. Reminded of the earlier incident, she asked Lottie when they were going to bed that night what had happened to damage the dress and why it had not been mended. In reply Lottie made a remarkable statement."

Hitherto Crocker had been sitting back in his chair, talking, as was his wont, rather to the writing-table than to his listener. Now he raised his heavy jowl and looked fixedly at Gladwin who stirred uneasily on his seat. It was obvious that the secret was out, and Paul was aghast at the prospect of what was going to happen.

"She said" resumed Crocker "that she had been ashamed to be seen mending the dress, and had left it in the drawer until now, when she could no longer do without it and must put it into service again. She guessed Sarah had found it and put it in the drawer originally, but she had said nothing for the same reason—that she was ashamed. She then proceeded to tell what had occurred.

"On New Year's Eve she, being alone in the kitchen quarters, was sitting by the fire in the Servants' Hall when a man came quietly in and, after talking for a few moments, made—er—advances to her. When she drew back he caught hold of her and, as she struggled, used force. He was proceeding to molest her in a most abominable manner and had torn her frock half off her back when something—she thought it was a noise in the front part of the house, possibly Mervyn (who you will recall was also at home that evening) moving from one room to another—startled him. He let go of the girl and ran away." After a pause he added solemnly: "That man, Gladwin, was you."

This appalling accusation struck Paul like a blow in the face. For a moment (as when years ago Sneade had suddenly trumped up a fantastic charge against him) he thought Crocker must have taken leave of his senses. But he had only to look at the cold expression in his employer's eyes to know that he was sane, inexorable and very angry.

He opened his mouth to begin an indignant denial, when he realised that anything he might say to exculpate himself could hardly fail to implicate Mervyn.

Crocker broke in on his panic-stricken search for words.

"As I recall you made an excuse to return to this house as we were driving to Colonel Charteris' party. I thought at the time it seemed curious to remember some unfinished accounts at an eleventh hour; but I can now understand that there was good reason for you to come back unexpectedly."

Paul remained speechless. If he said the girl had lied, they would confront him with her, and she, knowing he would not betray the truth, would lie again and probably elaborate her story. If he merely said he was innocent, they would enquire who else in an almost empty house could possibly have gone to the Servants' Hall, conversed a little (the fact of conversation proved the man to be an inmate and personally known to Lottie) and then assaulted the girl? There would be only one answer—Mervyn. All the staff were accounted for. Only he and Mervyn were outside the spheres of perfect alibi.

Paul bowed his head and sat for a few moments wrestling with the agony of his spirit.

Then he rose and stood respectfully before his employer.

"What is your will, sir?"

Crocker was taken aback by the absence of any protest or excuse.

"Have you nothing to say?" he demanded.

"No, sir. Nothing."

"You admit, then, having done this dreadful thing?"

"I have nothing to say."

The big man sighed deeply and blew his nose.

"This incident distresses me beyond measure, Gladwin, and Mrs Crocker is heartbroken. We thought you were happily settled here and had come to rely, more than perhaps you realise, on your help and good sense. But episodes such as this cannot be tolerated. I should be prepared to make some allowance for hot-headed youth, suddenly losing control under the influence of passion. But for a man of your age to use violence to a girl who is little more than a child, to defile my house in an attempt to slake a bestial appetite, is beyond excuse.

"I confess I had expected an indignant denial. I could hardly believe that you were guilty of this evil thing, although the evidence seems conclusive. But you have as good as confessed, and I have no option but to send you away. You will leave tomorrow and will find, in an envelope on the hall table, what I hope will be sufficient to tide you over till you obtain other employment."

When he had finished speaking, Mr Crocker, as a mental organism, faded out of sight. His physical envelope remained, filling the wide chair; but it was temporarily unsentient. Paul walked steadily from the room and went upstairs.

They wrote no word to Mervyn about Paul's disgrace. How should Mrs Crocker find language suitable in which to describe so shocking an affair? What reason could there be for causing the boy distress at this moment of his school career, or setting him to worry over an accomplished fact?

Consequently, when he came home for the Easter holidays, his father sent for him immediately and told him, briefly and in elaborately guarded language, what had occurred.

The boy listened without attempting to interrupt. He grew rather pale and a little frown was fixed between his eyes.

"I do not quite understand, sir. What is Mr Gladwin supposed to have done to this girl?"

Mr Crocker hummed a moment. The strictness of his son's upbringing now embarrassed him.

"He tried to—er—to kiss her against her will."

"But that's not a crime, is it?"

"I fear he—er—became—er—still more familiar, laid hands on her and frightened her badly."

"More familiar?—Oh, now I know what you mean, but it doesn't make sense. Not with Mr Gladwin. Did she go and complain to mamma? And what did *he* say? Besides he wasn't here; he was with you. I'm sorry, sir, but it sounds just mad to me."

The father found himself driven to be more explicit. He had assumed that Mervyn knew of Paul's return to the Park; so that detail had now to be added. He had avoided any reference to the torn dress—the material object upon which the whole revelation was based—and was now compelled to mention that also. Gradually, and with the inconsequent obscurity of a shy man frightened of his own theme, he told the whole story.

Mervyn heard him through in tense silence.

"I see" he said, when his father had done. "What a rotten shame. Please excuse me now."

And he went away without another word.

The loft over the carpenter's shop deserved a more generous name. It was, rather, an upper room in a building of recent date and, though small, had a good dormer window, plaster on its sloping ceiling and a stove. During the Christmas holidays Mervyn had contrived to install a piece of carpet, an old sofa which had formerly been in the nursery, two or three cushions from an upstairs room and a fragment of looking-glass. As no one used the shop below except his brother and himself, his few meetings with Lottie had been carried through without risk of discovery, thanks to his knowledge of John's whereabouts.

Today there was less risk than ever before, for John had not yet broken up, Georgie was out walking with her governess, his father was in London and his mother had gone calling. It was the afternoon following the disclosure of Paul's supposed wrongdoing.

When she played her little tapping tune upon the door, he opened it immediately and closed and locked it behind her. She was aglow with anticipation and excitement and, uttering a low cry, flung her arms round his neck. He took her

141

strongly by the wrists and pushed her from him. Holding
her firmly at a distance he looked at her a moment with
quivering lips. Then he set his jaw and released her hands.

"Sit down, Lottie."

The flush of happy expectation died from her cheeks and
her eyes darkened anxiously.

"Dearest, what is it?" She tried to come to him but he
thrust her away.

"Sit down, I said."

Trembling she sat as bidden, watching him with large
frightened eyes which slowly filled with tears.

"I have just heard what you have done, and that one of my
best friends has been dished for a fault of mine. I want to
know why this happened."

"But, Mervyn, for *you*, of course! He saw us; and he
would have blabbed on us and got you into trouble. Don't
you understand?"

"I understand perfectly what you have said. It's *you* do
not understand that what you have done is sheer beastliness.
You've smashed up a good man by telling a foul lie, and to
no purpose. He wouldn't have said a word. He *didn't* say a
word, when my father accused him. Oh, Lottie, how could
you do this filthy thing? Now we are all up the spout
together—he and you and I."

"But *why*, *why*? Darling Mervyn, be sensible! He has
gone and can't meddle with us any more. Bad cess to him
anyway! I hate him. But I love you. I'd do the same to
anyone who threatened you—over and over. Can't we be
happy again? Oh, my sweet—" She rose and came close
to him, pressing herself against him, but keeping her arms
carefully to her sides. "I am sorry if I have hurt someone
you like; but you are what matters to me, and to be able to
go on loving you—"

A momentary convulsion of grief and anger distorted the
boy's face. He stepped back a pace and raised a hand, as
though to strike her across the cheek. Instead he brushed
his arm across his eyes, went to the door, unlocked it and
threw the key on to the floor at her feet.

"There you are!" he said unsteadily. "That'll help you with your bitcheries. I hope I shall never have to speak to you again."

When his father returned from London, Mervyn made a full confession. Mr Crocker was wise enough to see the uselessness of reprimand. The boy was punished already, would continue to be punished as long as the memory of Gladwin endured. And the father had a further reason for not penalising or lecturing his son. He felt that he himself was by no means free from blame. The injustice done to Paul lay heavy on his conscience, for he was a man fair-minded to the point of pedantry.

Every effort was made to get into touch with Gladwin. Mr Meadows was asked to enquire of Matt Merton. He did so, and Matt undertook to do his best. But although he knew where Paul was, and urged him to respond to Crocker's invitation, Paul was obdurate. He would never return to a place where he had been treated with gross injustice, falsely accused and wrongly condemned, where every servant in the house knew of what he had been accused. He forbade Matt to breathe a word which might help them to find him. Matt submitted, and reported to Mr Meadows that his friend was no longer where he had been and had disappeared, leaving no trace.

The problem of Lottie promised to be a difficult one. Mr Crocker hoped to be able to place her in one of the reformatory institutions maintained by his Society. But she solved the difficulty for him by running away to London, boarding a train from the station beyond Lashwater on her free afternoon. She took with her over a pound's worth of miscellaneous change from the drawer where the dairy-money was now often left. Since Paul's departure the care of money and the keeping of accounts had become slovenly and irregular, so that to have engineered his dismissal proved, after all, of some advantage to her.

BOOK THREE

GIRL TO LET

THE VICARAGE

EVAN SLODE

CORNELIUS FLEISCHMANN

MENACE

A FREEHOLDER

WHEN LOTTIE REACHED London it was after five o'clock, and the light of an unkindly April day was already fading. The interminable and savage winter still lingered; and although there had been a brief respite from frost and snow, the air was raw, and sullen cloud lay over the city.

The girl was frightened and miserable. The desolation of spirit into which she had been thrown by Mervyn's contemptuous rejection had, at the end of a few days, hardened into a hatred of Lashwater and of everything connected with it. A reckless determination to get away and never to see the place again had buoyed her up during the preparations for flight and the flight itself. But now that she was free, and faced with the immense and menacing loneliness of London lying out there beyond the station walls under the darkening sky, bravado crumbled, and the bewildered misery of the last days under the Crockers' roof once more oppressed her. She was just not capable of understanding in what way she had so outraged the boy whom, according to her lights, she genuinely loved. Love to her meant only one thing— a thing precious to her because it gave Mervyn happiness and, for that reason, to be safeguarded at any cost. No one mattered except Mervyn; nothing mattered save that he should continue to enjoy the delights of their clandestine love-affair. Admittedly an element of vengeful anger against Gladwin had prompted her to the false accusation; but fundamentally her motive had been to keep her lover for herself and to shield him from discovery. And he had turned on her with bitter words and contempt in his eyes, so that she had lost, not only him, but her home and her livelihood also.

She stood on the dirty platform of the South Western

terminus, gazing wretchedly round at the smoky train-shed and the drab hurrying figures of departing travellers, asking herself what in the world she was to do.

A middle-aged woman, who had been watching her for a few moments from the entrance to the booking-hall, now approached.

"Can I help you at all, my dear?" she asked. "Are you expecting someone to meet you?"

Lottie started at being spoken to, but was reassured by the stranger's respectable appearance and pleasant manner.

"Thank you, 'm. I wonder if you could recommend me to a decent cheap lodging for the night. I must be at work early tomorrow and had to come up the evening before."

"Do you know London at all?"

"Not at all, ma'am."

"My dear child, you have no business to be all alone like this. You must certainly let me find you a suitable place to stay. Come along with me. That bundle is not too heavy?"

They went down the steps into Waterloo Road and, turning northward, walked side by side toward the river.

"What is your work to be?" the woman asked.

"I am a seamstress, ma'am" improvised Lottie.

"Ah, I envy you, my dear. I never was clever with my needle. And where are you to be employed?"

With an effort of memory the girl recalled the name of a dress-making establishment, seen on boxes at Lashwater.

"Indeed? A first-class shop. You are a lucky girl. I think I should like a cup of tea, and I am sure you would too, after your journey. Here is a quiet-looking place. Let us sit down for a few moments."

Even to Lottie's ignorant eye, the room into which she followed her companion looked an improbable source of tea. There was a bar with bottles on shelves behind it, and below the shelves barrels on trestles labelled Port, Sherry and Madeira. A plump highly-coloured young woman, in a tight blouse cut very low, stood behind the bar and, as the customers approached, raised her eyebrows and said "Yes?" rather pertly.

"You sit down over there my dear" said Lottie's guide "and I will order the tea."

A moment later she came over to where the girl was sitting, carrying two glasses of port.

"Most unlucky! The flues are being cleaned and the fire is out, so they have no kettle on the boil. We must put up with this instead."

While they sipped their port, Lottie stared out of the window through the gathering dusk. She listened to her companion's flow of conversation, and her native wit soon told her that an undue curiosity underlay the stream of low-toned and amiable commonplace. The wine was restoring her courage and quickening her intelligence. Carefully non-committal she parried the various enquiries as to relations living in London, whence she had come, her age, what money she had. All the time she looked through the window, and gradually there came back to her a memory of the big church just across the road. She had seen that church before; she had spent some days in a kind clergyman's house just behind that church, and once or twice his housekeeper had taken her out shopping in the morning and, coming home, they had passed close to those great pillars, with the shallow projecting gable on top of them.

Quickly making up her mind, she leant forward and whispered in the other's ear.

"Eh? Well, I dare say. I will ask the girl."

The woman had reached the bar and was murmuring an enquiry to the barmaid, when Lottie, catching up her bundle, was out of the door like a flash. She doubled to the right and down a narrow entry where, hiding behind a pile of broken cases, she watched the small section of pavement which crossed the entry's mouth. It was virtually dark in this tunnel-like passage, but there was still light enough outside for her to see who went by.

Almost immediately her late companion came into sight. She pulled up short within full view and a few feet from where the girl crouched in her corner. Looking rapidly to left and right, she took a step or two forward, then paused again, went to the edge of the pavement and scanned the opposite side of the road. A man came by. She stopped him with a brief enquiry and exaggerated gestures of distress. He shook his head and walked on. The woman moved beyond Lottie's radius, down the slope towards the station; but the girl remained in her hiding-place—and wisely, for very shortly the solid figure in its sedate black cloak and handsome but sober bonnet reappeared. The woman was now walking quickly, still glancing anxiously from side to side. Indeed so concerned was she with every direction save her own, that she almost collided at the mouth of the entry with, of all people, a couple of policemen slowly strolling in the other direction. Even Lottie could not fail to observe how, when she realised the nature of her near-collision, the anxious searcher swerved away. No enquiry this time; no appeal for help in re-capturing a runaway. The little incident confirmed the girl's suspicions. She was well free of that brand of friend-in-need. The next moment the woman passed out of sight and Lottie saw her no more.

After waiting several minutes, the fugitive edged cautiously toward the street. There was no sign of her pursuer. Dusk brooded heavily over the sour spaces of pavement and roadway. Owing to the toll-bridge, there was never much traffic over this upper stretch of Waterloo Road, and it was now nearly empty. The air was growing colder and smelt of snow. Taking a firm hold of herself Lottie stepped out of her refuge, flitted across the street, and down the narrow roadway opposite which ran alongside the church.[1]

It was almost too dark for her to recognise St John's vicarage, but a blend of instinct and memory took her to the right door. She knocked, at first timidly, then with the recklessness of semi-desperation. Nothing happened. There was a dim light in one of the ground-floor windows; and, having waited in vain for someone to answer the door, she left her little portmanteau on the top step, went a few paces along the pavement, and clambering on to the area-railing peeped into the room.

[1] See map, p. 32.

An oil-lamp, turned low, stood on a large bare table, and beyond the lamp crouched the figure of a man, his head buried in his arms which were flung forward across the table. She could see a shock of dark hair and two hands clasped so tightly that the whiteness of the knuckles was visible even in the dim light.

Dropping back on to the pavement, she returned to the front step and, in the shelter of the small projecting porch, considered what to do. The cold was striking through her cloak and dress, and her teeth began to chatter. Something thicker than oncoming night was pressing out the last greyness of the day. Undoubtedly it was going to snow.

Fear now took possession of her. At all costs she must find shelter. Across the road was the railed churchyard, with a few scraggy trees overhanging the cobbles. She groped in the darkness and happened on a low-growing branch. After two or three attempts she managed to break it off. The crack sounded so loud in the gloom and solitude that for a moment she shrank against the railings, hoping to be hidden from whomsoever should have heard the noise and come to investigate. No one came. Only the clack-clack of footsteps in the main road broke the silence. The light still shone in the window of the vicarage.

Once again she climbed the area-railing and, leaning over as far as she dared, tapped sharply on the window-pane with her broken stick.

The crouching figure leapt to his feet, staring wildly toward the window. He was a powerful, rather coarse-featured, youngish man, dressed as a clergyman. His hair stood out in a disordered brush, his face was haggard. Striding across the room, he peered out into the darkness. Lottie could see his nose pressed against the pane about a yard from her face. She threw the stick away and, holding on to the railing with one hand, beckoned with the other.

He turned suddenly away from the window and rushed toward the door of the room. Guessing what was to happen, the girl jumped down, hurried to the front door again and reached it to hear the sound of bolts being withdrawn.

The next moment they confronted one another across the
threshold.

"What do you want?" he demanded. "You can't come
in here! Go away: go away at once! Oh, my God, is it all
over the district already? I've no money, I tell you. Not a
penny—for the likes of you or for anyone else. You are only
wasting your time."

"Please, sir," she interrupted "please listen to me. I am
all alone in London and want shelter for tonight. I lived
here for a short while as a child, with a kind clergyman and
his housekeeper. I thought he might still live here and
remember me."

The man stared at her confusedly. Then he seemed to
become aware of the bitter air creeping into the passage. He
shivered, and stepping on one side said gruffly

"Well, come in for a moment. The place will be an ice-
house in a minute or two, if you make me stand here with
the door open."

She followed him into the room where the lamp stood on
the large table. He pulled a curtain across the window,
turned up the lamp and put a little coal on the fire.

"Who are you" he demanded "and who do you want?"

She told him her name and repeated her former story
about having to start work at a dress-shop the next morning.

"I have nowhere to go" she said "and the other clergyman was kind to me."

"What was his name?"

"I don't remember. It was years ago and I was a
child."

"What was he like?"

"He had big dark moustachios and a square face."

"That would be Dr Meadows. He's been gone from here
these six months. He has a parish in Marylebone. I could
give you his address—but what's the good of that?" he
added. "You couldn't find your way there tonight."

He stood biting his finger, a scowl darkening his heavy
face. Suddenly he threw at her a look of angry suspicion.

"You're lying! You came here to tempt me! You thought

I was finished and had money and—God knows, I *am* finished,
but—"

Her look of utter astonishment checked his tirade.

"Forgive me" he mumbled. "I am very unhappy and
forget what I am saying. What is it you want? A shelter
for the night? My dear young lady, this is the very last
house in London where a girl can stay tonight. You will
understand why, when you read the papers in a day or two.
What am I to do with you? Ssh!" (as she made to speak)
"let me think."

While he stood and thought, still biting his finger and
cupping the elbow of his bent arm in the other hand, Lottie
looked at him more carefully. The comparative warmth of
the room was restoring her native spirit, and she was once
more prepared to take the measure of whatsoever might
happen. He was a well-built man, over six feet in height
and with strong square shoulders. Lottie did not tell herself
that he was a peasant type, for the words would have had no
meaning for her; but she was conscious that he was of her
kind—not a gentleman, but a son of the people. She noticed
that his clerical dress was threadbare and crumpled, his shirt
cuffs soiled, and his large hands neglected and dirty.

He turned suddenly towards her and saw her watching
him.

"Why are you staring at me?" he cried. "How do I know
you are not lying?"

"I beg your pardon, sir. I did not mean to stare. Indeed
I have told the truth. It is not a night to be out in alone, for
choice."

He brushed aside with a queer vague gesture both his own
suspicion and her apology.

"There is only the Convent" he said. "I must take you
there. They will not have heard—yet—"

"Are you alone here, sir?"

He nodded abstractedly.

"Oh yes, quite alone. They walked out immediately it
happened."

She made a little movement of impatient bewilderment

"What is 'it'? What has gone wrong? You keep on hinting. Tell me what has happened and perhaps we can help one another."

He stared at her with puzzled apprehension.

"How help one another? How can you help me?"

"I have no idea, till you tell me your trouble. But we both seem to be alone, and two heads are better than one any day. What is your name? I have told you mine, and fair's fair."

Again he stared at her, and into his eyes came a strange red light, which shook the girl's new-found assurance.

"My name, eh? Then if you are not Delilah you are a nark!" He strode forward and stood towering over her. "Take off that cloak!" She obeyed trembling. "Turn round! Again! H'm, a pretty little nark too! You've come to the right shop, my copper's doxy, and we stock everything you want. 'The last house in London' I said 'for a young lady'; but the first for your sort. Let us eat and drink and be merry, for tomorrow—Tomorrow?" he repeated dully, putting his hand to his head and turning away. "There is no tomorrow. . . ."

With a great effort Lottie mastered her terror. The man was not sane. She must gain time.

"Please, sir, I am very hungry. You said 'eat and drink'. Is there food in the house?"

"Food? I suppose so. I do not know."

"Then show me where the kitchen is and I will get some supper ready. Then we can go to the Convent. It is not seven o'clock yet."

With a shrug of the shoulders he lumbered out of the room and down the corridor. The girl snatched up her bundle and cloak and followed him. Half-way to the servants' quarters, near the lobby leading to the front door, she thrust the things into a corner. There was no light in the passage save that which filtered through the open doorway of the room they had just left. She found him fumbling with candle and matches in a cold dark kitchen. As the flame struggled to life, it was as though a carpet of cockroaches was being

154

dragged scuttering across the floor. She shivered, and stood in her tracks while the beastly insects raced for cover.

"The larder?" she asked, and despite herself her voice quivered.

Again he led the way. In the larder the cockroaches were even worse. The shelves swarmed. As with a hateful rustling noise they fled from the light, she saw what they had lately overrun—half a pork pie, a loaf of bread, two or three eggs. Forcing back her nausea, she managed to say with comparative steadiness:

"Please take plates and things to the other room and lay the table. I will get the fire going and boil some water."

He obeyed without a word, loaded a tray and she soon heard in the distance the faint clatter of cutlery and crockery being set out on the polished table-top. She poked the dead ashes in the grate with a maximum of noise, dropped the tongs with a clang, and then sped on tiptoe back along the passage to where she had left her belongings. Snatching them up, she raced to the front door which, not having been rebolted, was on the latch.

Out into the icy darkness she went, leaving the door wide open, and scudded toward Waterloo Road, clutching cloak and portmanteau in her arms. Hardly had she turned the corner of the churchyard and entered the straight for the main road, when she heard the door of the vicarage slam violently. A sudden gust or the madman? She ran the faster.

Waterloo Road looked deserted. The widely-spaced gas-lamps guttered and burnt blue in the bitter wind. A few flakes of snow scurried by, almost level with the ground. Lottie made instinctively for the only hiding-place she knew, the entry near the wine-shop which had served her well before. Once plunged into its now black obscurity she felt safe enough to put down her bundle and wrap herself in her cloak. She was warm with the effort of flight, and hastened, while the warmth lasted, to consider her truly desperate position.

She had got no further than to admit it desperate, when a

door in the wall of the entry just behind her hiding-place opened suddenly and the light of a lantern shone across the dirty passage.

"Come in, you" called a woman's voice. "What's the row?"

Lottie had jumped round to face this new menace and now tried in vain, beyond the dazzle of the lantern, to make out the speaker.

"Gawblimey, come *in*! And look slippy about it; it's bloody cold."

Not knowing what else to do, Lottie obeyed, and found herself in a passage at the end of which a bright light and the sound of voices came through an open door. The woman who had let her in, having closed the outer door and locked it, came close and raising the lantern looked the girl up and down. She was the barmaid of the wine-shop.

"Lawsy, it's the kid who bolted from Ma Scratch! Smart piece of work, me dear, and ere's to you. My! Wasn't the old meat-merchant sick? Come and meet the rank and fashion."

She led the way into a cosy parlour where a bright fire was burning and three people were seated. In an arm-chair close to the fire was huddled a tiny bent old woman with white hair and rosy cheeks. In one hand she held a glass of grog, in the other an ear trumpet which she was holding out toward a stout ruddy-faced man who looked like a farmer.

"So I told im e couldn't stuff *me*" he was shouting into the trumpet "and e must shell out or take the consequences."

The third person was a good-looking young man, very smartly dressed, who wore several rings and a handsome tie-pin. His wavy black hair, shining with grease and faultlessly arranged, and the fleshiness of the upper lip under the neat little moustache betrayed his race. His nose was finely cut and his large soft eyes had wistfulness and charm.

"See what I've found" the barmaid began, as she drew Lottie into the room. "Idin in our passage without permission. Let me present—Auntie Jo, deaf as a doornail but spry, very spry; Uncle Tom, free vintner and boss of this

ere Cabin; Leo Arris, man about town I *don't* think, and"
(with a sweeping bow) "little Victoria the lady elp, God's
gift to wine-shops. Them's us. This young lady on the
other and—what is your name, my dear? Look out, the
child's going to faint! Quick, Leo, a bracer. . . ."

Lottie lurched forward, and if Victoria had not caught her
in time and laid her on the couch, would have fallen to the
floor. Lack of food, the excitements and exhaustions of the
last few hours, and now the sudden warmth of the parlour
with its bright light and strange faces had finally overwhelmed
her. The room had begun to swirl dizzily and her stomach
to heave. She had just been losing consciousness when the
barmaid realised her plight.

She came to quickly enough. They gave her brandy and
brought her soup and bread. Gradually her head cleared.

"Thank you" she said unsteadily "I am better now."

"She's starved" announced Auntie Jo suddenly, in a deep
strong voice which emerged almost alarmingly from her
miniature body. "Starved, that's what she is. Vicky, feed
her some more."

They fussed about her with generous solicitude. Uncle
Tom fetched a glass of his best port from the bar; Leo cut
thin slices of cheese and laid them on buttered bread; Vic
sat by her side, fondling her affectionately, coaxing her to eat
and drink. At intervals Auntie Jo issued stentorian orders, and
became impenetrably deaf, even at the end of her trumpet, when
someone tried to explain why they could not be carried out.

By the time the noise and hustle of the impromptu meal
had subsided, Lottie was fully recovered. Indeed, thanks to
the port (a very different affair from that administered by
Ma Scratch only a little while ago) she felt even better than
usual. They asked for her story, and devising a deft mixture
of falsehood and truth, she told it. She was shrewd enough
to guess that this was not the company in which it would
pay her to play the lily-innocent. Her version of the events
which caused her to run to London did not, therefore, conceal
the fact that she was to some extent a girl of experience.
She implied, however, that she had succumbed to persecution,

and then been unjustly blamed for another's fault. When she came to describe the adventure in the vicarage, the three whose hearing was unimpaired gave exclamations of astonishment and loud whistles. The latter attracted Auntie's attention, and a condensed version had to be yelled into the trumpet.

"Please" asked Lottie when quiet was restored, "who is that man and what is the matter with him?"

Uncle Tom cleared his throat and looked embarrassed.

"You tell her, Leo."

"No, Vicky tell her" said Leo.

"All serene!" Vicky was unabashed. "And in words of one syllabub. Well, Lottie me dear, e's the reverend Merrick —in a day or two e'll just be Merrick—and when Dr Meadows (your friend) left St John's to go north-west, they put in a parson who was ill in bed. Don't ask me why. Seems silly to me, but I suppose they'd promised im. Anyway e was so ill e couldn't expect to come and start the job for a few months, and this young chap was sent to keep things goin. Only a curate, you understand.

"Well, early on e made the oly Jemimas who run schools and girls' classes and so forth all twitchety. They *said* it was 'cos of the way e messed the kids about and looked em over —*you* know—but . . . Well, I dunno. E's not a gent, y'see— taught isself as it were—and they're an ighty-tighty lot for all their fiddle-faces and ell-fire. Daresay e *as* a list that way —most men ave—but no go in a parson. All the same from what we can ear they were sittin for im, and the other day e overdid it, preparing a couple of kids for something, and the kids were scared and told their parents who raised ell and tommy with the nobs.

"Oh, e's out, pore devil. Mebbe serve im right, mebbe ard cheese. Spose some kind of a fit seizes im. You did well to run, my girl—better even than the first time today."

At last Lottie got nervously to her feet.

"I must go" she said. "It is getting late. Thank you for being—"

"And where precisely are you goin, may I ask?"

"I—I—"

158

"Then don't talk nonsense. You can't stagger about in a snowstorm with no place to go. You'll sleep with me and we'll keep one another warm. Plenty o time tomorrow to plan what next."

The relief of finding a shelter was so great that Lottie made no attempt to protest. The plan was conveyed at full pitch to Auntie, who crinkled all round the eyes with amusement and uttered a sonorous chuckle which seemed equivalent to consent. Leo bade everyone good night with graceful courtesy and took his departure. Uncle Tom stumped about fastening doors and windows. Then Lottie climbed the narrow stairs in the wake of the brisk Victoria, and in a very few minutes was dead asleep, while the wind moaned in the chimney and outside the shutters the snow fell steadily.

UNCLE TOM'S CABIN (the name was painted over the wine-shop door), for all that its boss and personnel were genial and humane, worked as readily agin the law as did most establishments of the kind in that quarter of London. Tom Ormerod and his presumed mother, Auntie Jo, although they were small beer compared to many, were no less at home in the jungle than any of the other beasts of prey; but just as among real wild animals some take this line and some that, so among the prowlers of Lambeth and Southwark there were varieties of taste and activity, and the Ormerods, on their own lines, were out against society for what they could gain from it.

For a few days after Lottie's arrival Uncle Tom took little notice of her beyond a kindly nod when they met and some friendly chaff over supper. She was left to Victoria, who set her to menial jobs behind the bar, to laundering, to oddments of needlework, to holding skeins for Auntie Jo, and to brightening her own periods of leisure. Victoria's zest for life, like her conversation, was comprehensive and inexhaustible, and Lottie wished that she would relax some time during the twenty-four hours. But as the girls continued to share one another's company during the day and the barmaid's bed during the night, there was little beyond hoping to be done.

Victoria had a poor opinion of men. They appeared to her to be selfish, smelly and physically unattractive. Leo Harris she liked, in a chummy sexless way, because he kept himself to himself and was gentle and considerate and (though she put it differently) as intuitive as a woman.

"E'll talk to you like e'd talk to another feller" she said. "*And* keep is distance. It's them that start firkydoodlin

about with a girl as soon as they get within reach of er that
I can't stand. And breathin mother's ruin down yer neck
with their darlings and all."

"So you never have any truck with them at all?" Lottie
was genuinely curious.

"Oh, I wouldn't say that. Shines for shino's fair enough,
if you must. But I try all the tricks first."

Another time Lottie asked about Uncle Tom.

"What is a free vintner, Vicky?"

"E's a cove as can do any dam thing e likes in the liquor
line. Don't need a licence; can show a copper the door—"

"Then why aren't there lots of them?"

"They don't make em now. They go back into long ago.
And if one of em as no son to follow im, that partikler case
dies out. So they get fewer every year."

"And Uncle Tom has no son?"

Vicky winked.

"Not yet, he ain't. But we'll see."

Auntie Jo was present during this conversation and, in
the freakish way she had, became suddenly aware of what
was being said.

"What'll we see?" she demanded.

"Talking about Uncle Tom and a son" shouted the girl.

"Well, e does just as well, don't e?" enquired the old lady
complacently, and proceeded on her mistaken track. "Me
pore usband used to worry so. Never mind, I'd say to im;
there's ways and means. And no one can say it's for want of
tryin. That e *ad* to admit" (chuckling). "Then me pore
sister died and someone ad to look after the sweet little orphan
baby. Ah, dearie me, you've got ter help yourself in this life
for no one will do it for you."

The newspapers gave considerable prominence to the case
of the unfortunate Merrick. Headed "Serious Charge against
a Clergyman" or "Extraordinary Accusations against a
Curate", columns were devoted to the alleged outrage against
two eleven-year-old girls. The magistrates committed the
accused for trial at the Central Criminal Court, and offered to

take bail, the prisoner himself in £500 and two sureties in £250 each. No bail being forthcoming, Merrick was locked up.

Lottie read the accounts of the proceedings before the bench, and did not try to conceal from herself that she was deeply sorry for the man. He had frightened her badly; but now that she had escaped from that dreadful house, she had a feeling that in some degree the two of them were comrades. He was a rough and simple being, who for an unknown reason had become a parson and, by so doing, cut himself off from his kind. A momentary loss of control, or a momentary possession by some force stronger than himself, had wrenched him from obscurity and turned him into a hunted creature. Too broken even to try to escape, he had stayed where he was, awaiting capture. They would send him down for quite a term. What would happen to him when he came out?

She, too, had yielded to a sudden impulse of desire; became involved with persons higher in the social scale who, when trouble came, despised her and cast her adrift; she too had been ejected from a monotonous yet safe obscurity and left to perish. Forgetting her own part in the affair, ignoring the fact that thanks to her new friends she was far from perishing, taking no account of having been neither publicly accused nor sent to jail, she became intoxicated with large generalisations against the cruel persecution of humble folk by the rich and powerful. Finally she persuaded herself that both she and Merrick were innocent victims of a malign society, to whom they owed nothing save, in their own time, revenge.

To her, in this frame of mind, came Uncle Tom with a strange proposition.

It appeared that a year or two ago considerable stir had been caused by the alleged kidnapping for immoral purposes of a young girl. She had been the support of a sick mother and two little sisters, and after having disappeared for several days, had been found in a brothel in Pimlico. It had finally transpired that she had gone there of her own free will; but in the interval between the opening of the case and its disappointing conclusion, a number of worthy persons had subscribed money for the relief of the mother and two children. If only the pathetic story had not collapsed in so unsatisfactory a manner, quite a tidy sum would have been netted for the distressed family.

Uncle Tom now suggested a revised and improved edition of this appeal to humanitarian sentiment. He understood from Vicky that Lottie had ambitions to become a dancer, and that she showed a natural gift for making up dances as she went along. It appeared that she had danced an occasional improvisation in the privacy of the girls' bedroom which, to Vicky's perhaps prejudiced eyes, had seemed just beautiful. Very well then; a dancer she should be. A disappearing dancer would have a stronger appeal than a mere bread-winner. Further, she should have run away to London to avoid the brutish overtures of a drunken stepfather and, naturally, had changed her name. "Ilda Tremaine you shall be!" declared Uncle Tom, as in a moment of vision. "Ilda Tremaine. That's the ticket! And escaped from the clutches of a beast in uman form. The girl fightin for er honour always fetches em, while a fam'ly in the country and a different name will stop any nosin around."

He proceeded to outline his plan. A man who owed him a good turn, manager of a Greenwich music hall, would engage a new and unconventional dancer and make a bit of a splash about her. Lottie would appear on the stage for three or four nights; and then vanish. Rumours would get about of suspicious characters hanging around the stage door. Her humble but honest friends would bestir themselves. Something of an outcry would be raised in the Press. Finally, bedraggled and tearful, the lost girl would struggle home, fall on the doorstep in a state of exhaustion and, when sufficiently recovered to answer questions, would tell a pathetic tale of having been decoyed to a bad house and there (as the newspapers would say) forced to submit to the embraces of strange gentlemen. At this point a fund would be opened, the results of which, Uncle Tom anticipated, would be highly satisfactory to all concerned.

"But where will I have been all the time?" demanded Lottie. "I'm not spending a week in a bad house for anyone."

"No, no, me dear, nor shall you! You'll be snug as a bug at ome all the time."

"And where's home? Here?"

Uncle Tom shook his head.

"Wouldn't do. All of us ere got to be crazy with grief and worry. No. You'll first of all shift over to Leo's mother the other end o' the town. It'll be noticed she as a young lady lodger, and there'll be talk she's a new dancer come to try er luck. Good. That'll cut you off from ere. Then after the grab you'll ide up somewhere safe which Mrs Arris 'll find for ye, until it's time to do the prodigal's flop on the old woman's doorstep."

"But when I turn up again I'm to say where I was taken to, and they'll go and poke around and find I never was."

"Gammon and spinach, ducky. Trust yer old uncle. There's a madam in that line of trade who needs payin off— the very one, by the way, that employs Ma Scratch who nearly nabbed you the day you came ere—and this is when she gets it. You swear you was tricked into goin to er place —give the address an all. A course the old bitch will deny it; but she can't prove you weren't there, and the beak will note that she runs a flash-drum and out she'll go. It's a cert, me dear, and we split the swag."

Lottie was not greatly impressed with Uncle Tom's plan. She was at heart an egotist and far more interested in her own advancement than in the team work of a gang-swindle. But for two reasons she agreed to play her part. In the first place, here was a chance to vent her spleen on moneyed fools. In the second place, and more important, she had begun to regard the Cabin as a dead end, and it seemed possible that the suggested escapade might offer an opportunity of a wider personal existence.

The Greenwich manager was amenable enough. He watched her do a desultory solo dance, ran his hand up and down her legs, smacked her bottom and said she'd do prime. No doubt he would have suggested further compensation in return for an engagement; but Uncle Tom, who accompanied her, had evidently made clear that this was a special case and that the girl was not without protection.

During the few days' interval set aside for the rehearsal of her turn, she went with Leo to see his mother. Mrs Harris, a comfortable middle-aged Jewess with a husky voice and sleepy yellow eyes like a cat, occupied one floor of a house in Foley Street, Marylebone. She and her son were on the most affectionate terms, and clearly lived together in amity on a basis of mutual incuriosity as to what the other was doing. Lottie was shown a small but comfortable back-room, looking on to Ogle Mews, and made welcome whenever she wished to occupy it.

It was thought prudent that prior to her appearance at Greenwich, and perhaps during the few days of her activity there, she should be seen in Leo's company both in and about Foley Street and in the West End bars frequented by him and his kind. This would account for his later taking a prominent part in the hue and cry, and also explain the girl's presence near the Harris tenement before she actually went to ground. Accordingly she moved into her temporary home; and on a clear, cold evening, wearing a cheap fur cloak and a dress obtained on easy terms from one of Uncle Tom's slop-shop chums, she accompanied Leo to the Crown and Anchor in the Strand.

The big room was crowded. Down one wall were alcoves —not of the kind which permitted complete seclusion (the tavern was not that kind of place) but recesses in which a party of four or even six could sit comfortably withdrawn from the bustle of the floor. The opposite wall was shut off behind a long mahogany bar, at which clustered men and women of all ages. The Crown and Anchor was not a night-house nor, save incidentally, a place for a pick-up. It was one of the favourite haunts of the Swell Mob—smart thieves, billiard and card sharps, confidence men and tipsters—and the company virtually consisted of folk who, being in the same line of business, did not prey on one another nor interfere with one another's girls. An occasional flat wandered into the tavern by mistake and came to regret it; but such incidents were uncommon, and even slightly resented as contrary to the spirit of the place.

Leo, beautifully dressed as ever, introduced his companion to two or three cronies under her new and assumed name. They treated her with the greatest civility, offered her a stool at the bar, and slid easily into enigmatic chat with Leo on subjects of mutual interest. While they talked, Lottie sipped her port and looked about her with lively interest. This, she felt, was more like being alive than anything which had happened to her since her stolen meetings with Mervyn Crocker. The bright lights were repeated in diminishing vistas by the mirrored walls. The noise of conversation swelled and sank in an extraordinary and exciting manner. If you withdrew yourself into a kind of windowless listening post, so that you could hear but not see, the clamour of talk, the footsteps, the chink of money, the sound of glass and crockery on polished wood or marble-slab blended into an undulating howl, of a kind which might issue from a cageful of wild animals. Now it fell to a deep conspiratorial hum; now shrilled almost to a shriek; then on a slightly lower note soared into a rhythmic bang and clatter, such as a train makes passing through a deep-walled cutting. To Lottie it was the most thrilling noise she had ever heard. This was the big world; this was London; this was part of the far-flung battle for success, into which at any moment she herself was to plunge.

Not as a dancer. That casually expressed ambition might mean years of waiting and hard work. She was out for quicker results, and felt that she could get them. Also the coming imposture, which seemed so ingenious, so important to Uncle Tom, already struck her as stupid and trivial. She would go through with it for the sake of the new experiences and new contacts which it might bring her. But her eyes were set on horizons loftier and more distant. She, Lottie Heape, would dominate, in her own character and by her own qualities, the London of money and luxury, the London of men.

She came back to the present with a slight start to observe a big man, his fur-lined coat thrown open to reveal evening clothes, his silk hat set rakishly on the back of his head, throw his arm round Leo's shoulders.

"God's teeth, dear boy!" he boomed. "Where you bin? Not seen you for weeks. Thought you'd jilted me."

He had a big drooping moustache, eyes heavily pouched, and loose folds of cheek and chin which hung like dewlaps over his collar. A great paunch swayed shamelessly below his shirt front.

Leo simpered (there was no other word for it) and in his gentle caressing voice excused himself. He'd been busy over a hundred things : also his mother had been unwell.

"All's well that ends well!" the big man cried. "So long as I've found you again—and lookin handsomer than evah. We'll crack a bottle of fizz to celebrate. Heah, Mabel me deah! Give George one of the usual and tell him to bring it over theah!" He pointed toward a corner table, pressed Leo to his side and, still talking volubly, swept him away from the bar and across the room.

Lottie was looking after them with a flicker of amusement, when the only one remaining of the two men to whom she had been introduced bent toward her and said politely:

"I must apologise on Leo's behalf, Miss Tremaine. He should not leave a lady so unceremoniously. But if you will allow me to act as escort until he returns . . ."

She smiled at him brightly.

"That is very civil of you. But poor Leo could hardly help himself, could he? Who is it?"

"Lord Frederick Boreham, half-brother of Lord Candover."

"I'm sorry" she said. "I am a country mouse. These grand names mean nothing to me."

The man gestured apology. He had an agreeable open face, which, with a fluent tongue, was indeed his principal stock-in-trade and enabled him to inveigle well-to-do strangers into investments of a kind highly profitable to himself.

"I beg your pardon. The brothers are such a queer set-out that all London knows them."

"Please tell me about them!" She threw into her voice all that she knew of flattering eagerness.

He bowed acknowledgment.

"With pleasure."

Rapidly and with humour he told a tale of an elderly and impoverished Marquess, who married twice and had a son by each wife. The first had been an ailing aristocrat and her son took after her; the second was a bouncing beauty off the Olympic stage and a very shrewd woman indeed. Early in her reign coal was found under one of Candover's agricultural estates, and in a couple of years his lordship advanced from titled penury to affluence. The Marchioness now exerted her charms and her native wit to obtain control of his unexpected wealth.

"Don't ask me exactly How" said the man, "because I couldn't tell you with a lady present; but she wheedled almost all this brass out of the infatuated old fool (he was twice her age) and had the lip to tell him she was a better business man than he, and that she would manage his affairs for him. What she said was true enough, of course, if she'd meant it like that. But she didn't.

"Then the old boy pegged out. Her Ladyship (no longer a chicken) got the jitters because her stays would hardly meet, and took up riding. She'd never played this particular game in her life; but, obstinate as a mule, knew better than her groom, took out a half-broken gelding one day, was run away with and flung against a tree. Killed outright. When they read the will they found she'd left every damn penny to her own son Freddie! Of course it was really family chink and belonged to her stepson but there was no entail and she could do as she liked.

"So there you have them—little Candover, slipping along in the shadows with a paltry thousand a year, and Fred Boreham crashing about town with his pockets full of rhino. And keeping them full too. He's his mother's son is Freddie, as anyone in the City will tell you. But he knows how to spend as well as how to earn. He's a great one for making the feathers fly."

"Hens' feathers?" asked Lottie demurely.

The man stared at her a moment, and then gave a shout of laughter.

"Jolly good for a country mouse! We must have a drink on that!"

As he leant over the bar to give his order, she became conscious that another man was standing by her side.

"What's the joke and who's the country mouse?" demanded a full complacent voice.

Lottie's acquaintance turned his head.

"Oh, hullo, Slode; have a drink." He spoke to Lottie: "Miss Tremaine, may I present Mr Evan Slode? Slode, this is Miss Tremaine."

The newcomer bowed too elaborately over her hand. He was in his middle twenties, inclined to plumpness, and over-dressed in a black frock-coat of superlative material. His collar, shirt-front and cuffs were laundered to gleaming perfection; his black and silver cravat was centred by a large pearl pin; he wore varnished boots. His face was round and, where it was not shaved black, freshly coloured; his waved hair and opulent moustache were of the colour they now call "midnight blue".

"Charmed, I am sure." The self-confidence with which he uttered this cliché underlined its insincerity. "May I repeat my question? Who is the country mouse?"

"I am" said Lottie with pert unconcern. She considered that Mr Slode was over-pleased with himself. "Any objection?"

For a moment he seemed slightly disconcerted; but the next instant, with a languid wave of his hand:

"My dear young lady, if the cat won't go away, the mice have to, haven't they? That is if they want to play—as I presume you do."

"Miss Tremaine is to dance at the Greenwich Britannia" put in the other man. "She is a friend of Leo's."

"And how is our charming Leonora?" Slode asked. "I've not seen her lately."

"Here he comes" rejoined the other rather sharply (clearly

169

he disapproved of Slode's looseness of tongue), and in fact Leo was crossing the room in their direction. When he reached them, he nodded a little uneasily at Slode, then bowed to Lottie.

"Miss Tremaine, I am afraid we must shortly be going. If you would be kind enough to excuse me just for five minutes more—I already owe you apologies for deserting you, but it was important I should see my friend—I will rejoin you ready for the road. Perhaps these gentlemen—"

"You leave Miss Tremaine to me, old chap," said Slode heartily. "I'll look after her." To Lottie he said: "Literally two minutes with your permission" and swaggered away.

The first man looked at his watch.

"I must be off. No idea it was so late." With a hesitant smile he added in a low voice: "At the risk of being impertinent, may I beg a country mouse to keep an eye on Mr Ess? Not the most reliable of lady's men. Good night, Miss Tremaine. It has been a pleasure. . . ."

For the few moments that she was alone Lottie considered the evening's encounters. Lord Frederick and Leo were just grotesque. She was not censorious; it takes all kinds . . . But she was puzzled and faintly irritated by what seemed to her mere silliness. The second man (she never knew his name) she liked—friendly, amusing, well informed. And Evan Slode?

The surname seemed faintly familiar; but she could not place it forthwith and was not interested enough to try. At this juncture the original himself was put in evidence.

"Now" he said, settling on a stool at her side. "Let's talk. What shall it be?"

Lottie had drunk just enough to want more. But port had begun to cloy, and she asked for brandy and soda.

When the drinks were in front of them, Slode went straight to the point.

"Look here" he said. "I'm a fellow who always says just what's in my mind. Sometimes I give offence, sometimes not; but I always take the risk. Anyone can see you are a damned good-looking girl, but I can see also that you've got a head on your shoulders and plenty of spirit. With proper management you can crack this town wide open and pick out what you want to keep. Now tell me frankly—what's your little game? All Lombard Street to a china orange, it's not this dancing racket. Greenwich Britannia indeed! Never heard such bunkum."

"Bunkum or not" observed Lottie quietly. "It's true. I'm on there next week."

"Oh, I don't say you aren't going there" he rejoined. "What I do say is that that is only step one. Isn't that so?"

She nodded and looked him in the eye.

"That's so."

"Good. Now we understand one another. I will therefore go further, and say frankly that it is a rotten step and a waste of time. You don't start a tip-top whippet in the mongrel class and hope it will work its way up through the Dandies and the pugs and the spaniels till it reaches its kind. You bring it straight in among the whippets, and if it's a slapper, it wins. See? Well, when it comes to skirts, I can spot a slapper, and you're one."

He ran his eyes boldly up and down her body, as she balanced gracefully on the stool. This, thought Lottie, is as bad an egg as ever I smelt; but he's got his nut screwed on and he's talking sense. She was as unaware as he that they had seen one another before. As a child she had only seen him once or twice, and the scratches on his face had healed long since.

She showed no embarrassment at his scrutiny, but sipped her drink unconcernedly.

"Flattered you should think so well of me" she said at last, with a note of mockery in her voice. "What do you suggest—after Greenwich?"

He jerked his big frame toward her with surprising ease.

"Leo is getting up to go" he said under his breath. "No time now. Where are you living?"

"In Marylebone."

"Right! Meet me tomorrow evening, at nine o'clock at Mariotti's in Newman Street—few doors from Oxford Street." He rose to his feet and raised his voice. "I will surrender you to your lawful escort, Miss Tremaine, and wish you a very good evening." With a "Good night, Leo" thrown over his shoulder, he swung off into the crowd.

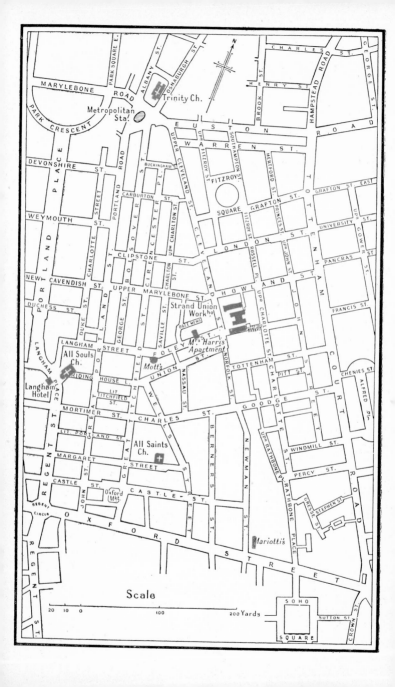

FOLEY STREET, MARYLEBONE, was an interesting specimen among London streets to anyone with a taste for interest of the kind. It was a continuation (at a slight north-easterly angle) of Langham Street, met Upper Cleveland Street at the Strand Union Workhouse, through which, if you knew the ropes, ran a passage into Charlotte Street.[1]   A London street to its foundations, it was nevertheless a good deal of a hybrid, with characteristics borrowed from adjacent and contrasting neighbourhoods. For this reason it had an attraction (doubtless an unconscious one) for Jews, who share the tendency to take surface-colouring from their immediate surroundings, while stubbornly retaining a basic individuality. The terrace of tall divided houses, in one of which dwelt Mrs Harris and her son, was predominantly a Jewish settlement. Decent in their habits, industrious and outwardly law-abiding, the inhabitants lived lives oddly apart from their neighbours. Each family was a close corporation, which watched its fellows narrowly lest it be over-reached, while combining with this needle-sharpness in detecting material gain or loss a complete indifference to moral values. How you got on mattered little, provided you got on: pander to the rhinofats in any way which paid, and no one would blame you. But as between rival panders the fight was on— early, late and all the time.

But the Jewish liking for Foley Street was not only an instinctive liking for their own characteristics in terms of bricks and mortar. It was partly also a highly realistic appreciation of its geographical advantages. Immediately to

[1] Upper Cleveland Street is now Cleveland Street : the Sick Asylum stands on the site of the workhouse and there is no thoroughfare (even for the best-informed) into Charlotte Street.

the west were the great houses of Portland Place, where were money and venal servants, and the recently finished Langham Hotel, whose luxurious appointments attracted wealthy visitors of many nationalities. To the south lay Oxford Market (a favourable pitch for those who could handle an open stall) and beyond, the loitering crowds of Oxford Street, peering at shop windows and only intermittently attentive to their watches, purses and pocket-books. To the east and north-east, a network of narrow streets led to the mixey-maxey of workshop, hide-out and miscellaneous opportunity which filled the angle of Euston and Tottenham Court Roads. Finally, athwart Foley Street's immediate hinterland, slanting south-eastward from the Metropolitan Railway Station at the top of Portland Road to where Rathbone Place debouched into Oxford Street, was an area favoured by harlots of every grade.

The north-westerly section of this area, centring on what had been Norton Street but by now (in the pathetic belief that a change of name meant a change of heart) re-christened Bolsover Street, was a low-class flesh-market of a rowdy and scandalous kind. It was not dangerous in the sense that Granby Street and its alleys were dangerous. Late at night its bullies and thieves might well molest unwary strangers, but it was too accessible from every side to function by day-light as a robbers' lair. It was, however, a public nuisance, and flaunted its trade in shameless squalor. Every house in Bolsover, Carburton, Clipstone and the two Charlton Streets, as well as in Cirencester Place and the upper part of Great Titchfield Street, was a brothel, a rooming house, a common lodging-house or a tavern with access to the upper floors.[1]

The Marylebone Vestry and the local clergy had struggled for some years against this scabrous portion of their in-

[1] The majority of these streets retain their names to this day (1946). Cirencester Place was merged in Great Titchfield Street in the late 'seventies, and Charlton Street was very lately re-christened " Hanson Street ". Bolsover Street was largely rebuilt about 1900 and has now no architectural character ; but I am glad to say that a portion of what is now Hanson Street survives unchanged, and gives an exact idea of what the whole area looked like at the time of this story.

heritance. They sought, under Lord Shaftesbury's Act, to borrow money for site-clearance and rebuilding on mortgage of the rates. But the selfishness of the well-to-do areas of the borough, on the ground that the cost would fall on the innocent as well as on the guilty, had burked every attempt to finance re-housing at the expense of the community, and even the smaller expenditure which would have been involved by large scale prosecution of disorderly householding. There were actually some who said that men of position in wealthy quarters of the borough had personal reasons for obstructing too searching an investigation into the uses to which certain of the house-property was put.

However that may be, little enough was done; and Bolsover and its supporting streets went their slatternly and raucous way, with Foley Street sufficiently withdrawn to keep its reputation, yet not so far away as to be out of touch.

Very different was the south-eastern section of this district of *chambres ouvertes*. Berners Street, Newman Street and Rathbone Place ranked almost with the purlieus of St James's for elegance and decorum. Of actual bagnios there were very few, and these were costly and luxurious. For the most part the ladies lived in well-appointed rooms and entertained a small and recognised clientele, or were under the direct protection of a single individual of influence and wealth. It was not to the disadvantage of Foley Street to be on terms with this discreet but spendthrift district. The demand for furs, jewels and clothing of all kinds was constant and extravagant; and such as were first on the ground with goods of sufficient price and splendour could hardly fail to get the business.

Some degree of these characteristics of Foley Street was revealed to Lottie during the day following the visit to the Crown and Anchor. She had all her time on her hands, and spent it exploring the neighbourhood of her new home. The weather, though still very cold, was dry.

In Foley Street itself she could not fail to notice the Portland Rooms, currently known as "Mott's". This establishment was the street's public acknowledgment of the proximity of fashion. Mott's was "smart", in the sense that evening-dress and *toilette* were de rigueur; exclusive, in the sense that only men of standing were admitted; and strictly decorous, in the sense that, no matter whom you brought or what you planned to do with her, she was for the nonce a lady and you mightn't do it there. Admittedly it was at Mott's that the irrepressible Lord Hastings let loose a sackful of rats one night, while a confederate turned out the lights; but that was an episode of which the administration was somewhat ashamed and, if mentioned at all, was shrugged aside with a brief reference to his lordship's "little way".

Lottie made a mental note of Mott's, but found more to interest and instruct her in the people in the streets. Several young bloods—less effeminate replicas of Leo—went purposefully about their business; low-toned gesticulatory discussions were carried on between men of affairs at street corners or at tavern doors. In the afternoon two or three spruce broughams drew up at different doors in Berners Street, gentlemen were admitted, and shortly reappeared with fur-swathed beauties on their arms, whom they handed cere-moniously into the vehicles. With the fall of dusk the Bolsover carnival opened up in earnest. Almost every door-way stood open, the lights from the passages showing in silhouette the cloaked or shawled figures of women standing on the threshold. The basement rooms were mainly lodgings for so-called "work-girls", who rapped on the panes as men went by or, from the top of the area steps, called and whistled.

The cold set a certain limit to the excesses of these wretched streets; but Lottie, after daring a few yards up one of them, saw and heard enough to send her hastily back again and scurrying past the entrance to the two or three more which lay on her way back to her temporary home.

Up in her room, she sat on the bed to consider what she had seen and relate it to the coming encounter with Evan Slode. With regard to the fundamentals of her position she had no illusions. A girl on the make had only one thing to sell, and no one was going to help her sell it in the best market. She, and she alone, must see to that. The carriage-beauties of Berners Street had somehow made a successful bargain; the screaming drabs in the stews, out there below her window, had not. She shuddered at the thought of sinking to their level of uncouth squalor. Going to the window she looked out into the darkness. The glare of the gin palace at the corner of Marylebone and Charlton Streets was reflected in the low cloud which had settled on the city during the afternoon. She fancied she could hear, even through the closed sashes, whoops of drunken laughter rising from these straight narrow streets, with their tall flat-faced terraces of dingy three-storey houses, their broken steps and crazy railings, their garbage-littered gutters, their brutish alternations of strident quarrelling and stupefied debauch.

Thoughtfully she began to change her clothes, putting on a new outfit, at once coquettish but restrained, which she had bought that day with the expert help of Mrs Harris and with money advanced by the ever-confident Uncle Tom. When she was ready, and had to the extent allowed by her small looking-glass approved her appearance, she went downstairs to supper. Neither Mrs Harris nor Leo had shown surprise or curiosity, when she stated she was going out before nine o'clock to keep an appointment. Leo had an engagement of his own, and his mother was indifferent to her lodger's plans, provided she behaved with propriety when in the house, and paid her way. At ten minutes to the hour, with the door-key in her bag, she emerged into Foley Street. She was well wrapped up against the cold, and had taken care to memorise the route during the day.

"Now we'll see" she said to herself.

As she turned into Norfolk Street, a snowflake settled lazily on her cloak.

*   *   *   *   *

Mariotti's occupied what is sometimes called the "mez-zanine" floor, over a large retail warehouse of fancy porcelain.

The interior of this warehouse, and its show-windows, were extra-lofty, with the result that the floor above was a low-ceilinged affair, stunted as to height and, as to floor area, a narrowish strip, squeezed between the Newman Street façade and the stair-well in the centre of the block. The visitor to Mariotti's had, therefore, the impression of entering the first of a series of railway coaches, leading one out of the other along the frontage of the building and with windows (they were in fact the top lights of the warehouse windows below) at floor-level.

Lottie stood for a moment at the top of the steep stairs leading from the street, and gazed about her. Such little tables as she could see were fully occupied, and immediately to her right was a miniature bar at which several men were standing. Most of those present turned and looked at her, but after an impassive glance they turned away again and resumed their conversations. No one came forward to ask her business; there was no sign of Slode.

Controlling a sudden feeling of shyness, she walked steadily through the first two railway coaches, scanning the tables furtively as she went. When she reached the innermost room she saw him, sprawled backward on a tilted chair, picking his teeth. He wore his hat pushed forward on to his nose and his overcoat was flung over the second and empty chair.

He made no effort to rise or move his coat; merely waved a casual hand.

"Here we are again!" he said. "Push the coat on the floor. What's it to be?"

While waiting for Lottie's drink, he neither spoke nor moved, but lounged there whistling through his teeth. Occasionally he broke off to hunt some fresh fragment of supper with his toothpick. At last he straightened himself, hitched his chair round so that they faced one another across the table, and began:

"What do I suggest after Greenwich? you asked me last night. Well, I'll tell you. But first of all get this clear— I'm not in this business for my health. If I fix you up, I've got to be paid, see?"

178

Lottie felt a sudden lifting of her self-respect. Here was a chance to assert herself, to display her worldly wisdom, to show this hairy brute that she knew how many went to a dozen. Pertly she took him up:

"You want me to be kind to you, eh? You surprise me. Well, there's time and all for that, when we see what's what."

He pooh'd rudely and gave a short snarling laugh.

"Don't be such a kid" he said. "Aren't you past thinking yourself all that of a treat? My poor little cotton-top, I can get all I want of that sort of thing without going to this grease about it! Pull-up now, and listen."

Lottie felt as though he had hit her across the face, and indeed her cheeks burnt and flushed scarlet with rage and mortification. With all her ambition, all her preparedness to sell herself at her own price, she had still retained the adolescent illusion that a girl's favours were the highest form of payment any man could desire. And now this lumpish cad had brushed them aside like change for a farthing. For a few moments she sat trembling with helpless fury, tears smarting behind her eyes. However, she was not going to give him the satisfaction of seeing her cry, and to gain time contrived a creditable sneeze and scrabbled in her bag, as though in search of a handkerchief.

She need not have worried. Evan Slode had not troubled to watch the effect of his words, but was snapping his fingers for the pot-boy to bring him another drink. When he turned to her and resumed the conversation, it was as though it had never been interrupted.

"And not only paid" he said "but paid by both sides. I'm a kind of matrimonial agent, I am—without benefit of clergy, as they say. The nobs come to me with their requirements, and I go about and find something to suit. It happens that I have on the books at the moment" (he winked crudely to emphasize his humorous business imagery) "a very wealthy cove who wants just what you've got. I can bring you two together and make a deal; but for God's sake keep off this schoolgirl bunkum about being kind to him. My client wants a warming-pan, not a pap-feeder."

She was now in control of voice and temper, and her hot rum-punch was beginning to take effect.

"Get me another of these, please" she said. "Who is this fellow?"

"Well, he's not exactly a beauty, but he's got the feathers, all right. City bloke. 'Bout fifty, I should say, and well on the flutter for several years yet. Sheeny, he is; which is all to the good for you. Like most of them when they're pleased, he's an open-handed sort of chap, and he's light on the drink."

"What's he bidding?"

"That'll be arranged when the deal is on. He's got to see you first."

She tossed her head.

"And I've got to see him!"

He swayed forward, frowning angrily a few inches from her face.

"Stow that kind of jabber, you little fool! I've told you once and I'm not going to tell you again. If you put up for this job you say 'Here I am. Will I do?' You're the salmon on the slab, and it's for him to buy a juicy middle-cut—or not. Your likes and dislikes don't come into it. If he says 'No', it's up the spout and I've wasted my time. If he says 'Yes', it's all over bar the cash settlement. That's my business, and I'll act fair by you as by him. So make up your mind here and now. Are you going to play?"

She took a drink and looked him sullenly in the eyes.

"All right; if you say so. When's the march-past and where?"

"Up at my place. I'll take you there. Afternoon's the best time for him. Say the day after tomorrow, just below here on the corner of Oxford Street at half-past three. I'll have a cab waiting. O.K.? Right; then run along to bed like a good girl. Ta-ta."

He took no further notice of her and began rummaging in his pockets for a cigar-case. As she made her way toward the exit, she heard him hammering for the pot-boy.

Outside it was snowing in earnest, and the pavement and

roadway of Newman Street were spaces of untrodden white, save for the wheel-tracks of a single vehicle. This she soon saw was a hansom-cab drawn up opposite one of the last houses in the street. As she approached, her footsteps muffled by the snow, she made out two figures—a woman and a man—standing on the door-step. He was holding both her hands and speaking urgently in a low voice. The girl's reply cut clearly across the silence.

"No, no, Phil. Not tonight. I'm tired."

He evidently pressed her once again, for she freed her hands with an angry gesture and almost shouted:

"Oh, go to hell, will you! I tell you I'm all out!"

He shrugged, turned away and descending the steps almost collided with Lottie as she hurried by, her head bent against the storm. Sweeping off his hat, he said, loudly enough to be heard by the woman who was now fitting her key in the lock of the door:

"Good evening, miss. A shocking night for a walk. Permit me to drive you home. My cab is here."

But she swerved aside, and without raising her head walked quickly on. A little scornful laugh came from the now open door.

"Stung again, poor little man! Got to go to bye-bye all by itself!"

"That's the way to treat 'em" thought Lottie vindictively, and sighed for the day when she also should stand firmly enough to crook her finger at a man and the next moment shoo him away. How soon?

The snow was now half hail, and tiny fragments of ice stabbed at her cheeks. She remembered the last time she had been out alone in a snow-storm, and the fear which gripped her as she ran from that awful vicarage toward the unknown. She was afraid again now, but no longer of the unknown. She was afraid of Evan Slode. "Not a very reliable lady's man" the kindly stranger had said. A shiver started at the nape of her neck and went rippling the whole length of her back.

When she reached Foley Street she felt bruised in spirit,

and exhausted by alternations of fright and anger. As she crept upstairs to the Harris door and tip-toed to her room, she was once again very near to tears. This time there was no need to choke them back. She flung herself on the bed and buried her head in the pillow.

* * * * *

The next evening was that of her first appearance at the Greenwich Britannia. The turn went neither well nor ill. The dancer felt listless and bored and showed it; an uncritical audience, out to enjoy itself and pleasantly full of beer, thought her a tidy little piece, and applauded her looks rather than her performance.

The day following, affecting a confident calm she was far from feeling, she kept her appointment at the corner of Oxford Street. The cab was there, and the massive figure of Slode stood on the pavement talking to the cabby. To her surprise he greeted her with graceful civility, removing his hat and opening the door for her to get in. As they jogged along he made conversation, but quietly and without a trace of the bullying insolence affected at Mariotti's. Mr Fleischmann was much looking forward to making her acquaintance; assuming that the interview passed off well, financial arrangements (which had already been discussed between them) would be submitted to her approval. "I am sure" added Slode "that you will find them wholly satisfactory."

He then relapsed into silence, sitting well away from her in his own corner and gazing out of the window at the untidy streets, already mushy with the melting snow. It was the last fall of a cruel season, and had hardly lain twelve hours.

The cab climbed the slope of Pentonville Road, turned north, forked east, took a narrow and dirty lane between high walls, passed under an archway and drew up.

Thus for the second time in her life Lottie Heape came to Larne Circle. She did not recognise it (how should she, who as a child had come and gone in a cab and, during her stay there, had never been allowed outside her prison?) nor, but for a mere chance, would anyone there have recognised her.

*   *   *   *   *

Mr Cornelius Fleischmann bowed low over the girl's fingers. He was a stout man of medium height, with thinning hair, no moustache or whiskers, and a large pendulous face, very Jewish, heavy but good-natured. He wore gold pince-nez on a chain, and a hot-house flower in the button-hole of his braided tail-coat. He smelt freshly of lavender water.

The two of them were alone in a room with a bright fire. Unobtrusively the man put the girl through her paces. He offered her a chair, then begged her to come to the mantel-piece to look at the picture hanging over it, then led her to the window. Although he talked all the time in a rapid throaty voice about nothing in particular, she was conscious of a continual scrutiny and of a tendency to circulate round her, in quest of a view from every angle. Mindful of her instructions she lent herself with docility to this elaborate inspection. Now and again, indeed, she threw in an attitude on her own account,—flashing her croup by changing stance from one foot to the other, raising her hands to her hair, throwing back her shoulders so that the dress tightened across her bust.

Finally he said:

"Well, my dear Miss Hilda—it is Hilda, isn't it . . .?"

"No" she replied at once. "It is neither Hilda nor Tremaine. My name is Lottie Heape. The other is just stage stuff."

"Lottie Heape" he repeated. "I like that much better, very much better. Lottie is just right, with those eyes and that colouring. It is a pleasure to invite you to share my leisure hours and honour me with your intimacy. I know you will be comfortable; I think you will find me a considerate and tolerable companion. Well, what do you say?"

Before she had time to answer, the door opened and a small man with baby-pink cheeks and sideburns came bustling in. He stopped short when he saw the room was occupied.

"Beg pardon I'm sure" he began, then recognised the man. "Why it's Mr Fleischmann! How are you, my dear sir? A long time since I had the pleasure. And this young lady?"

His small bright eyes fastened on her and would not let her go. She felt herself blushing under their pitiless stare and moved uneasily. Fleischmann assumed an air of haughty aloofness, very different from the engaging simplicity of his earlier manner. When he spoke, he managed to blend easy condescension with the semi-uncertainty of a gentleman groping after a servant's identity.

"Ah yes—er—Mr Slode Senior I believe. I am here by appointment with your son. Permit me to introduce Miss Lottie Heape, whom I am happy to describe as a friend of mine."

A tiny frown creased Slode's forehead and vanished. Without taking his eyes off her face, he bowed perkily to Lottie.

"Pleasure is mine" he muttered. Then turning to Fleischmann:

"I must not intrude any longer. Pray excuse my having interrupted your—er—conversation."

He slipped from the room and closed the door.

"Please don't forget the other one knows me as Hilda Tremaine" said Lottie quickly.

Fleischmann clicked his tongue.

"I beg your pardon, my dear. That was careless of me."

*   *   *   *   *

Half an hour later, Evan having reappeared, the necessary preliminaries were settled.

"Number Four Alpha Place, St John's Wood" repeated Fleischmann. "Don't forget it, dear child. In three days' time? Delightful. To you, Slode, I can only say 'thank you' for exceeding my wildest hopes. Charming, perfectly charming! I am sure we shall be very happy. Now I must really be off. My hansom will be waiting round the corner. Good day, Slode, and again thank you. To you, my pretty dear, au revoir!"

He kissed the tips of his fingers to Lottie and took his departure.

On their way back to Oxford Street she asked Evan how he suggested that she get to Alpha Place, indicating that it would be less noticeable if she kept her engagement in Greenwich and was then lost to sight, than if the journey were made during the daytime. He agreed, and gave her a five o'clock rendezvous two days hence at which he would report what arrangements had been made.

"By the way" he added "you'll need to cover your traces by a different name. Think of one, and tell me when you see me."

"I will" she said, with a nod and a little smile.

For the next couple of days Lottie took care to keep up appearances with all who were in the secret of her imminent "vanishing". She went to the trouble of paying a visit to the Cabin, in order to assure Uncle Tom that she had her rôle perfectly timed, that there could be no error of tactics, that all she needed was a little cash in hand. She accompanied Mrs Harris to the address in Camden Town, where she was to lie up for the duration of her supposed imprisonment at the hands of the ungodly, and made herself so pleasant to her promised hostess that the good woman was enraptured. In the late afternoon of the second day she met Slode at Mariotti's, and handed over to him the little portmanteau in which she had packed the few possessions she wished to retain. He handed her five pounds with Mr Fleischmann's compliments, told her bluntly that this was half the sum entrusted to him for her benefit, and that he was keeping the other half. "I'll call punctually every month for my commission on sales" he added, with the leer he kept for such as dare not hit him.

Before they parted he took her in detail through her instructions.

"Get out of the theatre a few minutes earlier than usual. Don't go to the station by the main road, but nip round

Skelton Street, along Straight Mouth and in from the river side. When you get to London Bridge, hurry out as slippy as possible to the corner of Duke Street turning up to the bridge. I'll be there with a cab, and we'll be off right away. Oh yes, and the name? Got one?"

"The name is Lottie Heape."

It was on the afternoon of the third day of this interval of suspense (a few hours before her eclipse was due) that, walking up Regent Street towards the Polytechnic, Lottie saw coming towards her a sturdy figure in clerical dress. The pavement was empty and she had an uninterrupted sight of him as he approached. There could be no mistaking those heavy moustachios overhanging that jutting jaw, the short stalwart legs, the dogged energy of the man's carriage.

Acting on pure impulse, as the two of them came level, she said clearly

"Good afternoon, Mr Meadows."

He stopped and looked at her keenly, but without recognition.

"I am sorry, madam. I am afraid I do not—"

"Do you remember taking in a little girl many years ago, and looking after her in your vicarage south of the river, and finally sending her to the country. . . .?"

He again studied her face with close attention; then his eyes softened and he smiled his astonishment.

"Upon my word, what a strange thing! Of course I remember perfectly. And now you are a grown-up young lady and, if I may say so, look both well and happy. It is indeed a pleasure to see you again. Have you time for a cup of tea? I should like to hear all about you."

Uncertain whether or no she regretted having declared herself, but pleasantly excited by the risk she had taken, Lottie walked at his side as he led her across Regent Street to his still bachelor vicarage adjoining All Saints, Margaret Street.

He talked away, asking no questions at present; and she was glad to listen, instinct telling her that one can never know too much of other people and their affairs.

"St John's got too much for me" he concluded. "I am not so young as I was, and I had had over a dozen years of it. So they were kind enough to move me to this small and easily conducted parish."

When he had busied himself with pouring tea and seen that she was supplied with bread and butter, he said:

"Here I am, chattering about myself, when I really want to hear your story! What are you doing in this part of the world, and what is your occupation?"

Lottie was ready for this. She spoke gratefully of the kindness shown by Mr and Mrs Crocker, under whose roof she had learnt to qualify for confidential service. She was now assistant to the personal maid of a lady with a house in Belgravia and another near Torquay. At this time of year, and particularly after so bitter a winter, the lady's health required the soft air of South Devon. She had sent her maid, with Lottie in attendance, to London to carry out certain commissions. These were now dealt with, and the two servants were returning to Torquay on the morrow.

"I have been looking in the shops" she said, naïve and a shade apologetic" and wandered further than I knew."

He congratulated her on her assiduity and success. Then, almost as an afterthought:

"By the way, I see one of your rescuers from time to time."

Her heart missed a beat. Danger? To gain respite she looked across in dim bewilderment.

"Rescuers? I'm sorry; I don't understand."

He laughed, embarrassed.

"Stupid of me! I cannot think of it all as having happened so long ago. Of course you would not remember. You were brought to me by two young men who saved you from a beating."

With arched eyebrows and great wondering eyes she gazed at him.

"Saved? From a beating?"

He shifted uncomfortably in his chair and made a play of watering the tea.

187

"Never mind" he said gruffly. "Much better you should have forgotten. But seeing you there, fully grown, telescoped memory. When you are my age, you will know how the years slide into one another."

The chance to drop the subject was ideal, and she knew it. But the spirit of mischief—the half-defiant impulse to tempt Providence a little further—combined with a rancorous desire to flout, in the person of this unsuspecting parson, the comfortable established world from which she had been ejected, captured her.

"But please tell me about this man—the man who rescued me. What is his name?"

"His name is Merton and he writes for the newspapers."

"And the other?"

"The other? Now what *was* his name? Gladwin—that's it. Gladwin. He went as tutor to the sons of the same Mr Crocker who took you in. You may even remember him."

She nodded. To the fun of deception was now added the vindictive pleasure of spiting Gladwin:

"Yes I do, vaguely. I was only thirteen or so when I left. But I'd no idea he had rescued me from anything. Better have spent his time rescuing himself."

Meadows looked at her sharply.

"What do you mean—rescuing himself?"

"Well, he got into a nice mess, didn't he?"

The clergyman rose to his feet and regarded her with dour suspicion.

"You seem to have learnt a great deal, young woman, about things not your concern. What manner of mess?"

"Oh don't you *know*?" she exclaimed, as though pitying his ignorance. "He—oh, I don't know how to tell you— he got into trouble over a girl. . . ."

"How is it that you are so precise over the misdoings of a man you only remember vaguely?"

"A friend—one of the maids—wrote to tell me all about it" she replied airily, and added, "Quite a young girl she was, too."

She hardly knew that as she spoke, she gave a tiny malicious smirk. The inner satisfaction of spreading in this vicarious manner the scandal against Gladwin betrayed itself in her eyes and in a twist of the cruel lips. Meadows read the omen instantly, and resentment at the insult put upon him blended with contempt for her lying impudence.

"I regret having to turn you out" he said. "My church-warden will be here any minute."

Striding from the room, he opened the front door and stood grimly aside while she passed into the street. She had barely set foot on the pavement, when the door was slammed to behind her.

That very evening Miss Hilda Tremaine left the stage door of the Greenwich Britannia as usual between ten and eleven p.m. She did not return to her friends in Foley Street, who were naturally thrown into acute anxiety. Time went by and there was neither sign nor news of her. Stories of dubious strangers frequenting the purlieus of the theatre led to mumbled suspicion, to raised eyebrows. Another case of kidnapping? The police instituted enquiries. The Press took the matter up, and demanded whether or no the streets of London were to be made safe for English womanhood. Sensationalism, hand in hand with moral indignation, advanced steadily toward a climax. "Wolves in Human Clothing"; "Social Hyenas with Dripping Fangs"; "The Blot on the Scutcheon"; "Who is to Blame?"; "The Truth about the Social Evil"—headlines sprang hourly from the fertile brains of cynical and alcoholic journalists.

The day appointed for the pitiful reappearance of Miss Tremaine—brutalised, terrified and fainting with exhaustion—drew near, arrived, passed by. Nothing happened. An urgent visit to Camden Town revealed that the girl had never turned up at all. Miss Tremaine had indeed vanished, for she was never heard of again. Poor Uncle Tom was distraught almost to madness. Mrs Harris, more philosophical, shrugged her shoulders and rejected any idea of tragedy. "Not that one" she said. "Too fly by a long chalk. She's snugged down somewhere, I'll be bound."

Up in St John's Wood, at Number Four Alpha Place, Lottie Heape drowsed deliciously in her soft warm bed. Her protector had left for business; the day was before her. Bunching the fine linen sheets about her shoulders, she slid back into dreamless sleep.

* * * * *

Arrangements at Larne Circle had been altered during recent years. When Evan had grown to manhood and displayed a talent for working the toffs by acting as liaison between them and their desires, William Slode had fitted up one of the smaller houses in the Circle as a bachelor-establishment for the junior partner, in which his business could be discreetly conducted. The relations between father and son had subtly changed. Evan looked as little the gentleman as could well be imagined; but his brazen aplomb and the ease with which he could pass from bullying insolence to flattering servility carried him into circles which his father could never penetrate. William Slode, insignificant and, for all his ingratiating giggle, spiteful as a ferret, could never impress himself in mixed company; Evan, on the other hand, though gross, bounderish and a swell-mobsman a mile away—had the flow of sporting chatter, bawdy stories and news from behind the scenes which made him a tolerable companion in hours of relaxation to men who at other times would cut him dead. Imperceptibly Evan had come to patronise his father, while retaining sufficient of his boyish fears not to carry the patronage beyond a certain point. He never meddled with his father's business activities, but in their personal contacts swaggered him down. William bore no resentment; indeed he rather liked to watch his son doing his peacock act. He thought him a smart fellow, and a credit to his dad.

On the afternoon when Lottie had been brought to Evan's house and submitted to the approval of Mr Fleischmann, William Slode had come across from his own place to see if his son were at home and, if not, to leave a message with the lascar servant who acted as the young man's general factotum. Finding the door on the latch, he had walked into the passage, listened for some sound of life, and then on an impulse entered the room nearest to him, only to find it occupied. His acquaintance with Fleischmann was of the slightest, and had to do with commercial rather than diversionary matters; so, as has been seen, he withdrew quickly and returned home.

Having regained his own little office, he plumped into a chair, covered his face with his hands and devoted his every faculty to an effort of memory. Where had he heard the name of Lottie Heape? He prided himself on never forgetting a name, and it was important for him not to do so, his business being largely of a kind unsuited to the keeping of written records. On this occasion his pride was not vainglory. After a few minutes' concentration he remembered.

The next moment the implications of what he had remembered came forcibly home to him. Lottie knew the secrets of the prison-house. Would Lottie also remember?

William Slode did not see his son for nearly a week after this incident occurred. Then he said

"That girl you introduced to Fleischmann—what was her name?"

Evan, with the air of a busy man asked to recall some trivial detail of the past, pretended to search his memory.

"Fleischmann? Oh yes, I remember. She was called Lottie Heape."

His father said nothing for a moment—just stood there, rubbing his chin with one hand. At last:

"I know the name. I know that name quite well."

Evan laughed.

"In that case it belonged to someone else. You can't possibly know that girl."

It amused him to mystify the old man who claimed that he never forgot, whose vaunted memory (on this occasion at any rate) was just a fraud.

the passage, listened for some sound of life, and then on an impulse opened the room nearest to him, only to . . .
occupied. His acquaintance with Fleischmann was of the slightest, and had to do with commercial rather than diver-sionary matters; so, as has been seen, he withdrew quickly and returned home.

Having regained his own little office, he plumped into a

18 : M É N A G E

LOTTIE, DURING HER prentice weeks at Alpha Place, was occupied in adapting herself to circumstances and studying the mentality of her lover. The glimpse of William Slode was forgotten. Evan on the other hand could not be for-gotten, and she kept him sufficiently in mind to forestall his threatened monthly visits by arranging meetings at Mariotti's, at which she handed over the agreed percentage of her earnings. For the time being this seemed to satisfy him. He was always boorish and often curtly insolent, but he kept his distance and showed no curiosity as to how things were going in St John's Wood.

Alpha Place was the upper section of a retired thoroughfare which, with an elbow turn, connected Grove End Road with Circus Road immediately to the north of Lords Cricket Ground. It consisted of about half a dozen small houses, each standing in its own garden, facing west and overlooking the considerable demesne of a large mansion whose gates were on Circus Road. Built about 1840, the low stucco building, with its plain pilastered front and elegant wrought-iron verandah, over which wistaria fell in a delicate cascade of violet and pale yellow green, was compact and comfortable. A double drawing-room ran from front to back on the left-hand side of the entrance hall, while on the right was a dining-room and, behind it on the garden, a small morning-room or study. On the first floor the two good-sized bed-rooms were intelligently planned to face east on to the back-garden and catch the morning sun, while a dressing-room, overlooking the roadway, was connected with each one and led into a bathroom which lay between them. A second floor with semi-attic accommodation and a basement supplied the needs of the staff and the various domestic offices.

As though in celebration of Lottie's emergence into the gay world, the spring won its final victory over winter during the first week of her new life. With a heady rush—the dizzier for their protracted enslavement at the hands of frost and snow—the trees burst into leaf, the grass turned green, and a jumble of late winter and spring flowers came simultaneously to life. The sun shone with increasing warmth; and the tall planes, the hornbeam and the weeping birches in the large garden opposite the house were loud and restless with the noise and movement of excited birds.

This violence of spring fever, coupled with the natural enthusiasm of a man trying out a new mistress, kept Fleischmann in a mood of delighted happiness.

Lottie's zeal and freshness—in hours of excitation she lost her glibness and became almost a child again—enchanted him; and being (as Evan Slode had said) an open-handed man to those who pleased him, he bought her jewels and pretty clothes, and after a few weeks increased the monthly sum he had promised to pay for the upkeep of the little house and for her services to its master. Of this increase she said nothing to Slode.

She revelled in the various little luxuries of her new life—in the hot water which gushed from its polished tap into the deep smooth bath, in the shining mahogany surface of bath-surround and lavatory seat, in the sweet-scented crystals she could scatter in the steaming water. She never tired of fingering brocades and chintzes, of polishing glass and ornaments, of putting on and off her smart new garments, and strutting in front of her pier-glass at every stage from mere chemise to hat and fur-lined cloak.

May blossomed into June, and June yielded before the golden splendours of July. Every morning at about ten o'clock Fleischmann left Alpha Place for his office in Old Jewry; every afternoon he was back again by five. He was reputed to have a Belgian wife—a Baroness, they said—and two grown-up children, all of whom lived in or near Brussels. His enemies declared the lady had been purposely installed there in order to prepare a comfortable asylum in a city which sooner or later would be called upon to give her husband refuge; the alternative, and perhaps kindlier, theory was that the two did not get on and dwelt apart for preference.

However that may have been, the financier lived in London as a bachelor, with a small suite at the Cannon Street Hotel.

For three months he was so engrossed in his new toy that, not only did he return in time to take a cup of tea with Lottie every afternoon, but he seldom showed any inclination to go outside the house and garden during the evening. Usually on Sunday he took her driving in Regent's Park; now and again they went to Lords for an hour or two, more to watch the spectators than the cricket; once or twice they visited the theatre.

On the second of these occasions an incident occurred. After the play had ended, they were moving slowly through the crowded foyer toward the doors, when a cheerful voice hailed them:

"By Jove, it's Fleischmann! How are you, old boy? Where have you been hiding yourself?" The speaker's glance now fell on Lottie, and with an impudent pretence of apology, belied by the quizzical and challenging look which he fixed upon her, he added: "Ooh, I see . . . I beg your pardon, old fellow. Won't you present me?"

With an easy civility, which Lottie now recognised as a habitual cloak in moments of irritation, Fleischmann did as he was asked:

"Miss Heape—permit me—Mr Dudley Frensham."

"Your devoted servant, madam" said Frensham, with a sweeping bow but a twinkle in his unswerving eye. Lottie inclined her head gravely, and stood looking straight in front of her until the two men had fallen into conversation and she could sense that the stranger was no longer observing her. She then glanced at him furtively. He was about thirty years of age, and handsome in the style affected at the time by actors playing the parts of junior officers in smart regiments. He had a smooth olive complexion; neat dark moustaches, with a parting in the centre and ends ever so slightly waxed;

a dimple in each cheek when he smiled; white even teeth; a nondescript nose, and eyebrows carefully plucked into thin arched lines. His hair was smooth, parted in the middle and glossily oiled. He wore full evening dress and carried a collapsible opera hat under one arm.

She took in all this while her escort and his acquaintance were exchanging commonplaces, and had just time to turn her head and resume the attitude of unassailable but well-bred boredom, when she heard Frensham say:

"Tip-top running into you like this! Won't you both join me at a bite of supper? Let's step across the way to the Albion. What do you say, Miss Heape? A cold bird and a bottle of Rhine Wine sound all right to me."

She looked to Fleischmann for a lead. His heavy face was expressionless, and though his lips smiled, his eyes were cold. But he spoke with his usual suavity.

"That is very hospitable of Mr Frensham, is it not? If you are not too tired, my dear. . . . An enjoyable place, the Albion. But it shall be exactly as you like."

She felt Frensham's eyes once more upon her, and a little tremor of excitement rippled over her skin.

"No, I am not at all tired. It would be delightful."

Supper passed off pleasantly enough, with light conversation and laughter and excellent food and wine. When Lottie and Fleischmann reached home he became amorous, and she used delaying tactics in order to interpolate a question.

"Who is this Mr Frensham?"

"Well my dear" responded Fleischmann readily enough (he was lying back in a comfortable chair, sipping brandy and water, with Lottie on the floor beside him and the nape of her neck with its cluster of soft curls within reach of his caressing fingers) "he is a bit of a mystery. He seems to know everyone and go everywhere, but how he lives at the scale he does can only be guessed at. They do say that he is, or was until lately, old Lady Pridgeon's lover, and of course if that were so, it would explain his economic survival. But

I have no personal knowledge of that matter, and never believe gossip. I would advise you—"

"Lady Pridgeon?" Lottie interrupted. "Who is she?"

He laughed indulgently.

"My little wildflower! I keep forgetting that my darling is truly as innocent as she looks, and knows none of the grotesques of the great Smoke. Julia Pridgeon—originally Judy Tapman from Shadwell, subsequently Julia Fawcett of the Soho Theatre—is the widow of old Tom Pridgeon, who got a knighthood and a fortune out of the Crimean War. He was a contractor and deserved neither, so maybe he was wise to contract out of this world aussi vite que possible. (How deliciously smooth your skin is my angel! Lean back a little more.)" She obeyed, and his hand slid forward to the base of her throat. "Well, contract out he did, and left his Judy with two hundred thousand pounds. She's sixty, if she's a day, and I suppose one must believe them when they say she was a good-looker once. Anyway—but it's just gossip, as I've said—"

She turned and looked up at him, incredulity and a spark of mischief in her eyes.

"You mean—she *paid* him?"

"Why not, little one?" he began. "Youth and strength are commodities like any others—to buy and to sell—"

He broke off, as though suddenly conscious of some hidden danger. Rising abruptly, he went to the tantalus and poured more brandy, which he drank neat at one gulp. Lottie felt a pang of alarm. He hardly ever drank with that sudden abandon, and something told her he was back again in the mood of irritation which had seized him in the theatre, but that this time the mask was off. He came towards her and, taking her by the wrist, yanked her to her feet. Holding her so that she faced him at a distance of a few inches, he said with quiet ferocity:

"That fellow is taboo. Do you understand? I know Frensham and his sort far better than you. They spell trouble; and I won't have their brand of trouble here."

"You're hurting my wrist!" Her wide eyes were scared and puzzled.

196

She struggled feebly, yet with sufficient energy to dislodge a corner of her corsage, which slipped down her upper arm and laid bare one swelling breast, pushed into extra plumpness by the pressure of the corset from below. The flush in his cheeks deepened, and she could see a tiny pulse fluttering in his temple. He relaxed his grip immediately, and was once again his controlled and punctilious self.

"My apologies, dear child, both for a foolish outbreak and for keeping you up so late. Bed-time and after."

The following day, when Fleischmann reached Alpha Place in the late afternoon, he said:

"Sweetheart, I want you to entertain two gentlemen and a lady at dinner tomorrow night. Look your prettiest and act your sweetest. We men have business to discuss afterward, so must leave you girls to your own devices for an hour; but perhaps we may be permitted to rejoin you in the drawing-room before the guests depart. All quite sans gêne and jolly, so don't be afraid."

She promised to do her best to please him, and first thing next day gave serious attention to her coming début as hostess to a dinner-party.

The staff of Number Four consisted of a cook-housekeeper —a severe but civil-spoken woman who, although she went through the motions of consulting the lady of the house, in effect catered and provided as she thought best; her husband; and a slow-moving dough-faced housemaid. The husband combined the duties of butler, gardener and handyman; he was also his wife's very obedient servant. The housemaid was a shade more pert than her appearance justified. Fleischmann did not keep a carriage of his own, but had a permanent arrangement with a near-by livery stable to retain for his use, subject to reasonable notice, a smart conveyance and a regular coachman.

When Lottie summoned Mrs Davies to a conference about the menu for the evening, she found that little was expected of her beyond satisfied acquiescence in the maintenance of

tradition. "The master likes . . . the master usually prefers
. . . at this time of year the master is accustomed . . ." As
the woman, in her precise sing-song voice, outlined what
appeared to be a more or less inevitable sequence of dishes,
Lottie found herself wondering—as from time to time she
had wondered earlier—who had been her predecessor at
Alpha Place and what she had been like. It had been obvious
from the outset that the establishment had not been suddenly
improvised. The furnishings, though costly and elegant,
were not brand new, and the household functioned with all
the smoothness of a going concern. Then one showery day,
finding time hanging even more heavily than usual on her
hands, she had taken advantage of the housemaid being out
and the Davieses enjoying their early afternoon siesta, to
investigate in greater detail than before her lover's dressing-
room.

She peeped into cupboards, opened such drawers as were
not locked and subjected the room to a scrutiny of the kind
already attempted—with meagre results—in the study-
morning-room. She found one drawer in the dressing-room
devoted to a promising miscellany of oddments—cigar-cases;
a bunch of seals; two or three theatre programmes; a few
very dull letters; a card-case with visiting-cards bearing
various names and addresses; a Paris hotel-bill and another
from Brussels, so oddly set out in columns that she could not
understand of how many persons the party had consisted.
Much disappointed, she sought to close the drawer, when it
jammed at the back. Coaxing it open again she found a
crumpled handkerchief, which her scufflings among the other
contents must have disturbed sufficiently to cause the edge
to catch on the drawer-side as it was pushed inward. It was
a woman's handkerchief, and across the corner was em-
broidered a name—"Coralie".

The memory of this handkerchief (which she had removed
to her own room and locked away) returned to her, as she
gave polite but fractional attention to the housekeeper's
recital; and when the woman concluded with the words:
"The wines, of course, madam, Davies will see to", Lottie

was seized by one of those impulses to run headlong into
danger to which a taste for crisis and a gambler's spirit
periodically exposed her.

"Thank you, Mrs Davies. That will do excellently. As
the gentlemen will sit over their wine, we two ladies will
take coffee in the drawing-room. And now tell me" she
added quickly, impatient to be reckless before the courage
failed her "What became of Coralie?"

The housekeeper showed neither surprise nor embarrassment.

"I think you should ask the master that, madam."

"Oh, I shall" declared Lottie airily "but I thought you
might be more likely to tell me."

Possibly her impudence appealed to Mrs Davies, for the
long straight mouth twitched at the corners.

"And why should you think that, madam?"

"Well, men are so stupid about their affairs, are they not?"
Lottie's air of weary tolerance was deliberately comic. She
knew she was acting caricature, and enjoyed doing so. "They
won't talk about one woman to another."

"Very sensible of them, if you ask me" said Mrs Davies
primly. "And if I may be so bold, madam, I should let be
the lady you mentioned. She—"

Lottie waited a moment, but the woman said nothing more.

"She . . .? Come on, Mrs Davies, you must finish what
you were going to say."

The housekeeper looked fixedly at the cornice over the
girl's head, and said in her low monotonous voice almost as
though she were repeating a lesson:

"She forgot that one can be overlooked."

With a stiff little bow she returned to her kitchen.

*　　　*　　　*　　　*　　　*

The guests arrived about six o'clock. First to come were
a lanky vacant-looking gentleman and a large genial young
woman, built like a Wagnerian Rhine-maiden and with thick
coils of ash-pale hair wound round her head.

"Lottie, my dear" said Fleischmann "allow me. These

199

are Jack and Jackie, known to the census as Major John Bulwinkle and Miss Jacqueline Sanderson. To you, my friends, let me present Miss Heape, who is as delighted to welcome you here as I am."

A hansom jingled to the door and the next moment Davies announced Lord Frederick Boreham.

"'Pon my soul, Flashy" thundered the newcomer, as he surged into the room, "thought I should nevah get heah! Demd jarvie took every wrong turnin' in Christendom 'cept the one we all like to take. Ha ha!" (screwing a monocle into his eye he looked about him) "Can this be Jacko that I see before me? *And* the lovely Jacquelina? Capital, capital—eh?"

He broke off, as Fleischmann took him by the arm and turned him firmly toward Lottie.

"Spare a moment for your hostess, me boy! Lottie, Lord Frederick Boreham; Freddie, Miss Heape."

"Ay say, shockin bad manners, what? Fratefully sorry, Flashy old man, and to you, madam, the humblest, the very humblest."

Lottie struggled with her gravity. It tickled her to be receiving this pot-bellied specimen of dudery in her elegant drawing-room, and to remember that not many months ago she had watched him from a stool in the Crown and Anchor, seen him greet Leo like a long-lost mistress, and heard his story. He had had eyes only for Leo, that evening in the Strand, and she doubted whether he had even realised the young man had a girl with him or would have cared if he had. She was too young to understand how various jealousies can be.

She responded demurely to his greeting and found herself standing between the two gentlemen, while Fleischmann strolled toward the open french window with Miss Sanderson.

"Chawming spot heah, Miss Heape" observed Major Bulwinkle. He had a long narrow face and a receding chin. "Smart fellah, our friend, and" (with a bow) "a deuced lucky one too. Chawming those ramblin roses. Haw haw! that reminds me. You'll like this one, Freddie. Deuced amusin, I thought. Did you know that out of a rose you can get two thingumibobs, one cold and the other hot?"

"I did not, dear boy. Pray expound."

"You can get cooler de rose and hotter of roses! Not bad, what?"

"Demmit, Jacko, you'll be the death o' me one day, trottin out these jew de motts—that's what the froggies call 'em, eh, Miss Heape?—and on an empty stomach, too! Not that you human skeletons set store by stomachs, anyway. Look at him, Miss Heape! What's the use o' askin a chap that shape to dinner? Now *me* . . ." and he patted his great paunch as though it were a horse's flank.

Fortunately at this moment dinner was announced, and further anatomical comparisons avoided.

It was a relief to Lottie to find herself alone with Miss Sanderson after the meal was over. The strain of pretending that she was in control of the repast and its service (whereas in fact she was nothing of the kind) had been considerable; and though, thanks to Fleischmann's training, she was sufficiently conversant with concerts, flower-shows, picture exhibitions and current politics to say "yes" or "no" intelligently when she had to, the task of keeping abreast of the smallest of small talk had not been an easy one. Fortunately, as dinner progressed and the glasses were refilled, Lord Frederick and Major Bulwinkle grew noisier and more talkative, while Fleischmann, with his quiet smile, sat at the head of the table and egged them on. But it was, all the same, a release when she could catch Jacqueline's eye and, with a bow and a smile to the standing gentlemen, follow her from the room.

As soon as coffee had been served and the drawing-room door was shut, the guest gave a deep sigh and threw herself back on the sofa.

"The Lord be praised!" she said. "We can now let down our back hair and be comfortable. I am dying to know about you. You look awfully young to take on Flashy. How's it going?"

Lottie made a suitable noise, and the visitor rattled on.

"You'd think Jack was an idiot to look at him, wouldn't

you? But he isn't. As much on the spot as Sultan Freddie. They're up to something, those three, I promise you. If only they wouldn't act so damned Belgravia, when they're 'out with ladies'. But Jack's all right. I've bin with him five years now and never regretted it. Not going to smoke? Come on, duckey, make a start. You'll come to it sooner or later."

During the next half-hour Lottie learnt a great deal about her new friend and, incidentally, about the hazards of the life she had elected to lead. Jacqueline Sanderson had been a sales girl at a fashionable milliner's, and Major Bulwinkle had seen her in attendance when he visited the shop with his wife. He had contrived to make her acquaintance, and had ultimately set her up in rooms in Rathbone Place, where an intermittent liaison had now lasted happily for a considerable time.

"Nothing personal meant" she said, "for Flashy's a good sort and plays fair by a girl, but I like diggings on me own a sight better than a two-cosy of this sort. Not so roomy, of course, and nix on the buttercups and daisies; but more doing. Still, you're new to it and this is a good way to start; but it'll turn out a bit boring in time—at least I found it so."

She surveyed Lottie with an expert eye and a kindly smile.

"My! you're a pretty thing! Stand up and let me look at you. All so compact, yet nothing missing. Thank your stars you're not my size. I was more or less this pattern when I was fourteen—and that's ten years ago."

She also rose, and twirled slowly round for the other's inspection. Lottie gazed at her in frank admiration. She was indeed a magnificent creature, her head with its great coils of hair set proudly on the neck and shoulders of a goddess, her breasts and flanks the generous symbols of triumphant femininity.

"I think you're lovely!" breathed Lottie. "I'm just a shrimp."

Jacqueline laughed delightedly.

"Wish we could change over—off and on, you know, like

the Arabian Nights. I wouldn't do it for keeps 'cos Jacko doesn't care for shrimpin. But I know one or two who do. Tell you what, when you're on your own—you will be, Flashy goes to the Continent now and again—come and see me and I'll introduce you."

They chattered on. When the light began to fail the falling dusk, as it often does, brought occasional silences, and in the middle of one of these Lottie said suddenly:

"Funny, you know, but I stayed in Foley Street before I came here, and I used to walk up Rathbone Place and those streets near by, and envy the girls going in and out of their houses, and wonder if I'd ever have a place of my own."

"Well, so you have, haven't you?"

Lottie shook her head.

"No, not of my own."

Jacqueline did not speak for a moment. Then she leant forward and spoke seriously:

"Listen to me, babe. You're only a kid yet, and a very new member of the sisterhood. Don't be in too much of a hurry. Learn the game before you start playing on your own. You've fallen on your feet first go off, and be thankful. Flashy, as I said, is a good egg so long as a girl behaves. But he's a devil if he's crossed; and the best way to cross him is to take on a freeholder. Compree? I knew one that tried it, and she got the goose all right. I don't say that to have a flutter or two at my place would do any harm. A girl must go after her own pin money. But no trespassers on the premises, that's flat."

As she thanked her friend for this advice, Lottie was thinking back to Coralie and to the words with which Mrs Davies had closed their conversation that morning. But she decided to ask no questions.

Then the gentlemen came in, and they all drank sherry-cobblers and the party broke up with great good fellowship. Fleischmann went to the porch to see the guests depart, leaving the drawing-room door open. Lottie heard Jack and Jacqueline call good night, and the crunch of their hansom getting under way. Then she distinctly heard Lord Frederick, in what he fondly believed to be an undertone, say to his host:

"So in due course, and if you can find him, you'll tackle this missionary bird and I'll look after Dirty Dick?" Inaudible response from Fleischmann. "Right you are! Good night, old boy; top of the evening to you!"

ABOUT THE MIDDLE of September Fleischmann said:

"I must leave my little girl all by herself for a while. There is business on the Continent to be attended to, much as I dislike having to bother with it. Is there any friend or relative you would like to visit you?"

Lottie, with a private giggle at the thought of inviting Vicky, shook her head.

"I shall be all right. I have plenty of sewing to do. And if I may go out sometimes to see Jacqueline . . .?"

"Of course, of course. The carriage has only to be ordered."

"How long do you expect to be away?"

"One can never be sure. For two or three weeks, I expect; and how glad I shall be to see my pretty again!" He took her by the shoulders and studied her face. "Seriously, darling, you get lovelier every day. A depth to your colouring . . . a richer womanliness. . . ."

She drooped her head so that she could rub her cheek against his hand.

"Thanks to my lord" she murmured.

The remark was pure *câlinerie*—and cribbed into the bargain from Eleanor of Castile, as presented in a historical romance which Lottie was reading in a desultory way. Yet in fact it was most of the truth. Under the influence of love skilfully interpreted, her young-girlish charm was giving place to the warm comeliness of womanhood in flower. The awakening of her passionate self, begun during the brief boy and girl entanglement at Lashwater, was now complete, and she glowed, as the man with his quick eye for beauty did not fail to notice, with a new and sombre wealth of colouring.

Fleischmann continued to look at her steadily.

"Salpi glossis in sequence" he said gently, and his tone was that of a connoisseur rather than of a lover. "When I found you, you were blush-pink and lilac and the markings on the calyx were pale yellow; now you are deep wine colour, shaded with purple and dusted with gold. And all the time the same grace of carriage. . . ."

She did not understand what he meant, nor cared. But he was praising her, and that she liked. She threw her arms round his neck and kissed his fleshy lips.

"Come back soon" she whispered. "Don't leave your poor Lottie for too long."

A few days after Fleischmann had gone, she drove by invitation to call on Jacqueline. The weather had turned very warm, and although there was certainly thunder about, the sky was cloudless and the afternoon sun beat down on almost empty streets. The carriage followed the Outer Circle for the sake of a breath of air, went straight down Portland Place, turned left at the Circus along Oxford Street, and then left again before reaching Tottenham Court Road.

The fragrance of womankind brooded deliciously over Rathbone Place. It came not only from the open windows of the apartments of a dozen little ladies, but also from certain shops and business houses which, most suitably, had invaded this favoured precinct of Paphian London. Two stay-makers; an importer of diminutive Swiss watches; a milliner from Paris; a dealer in perfumes and sweet-scented soaps; a painter of miniatures; a designer and manufacturer of artificial flowers; a dyer and cleaner—"Aux Milles Couleurs"—who offered a range of the subtlest French tints; a mantua-maker with a speciality of parasols—such were the merchants who, in this street of merchants, proffered their merchandise by daylight and in public.

The very atmosphere seemed heavy with mingled scents, urgent with the whisper of silk and linen rippling over a counter before a customer's eager fingers. One caught a waft of rare perfume, the scent of tumbled curls, the distracting exhalation of well-cared-for bodies gently perspiring in the stagnant air, and could imagine that they blended with the faint sound of beauty nestling silkily into delicate lingerie, and with the gentle rivalry of cog-wheel and heart-beat as a tiny jewelled watch rose and fell lazily on the left breast of a diaphanous summer gown.

Something in Lottie responded eagerly to this luxurious medley of scent and sound. One moment she felt a cold shiver of agitation, the next broke into a light sweat. At Jacqueline's door she dismissed the carriage, telling the man to call in an hour and a half's time, was conducted upstairs by a heated and rather dishevelled youth in livery, and ushered into a long comfortably furnished sitting-room, which at first sight appeared crowded with women, but when focussed was found to contain only half a dozen.

Jacqueline came forward to greet her, kissed her warmly and then, with an arm round her shoulders, swung her about for a general introduction.

"Here we are, girls—Miss Lottie Heape, the little beauty I promised you! Isn't she all I said and more? Lottie, my dear, four or five friends of mine—and yours too, I'm sure, after a few minutes—all dying to know you and not one of em any better than she ought to be."

There was a chorus of laughing protest, and the newcomer was given a comfortable chair, a cup of tea and a slice of one of Mr Gunter's most admirable cakes.

Conversation was general and, to begin with, extremely refined. The excessive sultriness of the afternoon most unseasonable . . . the latest bonnets and the pros and cons of transformations . . . reminiscences (mainly misfortunate) of Goodwood . . . social adventures at Brighton recently encountered by one of the company . . . miscellaneous yearnings after a breath of sea air . . . merits of Ramsgate and of St Leonards *vis-à-vis* Brighton . . . defence of inland Spas, in particular Cheltenham and Leamington, as against the sea-side . . . desultory counter-attack.

Boredom began to settle on the party, but there was a

general brightening when Jacqueline rang the bell and requested a neat-looking maid to "bring in the tray". After a second round of sherry-cobblers, conversation gained in volume what it lost in delicacy. The ladies rose and sauntered about the room. There was something of a General Post; and Lottie found herself on a sofa between a languid golden-haired beauty with a weak vain mouth, and a little dark French-woman all sparkling eyes and restless vivacity. Jacqueline came over to them, a cigarette in one hand, a glass in the other.

"Are you happy, my dear?" she asked. "Mind out now; your company is very mixed. The fresco on your left is Alice, who got Mr Leighton made an R.A. by sitting to him. Funny pose, I always thought, for giving a man a hoist."

The languid beauty pouted, but then, remembering that her smile was famous, unfurled it with gracious deliberation.

"Don't be low, Jackie. Never you mind her, my child" (half-turning to Lottie), "she *will* talk shop."

"But it's fact" protested Jackie. "Alice's performance as a virgin in a wall-picture for a church was so splendiferous —were you a wise or a foolish one, darling? Were you even a—"

"Yes, Jackie my angel, I *was*, if you want to know. That was four years ago, and four years are a long time when you're as young as I am."

"She youngs herself more each year, notre chère Alice" broke in the Frenchwoman. "One of these days she toddle again, hein?"

"Shame to tease the poor dear" said Jackie. "Lottie, this is Merlette—meaning Mrs Blackbird, dearie, in case your education has been neglected, and isn't she like one? But some call her 'En tout cas' because—"

Merlette waved her aside.

"Zut! How you talk! You frighten the little one with such stories. Listen, Meess Lottie, I choose my métier— yes?—and do my best. What more is there to do? And this great statue comes and makes a fool of me! Go away, you outsize Canova, and get back on to your pedestal!"

Jackie laughed and wandered off. The little Frenchwoman looked after her affectionately.

"Une brave fille, celle-là—a good girl, Meess Lottie, which all are not. And beautiful—! Quelle poitrine, my foi, quelle poitrine! We others, avec nos pauvres petits nichons qu'on ne peut pas même faire se trémousser sans effort. . . . Ah well, one is as one is, and it is useless to cry over the broken jug."

Lottie had no notion what Merlette was talking about; but she liked the kind, brisk little woman and smiled out of general goodwill.

Merlette spoke across her:

"Alice, chérie, you are always with Sir Edward, yes?"

Alice nodded; then with a shrewish glitter in her usually expressionless eyes said:

"Not for much longer by the look of things. He's playing about with a kid at Florizel. She can have him, if she wants, but it'll cost him something to be shut of me, and he's short on the dibs these days."

"Et alors?"

The other shrugged.

"Applications are invited. . . . I don't worry. My type is always wanted."

Two girls were standing by the window overlooking the street and one of them suddenly called across the room

"Jackie! There's Frensham. Two to one he's coming here."

"Damn his eyes for a nuisance" returned the hostess. "Please try to be nice to him all the same. I don't want a brush with him at this moment." There was a general titter. "That's right, dears, have your laugh out. I don't mean that, and you know it. He's an awkward customer, that bloke, and could muck up Jacko's business if he wanted to."

"You know this Frensham?" Merlette asked Lottie. "Un mec comme il n'y en a pas beaucoup! E smell the poules a mile away, that one. I ate im."

Lottie did not answer. Still uncomprehending, she was well aware of whom they were talking. She felt a stirring of pugnacity, as she recalled his shameless thrilling gaze that night at the theatre and his rumoured reputation. "Perhaps I'll take him down a peg or two" she thought.

The door was flung open and Dudley Frensham, in a suit of cream alpaca and a Panama hat, paused on the threshold and surveyed the room with his bold eyes, smiling his insolent smile.

"Good day, girls!" he said, sweeping off his hat. "Quite a bevy, 'pon my life. Jackie, my dear, how are you? I see there's a cool drink for a weary traveller. I need one, believe me. My God, it's hot! *And* Emmy, *and* Diana, *and* that wicked little Frenchie (Merlette, my soul, why will you never smile for me?) *and* the lovely Alice, London's arum-lily, *and*—Hullo? A stranger? Not quite. I know you . . . let me think . . . ah yes, ah yes" (and his smile widened until the glittering white teeth showed fang-like at the corners of the jaws) "I remember now."

He stood in front of Lottie looking down at her, and she, with perfect composure, gave him look for look.

"You're lucky" she said indifferently. "I don't."

His smile remained impudently fixed, but a shadow of a scowl flitted across his eyes. With a flirt of the shoulders he turned away to take the drink which Jacqueline was bringing him. Merlette nudged Lottie with her elbow.

"Ver' good" she murmured, "but take care."

Jackie approached.

"Mr Frensham wishes to be introduced, Lottie, and to apologise for mistaking you for someone else."

He bowed over her hand, but even as he did so he fixed her with a keen upward look.

Merlette rose from her seat, and without a glance at Frensham moved away. He immediately took her place.

"Truly I apologise, Miss Heape" he said in a low voice "but *not* for mistaking you for someone else. That I could never do. Rather for recognising you—aloud. And how is the excellent Mr Fleischmann?"

"Not very well" she replied. "He feels the heat rather and has stayed indoors today."

He pursed his lips and nodded.

"Very wise. Can't be too careful this weather. And when does he get back from Brussels?"

Lottie bit her lip. That was a bad slip. The next moment she gave him a mischievous smile.

"Suppose *you* tell *me*, then" she said. "I'd like to know."

He laughed.

"And I like your spirit" he said. "Let's go, shall we?"

Half involuntarily, half because she wished to see the adventure through, she began taking leave of the company. Jackie looked at her curiously, but bade her a cordial farewell.

"So nice to see you, dear. I'll look you up one day soon. So long, Dudley. You're a bad man to break up my party and steal the reason for it. But then men are so greedy. . . ."

Lottie's hired carriage was waiting at the curb a few yards away. It was a small Victoria, with a striped canopy to keep off the sun. He handed her in and took the seat at her side. During the drive he talked easily of ordinary things. He had an agreeable voice, and so managed what was virtually a monologue that she felt she had taken an adequate part in the conversation. Actually she felt hollow inside, and was too busy anticipating, with a mixture of alarm and curiosity, what would develop when they arrived at Alpha Place, to give more than a minimum of response.

At one moment she was aghast at her own temerity, for the Davieses were out for the afternoon and nothing short of an earthquake would rouse fat Annie from her hot-weather coma in the basement. But the next instant her spirit asserted itself. The way to finish this fellow slap-off was to play the timid innocent, and then, when he least expected it, burn him up.

At the garden gate she put out her hand.

"Thank you for seeing me home, Mr Frensham. Can the coachman drive you anywhere?"

"Nowhere, thank you" he replied, ignoring her hand.

Keeping her nerves well under control, she dismissed the carriage and walked up the short pathway to the door of the house. The man followed her without a word. As she fitted the key to the lock, she said over her shoulder:

"What time is it?"

"Nearly seven o'clock" he replied. "You dine late?"

Hardly aware of doing so, she answered:

"It is too hot to eat. I shall have some fruit on a tray. Any time—"

They were now in the hall and Frensham, hanging his hat on the hat-stand as though he were a family friend, turned to go into the drawing-room. She was already at the foot of the stairs.

"Don't be long taking off your hat" he said gently.

She felt that the moment had come, and summoning to her aid all that she felt of angry contempt for this brazen and impertinent parasite, she returned slowly across the hall. He was inside the room when he heard her step, and immediately faced her.

"I don't like to be inhospitable even to an uninvited guest" she said "but what exactly do you want in my house?"

"You, my dear." Respectful but blandly positive.

"Me? Really, Mr Frensham, your way of doing business is a little sudden. What if I say no?"

He shook his head with a tolerant little smile.

"You won't say no, you pretty thing, and as for business— I don't understand."

She jerked her head impatiently.

"Psha! I've got to spell it, have I? All right, then, can you afford it?"

He laughed outright.

"Charming! I hope I can. Most embarrassing not to pay the shot—after coming all this way. How much?"

"Couple of ponies, if I felt inclined. But I don't. Not this afternoon. Sorry to disappoint you."

"My dear Miss Heape, you haven't disappointed me." His tone became one of patient but courteous expostulation. "I seem to have given you a wrong impression altogether. I hoped we might continue our conversation in peace and quiet. That was all. It was you who introduced the subject of—what shall I say—quid pro quo? And defined the 'quo'. If I am in the way, I will leave you at once; but it

would be agreeable to make closer acquaintance, and if you
have nothing better to do—pending your supper-tray—"

The sentence trailed into silence. Was it imagination to
hear in the last few words—faint and ironical—a threat?
For the moment she was nonplussed. Impossible to repeat
to him some of the things he had said earlier; that would
show the attention she had paid to him. Impossible, under
the gaze of those compelling eyes, to say outright that he was
very much in the way and please to go. *Was* he in the way?
Did she wish him to go? She felt her annoyance and her
defiant self-control dissolving into uncertainty and—though
this she hardly admitted to herself—into an enticing sub-
servience. There seemed no alternative save to follow his
lead, to accept this pretence of conversational friendship.

"As you wish" she said, with a poor attempt at non-
chalance. "Please excuse me for a few moments."

Upstairs in her bedroom she sat in front of the mirror and,
with hands clenched tightly on her lap, talked to her own
reflection.

"Get a hold of yourself, you silly little idiot! What's come
over you? You challenged the man and he has taken the
challenge. He's to be pulled off his high horse, don't you
remember? Well, go down and tackle the job." "All very
well" the reflection replied "but he starts something simmering inside me. I'm not afraid of him, I'm afraid of
myself. I'll never face up to him—not in that way—because
when it comes to the point I shan't want to." "Well, if
you're such a funky little ninny, I'm not. I hate the man
and mean to tell him so. He can't do anything to me."
"He can; and you'll like it."

She jumped to her feet, smoothed her hair, dabbed her
neck, ears and arms with scent and went quickly downstairs.
Frensham was standing with his back to the room looking
out of the long window into the garden. He did not move
as she entered the room, and her agitation returned so suddenly that involuntarily she let go of the door handle. The
door swung to and closed with a click.

He whipped round at the noise, crossed the room with a few rapid strides and took her in his arms. Held so tightly against his chest that it was useless to struggle, she automatically drew her head away so that her face was tilted towards him. Instantly his mouth fastened on hers. She felt her lips parting under the long ferocious kiss. Her resistance crumbled. For a moment she lay limp in his embrace; then, with a little whimper of animal pleasure, clamped herself even more closely to him and fought his kisses with her own.

Next day was wage-day, and Mrs Davies attended with the household accounts, ready for the weekly settlement. When the business of staff-payments was reached and Lottie had handed over the regular amounts, the woman said smugly:

"There'll be two pound extra this week, madam, for Davies and me."

"What for?"

"Well, madam, company always makes for more work. There was the gentleman yesterday. . . ."

Lottie did not immediately take her meaning, and looked up in perplexity.

"But—" she began, then saw that Mrs Davies, as once before, was staring upward at the angle of the ceiling, her pale lips set in a close line. "She forgot that one can be overlooked . . ." the words raced across Lottie's memory. Silently she took two sovereigns from her purse and pushed them across the flap of the bureau.

* * * * *

In the afternoon of this same day, a second unusual episode occurred.

Lottie was sitting in the drawing-room sewing, with a small pile of underclothes and stockings at her side, when Davies flung open the door. He had hardly time to say "Mr Slode to see you, madam", when the caller stood before her. He gave a little ironical bow, put his hat on a tabouret and threw himself on to the sofa.

"Well, well" he said, lying back on the cushions with his legs stretched out at full length "and how are we today? I hope I am not detropp? That's capital. The guvnor's abroad they tell me, on—we must hope—his lawful occasions."

Lottie quickly recovered from the surprise of this unexpected visit, and fixed him with hard and hostile eyes.

"What do you want? You've had your divvy for the month."

He looked at her in mock reproof.

"Tut, tut! That's not a nice way to greet a friendly caller. What do I want? Perhaps just to see how a pretty little girl is fixed—whether she's comfortable and well treated and all that. Perhaps—"

She interrupted him tartly.

"Oh stow it, can't you? I'm busy. Once again what do you want?"

"Pray don't let me interfere with your interesting repairs" he replied. "No need to be bashful. Drawers are no treat to me. Just go on stitching away and I'll tell you why I'm here. Mind if I smoke?" Without waiting for an answer he pulled a cheroot from his breast-pocket and struck a fusee; then after a pause: "Care to turn a century on the side?"

She had resumed her sewing and did not look up.

"As how?"

"Just in return for a little information."

"Must be pretty hot information if it's worth that."

"It all depends; but if you can get it, it's worth all of that. Now listen carefully . . ." and he proceeded to tell her what she was to do.

After he had gone, she sat and thought over his proposition. It sounded feasible enough. She had already chanced on the discovery that, thanks to some peculiarity in the house's construction, aided possibly by the angle of the garden wall, it was possible, if one were near the window of her bedroom, to hear what was being said in the study immediately below. Into the bargain Freddie Boreham had a voice like a high wind and Flashy, though low-toned, articulated clearly and with precision. She had no idea what Slode meant, when he

215

said that her cue was to be "Homes from Home", but at least it was easy to remember and that was all that mattered. The thought of a hundred pounds was very agreeable to her, and she had no fear of being cheated by Slode. She knew that at the moment she represented to him a good investment, and that so long as it paid him, he would play straight.

BOOK FOUR
THE STREET
OF THE MONEY-CHANGERS

HUGH ST MAUR had just returned home from one of his occasional jaunts to London. He would stay away for two or three days, put up at Batt's, dine at his club, do a theatre or a concert, pay a few calls, visit exhibitions and, in among, spend an hour or two with his lawyer or a stockbroker friend, so as to give a business colouring to what was in fact a pleasure-outing pure and simple.

As he sat with his wife and daughter over dinner, he was full of the art of Gustave Doré. The religious pictures, over which ecstatic young girls of good family were raving in their hundreds, he dismissed as namby-pamby. "They are just haloes and treacle" he said "if a good Catholic be permitted such irreverence." But some of the illustrations, of which trial sketches and a number of originals had been on view—particularly those to Dante's *Inferno*, to *Don Quixote* and to Rabelais—filled him with enthusiasm. He had bought the Cassell edition of the first two, and staggered home with the heavy folios for the delectation of his family, emphasising, however—and rightly—that mediocre book-production had robbed the drawings of their full effect.

After Hetty had gone to bed, Mr and Mrs St Maur walked the terrace in the October moonlight, and then, feeling rather chilled, made up the fire in the small morning-room, which was the sitting-room used for preference when the family were alone. A protracted silence fell, and Mrs St Maur glanced enquiringly at her husband. He was frowning into the fire, and she saw that something was worrying him.

"What's the matter, dear?"

"Nothing exactly the matter, my love—not with us anyway. But I heard some distressing news in the City about our friends at the Park."

"About the Crockers? How—'distressing'?"

"Of course it may not be true, but they are believed to be in Queer Street."

"Nonsense, Hugh! It's the last thing which could happen to them. Why, he must be rolling in money."

"Well, my dear, I hope you are right. But that is what I was told. It appears that the Secretary of Crocker's what-d'ye-call-it Hair Tonic Company had for some while, in collusion with a shady stockbroker, been working a plot to defraud the firm. The fraud was discovered and the business was bound to crash, when suddenly Crocker volunteered to make himself personally responsible. That's all I know. The fraud was certainly committed. So much is known fact. The rest my informant had only just learnt at third or fourth hand, and it may of course be hearsay."

"But *surely* . . . Why, Mr Crocker would have got wind at once of any hint of crooked dealing—a first-rate business man like that."

Hugh shook his head.

"Not really a business man, Lola. An excellent fellow for all his solemn ways, but I suspect a good deal of an innocent. He came into that what d'ye-call-it tonic ready-made. His guvnor worked the thing up. *There* was an old nut and no mistake. I remember my father telling me about him. But our worthy Mr Gervase . . . What worries me is that it would be just like him to *offer* to carry the baby. He is high-principled to the point of morbidity, and would go out of his way to feel responsible to everyone and try to make it up to them."

"Is it a lot of money?"

"So I gathered. I don't know how much; but enough more or less to break the poor old bird. But perhaps it's all my eye. Let's hope so."

Lola St Maur sat staring in front of her, as she disentangled from her husband's words what she knew to be good-neighbourly optimism from what she feared to be sober fact. At last:

"Hughie, Mervyn has just gone up to Oxford. Will it affect him? And John and little Georgie?"

Like any decent man who regrets disaster to a friend's family but is all the more thankful that it has not struck his own, St Maur was by now ready to drop the subject. He yawned.

"I've no idea, darling. I hope not. Suppose we go to bed and see what's happening in the morning?"

She rose and began putting the room to rights.

"You must be tired. But what shall I say to Hetty?"

"Hetty? Why say anything to her? She'll be sorry, but she'll soon forget. Besides, it may not be true."

His wife smiled at him.

"You old silly!" she said. "Never mind. Let it stand over till tomorrow."

But the news reached Hetty before either of her parents saw her. She was down early on a glorious autumnal morning, ready to set off with her dachshund for a run over the dew-drenched meadows, when the old parlour-maid, who had been with the St Maurs since before the girl was born, stopped her at the hall door.

"Them Crockers have lost all their money, so the milk says."

"What do you mean, Annie?"

"What I says, dearie, and no more cos I don't know no more. But one hears of rich folk turnin poor overnight what with speckerlations and new-fangled mines and what not."

"Mamma" said Hetty at breakfast "what's this about the Crockers?"

Her mother was careful to show neither surprise nor embarrassment.

"We know nothing for certain yet, darling. Papa heard in London they have had losses, but I hope the story is exaggerated. I thought we might walk up there, and see if anything seems amiss."

With the swift fatalism of youth, always inclined to prefer outright disaster to anti-climax, Hetty assumed the worst. She had no idea what "losing all one's money" might mean in the way of domestic upheaval; but she realised that persons

of whom she was fond were in adversity and, for that reason
felt sad and sorry.

As chance would have it, they met Mrs Crocker a little
way from the gates of the Park, walking down the road
toward the town, a basket on her arm. She greeted them
with her usual pleasant smile, but there was a strained look
in her eyes and an artificial steadiness in her voice as she
said abruptly:

"I am glad to have seen you both. I would prefer to tell
our friends, rather than that they should hear gossip. We
are in bad trouble here, and I fear will soon be gone."

Mrs St Maur had to decide quickly whether to admit that
rumour had reached them, and that their morning's walk was
in fact a reconnaissance, or to feign ignorance and compel the
poor lady to confess the truth. She chose the former.

"I am so very, very sorry. My husband came back from
London last night and—er—was uneasy because of something
he had been told. Is there anything we can do to help?
You have only to say. . . ."

Mrs Crocker looked away, fixing the hedgerow with a
forced stare. She was fighting to keep her eyes open. They
were already bright with tears. She swallowed once or
twice and said in a low voice:

"Thank you, my dear Lola. You are a good friend, and
I will take you at your word. If you could have Georgie
for a little while . . . Mr Crocker is in London and I must
go to him. I am on my way to settle various accounts in
the town—and see the agents about the house. . . . It must
go now. . . . Everything must go."

She quavered into silence, and turning her back on the
St Maurs, struggled for self-control.

Mrs St Maur, deeply distressed, felt that relief for both
parties lay in action.

"Hetty" she said briskly "do you run on to the house,
find Georgie and help her to get her things together. Wait
with her until I send a cab from the town."

The girl hurried obediently away, and as soon as she was
out of earshot, her mother went to Mrs Crocker, put an arm

round the bowed shoulders of the older woman and, taking the basket from her hand, said:

"You poor, poor dears! I am so dreadfully sorry. Leave this settling-up to me. It will be a miserable ordeal for you to go from shop to shop. I will see to it all, and send Mr Etchells up to call on you about the house and grounds. A cab shall fetch Georgie straight away, and she shall stop with us just as long as ever you like. Now, please go back home and stay there in privacy. You must have a thousand things to do, and to meet a lot of people will be intolerable. Please, please don't thank me! It is the very least we can do after all your kindness to us. . . ."

She gently propelled the now weeping lady toward the drive gates and, once they were round the bend and out of sight of the lodge, bade her a brief farewell. She then quickly retraced her steps and hurried down the hill to Lashwater to carry out the melancholy commissions she had undertaken.

*   *   *   *   *

What had actually happened was this—

Fired, maybe, by the example of more than one trusted yet dishonest employee who, during the 'sixties and with varying success, had taken advantage of their superiors' confidence to defraud the firms for which they worked, the Secretary of the Delilah Hair Tonic Manufacturing Company Limited, in conjunction with a broker friend, had organised a traffic in duplicated shares.

It was undeniable that the Secretary, who was the originator of the scheme, planned and carried it out with great ingenuity and daring, taking full advantage of certain local conditions which were strongly in his favour. Delilah certificates required the Seal of the Company and the signatures of a Director and the Secretary. Signing certificates was one of the authoritative yet automatic duties which Mr Crocker liked to regard as a Chairman's prerogative. It gave him a pleasing sense of importance, yet required no special knowledge of the workings of the firm. Well aware of his Chairman's determination to keep this job of endorsement in his own hands and not to permit his junior colleagues to share in it, the Secretary took the opportunity, when Crocker was in his office, of putting before him from time to time a book of certificates, requesting that a batch of them be signed, and promising to attend to their completion when he was back in his own room.

As the bogus certificates were duplicates of existing issues, the necessity for fairly frequent signing indicated a brisk business in transfers, and Crocker's more or less ritualistic enquiry as to how things were going could be suitably answered. The share register was in the Secretary's care, and the names of the transferees were entered therein, as and when they were communicated by his broker-ally. They were marked with a secret sign, so that the buyers of duplicated shares could be distinguished from holders of genuine shares by the Secretary and by him alone.

So far the malefactor gambled on his Chairman's negligence and his own judgment of character. But he went further, and dared a bold stroke. Delilah dividends were paid annually. The shares stood high, for the Company was prosperous and the genuine issue not a large one. The Secretary asked himself whether, in order to have the best part of two years in which to develop his fraud, it might not pay him to risk a depreciation of the market value of the shares by persuading the board to pass a dividend. He knew that for some while the directors in charge of laboratory research, manufacture, bottling and other technical services had been pressing for better and more up-to-date equipment and accommodation. With their help and approval, he worked out an estimate of the expenditure such re-building and re-fitting would involve; wrote a report demonstrating the working economies and great increase in business which would result from the alterations; and suggested that, if a dividend were passed in order to provide funds for a large-scale factory reconstruction, such a decision (coupled with an informative statement to the shareholders explaining the important benefits which would accrue to the Company and to them, once the work was carried out) would only temporarily depress the market value of their holdings.

After considerable demur the Board agreed, and the dividend was passed. As anticipated the shares fell. But not catastrophically, the reason publicly announced for the Board's action being sufficiently convincing to prevent a serious loss of faith in the Company's future. At this juncture the broker gave confidential advice to a Financial Company with a taste for speculation to buy as many shares as they could lay their hands on. He made no secret of being a friend of the Delilah Secretary who, he said, had given him more details than those made public of the certain future advantages of the re-building of the factory. The Company were duly impressed, and during the next few months the broker bought for them large blocks, most of which were in fact duplicated shares, although a few were genuine.

The timing of the operation now became delicate. The next Annual Meeting was drawing near, at which, as the Secretary knew, it was Delilah's intention to announce the declaration of a good dividend. This statement would immediately send up the value of the shares; and as the Finance Company would be certain to send a representative to the meeting, it would convince them that they had been well advised and prevent any suspicion of irregular dealing. The conspirators, therefore, decided to take one final risk, and to stay at their posts until after the meeting had taken place. Prior to the meeting, the Secretary prepared dividend warrants for subsequent issue, carefully omitting all those shareholders distinguished by his private mark.

As the Secretary had anticipated, not many shareholders attended the meeting—for Delilah, despite the fall in share-values of a year ago, was still regarded as a solid and successful Company—but among those present was a representative of the Financial institution, which by now owned most of the shares. A dividend was announced. The shares rose, and the Finance Company were able immediately to sell a portion of their accumulated holding. At this moment, in the brief interval between the announcement of a dividend and the despatch of the warrants, the Secretary and his broker colleague decamped to the Continent, the former having posted a letter on his way to the boat-train to say that he was indisposed but hoped to return to work in two or three days' time.

With the distribution of the dividends, the fraud was immediately exposed. The Finance Company were still the principal holders of shares and, when an inadequate dividend reached them, demanded an instant explanation. It was discovered that the great majority of their shares were duplicates, and the fact that they had just disposed of a chunk of similar duplicates, whose whereabouts it was no easy matter to trace, made confusion worse confounded. Delilah was faced with liquidation.

So Hugh St Maur's story was substantially correct, and at no point more so than in the unconfirmed rumour of Crocker's personal intervention. No sooner had the scandal broken, and it had become clear beyond a doubt that the Delilah Company, in the person of its Secretary, had committed a criminal fraud on the public, than the Chairman showed as much constructive vigour as formerly he had shown negligence and want of acumen. By means of a prominent appeal in the Press, he summoned a meeting of all shareholders, irrespective of whether their shares were genuine or duplicated, and spoke from an empty platform. He declared that neither he nor the other directors were liable for a fraud perpetrated by one of their servants, nor were his co-directors morally responsible. He, on the other hand, felt himself personally to blame for damage done in the Company's name to many innocent people.

"You gentlemen" he went on "can, if you wish to do so, destroy Delilah as a trading concern and recoup your losses to whatsoever extent liquidation proceedings may make possible. I appeal to you to consider an alternative plan. Those of you who hold genuine shares in the Company know our record previous to this disgraceful affair; you have studied our Balance Sheets, watched our progress and drawn what I hope I may be permitted to describe as handsome dividends.

Those of you who have been inveigled into buying bogus shares are the poorer by the amount those shares cost you. If you will permit Delilah to go on working, to develop as it certainly will develop, I will myself, out of my own pocket, buy in every duplicated share at the price paid for it and the Company, which will not contribute in any way to this purchase, will continue its career without being penalised for the wrongdoing of a dishonest servant or for the negligence of its chief executive. In this way a prosperous and reputable business will survive, and a large number of blameless and hard-working folk will escape the terrors of unemployment. I need hardly add that I myself am resigning from the Board and will have no further connection with the Company. I now relinquish the Chair in favour of my colleague, Mr Brett, and withdraw, leaving the meeting free to ask questions and discuss my proposal without the embarrassment of my presence."

Before he was allowed to leave, a shareholder demanded how it was proposed to distinguish between holders of genuine and bogus shares, seeing that some of the former had passed into other hands since they were issued. Admittedly no warrants had been sent out on duplicated shares originally purchased by the victim of the fraud—the Finance Company—but he had himself encountered two cases of different persons holding shares with identical numbers, and other similar cases must exist.

Crocker replied that Delilah hoped, by patient investigation, to succeed in identifying the great majority of such duplicated issues; but that if any disputable cases proved to be insoluble, the rival holders could elect for joint reimbursement if they so desired.

There were some among the audience to whom the quixotism of Crocker's suggestion was so foreign to conventional business method that it appeared suspicious. No man, they felt, would be such a fool as to sacrifice himself to this extent, unless he had some trick up his sleeve. But during the long discussion which followed the ex-Chairman's departure, it became evident that his offer could only be a genuine one, and that prospects of profit for holders of real shares and of reimbursement for holders of duplicated ones were emphatically brighter than they would be, were Delilah destroyed. If the Company were liquidated, the directors would doubtless plead that they were not legally liable, and leave only the assets of the Company to meet the claims of creditors and shareholders. According to Crocker's scheme the Company would remain unscathed and continue to function, those who would be creditors in the event of its bankruptcy would be creditors no longer if the business went on, and the personal fortune of an individual no longer connected with the Company would be available to satisfy the claims of the creditors in respect of the duplicated shares.

Very few of the people present realised the effort which it cost Mr Crocker to make this public avowal of his culpability. To himself he would never have thought to make excuses, being a man whose moral courage was as great as his rectitude. But to appear before a hall full of angry and frightened people and confess himself a mere incompetent figurehead required social courage, and of this he had very little. He had moved impressively through life, accustomed to be treated with the respect due to an established institution. The rôle of prominent citizen had ceased to be a rôle and become a second self. And now, gathering all that he had of self-possession, shutting his mind to every thought of how he must appear to those rows of silent listeners, he had forced himself deliberately to shatter the legend of his own weighty integrity, which over years he had laboriously created. For half an hour after leaving the hall he sat in his private room, bowed over his desk in mortal shame, and sobbing because his heart was broken. Then he pulled himself together, and crept away from the office which was no longer his to the frowsy Bloomsbury lodging where, to escape casual contacts with acquaintances of earlier days, he had taken refuge.

There followed continual conferences with his man of business. Crocker was a rich man, but he had always spent freely and the bulk of his fortune had been derived from

228

he Hair Tonic. There could hardly have been a worse
moment for a forced sale of Delilah shares, yet sell them he
must. Even by throwing in his outside holdings and what
he had of chattels and real estate, he would be compelled
in order to honour the pledge offered at the meeting and by
a large majority accepted) to sacrifice the greater part of what
he possessed. This without hesitation he prepared to do.

Physically he was a pitiful sight. His complexion had
become yellower than ever, and his large full face had so
fallen in, was so runnelled with troughs and hollows, that it
is doubtful whether many who had known him formerly
would now have recognised him. Nevertheless he clung
piteously to his hiding-place, refusing even to go out into
the street, but sat all day at the table in the over-furnished
parlour, ruffling through papers, adding up lists of figures,
studying the market reports.

His wife had soon joined him in London and shared his
retreat. With head held high and a quiet courageous smile
on her lips, she did the simple shopping necessary for their
needs, carrying her purchases home in a string bag and
handing them over to the landlady, who undertook to cook
but not to cater for her lodgers.

Crocker's lawyer found that each visit to his stricken
client thrust him further into the rôle of devil's advocate.
He had had sufficient experience of persons plunged into
sudden financial trouble (though never before on the scale or
with the unexpectedness of this grievous disaster) to be
prepared to advise how something at least could be saved
from the wreck. But the present case was directly contrary.
Crocker was possessed by the demon of self-mortification.
He wanted to strip himself of every shred of financial covering,
so that, when at last he stood naked before those for whose
losses he felt himself to blame, they would see that, at least
to the limits of his power, he had made restitution.

There was little the lawyer could do to check his client's
extremism. He urged him to put in his wife's name sufficient
to make provision for the family's future, but only succeeded
to the tune of an annual two hundred pounds. He managed

to persuade him to let the elder boy finish his term at Oxford
rather than suddenly disappear within two or three weeks o
his arrival. The delay, argued the lawyer, would lighten th
emphasis on what had occurred, would lessen the embarrass
ment felt by the boy himself and would give the parents tim
to decide what should be done with him and even to re
construct some sort of family life. He further argued tha
John, now sixteen, should remain at school till the end o
the school year in July 1870. At the moment, there wa
plenty of cash in the bank to pay the fees ahead, and, after a
confidential word with the headmaster, it could be arrangec
that the boy's departure a year earlier than would have beer
normal should be rationally accounted for. With regard tc
Lashwater Park, the adviser pleaded with Crocker not tc
force a panic sale. The property was a valuable one, and for
that very reason not of a kind to fetch its price at a moment's
notice. By all means let the furniture and effects be disposed
of forthwith (the type of man who would ultimately pay an
adequate figure for the house and grounds would not require
the former to be furnished); by all means let the treasures
of the orchid-houses come to auction in London as soon as
they could be included in a first-rate sale. But for the free-
hold of the property as a whole it was essential, he urged,
to estimate its current value, fix the price accordingly, and
stick to it.

Crocker demurred. Not only was he obstinately set on
raking in as much cash as possible and with the least possible
delay, but Lashwater was in some sort a symbol of the old
self, of the Crocker whom he now bitterly designated as a
pompous sham. It was at Lashwater that he had lived in
thoughtless luxury, enjoying wealth he neither earned nor
even troubled to supervise. The sooner the place were sold
and could be forgotten, the more quickly he could lay the
humiliating spectre of his former life. The best the lawyer
could do was to secure a respite until the end of the year.
Within less than three months he must find a buyer, or the
property would come to auction and without reserve.

On a private list of his client's securities, which Crocker in

the first desperate days of wholesale realisations had taken from
a locked box and thrust into his hands, the lawyer observed
an entry recording a considerable holding in a concern called
Homes from Home Limited. This was a Company whose
shares were not quoted on the Stock Exchange, and enquiries
failed to obtain any further information about it than was
contained on the file. When he asked Crocker what he
knew of the Company, the haggard man showed signs of
embarrassment. He muttered something about having taken
the shares over in lieu of a bad debt, that he understood
the venture to be a more or less private one, that it had
paid him one and a half per cent for a number of years and
that he believed it was something in the hotel line. He
had no idea whether the shares were saleable, but would
himself approach the office whence the dividends reached
him. The lawyer was puzzled. Evidently his client did
not wish any steps to be taken on his behalf—a disinclina-
tion which, in another man, would suggest that he had
something to conceal. But that Crocker should have indulged in shady financial dealings was inconceivable. He
had been remiss in carrying out his duties as Chairman of
Delilah; he had lived on commercial profits, while affecting
the lofty attitude of a philanthropist hardly aware that such
a thing as commerce existed; but he was upright to the
point of absurdity, and would not have known how to dabble
in roguery, even if he had wished to do so. Clearly, however,
there was nothing to be done in the matter, so the man of
business shrugged his shoulders and presumed that his client
would report to him in due course.

Crocker was an unusually friendless man. He had been
too well-to-do to be "taken up" by warm-hearted acquaintances, drawn out of himself and given a taste for congenial
society; conversely, he lacked social talent and social ambition
and, in the days when the vast anæsthetic of charitable
endeavour had kept him happily floating in a mazy dream of
august beneficence, had never needed friends or noticed
that he lacked them. Now, however, he was down to earth

with a vengeance; and though he valued as they deserved
the love and loyalty of his wife, he felt desperately alone in
his struggle with unfamiliar mundane things.

This sense of solitude had never possessed him so menacingly
as at the moment when, after the lawyer had left him, he
faced the problem of the shares in Homes from Home Limited
and their conversion into cash. He bitterly regretted the
careless urgency with which he had handed over his private
list of holdings. Nowhere else were those shares mentioned;
no member of his family or of his circle of business acquaintances knew of their existence. He would have been
delighted to forget all about them, to disown them, to
return any future dividends to the source whence they came.
But this his conscience would not permit. If these shares
were worth anything, their value in money was due to the
poor people he had allowed to be misled. Therefore he
must find out their value, get possession of it and hand it
over.

But he could not bring himself to make a direct approach.
The background to the singular transaction which had brought
him these shares had lost none of its horror with the passage
of time. He had always prided himself on indifference to the
opinion of others—and certainly his bland imperturbability
had, in the happy past, done duty as indifference, and helped
him to override self-seeking opposition, to stifle ill-natured
mockery by ignoring it, or to invest the Chair at a difficult
meeting with an authority almost Divine. But he was now
compelled to admit to himself that, shorn of his prestige as
a being of wealth and eminence, and uneasily conscious of
dark possibilities behind his shareholding in Homes from
Home Limited, he was a frightened man—so frightened, in
fact, that he no more dared to face up to whomsoever represented this mysterious concern, than he had dared to hold
on to Granby Street, confess the truth about his own naïveté,
and take the consequences.

Then, as he sat in the stuffy parlour, listening to the uneasy
beat of his uneasy heart, to the late sleepy flies of a brilliant
autumn drumming hither and thither, plopping on to floor

and table, crawling disgustingly between the sheets of paper piled in front of him, he thought of Mr Meadows.

Mr Meadows had treated him as a human being, not as a mere money-bag to be tested and caressed and squeezed; Mr Meadows fought precisely the social evils with which the old ruffian John Gladwin had wickedly involved the Torchbearers; Mr Meadows had warned him against that red-haired scoundrel (what was his name?) who had plotted with Sneade and forced him—Crocker—into the humiliating position (oh, yes: fully deserved, but all the same humiliating) in which he now found himself.

Meadows would understand. Meadows would appreciate why his warning had had to be ignored. Meadows would agree that every penny must be got together for victims of the Delilah swindle, and discern that the ruined Crocker of today was at heart the wealthy Crocker of all those years ago, but shorn of his grandiloquence and frankly the shivering ingenuous simpleton he had always been.

"My dear" he said timidly to his wife "will you do me yet another service? The library at University College will have —or should have—a Clerical Directory, and I have no doubt the Librarian would allow you to consult it. I want to know the present whereabouts of the Rev. Alfred Meadows, at one time Vicar of St John's, Waterloo Road. It is important, or I would not add to your burdens. . . ."

*   *   *   *   *

Meadows made his way to Bloomsbury within a few hours of receiving Crocker's letter. It was a moving letter, pathetic in its naïve self-abasement, crying "Peccavi" without a word of self-excuse, appealing to the clergyman to come to the help of innocent people who were suffering for the writer's fault. Meadows had not seen Crocker for nearly ten years, and expected to find him aged. But he was shocked to see how sadly—age apart—the man had altered, as though internally the structure of his self-esteem had collapsed and, dragging his bodily envelope with it, had crumpled it beyond repair. He was careful, however, beyond expressing sympathy in the other's anxiety and pleasure at the opportunity of giving any assistance within his power, to show no visible concern and to ask no questions.

Crocker, with a deliberate precision which was obviously maintained only by an effort, proceeded forthwith to tell the whole story, from the reading of John Gladwin's will to the present necessity of realising on a shareholding in Homes from Home Limited. Speaking now with difficulty, he concluded:

"In those days vanity (which I mistook for pride) blinded me to everything save the necessity of keeping up what I took to be a worthy reputation. In fact I was nothing but a whited sepulchre, and its doors are now flung open, to reveal a heap of crumbling bones."

"A strange story" mused the clergyman aloud (he was seeking to give Crocker time to recover from his extreme of agitation). "Without your help I could never have uprooted the scattered weeds in my own vineyard, and all the time you were the blameless owner of that tangled wilderness near Waterloo. Of course I now see why Spelter crossed your path, though for whom he was acting or what devil's game was being played, I have no idea. Still, those are points which can be cleared up—must be cleared up, in fact, if we are to press this matter to a real conclusion. For the moment, as I understand you, the urgent task is to investigate this Company, and to sell your shares in it for the utmost they may be worth. I shall be surprised, however, if we find ourselves able to stop there."

Crocker passed a hand wearily over his forehead.

"I cannot think beyond the immediate future. If you can help me to turn these shares into money, I shall be content— and deeply grateful. I have not the spirit left in me to wish to probe further."

"Forgive me" said Meadows. "I had no intention of involving *you* in any crusade. My 'we' was an editorial 'we', signifying myself and such collaborators as I may be lucky enough to find."

"How will you start your enquiries into the Company's activities? Not personally, surely?"

"Oh, no: not personally. My uniform is nearly as stulti-fying as that of a policeman, when it comes to dealing with the sort of gentlemen who employ the Spelters to do their work. And I have not a policeman's authority. No: I shall set—"

He stopped short. On the point of mentioning Merton's name, he suddenly remembered that Crocker had given asylum to the child Lottie Heape; that Crocker had em-ployed Merton's friend Gladwin as tutor; that some mysterious wrongdoing had cost Gladwin his job; and that on the occasion of the chance meeting with the girl Lottie—not many weeks ago—she had first told him a pack of lies, and then had the impertinence to giggle at what she conceived was her own cleverness but was in fact her self-betrayal. He could now make a shrewd guess at what had happened at Lashwater, and would dearly like it confirmed. But he hesitated. On the one hand, it would be brutal to plague the unhappy man with questions likely to revive painful memories. On the other, it might well be now or never; and surely there ought to be full confidence between them, if they were to work together? Charity won the day. He had not the heart to force Crocker to think back to incidents pre-dating the present catastrophe. He took his leave, promising to lose no time in starting investigations into Homes from Home.

ON THE VERY evening of his conversation with Meadows, Crocker, sitting alone in the parlour of his lodgings, heard a knocking at the street door and, in due course, the shuffling footsteps of the maid-of-all-work on her way to open it. A minute or two later she entered the room, holding a card between her worn and dirty fingers.

"Wants ter see yer" she said.

Crocker took the card in uneasy surprise and read:

MR CORNELIUS FLEISCHMANN,
14A Old Jewry, E.C.
Commission Agent.

With a slight shrug he nodded to the servant to admit the visitor, and rose to his feet as a well-dressed stoutish gentleman appeared in the doorway, holding a silk hat in his hand.

"I must offer my apologies, Mr Crocker" the stranger began "for calling on you without an appointment and at this inconvenient hour, but Mr —— (naming Mr Crocker's man of business) encouraged me to believe that if I happened to be in this neighbourhood—which is infrequently—I might be permitted . . ."

"Please sit down, sir" said Crocker, walking across the room to make sure the door was shut and the key in the lock on the inside. "What can I do for you?"

He returned to his chair, and as Mr Fleischmann began to state his business, studied him with care. He saw a cleanshaven, jowled, but pleasant-faced Jew, radiating personal cleanliness and with a voice and manner controlled and courteous. Having swiftly registered this on-the-whole-favourable impression, he became immediately absorbed in what the man was saying.

"You will, I hope, believe me" said Fleischmann with a deprecating smile "when I say that I am diffident of intruding on a victim of undeserved financial misfortune. I have been in business myself too long not to be familiar with its ups and downs; but I know from my own experience that help —even a stranger's help—can be very welcome at certain junctures. Forgive my referring to the matter, but I must make clear that we City men, who earn our living by following the stock-markets, are aware of the recent mishap which has overtaken the Delilah Company, and deeply respect the generosity of its Chairman in assuming so great a part of the responsibility."

Crocker moved his shoulders impatiently.

"Let us take all this for granted. In what way can you help me?"

Fleischmann bowed assent.

"I beg your pardon" he said. "I will go straight to business. You are a largish shareholder in a Company called Homes from Home Limited. I am anxious to acquire shares in that Company, and when I learnt that you were concerned to raise a considerable sum of money without delay, I thought a deal might advantage both of us. As you are of course aware, shares of this kind are not easy either to buy or to sell. They are not quoted on 'Change, and dealings in them are not encouraged, without their knowledge, by those in control of the Company. Consequently such dealings are only possible at more or less chance encounters between interested individuals. Accordingly I ventured a personal enquiry of your Mr ——, who told me that you were indeed desirous of selling your holding, but preferred to do the business yourself and had informed him that you would approach the Secretary of Homes from Home Limited and enquire the value of the shares. Am I correct?"

Crocker nodded. He had dropped his head while the other was talking, and now sat playing with a penholder, his eyes on the table in front of him.

"Very well" continued Fleischmann. "Now I can save you the trouble of enquiring from the Secretary, and at the same time make you a much more favourable proposition than you are likely to obtain with his help—even if his help were forthcoming."

The man at the table raised his eyes and looked dully at his visitor.

"What do you know of this Company, Mr Fleischmann? I know nothing, though I am full of suspicions. I will confess to you frankly that my holding is a burden which I was forced years ago to assume, lest something worse befell an organisation for which I was then responsible. I put the thing out of my mind, accepting the trifling dividends which reached me regularly rather than probe into a question of which I wished never to be reminded. The shares are Founder's shares, carrying the right to appoint a nominee and a successor. I salved my conscience at the time by telling myself that this privilege would release me if, as I suspected from the first, the concern proved to be not everything it should be. But I could never bring myself even to investigate, much less to insist on exercising a Founder's privilege. Cowardly, you think? I agree; but then in some respects I have been a coward. It needed some such crisis as that which has recently overtaken me to force me to recall even the existence of these shares. Now indeed I not only want to be rid of them, but I *must* be rid of them. So you see I am very ready to hear anything you have to say."

Fleischmann listened imperturbably to this naïve, unprovoked and pathetic outburst of self-accusation. He maintained an attitude of polite attention, and when Crocker had finished, made a little gesture of sympathy with one hand. A song of triumph was ringing in his head (this was turning out better than he had dared even to hope), but not a muscle of his face betrayed his emotion and his voice remained level and quietly sincere.

"Thank you for your confidence. It makes my mission much easier. They are a bad lot behind this Company, and you would have had an unpleasant reception, had you called on them. The Secretary was very rude to me; but then I am an old hand with City wolves and know when to ignore insolence and when to punish it. For the moment I ignored it; but if you and I can come to terms over the shares, I shall lose no time in devising punishment.

"As for what I know of these fellows—it is briefly this. They started as operators of a chain of hotels—genuine hotels, and in some cases well-appointed ones on favourable sites—but soon turned them to . . . well, to improper uses. I and my associates think we can make money by managing these hotels as they should be managed—restoring them, you understand, to their rightful status. It will be open war between us and the men still in charge, for they are coining money out of their iniquities; so you see how important is your holding to our prospects and plans.

"Here then, Mr Crocker, is my proposal. Naturally, I cannot say for certain what the Secretary would have told you was the sale-value of your shares, but I guess at the very outside about twenty-five per cent of par. They are not interested in buying the shares except at a knock-out price, and would strongly oppose such shares passing into other hands. They make their money on the side, and all they want of the shareholders is silent acceptance of a very modest dividend. Are you aware that your holding is forty-nine per cent of the whole? No? Well, it is. The transfer of so large a proportion of the issue to other outsiders would cause considerable disturbance, whereas, if the men running the Company took them, they would expect to get them almost for nothing.

"Still, I give them the benefit of the doubt and assume they would offer twenty-five per cent. I, on the other hand, will give you sixty per cent of what you paid for them—or rather of the sum they represented when they were issued to you, for of course, in fact, you paid nothing—"

"How do you know all this?" interrupted Crocker, his voice shrill with alarm.

Fleischmann leant forward.

"Please, sir" he said gently "have no fear. The facts as to your original involvement in this affair are not our concern, nor of any interest to us save in so far as they affect our policy. It is our job to know everything possible about Companies and their dealings, and we collect information all the time, never knowing when it may be useful. I am being perfectly frank. I want those shares, and will pay in cash sixty per cent of the value they represented to you when you first received them."

Crocker shook his head in bewilderment.

"I do not understand why you make this offer" he said "and I doubt if I can recall what equivalent in money the shares originally possessed. . . . It was all so painful to me . . . and so long ago. . . ."

"I can tell you exactly, Mr Crocker. In return for those shares you surrendered the ownership of an area of house-property which brought in an annual income of, roughly, y hundred pounds. At a reasonably conservative estimate under present conditions that represents a capital of x thousand pounds. You hold z shares; so each share was originally reckoned as being $\frac{x}{z}$ pounds, and I am willing to pay per share three-fifths of that amount."

He took a piece of paper, made a rapid calculation and pushed it across the table.

"There you are, sir. That is the total of my offer in pounds, shillings and pence."

Crocker glanced at the figure, got up from his chair and began shambling about the room. He was clearly labouring under some melancholy excitement, and at the same time fearful that fate was playing him another evil trick. He stopped short in his agitated perambulations and stood close to Fleischmann, looking down at him, his features working and his hands clutched restlessly together.

"Do you *mean* this, Mr Fleischmann? You would not be so cruel as to torment such a poor creature as I now am, by dangling release in front of him and then . . . You will, for this sum of money, take those accursed shares and set me free of them for ever?"

Fleischmann regarded him steadily, with eyes grave and compassionate.

"Pray do not agitate yourself, my dear sir. I mean every word I have said, and do not for one moment make my proposition out of charity or pity. As I told you, I *want* these shares because I think I can make money out of them. I should be a fool indeed to try a trick at the expense of one who alone can give me what I want."

Crocker turned away with a deep sigh of relief and, stumbling like a tired old man, regained his chair. He sat silent for a moment, his head on his hands. Then:

"Thank God" he said "and thank *you* also! This is more than help in adversity. It is a remission of sentence."

Fleischmann began to feel embarrassed. The man was working himself into a state of almost tearful agitation and might break down completely. Let us, he thought, get back to business.

"Now, sir" he said "when can we close this deal? For my part the sooner the better. By what hour tomorrow could the certificate be available?"

"It can be available this minute. I have it here. I have never parted with it. I have always kept it where nobody could see it, for I hated to confess, even to myself, that I had it. I *knew* there were horrors behind it, but what horrors I never dared to enquire. I—"

Fleischmann cut him short.

"Then we can settle the matter out of hand. I have the money with me—and on chance brought also a transfer form, which only requires your signature. It is, as you will see, already witnessed—a little prematurely, I know; but between friends . . ."

He drew a bulky leather wallet from his breast-pocket and began counting out Bank of England notes. Crocker watched him with bemused fascination.

"If you would kindly get the certificate . . .?" the visitor murmured.

"Ah, yes. Of course, of course. Pray excuse me. This business has unnerved me."

He reached for a deed-box which stood on a shelf behind his chair, pulled a heavy bunch of keys from his trouser-pocket and began fumbling them over. When he tried to fit one into the lock of the box, his hand shook so badly that Fleischmann could hear the key rattle against the metal plaque. At last he opened the box, found the paper and handed it across the table. The other glanced at it, nodded and placed the pile of notes in Crocker's hand.

"Please check the amount" he said.

But the task of fingering each note and calculating the total was too much for the wretched man, and Fleischmann had himself to count them out, one by one, stating the rising total as he did so. At last the money was stowed away and the deed-box locked. The broker rose briskly to his feet.

"It only remains for the transfer to be signed. . . . Thank you. . . . I will say good night, and express my appreciation of your courteous reception. It is not always that a transaction proves so agreeable to both parties."

He put certificate and transfer carefully away in his wallet which he returned to an inside pocket, took up his hat and held out his hand.

Crocker saw him to the door, and stood for a few moments on the step, watching the portly figure fade into the darkness beyond the radius of the street lamp. Then he regained his room, and sank exhausted into the arm-chair. He was thankful his wife had gone away for the night. It would not have been easy to keep her in ignorance of this interview, of which nevertheless she could on no account have been told.

It was a fine night, but very dark. With a vague idea of cutting through to Portland Place, where he should be able to pick up a hansom to take him to St John's Wood, Fleischmann turned westward, intending to keep parallel with Euston Road. As he walked, he thought over his so recent achievement with glowing satisfaction. Now, he said to himself, we have really got them! His mind dwelt for an instant on the man who had sold him the shares. Poor devil, he thought. All to pieces. But the next moment he was gloating once more over the results of the deal he had just made.

Not the least satisfactory features of the affair were that he had only had to tell one lie (and a white one into the bargain), and that the man's desperate anxiety to be rid of the shares had enabled him to reduce the amount of money which he had come prepared to pay. The lie related to his visit to the Secretary of Homes from Home Limited. In fact the visit had been paid by one of his associates. The money saved was the difference between one hundred per cent and sixty per cent, which was not to be sneezed at for its own sake and appealed on general grounds to Fleischmann's business instincts.

For the rest he had not deceived Crocker in any respect. All he had told him had been quite true. It was true that he and his friends wanted these shares, that they hoped to make money out of them, that they were indifferent to the origins of Crocker's ownership. It was equally true that open war would follow if the shares passed into his possession, the position, briefly, being this:

Two groups of financial pirates were at grips with one another. The gang-warfare had already lasted for some while, the battle swaying now in Fleischmann's favour, now against him. The enemy had the advantage of greater resources, the bulk of which derived from Homes from Home. At the same time, this Company was their Achilles heel. Once Fleischmann and his friends could get a footing there, the screw could be put on with a vengeance. For months they had been working on this problem, making little or no progress. And now they had more than a footing; much more than a footing. . . .

With a silent chuckle Fleischmann thought further back than his interview with Crocker, and recalled the events of the last forty-eight hours, which had, as though by magic, transformed a stalemate into a certain victory.

Two days earlier he had been in Brussels. Returning to his hotel in the evening, after taking tea with his wife and adjusting her rather extravagant claims for maintenance, he was handed a telegram.

VITAL YOU RETURN IMMEDIATELY VERY IMPORTANT FREDDIE

Having complete confidence in Boreham's sense of what was important, Fleischmann made preparations to leave for London first thing next morning. He was there by evening, and at the Cannon Street Hotel found his bulky associate so manifestly bursting with sensational news that he appeared larger than ever. Boreham refused, however, to spill the beans while Fleischmann ate a hasty meal.

"Not here, old boy. Too many snitches hidin behind palm-trees and the like. You gobble up and we'll be off to Alpha, kiss the little lady good night, and get down to biz."

Lottie was picking out a waltz-tune on the piano with one finger when they entered the house. She greeted Fleischmann with demonstrative affection, rubbing herself against him like a kitten, clinging to his arm and looking up tenderly into his face. He kissed her fondly and said:

"Darling child! And how lovely you are looking! I was called home unexpectedly—and maybe only for a day or two —but I had to see my little girl. I want to hear all your doings, but not tonight. Lord Frederick and I have business to talk over; so run away to bed and get your beauty sleep—though I confess you don't seem to need one."

She obeyed prettily and left them. Fleischmann got brandy and water from the dining-room, lit the fire which was laid ready in the small study and the two men settled down.

Freddie's news was indeed important. The filed list of shareholders had told them nothing; but at last, through the good offices of an individual who had a foot in each of the opposing camps, he had secured a copy of the list of real shareholders in Homes from Home Limited. Among them (as they already knew) was a rich man who owned a Hair Tonic and was interested in missions. It had not been difficult, by a process of elimination, to put a name to him, and they now knew him as Crocker. But they had known nothing about him beyond his name, nor the astounding fact that his holding amounted to forty-nine per cent of the whole. In the second place, there appeared on the list a man who only held three shares, but was so greatly dependent on the goodwill of the Fleischmann group that he could easily be "persuaded" to part with them.

"And on top of all that, old boy" cried Freddie triumphantly "this jolly dog Crocker has suddenly got into the limelight by coming an almighty purler over the crash of his Hair Tonic. So not only have we got him sighted, but he is bound to be raking in the shekels wheresoever they may be found. In fact it is known that he *is*. Selling like mad. You twig me? First thing tomorrow you make up to Crocker's man of business—he is the chap whose job it is to raise the wind— and find how the land lies. Then, if necessary, you hunt out the old buffer himself. If you're the Flashy you were a few weeks ago, those shares will be yours; and they, mark you, *plus* the three from that tick Thingumbob will give us a majority! How's that, old cock?"

It was more than satisfactory, and left little further to be discussed. After a brief conversation on general matters Boreham departed, and Fleischmann sat a while thinking out his campaign for the morrow. Lottie was apparently asleep when he looked into her room on his way to bed.

"Dear little girl" he thought. "I'm a lucky fellow."

As he walked away from his triumphant interview with Crocker, Fleischmann ran over all this in his mind. Absorbed in planning how most crushingly to devise the destruction of his enemies, he lost all sense of direction. At last, in a lucid interval, he realised what a long distance he had already come. He had crossed Portland Place and Baker Street without noticing them, was now somewhere between Bryanston Square and Marylebone Road, and two-thirds of the way home. Surely better to walk on than search for a hansom in this unlikely area? Even if he pressed on into Edgware Road he could hardly hope to find one. It was only a little after ten o'clock—a dead period for wheeled traffic, too late for diners-out, too early for home-going theatre folk. He decided to strike diagonally north-westward, aiming at the junction of Harrow Road and Chapel Street. He was in a district of sour little lodging-houses, and the narrow and poorly lighted streets seemed deserted. Even pubs were lacking. He knew his general direction, but was uncertain which turning he ought to take to avoid a no-thoroughfare. He paused at a corner and, peering upward, tried to see the street name which presumably was painted somewhere above his head. There was a swift, almost soundless footstep, a moment of tearing agony and then blackness.

They found him next morning in a squalid court called Little Harcourt Street. He had been stabbed between the shoulder-blades, and before the knife was removed the body had evidently been dragged from near the corner of Upper York Street to where it was finally abandoned. The pockets were empty; but no attempt had been made to hide the identity of the corpse, whose coat carried the tailor's label and his linen the customary markings.

THE FLEISCHMANN MURDER was briefly reported in the evening papers of the following day, but as it happened neither Crocker nor Lottie noticed the paragraph. The former was too absorbed in his own troubles to read an evening paper at all, and the latter preferred to take the week's crime in a single orgy under the lurid auspices of the *Illustrated Police Gazette*. Consequently it was not until the next morning that they learned of the shocking event.

Crocker could not repress a little exclamation of horror as he turned the pages of his paper after breakfast. His wife, who had now returned, looked up in surprise.

"What is the matter, Gervase?"

It was a moment of considerable embarrassment, but Crocker managed to reply evenly enough:

"Nothing which directly concerns us, my dear; but an important City financier, of whom I have often heard people speak, has been murdered in the street."

"But Gervase how dreadful! Whereabouts?"

"Somewhere up in Marylebone. The police will say nothing, which means, I take it, that so far they have no clue and therefore have nothing to say. Did I not hear" (turning the subject) "that you had a letter from Mrs St Maur? How is little Georgie?"

But when he was alone, the thought of Fleischmann's tragic death took grim possession of his already tortured brain. That this should have happened so soon after the man had been in his company was, in some undefined way, sinister and menacing. Crocker was glad his lawyer was due to call during the morning. To him at least he could speak of the ugly business, and admit that Fleischmann had gone straight to his death from a *tête-à-tête* in this very room. But discussion of the matter, though it might give temporary relief, could not alter the fact that the crime had been committed, nor still the horrid suspicion that the victim's visit to Bloomsbury had been somehow connected with it. Crocker felt instinctively that in one way or another the incident meant more trouble. As he sat with bowed head, trying vainly to control the rabble of miseries which ran riot in his tired brain, he groaned aloud.

The news reached Lottie in a different manner. She had not worried when Fleischmann did not return to Alpha Place on the second night after his sudden reappearance. He sometimes stayed in town if business kept him late; and she concluded, seeing that he himself had described his return to London as a rush-visit, that he might naturally have had a full programme of engagements. But as the next day drew to a close and there was neither sign of him nor message, she began to feel puzzled. It was not like him to stay away for two nights without at least sending some word of explanation; and surely, having unexpectedly found himself once again within reach of his mistress, he would not lightly keep away from her. Lottie knew well that he was still abjectly in love with her and, Boreham's late call having kept them apart for the one night he had spent in the house, she was sure he would make every effort to rejoin her at the first opportunity.

But he did not come; and she was forced to conclude that he had gone abroad again and been unable to find time to let her know. There'll be a letter in the morning, she told herself.

There *was* a letter in the morning, though not from Fleischmann. It was heavily sealed, and put through the letter-box at so early an hour that no one saw the messenger come or go. Inside were two Bank of England notes for fifty pounds each. Nothing else. Lottie's breakfast tray was always brought to her by the plump pert Annie, and the envelope had come with it. She had opened it and was searching for some possible message or indication of its source, when the door was abruptly opened and Mrs Davies walked in, holding a newspaper in her hand. Lottie managed to push the bank-notes under the bed-clothes, and was turning indignantly to demand why the woman came into her room without knocking, when she saw that the house-keeper's usually expressionless face was ravaged and aghast.

"What in the world . . .?" Lottie began.

With a great gulp the woman thrust the paper almost in Lottie's face and jabbed with her finger at a column headed with bold lettering. The girl stared at it, unable at first to take its meaning. Then with a stifled scream she turned terrified eyes on the housekeeper.

Mrs Davies now broke down in an extraordinary and revolting manner. She stood stock-still with her mouth wide open, uttering a series of harsh strangulated cries. Her features were twisted, and her face went from red to purple-blue. Lottie forgot her own horror, leapt out of bed and slapped the woman violently on both cheeks. The screeching stopped suddenly and a stirring of anger showed in the blank staring eyes. In that instant Lottie took the housekeeper by the shoulder, almost ran her out of the room, slammed the door and turned the key on the inside. She then dressed herself hastily, locked away the envelope and bank-notes in the inner cupboard of the wardrobe where she kept her private belongings, and went downstairs to the basement.

Both Mr and Mrs Davies were in the kitchen, the latter snivelling quietly in a chair in the limp, martyred aftermath of her fit of screaming, the former striding up and down with brows knit and hands clenched, trying to look very formidable and revengeful but succeeding only in suggesting a *déraciné* in a tantrum. Lottie knew her instinct to be right, and that a firm hand was needed to prevent the couple going to pieces. Prospects were bleak enough without the added worry of a pair of hysterical servants.

"Mrs Davies" she said crisply "there will be plenty of time later to cry over this dreadful business. Just now there is a lot to do. We may have the police here any moment, wanting to search the place. You and Annie must see that all Mr Fleischmann's clothes and things are suitably in order, while I try among the papers in the study to find some clue to what has happened. Davies must go now to Mr Fleischmann's office, get the name of his lawyer and call on him at once. We must know who is left in charge of his affairs and where we all stand. If Davies can find Lord Frederick Boreham also, so much the better. They should know at the office where he is likely to be. Then"(for the first time addressing the man directly) "you must go to the Cannon Street Hotel, see what possessions there may be there and whether the hotel people know of anyone else who should be approached. The police are certain to have been there already. Find out anything you can. Now please get started *quickly*. There is no time to lose."

Her peremptory manner and rapid clear-cut instructions had their effect. The housekeeper rose and silently left the room, while Davies began putting on his coat and looking about for his hat. Lottie climbed the stairs, lit the fire in the drawing-room, and for the first time faced up to her own position.

This, with every moment of thought which she gave to it, seemed to become more horrific. Slowly she came to the inescapable conclusion that the report on the conversation of three evenings ago, which she had given verbally to Slode at a rendezvous where at a certain hour he was always to be found, had somehow led to Fleischmann's tragic end. She had not the least idea in what way the two were connected; but that a connection existed she was positive. Indirectly, therefore, she was responsible for the brutal murder of a man who had loved her, who had treated her with kindness and generosity, whose flattering adoration and skilful love-making had given her many hours of delight.

That was bad enough. But her share in the crime was the more vile in that she had been paid for betraying him to death. When Slode had bribed her to give her lover away, she had thought (so far as she had thought of anything beyond the money's usefulness) that business men were always spying on one another, that some commercial tip was wanted by a rival, and that Fleischmann was well able to look after himself, even if a secret or two did leak out.

But instead this awful *awful* thing had happened! She sat rigid, her hands pressed tightly to her forehead, her teeth clenched, as she fought down a rising nausea. At the thought of those notes upstairs in the wardrobe she felt physically sick. "Blood-money" was a favourite expression of the *Illustrated Police Gazette*, and hitherto she had liked its threatening sound and its suggestion of dark deeds and wages paid for crime. Now she shivered as the words flitted across her brain. "Blood-money"; that was what they were, those two crisp notes—money paid for blood, for Fleischmann's blood, and paid to her, his darling and the sunlight of his life. She had from the first disliked and feared Evan Slode, but had allowed these feelings to settle into a passive repugnance which accepted him as a disagreeable but necessary adjunct to her life with Fleischmann. Now dislike and fear flamed into repulsion and terror, then fused into bitter and implacable loathing. By God, she thought, he shall pay for this! If I have to wait for twenty years I'll find a way of dishing the bloody swine!

Next moment, with the quicksilver mind which was her best equipment for the life she had chosen, she challenged her own thought. So you'll wait for twenty years! And how will you live during them? Little fool, you are on the street! You have your savings, of course, but they'll be gone in twenty months. Find another man? No doubt; but of what kind? Not the best of recommendations to have been Fleischmann's girl when this horrible thing happened— especially if it ever got out about the eavesdropping. . . . Oh why, oh why, cried Lottie to herself, did I ever listen to that vile brute, tempting me with his dirty money? Just a filthy treacherous little tart, that's what I am; and that devil Slode, or any one of the other devils behind him, have only to say one word and the whole world will know it!

She sat dry-eyed, parched with self-contempt, for fully half an hour; then hearing Mrs Davies and Annie overhead, awoke once more to the needs of the present. What ought she to do? Her first impulse was to run away—pack a few things in a valise, slip out of the house and disappear into London. But she could hardly more effectively bring suspicion on herself; and although she did not try to imagine how suspicion could crystallise into a knowledge that she had overheard a conversation and repeated it, her sense of guilt was so strong that she scented danger of discovery in every quarter. No; she must stay and face the music. Her rôle must be that of the pretty plaything of a man of means, a refreshment for his leisure hours, a charming butterfly unconcerned with his business life and utterly ignorant of its incidents and its contacts. She had hardly decided the part to play, and was rehearsing in her mind how best to play it, when the door-bell rang.

Anxious to put into practice without delay the policy of being visible and on the spot, and preferring the servants to remain out of sight during these hours of critical uncertainty, she went to the door herself. Jacky Sanderson stood on the threshold. She was soberly dressed in dark colours, and kissed Lottie without saying a word. In the drawing-room she took the smaller girl in her arms and held her close.

"Poor little Lottie!" she murmured. "Poor, poor child. We are so terribly distressed for you."

She led her by the hand toward the large sofa, and with an arm across her shoulders made her sit close.

"Now, dearest, listen to me. I have come, partly to show you you are not alone, mainly to talk about what next. You are not mixed up in this dreadful business at all—that is the first point to get clearly into your head. You know nothing about it; poor Flashy never talked to you of his business friends or enemies; and you've no notion of any private feud which might have led to this—to this damnable crime."

Lottie lay for a moment against the warm, rounded shoulder of her handsome friend, while an idea flickered through her mind. To give the hint would in any event help to divert attention from herself; and conceivably there was an element of truth in it. She sat up and fixed the other with grave questioning eyes.

"Jackie" she said quietly "what happened to Coralie?"

Jackie puckered her forehead in bewilderment.

"Coralie?" she said. "What Coralie?"

"I don't know her other name" said Lottie. "What was it?"

Jackie's brow cleared, but she looked away as though embarrassed.

"Oh, you mean Melnotte, the girl who—er—who—"

Lottie nodded.

"Yes. Don't be shy about it. The one before me. She lived here didn't she? What happened to her? The first time I met you, you warned me about taking a freeholder and said you'd known a girl who had. You gave no name, but I guessed whom you meant. I was right, wasn't I? Well, what became of her? Could that possibly . . .?"

Jackie was frowning again, this time with concentration.

"Upon my word" she said at last "it hadn't occurred to me. She certainly chose an A1 squirt to gay it with, but I've not heard he stayed with her long. Someone told me a while ago she was mostly at the 'Gyle' these days, and that speaks for itself. All the same I suppose she might have kept up a grudge against Flashy—he threw her out on her ear quicker than hell would scorch a feather, and her trunk after her, and I daresay she didn't care much for that. But it seems going a bit far, doesn't it? And why should any thug risk his neck, just because a dolly-mop has a down on a has-been? Still—I'll pass the word to my Jack. He and Freddie Boreham are off on the war-path as you can imagine. We're not near the end of this yet.

"But now let us get back to you, my dear. You can't stop here, with peelers tramping all over the place and tearing up the floorboards. You must come to me for a bit, and then when the dust settles, we'll find you a decent chap to take poor Flashy's place."

Lottie shook her head.

"No, Jackie dear, it's very very sweet of you, but I shall stay here till I know what is to happen to the place, and then I shall try to get right away from anyone who knows that I was with Flashy. I've got to live this down, and I can't do it with people being sympathetic or turning up their noses. You shall know what becomes of me—that I promise you; but there's got to be a break."

The other pleaded and argued, but Lottie was obstinate. At last Jackie rose to go.

"Well, my dear, if you won't you won't. But you've promised to keep in touch, and if at any time there's anything Jack and I can do, you've only got to ask."

They kissed affectionately and the visitor departed.

THE CREDIT FOR the inception and organisation of Homes from Home belonged to a gentleman from Melbourne. He had been christened Jesse Burdock, but was generally known as "Banjo", which had been his father's nickname, earned by a lively talent for musical entertainment in the shacks and round the fires of mining-camps.

"Banjo" Burdock Jr. had found it desirable to leave Melbourne in 1859. He was then about thirty-five years of age. The son of an "old hand", who had made money in the first flush of the diggings and died very shortly afterward, he had inherited not only his father's soubriquet, but also (perhaps more deservedly) his father's wealth. This was mainly invested in house property in the north-eastern quarter of the city.

A crowded area of narrow streets, lined with a jumble of houses of all kinds from wretched hovels to two-storey buildings of some pretension to comfort and decency, this district was acquiring a bad reputation as early as the middle 'fifties, and Banjo was quick to see how, by making that reputation worse, he could make his inheritance more profitable. He installed bullies, fighting men, two or three American negroes, thieves and flash coves with a following of swells, called them "tenants", and encouraged them to cram the premises to bursting point with miserable and degraded women. Two years of Banjo's administration turned the district into an Alsatia. The magistrates would now and again be compelled to force the police to take action, whereupon Banjo's lawyer would come forward with bail for the arrested "tenant", a fine would be paid, and things would go on as before. The better class of house he rented to one of several Jewish pawn- brokers, who furnished the rooms with gaudy rubbish and let them off to prostitutes at exorbitant rates. The proceeds were divided between the pawnbrokers and their common landlord.

Then, however, luck turned. The local police-chief, who had been Banjo's friend and well paid for it, got into trouble on his own account and was cashiered. His successor and immediate underling had been well aware of his superior's corrupt practices, and that Banjo was the real boss of the city's "black spot". His principal piece of evidence was the private ledger of one of the pawnbrokers, which proved conclusively that money was wrung from these unhappy women by every kind of extortion, and that the lion's share of it went into the pocket of the rich Mr Burdock who lived in the fashionable quarter on the hill.

The new Superintendent had not been in office for a month when he took simultaneous action against half a dozen of Burdock's tenants. The case provoked horror and excitement, and the Press sent up a howl of execration against everyone who might be responsible for this blot on the Melbourne scutcheon. But Banjo had been warned; and by the time outraged respectability had stopped shouting and looked about for the required scapegoat, he was far away on the high seas, bound for New York City. He spent a short year in that town and then, feeling that he might find less aggressive competition in London, crossed the Atlantic in the early months of 1860.

He had his connections in the metropolis and, with their help, studied London conditions and prospects. He found a vast field for possible activity, but one at present uncoordinated and wastefully decentralised. Within the year he had planned a sequence of interlocking enterprises, which he proposed to operate as a Company under the ironic title HOMES FROM HOME LIMITED.

Banjo was a scoundrel of the first order, but he had a genius for organisation. There must be no loose ends nor improvisation at any stage of any undertaking controlled by him. In consequence, the procedure adopted for the large scale exploitation of prostitution was carefully designed in sequence. The chain of processes began under the auspices of William Slode, in and about Larne Circle. There little children—by purchase, kidnapping or seeming kindly rescue from misery and starvation—were collected, kept in mild bondage and groomed for the market. The next stage depended on the promise or otherwise of the leaving pupils. A few were drafted to the occasional West End houses which had dealings with the central office; some were sent to be "disciplined" in Granby Street, and either benefited by the treatment and were moved on, or were pushed into the streets (under observation), or were confined in low-class dress-houses, or even in extreme cases stayed where they were; others were despatched to associated addresses in Liverpool or Manchester or Glasgow or Plymouth. The majority, however, were booked for the Continent.

For the accommodation of these last, "hotels" were supplied at strategic points. In London there were several, adjacent to railway termini or ports of departure for packets bound for Europe. There was one at Liverpool for Ireland, two at Hull, one at Southampton. They were hardly hotels in the accepted sense; but they had been so once, and the names and exteriors were retained unchanged. Also they regularly advertised for domestic and kitchen staff, laundresses, sewing-maids and so forth, and attracted a steady flow of young women, who found themselves alone in the world and faced with destitution. Affiliated to the London establishments, but in more central parts of the town, were Employment Agencies, which offered attractive openings for nurse-maids, governesses and the like. Beyond the Channel other hotels—on the coast in Havre, Antwerp and Hamburg, inland in Brussels and Paris—served, first as reception houses, and then either as places to work in or as distribution centres.

Naturally this complex structure took some time to perfect. It was at an early stage of its formation that the windfall of Granby Street dropped at the feet of Banjo and his friends. That was a stroke of luck indeed! William Slode had worked with Big Jimmy of the "Mint" on isolated occasions, just as he had also his affiliations with two or three West End madams. But nothing approaching a central authority existed, able to regulate the flow of goods from one point to the other or (equally important) to discipline the barely human ruffians of both sexes who made hells-on-earth of the streets near Waterloo and the alleys in Southwark lying between Lant Street and the river.

From the very first Banjo had insisted that some means must be found to assert control over any district in which the Company planned to operate.

"Hells is O.K." he said. "The boys when they're scammered need a wallow, and don't mind payin for it. But it's got to be hells-on-a-string. Those muck-heaps will get the lot of us into chokey with their goings-on. Why the dam places are as bad as Tiger Bay!"

And at this juncture, like a gift from the gods, the Gladwin bequest was handed to him on a plate. To recompense Crocker with so large a slice of Founder's shares in Homes from Home was the idea of Malcolm Sneade, who saw clearly that his days as Secretary to a Missionary Society were numbered, and had been already encouraged by Spelter to go in with Burdock's crowd. He urged the suggestion, partly out of sheer malice against his still nominal Chairman whom it amused him to visualise an innocent collaborator in the work of the new Company, but partly also from a shrewd intuition that it might at some future date be convenient to implicate so wealthy and respectable a citizen with a concern liable at any time in the future to require money and an air of respectability.

During the next few years Homes from Home developed out of all recognition. The network of girl-traps, training depots and channels of distribution; the hierarchy of overseers, madams, accountants, lawyers, bullies and spies grew in size and complexity.

The profits were enormous; but they were never registered, even in the private books of the Company, as the earnings of Homes from Home, which was recorded as producing a steady and modest profit from hotel management, sufficient to pay a dividend of one and a half (occasionally of two per cent) and the reasonable fees of a small board of dummy directors.

Traffic in women, though immensely the most rewarding, was by no means Burdock's only activity. He had other more legitimate interests, and it was in connection with one of these that he was destined to come into conflict with the Fleischmann group.

Fleischmann and his friends were in their way adventurers no less thoroughpaced than Banjo and his; but there were classes of business they never touched, of which the principal example was the prostitution racket. Indeed, although Fleischmann was naturally aware of the widespread existence of what was generally termed the "Social Evil" and knew that there were men who profited by its exploitation, he had no idea that a powerful organisation had been built up to control and extend it. Hence the surprise which the following curious episode caused him.

He was paying one of his periodical visits to the Continent (this was a couple of years before he first made appearance in this story) and had a rendezvous in Brussels with a German manufacturer of optical glass, whose product his office had undertaken to finance for the English market. His secretary in London had noted this appointment in his employer's list of engagements, as due to take place on such a day at three o'clock in the afternoon at the Hotel Richer. Fleischmann duly presented himself at this hotel, which was not large but had an outward aspect of quiet solidity, and was surprised to find the front door closed. Supposing that the porter had had to go off duty for a few minutes or that interior alterations of some kind were being made, and having vainly looked about for an alternative entrance, he rang the bell. The door was opened on a chain, and an ill-favoured man-servant looked the caller over. Fleischmann stepped forward in the confident manner of one expecting immediate access to a semi-public place, and said "I have an appointment at three o'clock with Herr ———" The last two words were drowned by the noise of the chain being slipped from its socket and dropped, and the visitor was admitted into the hall. To his astonishment he heard the front door closed and chained behind him, and was about to ask for an explanation, when the servant—an ugly customer, dressed in gaudy but squalid livery—strode past him muttering something about "fetching madam", and disappeared through a curtained doorway.

Considerably puzzled Fleischmann looked quickly about him. The place gave an impression of sombre and rather tarnished comfort, with heavy portières in red velvet and tall receptacles for cigar ends. In the far left-hand corner a staircase rose on a curve, carpeted with red and with heavy stair-rods of gleaming brass.

Immediately to his right was a small reception office. It was unoccupied, and a wall-safe, as his sharp eye at once noted, was just ajar. Some papers, carelessly thrust inside, projected slightly, preventing the door from closing. Accustomed to rapid action, Fleischmann took three steps, glanced at the topmost paper, and saw a printed heading which was somehow suggestive. Obedient to the instinct which bade him pick up anything which might some time come in useful, and without waiting to ask himself in what way the words were significant, he whipped the thing out, slipped it into his pocket, and closed the safe-door. At this moment an angular woman, dressed in black and with hair piled elaborately on the top of her head, came through the curtains at the back of the hall. She moved toward him, stately and unsmiling, and he noticed that as she approached she glanced quickly at the little office, where everything now was neat and apparently undisturbed.

"Monsieur has an appointment?" she asked, now looking directly at him with a mixture of suspicion and uncertainty. "With which of the young ladies?"

"With—er—I beg your pardon? Did you say young ladies?"

"Certainly, monsieur. It is unusually early for a client and I am not aware . . ."

Fleischmann was completely nonplussed.

"I don't understand" he said. "I was to meet Herr ——

from Jena here at three o'clock. This is Hotel Richer, isn't it?"

"Yes, monsieur; but there is no gentleman from Jena here."

"But—but" he began, when the woman interrupted him.

"Clearly there is a mistake. Monsieur has been misdirected." Turning her head, she called over her shoulder "Pierre!", and as the man appeared said tersely: "Show Monsieur out." Bowing coldly she left him, going back the way she had come.

Fleischmann was aware of the servant standing at his elbow, and the next instant of the pressure of a massive shoulder about to propel him toward the door. He shook the man off angrily.

"Don't touch me! Open the door at once!" he commanded, and strode quickly forward. A few seconds later he was in the street.

Back in his own hotel he seized a directory, and found that there was in Brussels not only a Hotel Richer but also a Hotel Richepanse. "That damned idiot Gray mixed the names" he said to himself. Fortunately the Hotel Richepanse was near at hand, and he was not above twenty minutes late for his interview.

After dinner he reverted to the strange experience of the afternoon, and recollected the leaflet which he had taken from the office-safe and put in his pocket. It was a smallish four-page affair and near the top of the front page, which was otherwise blank, was printed:

HOMES FROM HOME LIMITED: MOST SECRET

Those were the words which had caught his attention, and he now knew why they had done so. Not long before, acting on behalf of a well-to-do client connected with a big firm of caterers, he had attempted to purchase two hotels—one in London, the other in Bristol—and had been just too late. The properties had been acquired—so swiftly after they were known to be available as to suggest a pre-commitment —by a Company called Homes from Home. But when

Fleischmann had attempted to make contact with this Company, so as to offer them a handsome profit to turn over the hotels to his client, he had been unable to do so. The purchase money had been paid by banker's draft, which had been immediately honoured, and no information could of course be had from the bank as to its customer's identity. His failure to carry out his client's instructions had rather annoyed him at the time, and for that reason the name of the buyers had stuck in his memory.

The other pages of the leaflet carried a brief but damning report of a Board Meeting, and a list of addresses, among them the two English hotels in question and the Hotel Richer in Brussels. There were other addresses, many of which appeared to be those of private houses.

Fleischmann spent most of the next day in making discreet enquiries from personal friends resident in Brussels. He visited Antwerp and returned to London via Paris. Once at home again, he instructed the most reliable of his investigators, and in due course a dossier began to accumulate which, with the original leaflet, was lodged in his private office safe. The dossier contained good inferential evidence that Homes from Home Limited were controlled by Banjo Burdock, but not what a Court of Law would accept as proof.

Then occurred the first direct business clash between him and Burdock. The details are of no consequence—the matter in dispute concerned the floating of some South American loan—and in the end Fleischmann won the day. To his surprise he received an invitation to call upon Burdock "with a view to discussing means of avoiding in future competitive action which must in the long run only be disadvantageous to both parties."

It was a typical interview between rival buccaneers. Burdock, who affected downright cordiality and no nonsense, was a lean active man, with surprisingly broad shoulders, an ugly mouth full of yellowish false teeth and long artistic fingers. He laughed a great deal and flung himself about in his chair, while Fleischmann—stout, suave and sparing of gesture—sat with his plump hands on his knees, and only with eyebrows and pursed lips expressed the mood of the moment.

With great mutual civility it was agreed that the next deal attractive to both groups should be handled jointly. Neither man trusted the other; but Fleischmann intended, as an experiment, to stand by his word and collaborate with Burdock when occasion arose. It did so before very long, and Burdock double-crossed him. From that moment he waited on revenge. The significance of Homes from Home Limited was carefully debated in company with his closest associate Freddie Boreham, and it was decided that the connection with Burdock was clear enough to justify their assuming it existed, and that the attack, when it was delivered, should be directed against this highly vulnerable spot in the enemy's defences.

The problem was to get the facts as to the finance of the Company. Evidence of its real nature they had in plenty; but it was essential to have allies inside the fortress before an assault were ventured from without. For long enough they discovered nothing. Then Freddie, over a good deal of champagne, picked up two hints from a dubious free-lance, who was on the fringe of several financial circles and made a meagre living by selling to one trifles of information let slip in another. He recalled that some years back he had heard a fellow called Sneade making merry at the expense of a man "who made money out of hair-grease and spent it on godliness", on the ground that the latter was a shareholder in an ostensible hotel business "but little knew, silly old fool, what a dirty pig in a poke he had bought." He further mentioned an individual known by name to Boreham, as having some mysterious affiliation to Burdock's lot and as being a possible source of information. It was within a day or two of this encounter that Freddie had dined in Alpha Place and, when leaving, promised to "look after Dirty Dick" if Fleischmann would find and "tackle this missionary bird."

THE SMALL LYCEAN GALLERY in the south-western corner of the British Museum was cold and shadowy in the dim light of the raw November afternoon. Already grey dusk like massed cobwebs clung to the row of ten seated figures, flanked by a lion and a sphinx, which had once lined the Sacred Way at Branchidae. The reliefs from the Harpy Tomb at Xanthus still held a gleam of daylight on their salient surfaces, which shone the paler for the dark concavities between.

The room attracted few visitors at the best of times (it was remote and its exhibits were of little interest save to scholars) and, as Crocker crossed the threshold and paused irresolute, it appeared to be quite empty. But forthwith the figure of a man emerged from behind a massive fragment of carved cornice, and advanced to meet him.

"Good afternoon, Mr Crocker. I see you received my note and wisely decided to do what it asked. You do not know me by sight—at best you might remember a name which is no longer relevant—but I will give you a hint as to who I am. Years ago you assisted a busybody parson to poke his nose into matters which were the concern of the Lambeth Vestry, with the result that I was publicly disgraced and lost my livelihood. At that time you were proud of your share in thus turning into the street a man who had never harmed you. You boasted of it. Well, the boot is now on the other leg. Do you recognise this paper?"

He was a nondescript sort of man of medium height, with a very pale face and a dark drooping moustache already going grey. His eyes were cunning and the rather prominent nose was veined with red. As he came close, gripping a sheet of paper tightly at each end and raising it to Crocker's eyes so that it should be legible in the half-light, a reek of spirits blended with the fusty smell of an ill-washed body and uncared-for clothes.

Crocker hardly took in what the man was saying. An immense weariness had slowly descended on him during the last few weeks, until, except for mulling endlessly over the calculations, additions, plans and counter-plans involved in implementing his promise to Delilah shareholders, he seemed almost incapable of mental activity. The shock of Fleischmann's death had galvanised him into a transient vitality born of panic; but as the days went by and there was no sign that the tragedy was in any way connected in the mind of Authority with the dead man's visit to the Bloomsbury lodgings, he began to relapse once more into apathy. Then had arrived a note without heading or signature, saying that if he would come alone to the Lycean Gallery on a certain afternoon, he would learn something to his advantage. At once his fears revived. This had to do with Fleischmann. He dreaded to go, yet dared not keep away. He must know the best or the worst, whichever was in store. On some pretext, when the appointed day arrived, he got his wife out of the house and plodded the short way to the Museum.

Now he stood peering uncertainly at the paper held out in front of him by this insanitary stranger. It was the transfer form which he had signed and Fleischmann had put carefully away in his wallet. He felt a sudden surge of anger pushing up through his infinite lassitude.

"That was in Fleischmann's pocket" he cried. "You killed him or know who killed him! I shall give you in charge. . . ."

He turned to hurry from the room when the other, letting go of one end of the paper, gripped him by the arm.

"Not so fast, Mr Crocker, or you will be sorry. Did you observe the number of shares transferred by this form? A very considerable number. Over ninety per cent of the entire issue of that excellent little concern known as Homes from Home Limited—now, alas, fallen on evil days."

"What do you mean? Impossible, impossible, I tell you! My entire holding was less than half."

1* 265

"Indeed? You know the amount of the issue?"

"I do." (He could hear Fleischmann's voice, smooth and deliberate, uttering the exact figures.)

"But this paper transfers to the late Mr Cornelius Fleischmann almost the whole of that issue. And is signed by you. And witnessed."

Crocker stared at the man in stupefaction. His energy had spent itself and he felt the will to fight back oozing out of him.

"I don't know" he muttered vaguely. "I don't know at all . . . how that can be." Then, with a flicker of renewed excitement, "The paper has been tampered with! Give it to me! Give it to me, I say. It is a forgery . . ." and he advanced threateningly on his tormentor, who once again caught him tightly by the wrist.

"Be quiet, man! You'll gain nothing by shouting. You shall have the paper—when it has been cancelled."

"Cancelled?"

The other nodded.

"You see" he went on smoothly "Mr Fleischmann, for some reason of his own, wanted these shares. The persons for whom I am acting—'we' in other words—do *not* want them. Therefore we are selling them back to you."

For a moment the unhappy Crocker stood speechless. He made little despairing motions with his hands, and his mouth opened and shut. At last he managed to stammer out:

"B—but I d—don't want them either. . . . I won't have them. . . . I tell you, I *won't*!"

"In that event" replied the other "this transfer remains as proof that an overwhelming proportion of the shares in a Company which was cloaking illegal and abominable practices was owned by Mr Gervase Wilbraham Crocker, and hastily disposed of by him to a financier of doubtful reputation at the moment when the Company's true nature was on the point of being exposed. For between you and me (this is confidential) Homes from Home Limited is at the end of its tether, Crocker. There's a hell of a shindy coming, and you can be caught in it or not, just as you choose. Only you've got to choose now."

The harassed wretch felt his head begin to turn. He groped toward one of the casts which stood in the centre of the room and supported himself against the pedestal.

"And if I buy them back . . .?" he whispered.

"This document, and the certificate, will be yours to destroy or keep as you wish."

"The price?"

"We will be generous with you. It would be reasonable enough to ask a premium on shares which have paid so steadily all these years; but we will part with them at par. You can work out the total in your head, Crocker. Got it?"

For a moment it seemed the victim would break into hysterical raving. His mouth fell open, his whole body quivered violently, he threw his hat on the floor. But the fit subsided as rapidly as it had risen. He gulped once or twice, and then said in a queer toneless voice which seemed to speak of itself and without his volition:

"I haven't the money. I sold about half that number of shares at about half the price you ask. To pay four times what I received is impossible. There is no more to be said."

He stooped and picked up his hat, buttoned his coat about him and moved in a dazed fashion toward the door.

The other man was at his side in an instant.

"Not without me, Crocker! We leave here arm-in-arm, like old friends devoted to antiquities; and don't try any funny business. You can only denounce me by showing a peeler this transfer form—if you can get hold of it—and that won't be very healthy for you when the train is fired."

So arm-in-arm they went, through the echoing gloom of the great galleries, out under the portico into the cold clinging mist of a foggy autumn dusk. Crocker was propelled southward until they were about to emerge into the homegoing crowds which filled New Oxford Street. The man stopped short.

"You are making a bad mistake" he said abruptly. "I will give you one more chance. If by noon tomorrow there is a letter addressed to Mr Jones at the little newspaper shop on the right as you go into Euston Station saying you have changed your mind and will buy, you will receive instructions how to exchange the money—in notes mind—for the transfer and the certificate. And don't trouble to watch the newspaper shop. I shan't come myself to collect the post, and the man who owns the place doesn't like strangers hanging about his doorway. Think it over."

He nodded an off-hand good-bye, darted round the corner, and was immediately lost to sight in the hurrying throng.

*　　　　*　　　　*　　　　*　　　　*

The new factory of the Delilah Company (to achieve which the last dividend but one had been passed, with the alarming results already described) was well on the way to completion. Externally it was virtually finished—that is to say the roof was perfect, the windows glazed, the main walls smooth and pointed. Inside, however, there was still a good deal to be done. Until the machinery was finally installed—with its attendant water-feeds, outlets and complex plumbing, its driving-belts, its communications with laboratories and testing-rooms—it was not possible to lay the whole of the upper floors. In consequence the interior was a very tall oblong box, its sides pierced with rows of windows and its loftiness from floor to roof marked off into layers at intervals by gridirons of joists projecting inward from the walls and ending abruptly on the brink of a central chasm. Across this chasm stretched iron girders, which would in good time carry the remainder of the floors, but at present were mere streaks across a well of space.

When the first workmen arrived on the morning after the interview in the British Museum, it was barely daylight. A harsh wind had risen in the night, blowing away the fog but turning the damp streets into canyons of bitter air and setting the grimy laurels planted in squares and tiny gardens rattling and rustling. Inside the unfinished building it was almost dark. Through a big ground-level gap in one of the walls (which like the upper floors had to await the fixing of equipment before it could be closed) the wind rushed, was caught in a fierce upward draught, and swept the whole height of the central well, only to strike against the roof, divide to right and left and come whistling down again through the skeleton floors on either side. The noise was extraordinary; and the workmen, with their bundles and lanterns, had to shout at one another as they dumped their reefer-coats, mufflers and dinner-pails, collected their tools and sought their various stations. The foreman slammed himself into his little office-hut, and tried to shut his ears to the racket while he went over the worksheet for the day.

Five minutes later the door flew open, and the wind, like a long invisible finger, flicked the papers from the table and scattered them in every direction. The foreman swore and, turning to close the door more firmly, saw one of his senior hands, white as a sheet and teetering against the door-jamb.

"What the devil—?" he began; then noticed that the man was mouthing inaudibly and pointing upwards. The foreman came out into the howling maelstrom of the hollow shell of bricks and mortar. Peering up in the greying light he saw a dark something, like a mammoth rotting pear, hanging from one of the girders far above his head, and swaying slowly in the wind.

The ex-Chairman of Delilah had come home to die.

*　　　*　　　*　　　*　　　*

Later that day Mr Meadows received a letter from the dead man.

DEAR MR MEADOWS,

You will remember your kind undertaking of a few weeks ago to enquire into a certain Company some of whose shares I wished to sell. I am now in the possession of two clues which may assist you to identify the persons behind this Company. On the evening of your call on me I was visited by the Mr Fleischmann whose brutal murder *that very night* you surely read about in the Press. He came in order to buy my shares in this mysterious Company, paid me well for them and took the essential papers away in his pocket. When they found him dead, his pockets were empty. Someone had stolen the papers. Whoever prompted that theft was responsible for his death.

Today I have had an experience which provides the second clue, and incidentally releases me from the *fear*— yes, the abject fear—which has hitherto kept me silent about Fleischmann's visit and purchase.

When you brought your successful action against the Vestry responsible for the maladministration of some street in Lambeth—the name escapes me—one of the Overseers was publicly reprimanded and later dismissed. I never knew what the man was called nor at that time did I set eyes on him; but if you can trace him, he should serve as a signpost on your way, and I believe the close associates of the late Mr Fleischmann, if you can identify them, will assist your search.

Be careful. There are dangerous people concerned in this affair—people who stick at nothing. But have no more fear on my account than I now have myself. They cannot reach me where I am going.

Good-bye and God be with you.

G. W. CROCKER.

BOOK FIVE
NINE YEARS RUIN AND REND
1869–1878

25 : HETTY ST MAUR

(i) AUTUMN 1869-JULY 1875

The St Maurs, as we already know, were far from rich, and
made no secret of their modest means. They were, however,
in the current phrase, extremely well connected. Hugh
St Maur's family was older than his wife's, but she could
muster a more impressive collection of uncles, aunts and
cousins, who were not only socially unimpeachable but also
still alive.

Prominent among these was Sir Peregrine Vesey, Bart. of
Temple Vesey near Cheltenham, the head of an historic
Catholic family, a great landowner and a wealthy man. Sir
Peregrine was Lola St Maur's second-cousin-by-marriage
once removed, Lady Vesey having been first cousin to Lola's
mother. While the latter was alive, she had spent much of
her time at Temple Vesey, for her cousin, of whom she was
very fond, had for years been laid low with a disease of the
spine and spent her waking hours prostrate on a wheeled
couch. The invalid came to rely more and more on these
visits for intimate talk and news of the outside world. She
led a lonely life. Her husband was greatly occupied with
his estates and county duties; her only child Arthur was
either at school or with tireless energy spending holidays in
ways suitable to his years, and she was not strong enough to
receive strangers or even acquaintances, who might in time
develop into friends.

It was, therefore, a sad blow to Lady Vesey when her
almost-sister and constant visitor died suddenly. Instinctively
she turned to the dead woman's daughter—not to take the
mother's place (that would have been impossible in view of
Lola's own family responsibilities) but rather to remind her
of the beloved companion who was no longer there, and to

be able to talk of her and to relive memories of their affectionate intercourse.

So it came about that Lola, with her husband and daughter, grew into the habit of a twice-yearly visit to Temple Vesey. They would go for a month or more in the summer and again for Christmas, and certainly it would have been hard to find a pleasanter or a more beautiful place in which to enjoy—and at no cost—a change of scene.

When they first went there, Hetty was seventeen and Arthur Vesey, an undergraduate at Christ Church, three years older. He was not always at home on their summer visit, but they met him regularly at Christmas, and it soon became evident, to Mrs St Maur at least, that he was greatly taken with the gay high-spirited young girl. It was, of course, the kind of cheerful, teasing, frolicsome relationship one would expect between an active, normal lad at the Varsity and a girl in her late 'teens, still half a child and young for her years. But there could be no doubt that the boy liked her very well indeed, felt at ease with her, and laughed more gaily when they were together than in any other company. Nor did he try to hide his liking. At the celebrations held for his coming-of-age, he had led her out to the first dance (somewhat to the annoyance of neighbouring mothers with daughters hopefully in tow) and earlier in the evening, during the firework display, had caused considerable consternation among staid onlookers by chasing her through the crowd letting off crackers at her heels.

As time passed and Hetty became nineteen and then twenty and grew up once and for all, Arthur's manner towards her significantly changed. He followed her with his eyes; he ran her errands; in the middle of a brisk exchange of banter he would suddenly draw in, choke back a repartee, seem almost nervous of offending her. She seemed quite unaware of any alteration in his manner. Though she had outgrown her schoolgirl spirits—had, indeed, become rather a serious young woman—she was still innocent at heart, without self-consciousness or vanity, and not as yet awake to the deeper implications of contacts with the other sex.

When Arthur came down from Oxford, he at once took over from his father some of the duties of estate-ownership. Sir Peregrine had married rather late in life, was now well over sixty and had recently begun to feel the burden of his years. It seemed that almost overnight the strain of his wife's prolonged and pathetic helplessness attacked and breached his physique, as for years, but more gradually, it had depressed his spirits. He was a tall handsome old gentleman, with a fringe of pure white whiskers and a strongly wrinkled face. His upright carriage had been the admiration of the neighbourhood, but lately his shoulders had suddenly sagged and at times he dragged his feet. Naturally autocratic, his temper grew more gruff, as gradually the strain of living with, and grieving for, a hopeless cripple wore him down. His agent, his tenants, his colleagues on the bench all found him increasingly difficult to work with; although, owing to the great respect in which he had always been held, they bore his often unreasonable perversities with admirable patience.

This painful ageing of a proud and conscientious man was the sadder in that he himself was perfectly alive to it. He knew already that he was frequently irascible, obstinate at wrong moments, deliberately unreceptive of suggestions from his agent or requests from the tenantry: he now knew also that his body was failing him. It was therefore with grim satisfaction that he welcomed his son home from college, and installed him as regent in those minor spheres which, with the agent's help, the boy should soon learn to control. Arthur applied himself with industry and enthusiasm to his duties. He loved country life and country things. Jaunts to London or Paris were not his idea of pleasure, and he was content to spend nearly all his time at Temple Vesey, finding his work in serving its interests and his pleasure in carrying a gun or in the strenuous comradeship of the hunting-field. He was a genuine sportsman, devoted to the arts of game-shooting and of riding to hounds, even at their most laborious. A foot-slog after wild partridges, a long ride to cover in drizzling rain with a certain prospect of a day of unremitting wet, were to him as much a part of the sports he loved as occasions when game was easy and plentiful and the sun shone on a long fast run without a check.

It was in connection with this love of field-sports that, for the first time in the history of their friendship, he had come into spiritual conflict with Hetty. The incident occurred shortly after she had turned twenty-one. There was a shoot in the Temple Vesey woods, and it had been suggested that a party from the house should meet the guns in the hut designed for such gatherings, bringing the luncheon with them.

The non-shooters arrived a little ahead of time, and, while servants were unpacking the hampers, strolled along the open rides. It was a brilliant winter's morning, and the world was hung about with the glitter of white frost, like a Queen Mother under her panoply of diamonds. The sunshine sparkled on the rime which settled on fur collars and caps as their wearers brushed against trees and shrubs ashimmer with hoar frost. An occasional shot sounded from the depths of the woods; the ice on shallow puddles tinkled as it broke, and the frozen grass whispered crisply beneath their feet. Through this perfection of a December day, the walkers, well muffled against the cold, wandered a little further than they knew.

When they regained the hut, the guns, with one or two exceptions, had already arrived, and keepers were laying out the morning's bag. Several brace of pheasants, four hares, any number of rabbits—the furred and feathered corpses slept limply alongside their fellows. Arthur was standing by the array of victims as Hetty approached.

"So here you are at last" he said cheerfully. "What do you think of this lot? Not bad for three guns, eh?"

She shivered slightly.

"I hate to see them all laid out like this" she said. "They were so happy."

He laughed.

"Oh, well. Got to keep 'em down, you know."

"I suppose so. But need it be a Roman Holiday? They may have a chance to escape, and to be a good shot means skill. But they can't hit back, poor little things. Oh!" she broke off, shrill with distress "Look, Arthur, that one's not dead!"

And in fact, from a tumbled heap of rabbits just thrown down by a beater, one little blood-stained creature crawled feebly out. Its back legs were shot to pieces, and it tried to pull itself along with its front paws.

"Arthur!" she cried. "Arthur! Do something. It's horrible" and turning away, burst into tears.

She hardly spoke during luncheon, and slipped back to the house the moment the meal was over. In the evening he came and sat by her in the drawing-room.

"Hetty, dear" he said humbly "I am so dreadfully sorry you were upset like that in the wood. Gross carelessness on that fellow's part. I dealt with him faithfully, I can assure you."

She would not look at him, but with heightened colour continued her needlework.

"I hate it all—shooting and hunting and all of it" she said in a low tight voice. "I hate the slaughter of birds and animals being turned into a game for rich idle folk."

He was deeply hurt and got up from his chair.

"If that is your opinion of us" he said stiffly "there is no more to be said, except that I greatly regret it."

The episode passed, and the cloud on their friendship thinned and passed also. Tacitly they avoided the subject; and when his favourite sports were to be practised near home, she kept out of sight and did not join the fringes of the shooting-party or the onlookers at the Meet. On off days, however, the two of them went riding, and on all normal occasions were back on their old footing of easy intimacy.

When the time grew near for the St Maurs' next summer visit to Temple Vesey, Arthur, who regularly sat with his mother at certain times of day telling her of all the little occurrences about the place, sometimes reading aloud from the newspaper, sometimes playing cards, suddenly said:

"Mums, I am going to ask Hetty St Maur to marry me."

She stretched out a hand and placed it on one of his.

"I have wondered when you would tell me that, my dear" she smiled "and it makes me very happy to hear it now. There is no better fate I could wish for either of you. She is a sweet good girl, and my boy's wife will also be my daughter."

A few weeks later Hetty received her first proposal of marriage. It was made between high clipped hedges of yew, on turf as smooth as velvet, near the centre of the long walk leading from the garden-terrace of the house to the little pavilion, in which a romantic Vesey in the late eighteenth century, passionately devoted to his beautiful wife, had installed a life-size image of her in plaster of Paris, with another of himself, kneeling in adoration at her feet.

She did not immediately reply to the young man's somewhat halting words, but looked at him, at first in surprise, then, as the meaning of what he had said became clearer to her, in thoughtful perplexity.

At last in a low but steady voice:

"I don't know what to say. It is very dear of you, Arthur, to want me like that, and makes me very proud. But I am taken unawares. I have never thought of marriage with anyone. I am so young and know so little. Certainly I am fonder of you than any other young man I see nowadays; but marriage . . ."

"Do not be frightened, Hetty. I could not bear to frighten you. There is plenty of time, only I dared not keep silent any longer, in case someone else came along."

She smiled and put her hand on his arm.

"No, nobody else; nor likely to be. I see so few people. And *you* have not frightened me. Not an atom. You have made me as vain as a peacock. But marriage *does* frighten me a little—it is so big and for-everish. I must think about it a lot, before I can even imagine it. Does anyone know you were going to ask me?"

"Yes. Mother knows, and father too. They are delighted."

She flushed with pleasure, and for the first time showed some embarrassment.

"How sweet you all are to me" she murmured. "And the idea never entered my head."

"Now that it is there, it must stop there" he said "right in the middle of that lovely little head; and you will get so used to it that finally—Well, we shall see. No more about it now. I shall be round again before long."

That was in July 1875; and thereafter he asked her twice a year for three whole years. The first once or twice she pleaded for longer respite, but then began, with gentle obstinacy, to edge towards a definite refusal. Her attitude perplexed poor Arthur and finally baffled him completely. He was aware that she had told her mother of the original proposal, for Mrs St Maur had spoken to him with warm approval, urging him to be patient and all would come right. There was, therefore, no home opposition behind Hetty's stubborn evasions. He clung pathetically to the belief that the only obstacle was girlish timidity, and that if he stuck to it . . .

Yet, had he but known, his cause had been hopeless ever since, in the autumn of 1875, she had paid a visit to London and stayed with an aunt (her father's sister) who lived in Devonshire Place.

(ii) OCTOBER 1875

As chance would have it, there was delivered on October 3, 1875—the day after Hetty's arrival at this aunt's house, the current issue of the *Borough of Marylebone Mercury*. Mrs Easton was interested in local affairs, and always read the local paper with as much care as if it were *The Times*. Studying it in the evening, as she and her niece sat by the fire in the comfortable drawing-room, she gave a little exclamation and said aloud, but as much to herself as to Hetty:

"So she is calling a meeting! Good for Octavia."

The girl looked across in amused enquiry.

"What about, and who is she? Come on, Aunt May, you can't keep it to yourself now."

"Very well, my dear. I ask nothing better than to ride my hobby-horse, but you may find it a dullish jaunt from your point of view."

And she proceeded to relate in detail the story of the conflict which had arisen between Miss Octavia Hill and the Marylebone Vestry over the management of Barrett's Court.

"They have had the hardihood to order the immediate demolition of the whole Court, just in order to save Dr W's silly face" concluded Mrs Easton—"and that after Miss Hill had worked there for the best part of three years and already transformed it! Disgraceful, that's what it is!"

Hetty was more entertained by her aunt's vehemence than interested in the point at issue. Like not a few enthusiasts, Mrs Easton assumed that others had a background knowledge of her special subject, and treated the Barrett's Court affair as an instalment of an exciting serial, the earlier parts of which were familiar to her hearer. Consequently Hetty gathered vaguely that this Miss Hill was some sort of building contractor, who had started work on certain houses which were now to be demolished. Admittedly it was tiresome for her to have wasted her time and trouble; but why such excitement, and why a meeting?

"And the meeting, auntie?"

"Tomorrow night" replied the other briskly "at eight o'clock. I shall certainly go and will, if you like, take you with me. It is close at hand."

"Thank you. That will be very nice" said the girl politely, relinquishing the idea of finding out what their funny meeting was about. "Can't be duller than sitting indoors on my lonesome anyway" she added to herself.

Hetty returned from the meeting silent and preoccupied. When she was in bed, she lay wakeful for a long time and then dropped into a haunted sleep. Waking and sleeping, what she had heard, what Octavia Hill had said, and above all the impression made by the personality of the speaker revolved incessantly through a mind exhausted with excitement yet eager for more. When she came downstairs next morning she was in an advanced state of heroine-worship. Never in her life had she fallen so abjectly under the spell of another human being as she lay now under the spell of Miss Hill. The squarish figure with its long body and short legs, its broad shoulders and massive head, bundled haphazard into a heavy drab coat and with a nondescript hat pulled over a mass of soft brown hair, blazed in the girl's imagination like the Sun of Righteousness. The face was at once serene, passionate and profoundly human; and Hetty, who had sat for an hour and a half gazing steadily at it, still saw before her, as clearly as though they were in the room, the wide forehead, the large luminous eyes which changed their message with every turn of the speaker's argument, the mobile generous mouth which told of such dreadful things, yet promised with such confidence to mend and end them.

As for the subjects discussed at the meeting, they were little less of a revelation to Hetty than was the personality of the central figure. She had never for one moment conceived that human beings in this great city lived their lives in the conditions she heard described. She had known that some folk were better off than others, some folk more respectable than others; but by her standards poverty as opposed to wealth was as one pound to five pounds, and respectability as opposed to disrepute as unobtrusive good manners to vulgar rowdiness. Now she felt that the bottom had fallen out of her conception of the world she lived in, letting her tumble headlong on to the floor of Hell, where were starvation and cruelty and filth and misery and hopelessness.

All the morning she brooded over this tremendous revelation of the true meaning of poverty and the depths of degradation to which it can drive human beings. At luncheon she said suddenly:

"Auntie, I would like to know more about Miss Octavia Hill and her work. How is that possible?"

Mrs Easton, greatly pleased that her niece showed interest in a subject near to her own heart, lent her the numbers of *Macmillan's Magazine*, in which four essays by Octavia Hill on her work and her ideals had already been printed. She also filled in much of the background history of that remarkable woman, which history, two days earlier, she had omitted from her indignant narrative of the sins of the Vestry. Finally she hinted that there might some time be an opportunity to introduce Hetty to Miss Hill herself. The girl's eyes shone.

"Oh!" she cried. "That would be wonderful!"

After every word of Miss Hill's four articles had been read and re-read, Mrs Easton was asked for more material on the subject of London poverty. The good lady felt that discretion was necessary. The girl was very young; and this sudden uprush of sympathy with the underdog, admirable though it was as an expression of youth's generous ardour, sprang from emotional reverence for one noble individual, and had no glimmer of understanding of the horrors which lurked under the visible squalors of slumland. She, therefore, concealed the fourth volume of *London Labour and the London Poor* and Greenwood's *Seven Curses of London*, but lent her niece Mayhew I to III and, having looked over Mr Greenwood's new book *The Wilds of London* at a bookshop in Oxford Street, decided to risk "Tiger Bay" and took the volume home with her.

Hetty could hardly be persuaded to take a walk in Regent's Park, so absorbed was she in her new subject of study. But there came a day when she had finished her reading, had returned once more to refresh her memory of Miss Hill's inspiring essays, and was ready for the next stage. Slowly an entirely new conception of London had developed in her mind. Hitherto it had been a smoky wilderness of houses, to one of which she paid an occasional visit and, from its cosy interior, sallied out in company with her mother and Mrs Easton, to attend Mass in Spanish Place, or to shop in Regent Street, or to visit the Egyptian Hall or to attend a concert or even, though rarely, to enjoy a theatre. She had never thought to imagine how far the houses spread, what shades of difference there might be between one neighbourhood and another, what infinite varieties of ways of life were progressing alongside one another and all the time. Now she was becoming conscious of the vast city sprawling under its sulky sky—a maze of big streets and small, of parks and alley-ways; now she began to visualise the contrasted existence of the tens of thousands of men and women who, jostling one another along crowded pavements, constituted the town. Some sought pleasure, others livelihood, others rest after labour, others merely oblivion. Each one of them had an individuality, each one a secret life, yet in the mass they were London. Whether they lolled in the luxury of a great mansion, or dragged wearily from work to the one dirty room which stood for home, or tramped the pavement from dawn to dark, huddling finally into a doorway to find that much of shelter for the night, they were citizens of the same city, and had equal claims on its resources and its protection.

One day, when her aunt had gone to fulfil a long-standing promise to visit a friend in Hampstead, Hetty went out by herself. She had only been allowed to do this once or twice, and then on the understanding that she went straight into the Park or slanted down through Cavendish Square to Oxford Street on some specific shopping errand. Today she did neither. She walked down Wimpole Street, and west-ward along Great Marylebone Street. At the next turning she chanced to look to her right and a little behind her. Her new sense of London immediately awoke; here was one of the contrasts which she now understood must exist, but had never yet seen. Extraordinary that within a few minutes of Mrs Easton's house her imaginings should thus be verified.

Over her shoulder towered the backs of the tall Wimpole Street houses—dignified, well-cared-for houses, with large gleaming windows set in semi-circular bows, with pointing white and perfect on the dark brickwork, with paint spick and span. Backing immediately on to them, with only a mews between, a dingy row of slatternly three-storey dwellings faced another even dingier. At the corner was a garish public-house and fifty yards up the street a second one. The roadway was strewn with refuse; dirty children ran shouting along the pavement, running in and out of the open doors, pelting one another with cabbage stalks and orange peel.

Hetty took a firm hold of herself and walked steadily up

this unexpected street of poverty. Narrow roads went off on her left, and seemed to lead further into the heart of a huddle of squalid dwellings. Outside the second of the two public-houses stood a broken-down perambulator. The girl looked over the edge as she reached it, and saw a puny baby, its face parchment-yellow under smears of dirt, its mouth raw with ulcers. A sour reek of a kind to turn the stomach rose from the torn blankets in which the child was wrapped.

Hetty struggled with a sudden nausea, but forced herself to stand a moment longer gazing at this pitiful offshoot of a race who never will be slaves. As she looked, the tiny creature whimpered and struggled to free its arms from the filthy wrappings. One came clear—a match-stick of an arm, with angry red blotches near the wrist—but as the child wriggled feebly to release the other, there rose before Hetty's eyes the vision of the little wounded rabbit at Temple Vesey, straining to crawl away from death on the only crutches left to it. She thrust her handkerchief into her mouth and ran blindly up the street.

It was lucky that she had strayed into a mere pocket of slumland—a curious little enclave of bad property, over from the days when the northern sector of Marylebone High Street was fringed with alleys of evil repute. Had the area been larger she might well have lost herself, for her mind was so distracted that she took no account of her route. As it was, she scurried up Beaumont Street to the intersection with Devonshire Street, westward along its comforting breadth to High Street, westward again and first to the right, and found herself out in Marylebone Road, with the church and the Charity School close at hand and the familiar opening of York Gate immediately opposite.

Though she did not know it, she had passed within a few yards of her new Divinity; for her way took her up Nottingham Place, and in the front room of Number Ten, which overlooked the street, Octavia Hill was at that moment seated, making up her rent-book.

The visit wore on and Hetty was due to go home in three

days' time. She was still in the mood of serious endeavour which had possessed her since attending the meeting concerned with Barrett's Court, but on the day following her journey to Hampstead Mrs Easton was conscious of a new intensity in her niece's concentration. She knew nothing of the girl's adventure behind Wimpole Street. In reply to her "And how have you fared, my dear?" she had been told "Quite well, thank you, Auntie. I went out for a little and read a little. Nothing exciting." But though ignorant of the cause, the elder lady felt instinctively that Hetty's mind was on the simmer, and would not be long in coming to the boil.

Nor was she mistaken. In the evening Hetty said rather solemnly:

"Please listen to this, Aunt May. It is out of Miss Hill's article on the Work of Volunteers in the Organisation of Charity."

She opened the bound volume of *Macmillan's Magazine* for 1872 and read:

"Charity owes all its graciousness to the sense of its coming from a real friend. We want to bring the rich and poor, the educated and uneducated, more and more into direct communication. We must beware of raising up barriers of committees between those who should meet face to face. . . . In the same way much has been written of late on the subject of Sisterhoods and of 'Homes', where those who wish to devote themselves to the service of the poor can live together, consecrating their whole life to the work. I must here express my conviction that we want very much more the influence that emanates, not from a 'Home', but from 'homes'. . . . The work amongst the poor is, in short, better done by those who do less of it, or rather, who gain strength and brightness in other ways. . . . I believe that educated people would come forward if once they saw how they could be really useful. . . . Let each of us not attempt too much, but take some one little bit of work, and, doing it simply, thoroughly and lovingly, wait patiently for the gradual spread of good, and leave the professional workers to deal for the present with the great mass of evil around."

She closed the volume and sat for a few moments staring in silence at nothing in particular. Then she said:

"I would like to be one of these volunteers whom Miss Hill asks to come forward. I have thought it all out. I cannot go on living comfortably at home, wasting my time over fiddling bits of housework or chattering at tea-parties. I want to learn about—er—about things generally, and I want to do something useful. Supposing I came to London to study—oh, anything, music or drawing or languages— and gave part of my time to undertaking 'some one little bit of work among the poor', would you . . . I mean . . ." She blushed confusedly and clasped her restless hands, twisting the fingers in and out. Then with a rush "what I wanted to ask you was whether I could live here with you."

Mrs Easton managed to control her features and to show no sign of surprise, although in fact the suggestion took her very much aback.

"My dear child, I should like nothing better than the pleasure of your company. But you must get your parents' consent before a word is said to anyone. I am afraid your mother will not like the idea at all. Even though, as will certainly be the case, you are thought to be too young to visit alone, the work is often painful to a degree, and—well, it is good to keep the bloom on the fruit as long as one may."

Hetty rose, tucking the book under her arm.

"Thank you, Auntie" she said primly. "It is very kind to say you will have me, if mamma agrees. I shall tackle her as soon as I get home."

And she went upstairs to bed, leaving her aunt in a state of great perturbation. Oh dear, she thought, I'm to blame for all this! If I hadn't blurted out about that meeting. . . . What *will* Lola say? I fear she will be very cross with me. Of course neither she nor Hugh will hear of such a thing; and then the poor child will be bitterly disappointed and

also, I dare say, turn on me! Ah well, these sudden en-
thusiasms pass. Perhaps the child will fall in love, and that
will drive Octavia and the poor and the whole collection of
us out of her head.

But the stars in their courses fought against prudent age
and on behalf of impulsive youth. The very next afternoon
—the last full day of Hetty's visit—there called in Devonshire Place the Rev. William Fremantle, Rector of St Mary's,
Marylebone, and with him a youngish couple, the Rev. and
Mrs Samuel Barnett. Mr Fremantle had been a friend of
Mrs Easton for several years, and as Mr Barnett had been one
of his curates, he also was acquainted with her. Three years
ago the Bishop had offered Barnett the living of St Jude's in
Commercial Street, Whitechapel—a parish described by his
Lordship himself as "the worst in my Diocese, inhabited mainly
by a criminal population and much corrupted by bribery."
Barnett, with the courage of enthusiasm, had accepted; and
he and his young wife had now for over thirty months been
at grips with their terrifying problem.

Inevitably talk over the teacups turned to the fight against
poverty and ignorance and disease and crime. Inevitably the
name of Octavia Hill came into the conversation. Both
Fremantle and Barnett knew Miss Hill intimately. Indeed
the former was almost the first clergyman to appreciate her
ideals and her gifts. In 1869 he had handed over to her the
apparently hopeless task of raising a patch of wretched lanes
called the "Walmer Road Area", which lay just behind the
Yorkshire Stingo and within a stone's-throw of the alley
where, in the same year, was found the body of Cornelius
Fleischmann. From that time onward he and his curates
had worked intimately with Octavia Hill and her colleagues,
and the discussion of Barnett's difficulties in his new work
could not fail to dwell continually on the analogous problems
which she had faced and overcome.

"If only" cried Barnett "we could get a few helpers who
are not so-called 'Social Workers' nor paid investigators nor
undisguisable missionaries! The little children are the vital

people. The adults, even the adolescents, in my worst streets are irreclaimable—yes, Fremantle, despite your protests I must repeat *irreclaimable*. They are poisoned through and through by the bestial life they have led, by the horrible conditions in which they have to live, by the sense that every man's hand is against them, and that anyone who speaks to them kindly is fair game for cadging."

The talk swung to and fro, and Hetty, pale and motionless, sat listening, her eyes gleaming large and dark like moorland pools in a stormy dusk. Suddenly she got up and crossed the room to where young Mrs Barnett was sitting. The men and their hostess were now bent over the printed text of a Report made by Octavia Hill to the Local Government Board in January of the present year.

"Mrs Barnett" said Hetty breathlessly and almost in a whisper, impatient to say her say while there was opportunity, "I would like to come and help you. I have no experience, no knowledge. But I am strong, and I do not think I should be afraid. Not of the babies in any case, and they are the ones I would most love to do something for. Would there be *any* chance? Please, please think of it. Tomorrow I go home—not far away, to Lashwater in Surrey. Will you write to me? I have the address all ready; I wrote it down a few minutes ago, waiting for the chance to speak to you alone."

She thrust the fragment of paper into Mrs Barnett's hand, and turned to meet three pairs of eyes. Two of them smiled indulgently at the pretty group—the young wife seated, the girl on her knees beside her, talking so urgently; the third showed perplexity touched with uneasiness. The moment of scrutiny held them motionless, then passed. The visitors rose to take their leave.

"Good-bye, Miss St Maur" said Mrs Barnett. "It has been a pleasure to meet you."

Nothing more.

When they had gone, Mrs Easton put her hands on Hetty's shoulders.

"What were you saying to Mrs Barnett?" she asked severely.

The girl told her frankly, without apology or evasiveness.
"I am very much displeased with you" said the lady.
I told you yesterday that nothing must be said about this
sudden craze for social work until your parents' permission
had been given. It was wrong of you, Hetty, to snatch an
opportunity to disobey me. I shall write to your mother
and tell her that you are obviously not yet sufficiently mistress
of yourself to be trusted to manage even little children."
Hetty tossed her head.
"You needn't write" she said mutinously. "I will tell
mamma the whole story—that I promise you! " Her flare of
temper quavered and died, and she began to cry. "I am so
sorry I was rude" she faltered "and that I disobeyed you.
I went over to Mrs Barnett without thinking of anything
except that here was a chance. And it's not a craze—truly
it isn't—it's what I have been looking for, without knowing
it, for -oh, for years!"

(iii) NOVEMBER 1875-SUMMER 1878

Mrs Easton's forecast of the reception at Lashwater of
Hetty's crusading ambitions was only too accurate. The
girl's parents were horrified, and in their mood of shocked
distress vetoed the whole scheme with imprudent harshness.
Mrs St Maur wrote an indignant letter to Devonshire Place,
commenting with such asperity on Mrs Easton's interpretation
of an aunt's duty as to cause great offence.

There began, in consequence, a period of stress and discomfort for everyone concerned. Hetty pleaded and argued
and pleaded and wept and then relapsed into sullen defiance.
Her mother, having at the outset adopted an attitude of
blank negation, found herself bound to maintain it. This
she did by not mentioning the subject at all and ignoring it
if it were mentioned, and, with pinched lips and small unnecessary nervous gestures, by enlivening family meals with
trivialities on themes in which no one—not even herself—
was in the smallest degree interested. Hugh St Maur fluttered
uneasily round the perimeter of the battlefield on which his

womenfolk were so bitterly at odds. From loyalty and from conviction he supported his wife; but he grew daily more sorry for his daughter, suffering the agonies of rebellious but helpless youth, and resentful for the sake of an ideal, unthought-out but passionately upheld. He felt that if Lola would only recede a little from the position of "the whole thing is sheer nonsense and completely out of the question and I don't want to hear another word about it", the girl might respond. She had always been a "biddable" child, sweet-natured and reasonable; and the rôle of cross-grained martyr was at times clearly sustained only with an effort. But he knew that any attempt on his part to modify his wife's conception of parental authority would probably make matters worse for Hetty and certainly get him into serious trouble.

At last he decided to try an indirect approach. One day, when he had a good reason for going to London, he paid a surprise call on his sister. He plunged into an unreserved apology for the letter written by his wife in a moment of angry distress; and, before the lady had a chance to close the interview, implored her to help him resolve a deadlock which was making home life intolerable.

"My dear Hugh" said Mrs Easton, mollified by the apology but still on her dignity "you surely do not expect me to risk a second reproof for meddling in the affairs of your family? If you have now changed your mind, say so, assert your authority and let the girl do whatever she wishes."

"*My* authority?" he smiled ruefully. "What about maternal authority where a daughter is concerned? But seriously, May—that apart—you misunderstand me. I have not in any way altered my opinion as to the unsuitability *at this juncture* of what Hetty wants to do. But I have watched the child carefully and have come to believe that her wish to help in Social Work is not just an excited whim, but an indication of some element in her make-up, struggling to find expression. Of course she has gone too far and too fast. She does not understand—cannot understand—what life in a really bad slum is like. Nor of course does Lola; but she forms a general idea of physical dangers and risk of infection and glimpses of wickedness no girl should be allowed to have, and just says 'no' and again 'no'. I do not blame her. I cannot myself pretend to much experience of slum conditions; but I spent a few months with a Catholic Mission in Liverpool before I was married, and saw sights and smelled smells which I can still recall twenty-five years later.

"I have no hesitation at all in saying that it would be criminal to expose a girl like Hetty—who has lived at home all her life, is not yet twenty-two and young at that—to the sudden shock of seeing and hearing what she would have to see and hear, if she went to Whitechapel.

"But this is not quite the same as repeating 'I will never permit it'—a stupid remark in any case, because if a young thing means what it says, it will ultimately do what it likes, and if it doesn't mean it, permission or otherwise will not arise—and I have come to submit to your judgment a possible way to compromise."

"I warn you" Mrs Easton put in "that I am taking no initiative. I was only indirectly responsible before, yet was abused as though I had preached red revolution in my own drawing-room—"

"Oh, please, please! I beg of you to forget words written in heat and dismay. And no initiative is to be taken. What I have in mind is this: Hetty is very musical. She plays the pianoforte with a natural skill and grace; but she is quite untrained. If I could manage the fees and persuade Lola to agree to the girl coming to London to study, will you take her in—"

"She will not be allowed to pass this dangerous threshold."

"Oh, yes, she will—if Mrs Barnett will play up, and you alone can ask her to do so."

"I've no idea what you mean, Hugh."

"Just this. I want you to get Mrs Barnett to write to Lola. (I presume that she did *not* write to Hetty, as the child asked her, because you warned her not to do so?) If she would say how sorry she is to hear of the trouble caused by an impetuous and premature enthusiasm; that she fully agrees with the mother's view that the girl must walk before she runs; but that the work is noble work and the labourers sadly few and would there be an opportunity to talk matters over . . .? Something on those lines. . . . Then I will bring Lola to London and we will go to Whitechapel and see the Barnetts."

Mrs Easton looked dubious.

"And then?"

Hugh shrugged.

"I can't tell you. I never try to forecast too far ahead. But I believe in getting a conversation going, and I know my beloved Lola. She has the warmest heart in the world under a tigress determination to protect her young; and, as she always looks on the blackest side of every new possibility, the young appear in constant need of protection. I'll take the risk of the visit to Whitechapel proving a failure. All I want you to do, dear May, is to say that in principle you will give Hetty a home while she is working at her music, and to persuade Mrs Barnett to write that letter."

"Very well. I'll try. As for having the child here I would enjoy nothing better. She is a dear girl and her company is delightful. But I rely absolutely on you to keep me out of it, if things do not turn out favourably."

"You may safely do so. That I promise you. And now good-bye and thank you a thousand times."

That Hugh St Maur's strategy succeeded was due mainly to the tact and charm of Mrs Barnett's letter to Hetty's mother. She seemed to know by instinct just how to reassure maternal fears, while stimulating maternal interest in a child's aspirations. She concluded by saying that, if there were ever an opportunity, she and her husband would be glad to make the acquaintance of the parents of a girl whose appearance and manners had impressed them both most favourably.

Hugh affected not to notice this suggestion of a possible meeting, contenting himself with saying that the letter was civil and attractive and that Mrs Barnett must be a nice woman. During the days which followed he made no further reference, either to the lady or to Hetty's thwarted ambition,

and his apparent indifference to both so far irritated his wife
that she began to feel slightly injured on Mrs Barnett's behalf.
By slow degrees she came to a reconsideration of Hetty's
present life at home, and admitted to herself that it had a
solitude and an aimlessness which might well prey upon a
high-spirited young girl. She began to realise that it was
not reasonable to compare in her mind Hetty's circumstances
and her own girlhood. She had been one of a large family
in a sprawling untidy house deep in the country, at a period
when communications were so slow and difficult that households became communities sufficient to themselves. Hetty
was an only child; Lashwater, for all that it had a certain
longevity as a township, was becoming more and more an
adjunct of London, with interests and activities affiliated to
the metropolis. There was little local occupation for a girl
who was not content to shrill her days away in giggles and
flirtations, whose tastes—simple and immature though they
might be—were not those of most of her contemporaries in
the neighbourhood and seemed to them over-erudite and
boring.

When Hugh St Maur judged that his wife's change of
heart had sufficiently progressed (he could gather frequent
hints of the way her mind was moving from things she half-
said and from things she said no longer), he broached the
suggestion of Hetty's musical education. It was well received.
That the girl had talent was evident; that she was badly in
need of a real interest in life was obvious. She would return
home at regular and frequent intervals; she would be cared
for and comfortably housed by Mrs Easton, against whom
Lola might never have felt the least rancour, so warmly did
she now speak of her.

In due course everything was arranged. Hetty became
once more her cheerful affectionate self; and, as the months
went by, the shadow of that miserable period at Mount Felix
when the family was divided against itself, passed and was
forgotten by all concerned.

Not for a year or more did Hugh venture to revive the
memory of Mr and Mrs Barnett. Then he arranged with

Mrs Easton (who was both impressed and delighted with the excellent results of her brother's diplomacy) to invite the Barnetts on a day when Hetty's parents were due to visit Devonshire Place. In half an hour the two sets of visitors were talking like old friends. Hugh and Lola were invited to Whitechapel, went and were conquered. When next Hetty came home, her mother made a complete retraction.

"Your Mrs Barnett is an angel, darling, and I am ashamed to have doubted your judgment. You are now twenty-four; and if a year from now you still want to go and help her, and meanwhile, in your spare time at Auntie May's, will try to get a little experience of what the work means, I shall say God bless you and more power to your elbow."

Then the two of them cried a little in each other's arms, and at dinner triumphantly informed the master of the house that he had been quite wrong in opposing Hetty's wishes, and should merely have declared she must wait till she was older. He accepted the reproof with becoming humility.

So it came about that in the summer of 1878 it was arranged that Hetty should go to St Jude's Vicarage in Commercial Street, Whitechapel; and that, if things went well during a trial period of three months and she wished to remain, she should be allowed to do so. The trial period passed and she elected to remain.

(iv) CHRISTMAS 1878

When the St Maurs reached Temple Vesey for their usual Christmas visit, Arthur made one more desperate attempt. He and Hetty were alone in the tall shadowy library, and, mastering a sudden breathlessness, he began to plead in a low urgent voice:

"Hetty! Dear Hetty—let me for once say all I have to say, and then if it is still 'no', for ever after hold my peace."

She kept her eyes fixed on the warm bright fire—golden eyes, clouded by the thought of giving pain but with gentle determination in their depths. She wore a tight-bodiced dress of pale grey silk with a full skirt falling from a bustle

nd coiling about her feet, and her dark hair was drawn
moothly back to a chignon low on her graceful neck. One
and rested on the mantel supporting the huge carved structure
of the chimney-breast, the other hung motionless at her side.
She was neither agitated nor confused; merely sorry to have
o deny one she liked and respected, and anxious so far as
oossible to spare him.

"It is no use, Arthur" she said quietly, still staring into the
fire. "It will only hurt you all over again to—"

"I would rather be hurt" he interrupted "than not try once
more. So *please* listen to me. I love you, Hetty; I love you
distractedly. I suppose I began loving you when you first
came here on a visit as a growing girl (and that is long long
ago), though it took me, oaf that I am, some while to realise
it. But I realise it now only too well, and must once more
insist that to me nothing matters, except that you should be
my wife, and in due course reign over this house in which
everyone adores you. Never was there a match with fewer
obstacles. *My* parents want it; so do *yours*. We have youth
and health, and as for the good things of this world they are
lying at your little feet. You have only to stoop, dear dear
Hetty, and pick them up—and me with them."

She turned slowly and raised her eyes to his pleading face,
which he had thrust forward to within a foot of her own.
There were tears in those eyes, and a sorrowful tender little
smile set a dimple trembling in her cheek.

He laid a hand lightly on her arm.

"No! Don't say anything yet! I've not quite done.
'Stoop, and pick me up with them' . . . I know very well
it *is* a case of stooping. I am a stupid sort of fellow from
your point of view, and don't understand much about books
and music and all that. But I think I could make you happy;
and if I may do that, I am content. We will go abroad and
to London and I will try to learn about the things you care
for. We will live in London, if you like, and only come here
from time to time. While we are here, you shall have nothing
to do with the sports you dislike—although" he added wistfully "you *do* enjoy riding a little, don't you? Oh Hetty,

if I could only find words to tell what I think of you, I am sure you would pity me, and out of pity, if for no other reason—"

He seemed to collapse under the strain of his own urgency. Moving away to the other side of the fireplace, he pressed his hands to his forehead and gave a deep sigh.

"Forgive me. I am talking too much. One last request. Sleep on this; think of it—and of me—as kindly as you can and give me my answer tomorrow. I have promised that if it is again 'no', I will not pester you any more; and that promise I will try to keep, though Heaven knows whether I shall be strong enough."

Hetty had resumed her former pose while he said out his say, and did not now look up when she replied to him.

"You must try to believe me, Arthur, when I say that if I could possibly do what you want I would—and with all my heart. You are all dear dear friends, here in this lovely place, and I tremble to think that having to say 'no' may even to a tiny degree spoil that friendship.

"Yet I *must* say 'no'. I told you, when you first spoke to me about . . . about . . . well, about you and me—and that is three years ago—that I was not ready for marriage. You see I remember quite clearly, because it touched me deeply that you should want me, and has touched me more deeply each time you have said so. I said that I did not think I understood this 'love' business; that I 'loved' mamma and papa, and that before you talked of love to me I should have said I 'loved' Sir Peregrine and Lady Vesey and their son Arthur whom I've known so many years. But since you spoke, I have not been able to say that any more, because when you tell me you 'love' me, you mean something quite different—something I know to be different, but even now do not understand.

"Please do not imagine I have ever under-rated what you offer me. We are badly off, as you know, Arthur; and though we are gentlefolk, we are obscure nobodies beside the Veseys. I am not such a fool that I do not appreciate the honour you do me. *Your* loyalty, *your* protection, a great social position, everything a girl can desire—what more overwhelming good fortune could I hope for?

"But I cannot accept it. Partly, as I said, because I do not 'love' you in the mysterious way I ought to do if I am to be your wife. But even more—this will sound priggish, I fear—because I want to be of some use in the world. In a vague muzzy way I have wanted this for a long while, and went groping about after the right kind of use. I found it, to my own satisfaction, even before you first asked me to marry you; but I was forbidden to do what I wanted, and therefore could not say anything about it. Now—"

"But, my darling, what could be more useful than to care for all the tenants and the people hereabouts? They need someone so badly to help them in hard times, watch over their children, take them out of their narrow lonely lives. My poor mother has been an invalid for so long that they have almost forgotten what it is like to have the lady from the big house paying them regular visits, always ready to advise and cheer them."

"No, Arthur. All that is quite true, and as between rich and poor the task would be worthy and worth doing. But as between me and them it would not be what I want. I should be safe; I should have climbed on to a peak above the clouds where the sun is always shining, and at intervals descend with my basket of comforts into the cold and rain, distribute them, and go back to warmth and luxury where they could not reach me, and become a different person."

He watched her in growing bewilderment.

"I don't think I understand you, Hetty. How can you be of use', as you say, without some solid ground to work from? It would be the very fact that you yourself are not exposed to hardship that would set you free to give all your thoughts to others. I do not see how you can combine helping the unfortunate with being yourself in little better case, unless you go and live in the slums, cheek by jowl with the slum-dwellers themselves."

She threw up her head and looked at him with mild defiance.

"That," she said (a shade misleadingly) "is precisely what I am now going to do."

K*

(i) OCTOBER 1869–MARCH 1870

THE FLEET STREET offices of the influential weekly paper *Diogenes* were about half-way between Temple Bar and Ludgate Circus, on the left-hand side going east. *Diogenes* had been launched in 1869 by an enterprising man (who had had the foresight, over a dozen years earlier, to purchase all the rights from the proprietors of a journal with this title in 1855) and had quickly established itself as a fearless opponent of every kind of social injustice. It attacked official or administrative oppression; it exposed fraud and corruption; it championed the weak in any walk of life; it was vigilant in exposing abuse of power by such as were strong. It lasted for ten years (ceasing publication with the sudden death of its gifted creator) just long enough to witness the début of *Truth*, whose founder Labouchere undoubtedly owed something of his brilliant technique in unmasking money-sharks to the example of the less-specialised *Diogenes*.

On the second floor of the paper's offices was a door with an upper panel of ground-glass, across which, during the year 1870, were painted in black the initials M. M. This inscription celebrated the change of fortune which had befallen a large untidy young man, who formerly picked up a meagre but sufficient living, writing about the Fancy for *Sporting Life*.

Matt Merton's success had originated in two coincidences— the first that he was friendly with the Rev. Alfred Meadows of All Saints, Margaret Street; the second that poor Mr Crocker, formerly of the Delilah Hair Tonic Company, had asked Mr Meadows to make an investigation on his behalf and, the very evening on which he hanged himself, had written the clergyman a note giving two clues likely to be of help to the investigator. That had been in October 1869.

Before he received this note Meadows had already consulted Matt (still a hack-journalist and a happy-go-lucky bohemian), who had undertaken to make some enquiries into the matter under discussion, without having, in fact, the smallest idea how to start. When, however, after a week or two of bewildered inaction, he received from Meadows a copy of Crocker's letter, to which the clergyman had added from his own private diary the name of the Lambeth Overseer who had lost his job because of the Cross Street scandal, Matt had something to go on, and without losing a moment, tracked down Lord Frederick Boreham.

At the outset of the interview the fat grotesque was suspicious of the slovenly young stranger, with his talk of an enquiring clergyman who had somehow been connected with the recent suicide; but as the visitor filled in the outlines of the story, and revealed the startling fact that Fleischmann had been murdered on his way home from calling on Crocker, Boreham became interested and followed the exposition with close attention.

When the young man had finished, he was put through a short catechism, designed to test his consistency and to convince Boreham finally of his reliability. Why had Crocker asked Meadows to find out about Homes from Home? Matt did not know; he only knew that the two men had been jointly concerned in some social crusade years ago, and had become friends. Why had Meadows chosen Matt to investigate the matter? Merton shrugged. "I have done him odd services before. I'm a journalist of a sort, and knock about newspaper offices and meet the kind of fellows Mr Meadows would not know. He has had need of bits of information to help him in his work, and I could sometimes pick up gossip or intelligent anticipation or facts about people, which he could hardly get for himself. I like Mr Meadows. He is a good man, and I am glad to help him."

"How did you come across him?"

Matt gave a brief account of the Granby Street adventure,

adding: "It shows that, as long ago as that, he and Crocker were fairly intimate, for Crocker took the kid Lottie Heape to live on his place in Surrey."

Boreham sat up with a jerk, for a few moments stared at Matt open-mouthed, and then burst out:

"Here, hold on! Say that again—the kid *who*?"

"Lottie Heape she said her name was" replied the other, surprised by the vehemence of the question.

"*Lot-tie Heape!* Well, I'm damned! It can't be. Must be another. This was when?"

"Oh, eight years ago or more."

"And she was how old when you found her?"

"Nine, I think, or ten. Something like that. Why?"

Boreham frowned in silence at the opposite wall. When he spoke it was to cap Matt's question with another:

"What became of the girl? Was she still with Crocker when the crash came?"

"No. She ran away some months before. There was trouble of some kind."

"What became of her?"

"I've no idea. What's the point of all this, Lord Frederick? What are you driving at?"

The big man gestured for silence.

"Let me think. . . ."

At last he heaved himself out of his chair and, crossing over to where Matt was sitting, stood on the hearthrug near by. Hands in pockets, a coat-tail tucked under each arm, he teetered backwards and forwards on the balls of his feet. Beneath his sealskin waistcoat his great belly swayed like a haggis as he moved.

"Listen to me, young man" he began. "You have told me an interestin story and several highly interestin facts I did not know. I will now return the compliment; we will then pool our resources and see how we stand."

He proceeded to improvise a condensed but admirably clear account of the events leading up to the murder of Fleischmann. "This chap looks a bloated freak" thought Matt "but he's no fool"; and indeed the monstrous creature was almost impressive, as he rolled out in his deep hoarse voice a concise narrative of the mounting struggle between the group to which he had belonged and that commanded by Banjo Burdock. It was a verbal précis of the first order, faultless in perspective, adequate in detail, detached in manner yet devastating in implication.

"What then is our position?" he concluded. "What do we know? We know that Homes from Home belongs—or belonged—to Burdock, and that Crocker had a big shareholding. We know that Fleischmann visited Crocker to get a controllin interest in Homes from Home, and damn well got it. Before he could get home he was killed and robbed of that controllin interest—obviously at Burdock's orders, though we can't prove it. We know finally that one of Burdock's jackals is this Overseer chap—what's his name? Oh, yes, Waters—and Waters is sent to blackmail Crocker into payin out a lump of money for the privilege of coverin Burdock's tracks.

"What *don't* we know? Primarily this—who told Burdock that Flashy was goin on that particular evenin to see Crocker on this particular business? Flashy and I arranged that he should do so only two days earlier. We were absolutely alone in a small back room in his house when the plan was decided, and neither of us was such an idiot as to breathe a word to anyone else. I can only think of one possibility (which, to be Irish, seems impossible) and that is that someone in Fleischmann's house somehow overheard and for some reason gave us away. Who was in Fleischmann's house? Servants—a couple and a maid—and Fleischmann's girl; AND—this will bring you up short, me boy—Fleischmann's girl's name was Lottie Heape!"

He broke off triumphantly, and thrust his red creased face with its dangling folds of skin almost into that of the astonished young man. For a moment they stared at short range into one another's eyes. Then Matt gave a low whistle.

"Well!" he cried. "That's a corker and no mistake! *Can* it be the same? Where did he find her?"

"I dunno. Flashy kept his private affairs private—and

very sensible of him. Nobody's business but his own. It didn't matter to me or to anyone *then*, where he got her from. But it may matter a good deal to us *now*, and it's on the cards that I may be able to find out. You see how the Crocker connection ties up with the rest? That's what makes me feel it *must* be the same girl. But how the devil she got to know —well, never mind about that for the present. Enough that my first job is to track down where she came from.

"*Your* first job is a bigger one. We've faced up frankly to what *we* don't know; here's somethin the swine Burdock doesn't know." He swayed across the room, felt under a picture hanging on the wall, manipulated a spring of some sort and opened a panel in what appeared to be an unbroken space of wall-paper. Behind the panel was a small safe, from which he extracted a piece of paper. "Have a look at that" he said, and handed Matt the leaflet pocketed by Fleischmann in the Brussels hotel. "That's the amusin bit of bumf I said poor old Flashy pinched on his last trip abroad."

Matt examined the paper carefully.

"No getting past that" he said at last.

Boreham's heave of triumph suggested a sea-lion trying to clamber on to a rock.

"You're right, me boy. The whole set-out in words of one syllable *plus* an address-book for the use of trusted clients. No one but Flashy and I knew he had it. As soon as he got to London, we put it in the safe. We had an inklin we might need it one day, and that day's today. Your job is to smell out all the places it mentions in this country, and not to be nabbed doin so. We made a start, Flashy and I, and here are such odds and ends as we collected. But the work's got to be done from A to Z this time. Copy 'em down and I'll put the real baby to bed again."

While Matt was doing this, Boreham continued:

"Another job for me is to keep a tag on Waters. I'll put a private detective on to him. You never know where any trail may lead. Naturally" he added "the cost of all this is on me."

They met early in the New Year to report progress. Matt's

descriptions of the various hotels and private houses, which personally or through the agency of ingenious and unobtrusive cronies he had reconnoitred, added up to the result expected.

"There's enough dirty water there to sink a battleship" declared Boreham with grim satisfaction. "When the reservoir's full and we open the sluice—swish goes Mr Bloody Burdock for many a long year!

"Now for my little games. First, Miss Lottie Heape. I've seen that young lady four times in my life. The fourth was just after Flashy's death; the third was the night the poor chap and I fixed his visit to Crocker; the second was at dinner, also in Flashy's house; *the first was in a pub in the Strand*, where—as they say—we crossed eyes for a moment, but neither met nor spoke. Lucky I've a good memory, both for names and faces, and that first time has done the trick. She was with a Jew-boy who's rather a pal of mine, and as I wanted a few words with him in private, I took him to one side. Casually I asked about the girl, and he said her name was Tremaine, that she was a dancer or somethin, and was stayin with his mother. Not so very long after I am introduced to her by Flashy, and her name is Lottie Heape. Same girl, though. Not a doubt of it. So while you've been nosin out jolly old Banjo's nanny-cribs, I nosed out my pretty little pal and asked some questions. He didn't know much—hadn't seen the girl since she decamped from his mother's house not long after that night in the pub. (She seems to make a speciality of runnin away.) But one thing he remembered—that when he left me and went back to her in the pub, she was talkin to a feller called Slode, and that they shut up quickly as he got near and Slode vamoosed. He told me a bit about Slode, who seems to be an out-size stinker, and I wouldn't be surprised if he had been the bridge between Miss Heape and Flashy. In that case he'll likely have been the bridge also between Flashy's secrets and whoever wanted to know em."

"What's become of the girl?" Matt asked.

"There you have me—and force me to confess into the bargain that me kind heart made a fool of me. I'd liked the

kid well enough the two times I saw her while Flashy was
alive, and he was nuts on her; so when the poor chap was
killed, I thought that for his sake I'd give an eye to her.
The manservant came to my office the day after the murder
and said the girl was still in the house. So I went up there
with the bobbies; and on the way told em Flashy's bit of
stuff was still on the spot, and that I would find her somewhere to go and see she had money. And then—here, as it
has turned out, I was too soft—I gave her a different name.
I thought she ought to have a chance to get away and start
afresh; and with those fellows on her tail she would never
be free of a crime about which she knew nothin. That's
what I thought at the time. Not so sure now. Damn silly
of me, of course. Still, there it is. Where she is or what
she calls herself, I've no idea. Fortunately she'd be no good
to us in this immediate job of cuttin Banjo's braces. More
to the point is Mr Waters. He's small fry, but he's served
one good purpose. He's led us to their committee room,
and with any luck, when we're ready, we'll nab the lot. So
now for the plan of campaign. . . ."

One of the first of the major engagements in the War
for London Purity which was fought during 1870 was the
implementing of this very campaign. Fleischmann's avengers
were lucky in that they happened on a moment when Authority
was peculiarly receptive. Two years earlier, two years later,
there would have been obstruction, tergiversation, timidity
disguised as bellicosity in yards of bright red tape; but at
this precise juncture orders had gone out to clean up the
city—orders which for once meant what they said. There
were simultaneous raids on the various establishments formerly
operated as Homes from Home; which raids, having been
totally unexpected (for when Waters had told Crocker that
the game was nearly up and exposure on its way, he had been
bluffing, in order to frighten his victim the more), resulted
in the capture of ample evidence connecting the organisation
with Burdock and his principal associates. They were arrested
before they had time to escape, in the handsome City offices

where their lawful, if predatory, businesses were transacted. Banjo was returned to Australia with thanks, and suitably dealt with by his compatriots; the others were sentenced in proportion to their crimes. Among them was Mr Malcolm Sneade who, eager to hitch his waggon to a radiant star, had unwisely chosen Lucifer.

With what Boreham had called the "Committee room" the attackers were less fortunate. As fry goes Mr Waters may have been small, but he was also spry. He spotted his shadow after a few days, reported to headquarters that he was being followed, and was instructed to lay a false trail. When, therefore, the police closed in on the obscure tavern which had been chosen to masquerade as the meeting-place of the active members of the gang, they found nothing and nobody, because there was not anybody or anything to find.

That a private detective was shadowing Waters had been instantly recognised as a move by Fleischmann's friends, and countered accordingly. But for the seizure by the police of their secret houses, the Burdockites were wholly unprepared, because they had no suspicion that the address-list was in the hands of their enemies. This address-list had been compiled, as Boreham guessed, for the use of dependable clients. But there were certain features of the Banjo organisation which were secret even from the most sympathetic customers; and among them were the Slode incubator in Larne Circle and the channels through which the merchandise passed from there to the market. These, therefore, were not recorded in the leaflet and remained undiscovered and undisturbed.

All of which is preliminary to Matt Merton's rise in the world of journalism. During the period of his private investigation into Homes from Home he had kept careful notes, and, by the time the snares were laid and ready, had written his material into a piece of front-rank sensationalism. On the morning of the evening appointed for police-action, he asked to see the editor of *Diogenes*, and after a few words of explanation, handed over his manuscript with the request that it be read then and there. The editor raised humorous eyebrows at the young man's audacity, but liking the look of him, glanced at the first sheet. He neither spoke nor looked up until he had read straight through to the end. Then he smiled at Matt and said:

"That's first-rate stuff, Mr Merton. The best thing of its kind I've ever had offered to me. I suppose it's true?"

"It's true all right" replied Matt. "I couldn't have invented a quarter of it."

"Suppose I doubted it being true—I don't say I do, but suppose I did—could you convince me that all this has really been going on, and that it's break-up day tomorrow?"

"No, sir. Frankly I couldn't. The story is absolutely secret. It must be, or the birds will fly. I came to you because your paper has courage and you have the reputation of an honourable man. I give you my word that I have written nothing there which I have not either seen myself or know for certain to be just so; but beyond that I cannot offer any proof—until tomorrow, when proof won't be needed."

The editor pinched his lower lip, as he turned over the pages of the manuscript once more.

"I'll be ruined if it's a wrong-un, you know", he said cocking an eye at Matt. "Was it *Sporting Life* you said you wrote for?"

Matt smiled and shook his head. "It's not that at all, sir. I swear it isn't. But I do write for *Sporting Life*. . . . Till I get something better" he added.

After another pause for reflection the editor flicked the papers back on to his desk, gave them a sharp slap with an open hand, and said:

"I'll risk it. It's too big a chance to miss, though I shan't sleep a wink till tomorrow night." He rang a bell and a middle-aged clerk came into the room.

"Grayson, this is the lead for the number now at press. It is highly confidential and should be comped, proofed and corrected in the small room. No one is to see it except the section who handle the secret stuff. I will attend to the make-up myself. Tell Hinkins to prepare for double the usual printing number."

AT THE FIRST EXAMINATION

AT SUBSEQUENT EXAMINATIONS

Next day *Diogenes* left its competitors at the post. The scandal of Homes from Home as exposed by "Our Special Commissioner" swept the town. Three months later Matt was invited to join the paper's staff, and became M. M. He would chuckle sometimes at his own foresight in manœuvring the police (without seeming to do so) to plan their raids for the night before *Diogenes*' publishing-day.

(ii) APRIL-MAY 1870

Clean-ups can scour both ways—as Freddie Boreham, whose personal position *vis-à-vis* the moralists was not unassailable, learnt to his cost. He had won his victory over Burdock, and put an emphatic "Paid" to the vengeance-account which had been owing since his partner's death. But although the bosses among his enemies had been downed for years to come, many of the hirelings who had worked for them, thanks to the perspicacity of the despised Waters, were still at large. These men—and they were as pretty a collection of ruffians as could well be imagined—knew nothing of Matt Merton. Before the volcano erupted they had never heard his name; after it had done so, he receded into closely guarded anonymity. Banjo's henchmen were, however, fully aware of the part Boreham had played in their employer's downfall, and with malevolent resource devised their Day of Reckoning.

At the end of April, in the year 1870, began the hearing of one of the most extraordinary cases of the Victorian era. The clean-up, after its flying start, was well away.

Two young men, Ernest Boulton aged twenty-two and Frederick William Park aged twenty-three, were charged at Bow Street with frequenting the Strand Theatre with intent to commit a felony. When arrested they were "in drag" (that is to say wearing women's clothes), and at their first Examination appeared in the dock thus costumed. Among their intimates Boulton was known as "Stella" and Park as

"Fanny Winifred". Both had a liking for theatricals, and played female parts with zest and talent.

The phrasing of the charge was, of course, a piece of formal discretion. As the Examinations proceeded, it became evident that the "felony" of which they were accused was of the gravest nature, and involved a large number of persons who over a period of two or three years had associated with them. Testimony was given as to their frequenting the Burlington Arcade, now in male, now in female dress, where they mingled amicably with the genuine young women who made the Arcade their beat; as to their behaviour at a ball at Haxell's Hotel at which many of the men present, including the host, were dressed as girls; as to their comings and goings to and from their lodgings, where they generally wore men's clothes until late afternoon, then changed and went out, returning at all hours usually accompanied by gentlemen; as to the extraordinary quantity and variety of scents, creams, aids to beauty, dresses, furs, high-laced boots, dancing-shoes, corsets, lingerie and miscellaneous feminine fripperies, discovered by the police in their rooms.

It was an amazing case, which caused great public excitement, and provided disreputable pamphlet and broadsheet printers with material after their own hearts. Not the least sensational passages related to the intimacy of Stella with a man of title. It was deposed that for a time Stella lived with his lordship as his wife, wore a wedding-ring, used engraved visiting-cards and had a hairdresser call every morning to do her hair. During the hearing the peer was too ill to be called, and with his sudden death a month after the verdict, the possibility of further probing into the strange relationship was ended.

But in the course of the last Examination but one, another man of title became involved in the affair, although his name was never mentioned. A certain Francis Snaith was put into the witness-box. He was in business in the City, and told an extraordinary story of a chance meeting with Boulton, whom he alleged he had never seen before, at Izants in Bucklersbury. The lad was in company with "Mr Roberts of Moorgate Street and a nobleman." The four of them adjourned to offices in Gresham Street. There they drank champagne, and got merry and playful. Stella was "in drag" and behaved, according to Snaith, exactly as a fast girl out for a bit of fun would behave. The horseplay became more and more extravagant, and the witness' account of how the afternoon ended was heard after the court had been cleared and was not reported.

"The nobleman" was Freddie Boreham, and Messrs Snaith and Roberts, acting under instructions, had set out to trap him. It is true that Snaith's evidence was badly mauled and had little effect on the jury, who on May 15 found the defendants Not Guilty on all counts. But mud can be made to stick, and the identity of the "nobleman" soon went the rounds of clubland. The widespread incredulity with which the verdict was received (despite a Te Deum intoned by *The Times* in praise of national morals now satisfactorily vindicated) deepened the stain set upon all concerned. Indeed, had Boulton and Park been found guilty, general opinion might well have considered honour satisfied and the affair better forgotten; but an acquittal, in the teeth of what had been made public, was such an outrage on commonsense that the case rankled and festered into malevolent prejudice against individuals officially exonerated. So the official zeal for Public Morals, which had helped poor Freddie against Homes from Home, turned like a boomerang and hit him in the eye. In business his coolness and acumen belied his appearance of Falstaffian dissipation; but in his personal pleasures he was intemperate and foolhardy, with a genial shamelessness which might have got by a century earlier, but could only bring disaster—if anyone desired it to do so— under a régime of surface decorum, such as governed the polite society of mid-Victorian London. Boreham was finished by the affair of Boulton and Park. His appearances in this story have shown only the jungle side of his existence; but in those days a man of family and wealth could live two parallel and contrasted lives (provided they were not allowed to overlap), and Lord Frederick Boreham had been as much a figure at the dinners and soirées of Belgravia and Mayfair, as was Fat Freddie at the Crown and Anchor or haunting the purlieus of the City at grips with other cut-throat money-spinners.

Now both arenas were closed to him. Belgravia was locked and bolted; and without the prestige of Belgravia behind him, he was lamed for life as an active competitor in the race for wealth. He might, of course, have turned to outright banditry and, pitting his wits against the law, have struggled on for a few adventurous years. But he was not by nature a crook. He was a filibuster; and financial filibustery requires some basis of good repute, which last he no longer possessed.

It was his further misfortune that, once seen, he could never be forgotten. A man of nondescript appearance might have faded from public view for a while, and then slowly have resumed his former rôle of commonplace fragment in a general human background, indistinguishable from a hundred others. But Freddie Boreham was a marked man, physically as well as morally. He made no attempt to outstare catastrophe, but withdrew to Brussels and was ultimately lost sight of altogether.

(iii) NOVEMBER 1878

Matt Merton, still "Special Commissioner" to *Diogenes*, came out into the dusk of Fleet Street late on a foggy afternoon in November 1878. He wore a handsome ulster of excellent material, a billycock hat whose nap was sleek and new, and square-toed shining boots such as only Dover Street produced. He looked, in short, an exceedingly prosperous person; and so he was. His success was well deserved, and he had worked hard for it. In his middle forties, he was broader and thicker and shaggier than when we last saw him; but he was not flabby, and success, so far from tempting him to rest on his laurels, had given him an energy of movement and of mind which, except in moments of crisis, had not distinguished him in earlier years.

One particular episode of these busy successful years belongs to this story.

Returning home to his lodgings (at that time still the two untidy rooms in Adam Street) some three years after the exposure of Burdock, Matt found a letter lying on the floor just across the threshold of his sitting-room. It had been brought by hand and pushed under the door. The envelope contained a single sheet of paper and a second smaller envelope, sealed down and enclosing a letter addressed to himself in the hand of Dr Meadows. The clergyman wrote:

> The bearer of this note is the son of poor Mr Crocker who committed suicide two or three years ago, and on whose behalf and at my request you kindly started the enquiries into the so-called Homes from Home, which led to the big scandal you remember better than anyone.
>
> It seems that the young man has for some little while been anxious to know more of the circumstances of his father's death. He has recently taken his degree, and is now in the interval between leaving the University and starting to earn a living by teaching. He consulted his mother, who died not long since, but she could not suggest any line of enquiry except an application to me. She found a letter or two of mine and recalled having heard her husband speak of me during the last weeks of his life.
>
> The boy seems a wholesome straightforward person, and it would be a kindness on your part to have a talk with him. Naturally I have said nothing about your real share in the business—merely that you had kindly helped me with certain items of information.

The single sheet, folded round this letter, was a civil request for an interview at Mr Merton's convenience, headed by the address of a scholastic agency and signed "Mervyn Crocker". "Must be the boy for whose sake old Paul took the sack" Matt said to himself. "I'd like to have a look at him."

The desired meeting took place a day or two later. Matt explained that he had not known the late Mr Crocker personally, but at Dr Meadows' request had investigated a suspicious Company, with which Mr Crocker had been involved in such a way as to cause him great distress of mind. What had occurred to drive the unfortunate man to take his own life Matt did not know, nor had he ever come across anyone who did. He showed Mervyn the last letter written by Crocker to Meadows, and said that from that point the problem of Homes from Home had ceased to be a matter of personal tragedy and became one which concerned Society as a whole. He implied that his own share in the examination and exposure of the Company's true nature had been quite a minor one, and referred his caller vaguely to a paper called *Diogenes*, in which, he seemed to remember, a long article dealing with the question had appeared at the date when the scandal broke.

In a fortnight's time young Crocker asked permission to call again and, when he appeared, said he had read everything he could find relating to the case, but was as far off as ever from understanding how his father had been involved.

"Can you tell me" he said "how thoroughly the persons responsible for this organisation were tracked down and punished?"

"Not with any certainty" replied Matt. "But I do know that most of the subordinates—those employed to do the dirty work—were never traced. Several of the big men at the top, who financed and organised the traffic, were identified and convicted; but the underlings laid a false trail and got away."

"And are still at work somewhere?"

Matt shrugged.

"I couldn't tell you. Very possibly; but hardly on any coherent plan. The running of such a complex affair as Homes from Home needs the sort of mind no common thug possesses. Why do you ask?"

The boy blushed in embarrassment and shuffled his feet.

"Just that, if one or two *were* to turn up again, I'd love to have a smack at them."

Matt laughed.

"Well said! And so you shall! Should any likely-looking gentleman of that persuasion cross my path again, I'll send you word by the electric telegraph."

Mervyn was perfectly serious.

"Is that a promise, Mr Merton?"

Matt held out his hand.

"A promise."

During his eight years with *Diogenes* Matt had conducted a number of "investigations", and with each one his touch had become firmer, his power of presentation more controlled and more compelling. The subjects treated had been very various. No one of them provoked the horrified excitement of the exposure of Homes from Home (that particular sensation was to remain unrivalled until in 1885 W. T. Stead and the *Pall Mall Gazette* took their lives in their hands and, touching off the dynamite of *The Maiden Tribute of Modern Babylon*, blew corruption, hypocrisy and complacent prudery sky-high) but each had meant toilsome collection of material, which involved acute discomfort and often grave personal risk, scrupulous testing of facts, and finally the close concentrated labour of writing a mass of detail into an ordered and well-proportioned report.

He had, for example, described the inarticulate sufferings of thousands of sweated seamstresses, and the lengths to which they were driven to keep themselves alive. He had forced on the attention of the comfortable public the methods of one of the worst pests which plagued the decent working-men of England—the tally-man or credit-draper, who, while husbands were at work, tempted silly wives with tawdry finery, asking in return no money, but merely the man's ostensible signature to a printed form, promising weekly payments to the tune of three or four times the value of the goods. He had gone the round in person of the lowest common lodging-houses of the town, and painted an appalling

313

picture of their filth and promiscuity and threat to public health—with men, women and children of all ages and kinds herded into a single kitchen, sleeping in packed rows on the floor, many with contagious diseases which next morning were carried away and spread in every quarter of London. He had taken his readers into certain City billiard rooms, past the well-dressed sharpers hanging about the door, through the divan where others and their intended dupes sat smoking and drinking, into the long room where the tables stood. There he put the flash mob through their paces, exposing one trick after another, until the nervous reader felt himself identical with the plucked gull creeping miserably away with empty pockets or, worse still, in debt to some rascal and his accomplices to the amount acknowledged on an inescapable I O U.

These and other pilgrimages were not only strenuous, they were also dangerous; and Matt had become an adept at disguises. He earned his bread by creating successive groups of ill-wishers; and plenty of embittered persons—out of a job or recently out of jail or both—would have been glad to know that the massive well-dressed figure now moving toward St Paul's was indeed the architect of their misfortunes.

Matt turned into Black Horse Court and soon reached the first of a series of great plate-glass windows, which broke the left-hand wall. Set in an ornate and freshly painted frame each window bore in large gold letters the words: THE MARIGOLD DIVAN AND GRILL. FULLY LICENSED. A main entrance, surmounted by a projecting canopy of wrought iron and glass, gave access to this imposing establishment; and as Matt let the swing-door puff-to behind him, a comfortable warmth, a hum of conversation and in the distance the chink of glass and pewter on polished wood or zinc, set up, as always, a glow of contentment which spread over his whole being.

The Marigold, no less than Matt, had gone up in the world. Toby Langrish had demonstrated that he possessed a genius for tavern-keeping and, once he had formed for himself a nucleus of goodwill, had never looked back.

Gradually he had enlarged the small and outwardly dingy pub of not so many years ago, taking in this house to the right, that to the left, extending inwards and upwards. Indeed the Marigold had now so far imposed itself, that locally "Black Horse Lane" (though it still survived in flaking black paint, high on the dingy brickwork of the corner house) had fallen into disuse. One said "Near the Marigold" or "You know, just opposite Toby's."

Matt passed through the divan to the main bar, which stood in a short stretch of wide corridor or hall-way linking the divan with the big grill-room beyond. At this hour the grill-room, though open (one could see the great fire glowing under the gridiron of sloping bars), was deserted; but several men were seated or standing at the bar, talking or laughing together and exchanging occasional jokes with two pretty barmaids. To the latter Matt touched his hat and was received with smiles. Greeting one or two of the men, he said to the nearest of the girls:

"Toby in?"

"Yes, Mr Merton, he's in the office."

And there sure enough, beyond a thick curtain which hung to the right of the bar-counter, in a small room with a desk, two or three chairs, a bright fire and a parrot in a cage, sat the proprietor of this most flourishing house of call, nowadays something more than plump, and his large face something swarthier than rosy, but with no dulling of the twinkle in his eye nor the shining dome of his bald head.

"Wotchere, Toby" said Matt.

"Evenin Mr Merton" said Toby.

They met so frequently, even if it were only to wave a hand, that the laconic greeting was standard form. Nor was the ritual over. A kettle sizzled on the hob, and the landlord, without saying another word, got a black bottle and two glasses from the wall-cupboard and a box of cheroots from the drawer of his desk. Mixing two toddies he handed one to his visitor and waved him to a chair and cigar. For a few minutes both smoked in silence, sipping at their drinks.

Then Toby said quietly:

"I thought you might look in about this time; and, as I've a bit o' news for you, I stayed in the office. Gladwin's back."

"Phew! Is he now? For better or for worse?"

Toby shook his head.

"For worse, I'm afraid. I ran into him purely by chance yesterday on the way home from the Oddfellows. Lodge-night you know. He was three sheets in the wind, if not four or five, and looked like nothing on earth. A wretched sight, Mr Merton. I brought him here by the little door and tried to get him to eat something. But he was almost too far gone to swallow."

"Dear, oh dear, I'm sorry to hear that. Did you get any sense out of him?"

"I don't know for 'sense', but he talked plenty. Doesn't seem to have cared for the great You Ess, though it wasn't easy to find out what he'd done with himself there."

"Broke?"

"I suspect so. The point didn't arise and I couldn't very well ask him outright; but we'll have to see what we can do with him, and I got him to promise to come round here this evening. You'll be dining?"

"Do I ever miss your steak and kidney, Toby, except under force majeure? Indeed I shall be dining!"

"Well, he *said* he'd be here about half-past eight."

"Right you are! I'll be back for food about seven. Ta-ta."

And he made his way to the private hotel in Norfolk Street where, still a bachelor but now one able to pick and choose, he had comfortable rooms with excellent service and no responsibilities.

While he changed his clothes he pondered with some concern the fact of Gladwin's reappearance in London.

"Poor old chap" he thought. "He's been his own worst enemy so long now, that maybe he just can't make peace with himself. Still, we must see what we can do."

(i) MARCH 1869

When Paul Gladwin reached London after his dismissal from Lashwater Park in March 1869, he went straight to Matt Merton's rooms in Adam Street, Adelphi.

He had left Mr Crocker's house early in the morning, after a night spent in desultory bouts of packing interspersed with periods of moody indignation, and had seen no one of the family again. An envelope, as promised, lay on the hall chest, and inside it were a month's pay and five five-pound notes. It never occurred to him to do other than accept this gift of money from the man who had grievously misjudged him. He was no striker of attitudes in any circumstances; and less so than ever at the present crisis, because his anger was principally directed against Mr Crocker who should suitably be made to pay for his injustice. The degree to which Lottie Heape had established an ascendancy over him was shown by his refusal, even to himself, to condemn her for her treachery. The poor child had been frightened, and in a moment of panic had bolted to covert without a thought of the consequences to any but herself. The person really to blame was Crocker, who should have seen the absurdity of a story told by a terrified young girl caught out in a clandestine and precocious love-affair. He should have pretended to accept it, and then done nothing until he had privately examined the matter from every aspect.

Each time that Paul reached this point in his repeated mulling-over of the disaster which had overtaken him, he was forced in all fairness to ask himself whether, if Crocker had behaved thus correctly, he would not inevitably have found out the truth. "You acted as you did" said one Paul to the other "in order to shield Mervyn. Now you wish

Mervyn's father had acted in such a way as to ensure sooner or later the boy's exposure. Don't be a fool." Not caring to confront this awkward obstacle, he would go back to the beginning again; re-live each stage of the mounting catastrophe; wonder whether at any one stage he should or could have acted differently; and so gradually work himself up into a fresh fever of resentment against Crocker, only to collapse once more before the logical consequences of what he blamed Crocker for not doing.

Matt was out when the refugee arrived, and was surprised, on his return about noon, to find Gladwin on the landing, unshaven and untidy, propped against the locked door of his sitting-room and fast asleep. The visitor's hat had fallen off, and he was snoring in a desolate manner, with a small portmanteau wedged under his knees.

Roused, dusted down, settled in a comfortable chair and given a hunk of bread and cheese and some beer, Paul gave a severely condensed account of what had driven him from Lashwater. He had been accused of assaulting a young maidservant, had been too proud to deny so ridiculous a charge, had been sacked, and had left the house without another word to his employers. He mentioned no names and Matt asked for none, though the story was so pathetically inadequate that obviously, if it were true, its whole significance lay in the personalities involved. Instead he said drily:

"And *did* you rape the kid?"

Paul was furious.

"How dare you!" he gasped. "Haven't I just told you I didn't?"

"No, my dear chap. You merely said you were too proud to deny it. Not necessarily the same thing; indeed hardly ever the same thing. But I now conclude you did not, which may or may not have been a pity—"

"Look here, Matt. If you are going to be cynical and sneering about this, I'll be off. I came to see you because I thought you were a friend and would be sorry for what's happened. . . ."

"I *am* sorry, my poor fathead, that you've lost a good job;

318

but so far as I am allowed to understand *why* you've lost it, it is because on general principles you disapprove of assaulting maidservants. That doesn't make sense. Therefore, either you *did* assault the girl and were sacked, or something happened you don't want to tell me. All right; I won't force your confidence; but I had to find out which of the two it was. Enough of that. The point now at issue is 'what next'? How are the dibs?"

"Plenty for the time being. I've been saving for long enough—nothing to spend money on down there—and the old swine slung me a pony as a good-bye kiss. To salve his conscience I suppose."

Matt looked curiously at the friend he had seen only intermittently of recent years. The funny old fellow had learned to be angry, anyway, if only with a transient uncertain anger like the flames of coal-gas which flicker and die above a sullen fire. Physically, also, he was twice the man he had been. But the fundamental timidity, the desire to swerve away from unpleasant facts were still there. Why else this touchiness and these evasions? Oh, well; he would hear the story in due course. It did not particularly matter now.

"There's nothing I know of, just at this moment" he said. "But then I haven't been on the look-out. I'll make a few enquiries. The immediate job is to get you a proper meal and find some sort of a room. You're welcome to doss on the couch here for as long as you want; but it's not a bed of roses and I expect you've got a heap of stuff to come up after—how many years?"

Paul shrugged.

"Not so much. Books mostly and scribblings. I packed it all, and left a note for it to come by train to the Parcel Office. It can lie there till I'm fixed. You're a good sort, Matt, to do all this for me, and I'm sorry I flew out at you."

"Lor bless you" said Matt "that's all right! I like it. Now do you have a shave and a wash and a clean-up generally, and we'll go and get some bub and grub, pay a call on old Toby, and start a hunt for diggings."

* * * * *

319

Percy Clegg—the "son" of Clegg and Son, Tailors and Outfitters, Shoreditch—was a young man of enterprise and ambition. He had the appearance of a coarse-grained lout—and so, under certain provocations, he was. But in his make-up was a flair for business of a quality unusual in one of his type. Due to inherit a concern built up by the industry and integrity of his father, he combined a respect for parental achievement with an urge to modernise the methods of salesmanship and generally to put the firm on the map of Tailordom in letters as large as possible. A couple of years in the United States had made him a worshipper of "hustle", and when he returned to London and was given charge of the various outward manifestations of Clegg and Son—from press, catalogue and out-of-door advertising to literal window-dressing—he lost no time in thrusting his ideas of publicity on the citizens of the metropolis.

A certain degree of unconventionality in self-advertisement was traditional in the tailoring trade. Messrs Moses of Aldgate, for example, had secured the outside back covers of several part-issues of popular new novels between 1849 and 1860, and drafted "copy" whose sprightliness exceeded its syntax. They had a taste for humorous verse with punning titles ("Frankly and Fairly" was the ingenious heading of doggerel supplied for the part-issue of *Frank Fairlegh* by Smedley), and were certainly years ahead of their time in devising lay-outs which kept the firm's name, occupation and price-lists well in the background, while featuring jingles and witticisms which did not at first glance look like advertisements at all. Then in the late 'sixties Hatman & Co. of Ludgate Hill began to advertise widely in periodicals of various kinds. They were less sportive than Moses, heading their copy with the ambiguous and disputable slogan: ADORNMENT OF THE HUMAN FIGURE DESIRED BY ALL, and presenting a cut, three inches high, of two stuffed gentlemen wearing silk hats and single- and double-breasted Chesterfields. But the principle was the same; and there was no blinking the fact that competitive tailoring was out and about.

Percy Clegg studied the efforts of his rivals and determined

go one better. These Jew-boys, he said to himself, shall
ot have everything their own way. Clegg of Shoreditch
ere Cockney to the core, and if Cockney tailoring couldn't
ut-advertise a gang of sheeney sweat-shops it was a pity.
o he decided to issue a magazine—or rather a House-Organ
hich might be mistaken for a magazine, though supplied
ratis—and laboured during the autumn of 1868 to realise
is plan.

Percy had energy and dogged self-confidence. He knew
at the clothes made by his father's firm were good clothes;
ut he knew also that quality, if it is to prevail, must beat
oddy at its own game. Hence his scheme for a magazine,
hich would be costly to produce and distribute but, if
roperly designed, could not fail to attract attention. His
spiration was a shrewd one, but his capacity as writer and
ditor inadequate. He struggled along, and by sheer per-
verance produced a slim volume bound in limp cloth and
alled *Our Journal*. It was neat in appearance, and had a
rge folding lithographic plate depicting no fewer than
wenty-five styles of suit, overcoat and jacket for men and
ouths. But textually it was little more than a glorified price-
st and the first paragraph of the two-page editorial address
he spelling corrected before printing by the stationer next
oor) showed that composition was not up Percy's street:

> "In the small space which the circumscribed limit of these
> pages afford for a few observations, we shall possibly expose
> ourselves to a charge of egotistical pride by some of our
> readers, while by others our remarks may be deemed
> unnecessarily diffusive and elaborate,—but we trust there
> will be none who deny us the credit of truthfulness, sincerity
> and earnestness."

The production made little impression on the public, and
Clegg Senior shook his head over what, in his old-fashioned
yes, had been sheer waste of money. But Percy stuck to
is guns. The idea was a good one. The trouble was that it
ad been badly carried out. And, being naturally as honest
vith himself as the firm had always been with their customers,

he admitted frankly that he had bungled the job. "I'll fin
someone who knows ow to do it" he said.

To a modest degree an amateur of the Fancy, Percy Cleg
had a ringside acquaintance with Matt Merton; and runnin
into him one evening in April enquired after a possibl
"editor" of a Clegg house-organ. Matt promised to bear th
matter in mind, and did so with such fidelity that the ver
next day he sought out Paul, who had now for three month
occupied what he insisted was a clean and adequate room i
the equivocal purlieus of Catherine Street. ("I say, old boy
Matt had protested. "*Must* you live in Pussy Lane? You'
be awake half the night with caterwaulings, and anythin
filchable will be gone in a flash." Paul had laughed. "No
being a pretty girl or a toff or a pinch-bottom, they'll leav
me alone and I them. The place is cheap and will get an
sun there is and I like to be able to run into Somerset Hous
and check up on my rich aunts when they peg out. Beside
it's near enough Adam Street for me to keep a fatherly ey
on you.")

This April morning (it was about eleven o'clock) Paul wa
discovered in a dressing-gown, cooking a herring in a frying
pan over a small oil-stove.

"Lazy devil" said Matt. "I've been up for hours."

"More fool you, old fellow, for being a wage-slave
Literary chaps like me keep hours suitable to genius.
finished a story at four a.m. True the lady in the roor
opposite had been a little intemperate and disturbed me onc
or twice, so that the plot is a bit ragged; but it's not so bad
Like to read it?"

"Not a bit. I've found a job for you and we're going t
nail it down forthwith. Get dressed at once. I'll have deal
with this nasty-looking fish by the time you're ready."

In due course, still grumbling over his hurried breakfast
Paul was dragged to Shoreditch, introduced to Percy Clegg
and engaged on a trial basis to produce a scheme for a secon
and more ambitious volume which, to the glory of Clegg &
Son, should enchant the reading public. Mr Clegg wa
emphatic that the thing was not to be rushed. It must b

eally good and really original. There must not be a second
alse start. As his visitors took their leave, he hinted that
 success in this particular assignment might mean a full-
ime job as copy-writer in general.

It was almost at this moment that Matt Merton received
rom Mr Meadows on behalf of Mr Crocker the urgent
nessage begging that Paul Gladwin should return to Lash-
vater. "I wronged the young man" Crocker had written
'and wish not only to beg his pardon, but to ensure for him
 livelihood."

Matt pondered this curious summons for a day or two.
'I must tell him of it" he reflected "but he'll really have to
ell *me* what happened."

Sitting with Paul that evening he pulled Meadows' letter
rom his pocket and handed it over.

"Read that."

Paul did so, and as he read his face flushed with annoyance.

"Certainly not" he snapped, handing the letter back.
'Not for any consideration whatsoever will I go back to a
place where I was so treated."

"Paul, you'll have to tell me about it" said Matt gently.

The other did not reply immediately. He sat and stared
t the floor, his lips working, his cheeks and forehead still
ot with his vehemence. At last:

"Only this much. The son of the house had been fooling
bout with this kid—she *was* just a kid—and by a queer
oincidence I was put in the position of seeming to be the
hap involved. I was fond of the boy; there'd have been
ell to pay if the truth came out, for the Crockers are strait-
aced and would have believed the lad on the brink of per-
lition. So I just didn't deny it. That's all."

It must be remembered that Matt's consciousness of Lottie
Jeape was of the slightest. He had never set eyes on her
ince the time of the rescue; and after the early days of her
ojourn as a child in one of the cottages on Crocker's land,
Paul's occasional letters from Lashwater had hardly mentioned
er name. Not unnaturally, therefore, he gave no thought to

the identity of the young girl involved in this trouble, but concentrated on the case as it concerned his friend.

He found himself in some embarrassment. "That's all" Paul had said. If that were indeed all, the passionate refusal even to consider reinstatement was ridiculous. If Crocker had merely accused Gladwin on circumstantial evidence and, the charge not being denied, had dismissed him, and if now, further evidence having come to light, he wished to reverse the verdict and make a handsome and concrete apology, the obvious course was to make it easy for him to do so. Matt had promised not to ask unwelcome questions; but the situation bothered him, and he fidgeted in uneasy silence under the suspicious eyes of his still simmering companion, who broke out aggressively:

"What's the matter now? Surely it's obvious that I can't go back and have everyone on the place nudging one another and pointing at me as the brute who attacked a little girl under his employer's very roof? Crocker may wish to apologise and all that; but you can't make people forget a charge of the kind just by reversing it three months later."

So "everyone on the place" knew about it, said Matt to himself. The clue to the whole affair is missing. There's nothing more to be done.

"Sorry, old chap" he said aloud. "You know best, of course, and it's your business not mine. Shall we therefore pursue Mr Clegg's offer?"

This conversation—or rather this avoidance of conversation —had the effect of putting an embargo on Lashwater and on all connected with it as a permissible topic between Merton and Gladwin. The former tipped Toby Langrish the wink that the subject was taboo, and the three of them entered upon one of those absurd and unspoken conventions to dodge a certain subject which, if they go on long enough, become second nature. So established after six months had this system of mutual evasion become, that when for several days the newspapers carried facts and theories regarding the Crocker suicide, not a word was said in Paul's presence by

ither of the other two. Only when Matt and Toby were
lone was there mention of the tragedy or speculation as to
s cause.

Then came Matt's personal and intimate involvement with
he background of the affair, first on behalf of Meadows, then
s colleague of Lord Frederick Boreham. Immediately, from
he moment when he first learnt the astounding fact that
Fleischmann's girl and the child sent to refuge at Lashwater
were one and the same person, instinct told him that here,
very possibly, was the key to the mystery of Paul's dismissal.
But once again nothing was said to, or in front of, him.
Only when Matt and Toby were alone did they agree to keep
Miss Lottie Heape safely at the back of their minds.

"She sounds the sort that may crop up again in connection
with almost anything" said Matt.

"Strike me pink she does" agreed Toby "and the rummier
he better."

(ii) APRIL 1869-MAY 1875

After fifteen months of preparation and experiment Paul's
first venture appeared, and for the next five years he produced
each year a "Winter Magazine" and a "Summer Journal" for
the firm of Clegg. His aim from the first was to achieve
something as nearly as possible on the lines of the popular
"Annuals" and "Summer Numbers" issued by *Belgravia*,
London Society, *St James's Magazine*, and many other periodicals,
as well as by a few book-publishers such as Routledge,
Tinsley and Beeton.

Percy Clegg's limp cloth cover was substituted by paper
wrappers printed in bright colours and re-designed for each
issue in the clamorous (and by the standards of other periods
frankly hideous) style fashionable in the 'seventies. Percy
Clegg's carefully modest title was dropped in favour of
allusive and alliterative facetiae, which must have mortified
the soul of the precursive but out-distanced Moses. Thus in
the autumn of 1870 Paul led off with *Fun and Fashion*; con-

tinued the following summer with *Smiles and Styles*; passed
on to *Wit and Wear*, to *Novelettes and Novelties*, to *Merriment
and Modes*, to *Drollery and Dress*, to *Attire and Attraction*. In
the summer of 1874 he became a little repetitive and sank to
Stories and Styles, but pulled up in the winter with *Jokes and
Jackets*. Summer 1875 he decided to take a risk. A tentative
suggestion of *Toggery and Cleggery* having been abruptly
negatived, he cast about for something a shade provocative
but impersonal. He found it. The new number should be
called *Teasers and Trousers*, and textually should strike a
mildly daring note. But that number was never published.

In contents this series of pioneer experiments in sartorial
publicity resembled the regulation Annuals as closely as did
their format and appearance. There was of course no star-
novelist to dominate the cover—no Miss Braddon, no Helen
Mathers, no Mrs Riddell, no B. L. Farjeon; but on the level
of semi-amateur story-tellers, versifiers, cartoonists and table-
talkers—above which Paul, even had he the money to pay
for headline stuff, would have been unable to aspire—Clegg's
magazines were content to strive after variety and tolerable
competence. Occasionally a name known even beyond the
bar-parlours of Fleet Street made its appearance. The celebrated cartoonist Matt Morgan, for example, out of the kindness of his heart, provided a story and a drawing for the
second issue, and the same number had a restrained fragment
of Bracebridge Hemyng. Charles H. Ross appeared in *Drollery
and Dress* and E. L. Blanchard a half-year later. But these were
exceptional cases, and the most Paul could hope for was to
maintain a passable mediocrity. Admittedly he was sometimes forced to include very poor material indeed (every now
and again Percy Clegg himself produced a contribution which
could hardly be rejected), but the audience to whom the issues
were addressed were more critical of clothes than of literature.
They took their reading matter as they found it, provided the
Yachting Suit (at 47/-), the Imperial Suit (at 84/-), the Sealskin
Vest (golden seal at 60/-) or the Hessian Suit for little Jackie
eight years of age (at 40/-) were as described and up to Clegg
standards.

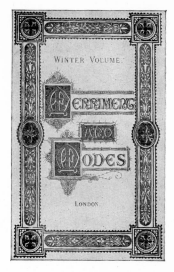

Paul became a regular member of the firm's publicity department at an early stage of his connection with it. He was an orderly, conscientious and reliable worker who kept himself to his job, created no jealousies, was pleasant with everyone and intimate with none.

"Oh yes" Percy Clegg would say "Gladwin's O.K. Useter ift the elbow, they tell me, at one time; but I've never seen a sign of it. Everyone likes im—or rather no one *dis*likes im. Or *knows* im, if it comes to that. Well, that's is affair, and I don't mind. I could do with arf a dozen more like im, noll take care o' my business and mind their own."

So the months and years passed in tranquil routine. When Matt Merton made his sudden reputation, became a person of means and moved into Norfolk Street, Paul was careful to make no change in his relationship with his friend. He neither forced his company on the great man nor kept aloof as though in diffidence. Between him and Matt and Toby Langrish the relationship was singular. The trio met more or less regularly; but whereas Matt and Toby (who met more frequently still) were genuine intimates, Paul's presence set the three of them on a level of incurious friendliness. He would talk of his work, but never of his private affairs. If he had successes, he never spoke of them; if he had troubles, he kept them to himself. Nevertheless he appeared to be happy in his remote inexigent way, and Matt gradually relaxed the vigilance with which unostentatiously he had from the first watched over his weak and wayward friend. It looked as though old Paul were on an even keel at last.

(i) OCTOBER-NOVEMBER 1869

WHEN—on that dreadful morning in October 1869 which brought the news of Fleischmann's murder—Jackie Sanderson had left her, Lottie remained in the drawing-room of Number Four Alpha Place, half on the alert for the police invasion and the catechism which were sure to come, half-relapsed into the slough of bitter self-reproach from which her friend's visit had summoned her. She gave no further thought to the future. Partly she was confident of her power to master any event which might arise; mainly she was possessed and tortured by the present and the immediate past.

In due course Davies returned. He had found Lord Frederick Boreham, who intended to call on Miss Heape at the first opportunity. The police had taken possession at the Cannon Street Hotel, and Davies had been careful not to be seen by them or to betray to the hotel staff his connection with the murdered man. Mrs Davies and Annie had accompanied him into the drawing-room, and stood sullenly silent while he made his report. Then the former said, in her tight toneless voice:

"And now, madam, we are leaving this house—all three of us—*when we have been paid*."

Lottie neither moved nor spoke. She remained sitting on the edge of an arm-chair, her eyes on the carpet. She seemed not to have heard what Mrs Davies said, and the woman repeated sharply:

"When we have been paid", adding "and look sharp about it!"

Slowly Lottie settled herself into the depths of the chair, clasped her hands behind her head, crossed her legs and looked contemptuously at the housekeeper.

"Paid for what? For running away?"

She had been thinking rapidly. Far better get this riff-raff out of the house. Her own forlorn situation would seem the more pitiful, were she discovered here alone and deserted; also (who could say?) it might be convenient to have further scapegoats. She knew well enough the basis of Mrs Davies' demand; and that if the couple denounced her as having on one occasion received a visitor in Fleischmann's absence, she might be involved in troublesome questioning, which could lead nowhere but would delay her escape from this memory-haunted place. At the same time she also knew the people with whom she had to deal. Annie was just a stupid lump; Davies, behind his impressive manner, was a coward; only Mrs Davies had to be reckoned with. Lottie decided, in those few moments of apparent unawareness, to make the woman lose her temper and then to bluff her.

Her deliberately insolent response to the housekeeper's demand achieved its purpose. Mrs Davies gave a gasp, drew back her lips so fiercely that they went white against her discoloured teeth, and trembling with passion burst out:

"Paid *to* run away, more nearly—and at double the rate intended, now you choose to be fresh! Mind your p's and q's, my saucy little trollop, or you'll find yourself somewhere money can't buy you outuv! You'll shell out fifty quid apiece to me and Davies and twenty-five to Annie here—and cash on the nail too—or your goins-on will come to the ears of them as'll soon find out what's what."

Lottie eyed the woman steadily during this tirade, a scornful little smile on her lips.

"Don't howl, Mrs Davies" she said superciliously. "You aren't a hyena, though you look uncommonly like one. So unless you precious trio of 'faithful servants' get your palms greased, you'll fake up some story about me? Right; go ahead! I don't have to fake stories about you, and we'll see who's believed. You got in first with poor Miss Melnotte once, but you won't do it again—that I promise you. When you were fool enough to refuse to talk about her to me, I made it my business to find out for myself, for I guessed

L*   329

there was her side to the story and that if ever you and I had differences . . . Well, I'm all primed ready. Now skip. I give you quarter of an hour to get out of here and never come back."

Mrs Davies was too staggered to make an immediate reply. She stood there with her mouth opening and shutting, while patches of angry red blotched her pasty cheeks. Suddenly Davies reached out and caught her by the wrist.

"Hold yer tongue, you!" he said savagely. "We're gettin out here and now. Go and pack the portmanteau, and not another sound or I'll slog you one you won't forget!" As his wife, with a single convulsive sob, almost ran from the room followed by Annie, he turned deferentially to Lottie, and resuming the voice and accent of a trained man-servant said:

"I trust, madam, you will forgive Mrs Davies' rudeness. She is—we both are—greatly upset over this terrible affair and for a moment she lost control. With your permission I will take her at once to some relatives, leaving the girl here. I will then return, and Annie and I will remain in the house so long as you wish us to do so. It is not fitting that you should be here alone; and after working for the late master for a few years we have naturally a good deal to get together for removal."

Lottie replied immediately.

"Thank you, Davies; but for the present I prefer to be alone. Take Mrs Davies away, as you suggest, and stay away—for tonight at any rate. I can manage for myself and need time to realise what has happened. If you care to return alone tomorrow to start your packing, I have no objection. Indeed I should be glad. I should not like us to separate on bad terms, and I know Mr Fleischmann would wish you to have some parting gift. Annie can please herself whether to go or stay. You will understand me when I say that I do not want to see Mrs Davies again."

The man bowed and withdrew. The brief interlude of artificial formality, carried through on both sides with due solemnity and of set purpose, was over.

Ten minutes later she heard the back-door close and the sound of retreating footsteps on the path which ran down to the road along one side of the little front-garden. The house was perfectly quiet. Whether Annie were still downstairs, she neither knew nor cared. Lying back in her chair she began once more to brood over her position.

This time her preoccupation was with the present. She chuckled inwardly at the success of her gamble on Coralie. That had been a bow at a venture, and no mistake! And how fortunate that she had asked Jackie for the surname! Clearly there had been more to the poor girl's undoing than refusal to pay blackmail after a little flutter on the side. She knew more about the Davieses than was healthy, and betrayal was her punishment. "Oh, well" said Lottie to herself, "she did the trick for me anyway."

She remembered her expressed intention of going through the papers in the little study, but now decided to do nothing of the kind. She must seem utterly helpless, so wholly the pretty little fool that she had not even the wit to think of looking for evidence concerning her lover's death. With Lord Frederick, perhaps, she could relax a little; but her line must throughout be one of frightened bewilderment, and that would not have been an easy line to maintain with Mrs Davies on the spot.

Once again she congratulated herself on the lucky victory over that detestable woman, and her mind switched back to her worse and still unchallenged enemy Evan Slode. Somehow, sometime there must be a reckoning with that blackguard; and a second uprush of hatred for him shook her like an ague.

Then a curious thing happened. For no conscious reason, she was back in a room with a bright coal fire, in a tall house somewhere behind Upper Street, Islington—the room in which she had first seen Flashy. Flashy was there with her. They were standing by the fire-place a few feet apart, and he was putting her through her paces, and she was doing her best to show him what he wanted to see. And the door had opened and a little middle-aged man had come in, and seemed surprised to find them there. He had only stayed long enough

331

to greet Flashy in a constrained way (who replied offhandedly and called him Slode) and, bowing to her, to apologise for his intrusion. Then he had gone out again. Since the incident occurred Lottie had never given him a thought; but now she saw him as clearly as though he were once again standing a few feet away from her. Also she realised that many years ago she had seen him before; and where she had seen him; and who he was. The question which William Slode had asked himself six months earlier was answered. Lottie also had remembered.

"Jiminy-figs!" she cried aloud, sitting up straight in her excitement. "The kid-breaker! And that lout of a boy—his son—is, *must* be, Evan Slode. Godamighty, I've got him now!"

At that moment there came a knocking on the front door. She opened it, to find two police-officers, Lord Frederick Boreham and Major Bulwinkle, standing on the door-step.

Boreham was ampler and the Major more vacuous even than she remembered them. Both raised their hats and the former turned to the police-officers.

"This is the young lady I was tellin you about."

Hearing him speak, Lottie realised that this was not the roaring Freddie of her earlier brief experience. There was about him a tenseness, a quietude, which seemed to brace him together. For the time being that sagging paunch was gripped in a mould of righteous anger. He is grieving for his friend, she told herself—grieving and out for vengeance.

"Please come in" she said; and the narrow hallway was full of men.

Boreham said:

"If you gentlemen think well to go over the house with Major Bulwinkle, I will have a few words with Miss Osborn on business, and then I am sure if you have any questions . . . You need not be afraid she will run away."

The two officers trod heavily through the ground-floor rooms, while Lottie, with downcast eyes and hands nervously clasped, stood timidly by Boreham's side.

"Has the writing-desk in the small study been touched?" one of them shouted.

She shook her head.

"Tell him, please" she said to Boreham in a small tremulous voice "that I have not been in there at all. Mr Fleischmann used that room for his business."

The message was shouted back. Soon the officers reappeared.

"And the servants?"

This time Lottie herself replied.

"The housekeeper and her husband have gone" she said.

"Gone? Why? Where to?"

She seemed on the edge of tears.

"I don't know. They came and said they were getting out of here. Where they've gone I don't know. The housemaid may be downstairs, but I haven't heard her. I think —I—I—am all alone."

Bulwinkle now led the way upstairs, followed by the police.

"Come into the drawin-room, my dear" said Boreham. "I am very sorry for you, placed in so miserable a position. It seemed better not to mention the name by which poor Flashy introduced us. These fellows are apt to persecute whomsoever they lay their hands on—and the more so if they fail to find other clues. You heard me say Miss Osborn? Understand?"

"Oh yes, sir" quavered Lottie. "And I am very grateful—"

"That's all right. Now anythin you know of this tragic affair you must tell to the police. My concern is what is to become of you. You can't stop here—especially alone. Have you any friends you can go to?"

"Well, sir, Miss Sanderson—Major Bulwinkle's friend—was here this morning and most kindly asked me to go to her. But I said no. I would prefer to go where no one knows me—for a while at any rate. I will find a lodging somewhere out of sight, and consider what to do next. Oh, sir, what a *dreadful* thing to happen to poor Mr Fleischmann! What a horrible, horrible thing. . . ."

She broke down in earnest, the strain of the last few hours suddenly overwhelming her. When a minute or two later the police and Bulwinkle came into the room, she was racked with real sobs, and genuine tears were streaming between the fingers pressed tightly against her eyes. Boreham loomed over her, like an embarrassed walrus.

Gradually the fit of weeping spent itself, and raising her head she saw the four men standing in silence watching her. With an effort she got control of her sobs, blew her nose, wiped her eyes and looked miserably up at them. She had a part to play, and the curtain was about to rise. For a few moments she would be the stray kitten or the whipped puppy—deprecating, pitiful, hoping for kindness yet fearful of a blow.

"I am so sorry" she murmured. "Please excuse me. . . ."

"Now, Miss Osborn" said one of the officers briskly. "Have you any idea who could be mixed up in this affair?"

"None at all . . . absolutely none. You see—"

"What enemies had Mr Fleischmann?"

"I think Major Bulwinkle and I can answer that better than Miss Osborn" put in Boreham. "She knew nothin of our friend's affairs. That I can say from my own knowledge, for we three associates often talked business in this house and never in the presence of ladies. Anythin you want to know about Mr Fleischmann's—er—competitors, we will be glad to tell you."

The officer smiled unpleasantly.

"There are other—er—competitors than business ones, Lord Frederick. This very attractive young lady . . ."

"Damn your eyes!" interrupted Boreham angrily; while Bulwinkle said: "Oh I say, none o' that sort of drivel, dontcherknow!"

Lottie interposed. Her voice was low but steady.

"Thank you two gentlemen, but I will answer the officer's question. I was very fond of Mr Fleischmann, and he was very very good to me. I was only—er—with him for about six months, and whatever you may think of a girl in my position, only a fool would risk losing all the advantages I had just gained. No; you may be assured that Mr Fleischmann had no enemies of the kind you mean."

The man bowed and spoke more civilly.

"Your relationship with the dead man, madam, is not our affair, except in so far as it may lead to the solution of this mystery. It is therefore with no suggestion of moral dis-approval that I ask how you first came into contact with Mr Fleischmann?"

Danger. On the one hand a chance to implicate Slode; on the other the absolute necessity of keeping secret her eavesdropping. The pause was almost imperceptible; yet to her it seemed a full minute long, with four pairs of ears—two friendly, two hostile—alert for her reply. She dropped her eyes again and, plucking at her handkerchief, replied:

"I was on the stage for a short time—dancing—and Mr Fleischmann saw me—and came behind—and proposed that I .... that we .... I called myself 'Tremaine', not—er—Osborn." Even in this precarious moment her sense of humour dared to flicker. "How many more names before I'm done?" she wondered.

While the man was writing down the details of her brief stage career, she was testing her story at top speed and from every angle. Yes, it would do. The name of the theatre and the date of her appearance were true; if by a remote chance Boreham remembered seeing her in the Crown and Anchor and, by one still more remote, had asked about her, what he had heard would tally with what she now said. Her vanishing from Greenwich after four days, direct to Alpha Place, could have been in Fleischmann's company, for no one knew any better.

The officer was putting away his note-book.

"Now, Lord Frederick, I presume you have no objection to our taking possession of the house for a while. As Mr Fleischmann's executor, your permission to search for papers or other evidence would make a warrant unnecessary. As for this young lady—"

"I will ask Major Bulwinkle to see to her. She cannot of course remain here."

335

Taking Jacko by the arm he drew him aside; then returned to Lottie.

"Miss Osborn, will you please go upstairs and put your things together? The Major will return in an hour's time and take you to Rathbone Place. I shall stay here and help the police with their search, so will be at hand if you want me. You must stop with Miss Sanderson until I communicate with you again. When our poor friend's affairs are settled, you shall be treated as he would have wished. Meanwhile" (handing her an envelope) "here is somethin to be goin on with. Now lose no time, please. Your trunks shall be sent after you; for the moment a valise is sufficient."

*   *   *   *   *

Lottie had no option but to do as she was told. So to Rathbone Place she went; and there remained, occupying a tiny back room which, with the double-parlour, Jacqueline Sanderson's bedroom and that of the maid, made up the first floor apartment in which Major Bulwinkle had established his mistress. She was made warmly welcome, and responded gratefully to her hostess' sympathy and kindness.

"But I shan't stay a moment longer than I must, Jackie. You are perfectly sweet to me; but I want to hide. When you have visitors I shall stay in my room, and if I ever suspect you are *not* having them on my account I shall disappear at once."

"My dear, you shall do exactly as you like. But you won't mind Merlette? She is such a friend of mine, and liked you so much. She would be hurt if you avoided her."

"No" replied Lottie thoughtfully. "I don't mind Merlette."

A few days later the Frenchwoman appeared. She took Lottie by the shoulders, kissed her on both cheeks, and looking at her affectionately with kind shrewd brown eyes, said:

"Pauv' p'tite! A cruel début! I do not refer to this horreur one single time more, but I must tell you that Jackie ere and I wish to elp you at any time. You ave only to whistle us and we come. N'est-ce pas, Jackie?"

Over the teacups they talked of Lottie's future.

"She insists on doing a vanishing act" said Jackie. "I see her point, of course; but only for a short time. This business will blow over, and in a few weeks no one will remember to connect her with it at all. Then we must find her a nice reliable fellow with plenty of what it needs."

"Parmi ses meubles, is it, once again? Well, each to her taste, but that as you know is not mine."

"And what is yours?" asked Lottie.

"Independence, chérie. I like to manage my affairs. I am my own—n'est-ce pas? And I wish to own myself, not to be locked away by some man, derrière une vitrine d'armoire like I was porcelaine de Dresde and all the third days taken out and dusted."

"Don't listen, Lottie—even to the English bits! She's an adventuress, and to be an adventuress you need to like living an adventure. Well, I don't. I want to be safe and settled; and you take it from me that a steady tie-up with a decent chap and a comfy little place of one's own is worth all Merlette's 'independence' three times over."

The Frenchwoman shrugged.

"A quoi bon? If I may not preach, at least I may eat! Please, Jackie, one of those macarons. . . . Délicieux! And now for our little Meess Lottie. What are we to do for er?"

Lottie shook her head vigorously.

"Nothing. Nothing at all. When I go away from here, I shall find work of some kind and be one of a hundred thousand working-girls: I am through with the game—at present anyway. Merlette's line frightens me. Yours, Jackie, I could not bear at present. What has just happened haunts me and will haunt me . . . for years . . . and years. . . ."

She began to cry, and Jackie put an arm round her and led her gently to her room.

"There, there" she said. "Have your cry out, poor little soul. You shall please yourself entirely, but you have had a shock and must rest."

When she returned to the sitting-room, Merlette was smoking thoughtfully and staring into the fire.

"The child is right, Jackie" she said. "Let er go er way

337

for the moment. Later on, per'aps—She is ver' young, and une vie d'ouvrière will not suit er for long. You call me 'adventuress', but that little one is more so than I. Assurément 'y en a qui sont grues de naissance. Tu verras."

It was a short month after Lottie had been installed as the guest of Jackie Sanderson that the newspapers carried the story of Crocker's suicide. As she read the brief description of the corpse dangling over the gulf of the unfinished factory, swaying this way and that in the howling wind, her heart turned over. Tragedy seemed to dog those with whom she had been associated. Worse than that, this last grim gesture of a beaten man was a consequence, direct or indirect, of the Fleischmann murder, and that had been a consequence—she dared not ask herself how direct—of her own venal disloyalty.

Panic seized her, a panic unreasoning and beyond control. She was incapable of coherent thought. Back at Alpha Place, after Flashy's death, she had at least held on to her sanity and realised the folly of flight. Had she now been able to weigh even the more obvious pros and cons, she would have understood that no one formerly in Flashy's entourage, from Boreham to fat Annie, could possibly connect her with Crocker or guess she had ever heard the name. From that point she would have progressed sufficiently to remind herself that Boreham had befriended her, and had bidden her stay where she was, until such money were paid to her as would fairly represent the dead man's gratitude to a love-girl of six months' standing.

But this time she was utterly distracted with fear and with remorse. Jackie was out; the maid was marketing; she was alone in the apartment. Thrusting a few clothes into a valise and cramming all the money she possessed into her reticule, she dressed for the street and, back in the parlour, scribbled a hasty note:

DEAR JACKIE.—I've cut and run. Never mind why or where to. Just be an angel and let the rest of my things stay here for the present. I have already promised once to keep in touch with you and now do so again. But don't worry if you hear nothing for quite a while, and when you do it won't be from "Miss Osborn" but from

Your loving

LOTTIE HEAPE.

The omnibus set her down at the corner of the Strand and Wellington Street, and she walked quickly to the toll-house and across the bridge. As she approached Uncle Tom's Cabin, her courage began to waver. After the shock of the morning paper, she was uncertain whether she could face up to the sort of reception she was likely to get, probably from Uncle Tom himself, certainly from Vicky. A few doors away from the wine-shop she stopped, put down her valise and for a full half-minute held on to a railing while she took a firm grasp of her nerves. "Now then" she admonished herself. "Have a go at it! It's got to be done."

At that moment a fortunate thing happened. Uncle Tom himself emerged from the Cabin and came slowly up the street toward her. She waited till he was abreast of where she stood and then spoke to him with controlled humility:

"Mr Ormerod! I owe you some money and I have come to pay it. I am very sorry not to have done so sooner."

He had been walking abstractedly, with bowed head and hands in coat-pockets. Startled at being addressed he looked up sharply, and for a few seconds stared at the strange young woman.

"Eh?" he said. "What did you say?" His preoccupied gaze gradually focussed into one of uncertain recognition. "Hey, there! I know you, though oo the ell . . . I got it! The kid as skipped and dished the lot of us on that kinchenlay! Well, I'm damned; and you got the nerve to show your fiddler's face in these parts. . . ."

"Please, Mr Ormerod, listen to me. I've come to pay you back what I borrowed—with interest if you like. It wasn't my fault that I boshed the game at Greenwich. Something *really* happened uncomfortably near what we planned to pretend. I can't tell you any more, nor say fairer than that here I am, money and all."

Uncle Tom was placable and good-natured. He had always liked the girl, and was not without practice in spotting a yarn-spinner. She admitted a debt and had come to settle it. That in itself was good enough. Her refusal in advance to say what had happened to her neither surprised nor irritated him. A man cannot spend nearly fifty years in small-scale social piracy without learning discretion, both in asking questions and answering them.

"That's prime, me dear. Come along to the Cabin and ave a drink on it. Don't be waxy with yer old uncle breakin out like that. Kind of took me by surprise. No offence, eh?"

She shook her head and smiled.

"None at all."

He entered the wine-shop ahead of her, shouting as he crossed the threshold:

"Vicky! Vicky! See oo's ere! And keep a civil tongue in your ead, for it's all serene and no callin names."

The buxom barmaid, her back to the street, was behind the counter filling a cask through a funnel fixed in the bung. She turned quickly, and did not at first recognise Lottie whose face was in shadow, silhouetted against the daylight beyond the door. When the identity of the visitor dawned on her, she flung up the flap of the counter, took two rapid strides and, arms akimbo, thrust her head forward and glared at the girl from such short range that their noses almost touched. Her lips were drawn back in an angry snarl, and during the few seconds of menacing silence which followed, Lottie needed all her pluck to stand her ground. Then, in a voice which rose from a rough whisper between clenched teeth to a wide-mouthed raucous scream, Vicky began:

"I'll be ——! Of all the —— sauce, comin back ere bold as brass after fakin er only friends—the folk as took er in and saved er life I wouldn't wonder! You bloody little welsher! You snivel your way in, collect the dibs, and then off and away, gayin it and flashin your meat I've no doubt,

wherever there are fools to pay for the sight of it. Ooh!!
Let me get me ands on yer—"

She had just begun to raise her arms, when they were
gripped from behind by Uncle Tom. Swinging the girl
round he slapped her face hard, first on one side, then on the
other.

"Stow yer mag, you hell-cat! I told you no back-bitin.
The kid's come on purpose to settle up, and if I'm satisfied
that's enough. Don't you mind Vicky, me dear" he said to
Lottie. "She blows up easy, but down again ditto. Now
kiss and be friends, you two, and we'll ave a glass all round
and work out what's owin."

Vicky, fingering the angry flush on her right cheek, eyed
Lottie sullenly. Once or twice her glance flickered nervously
toward Uncle Tom, who stood there, massive and ruddy,
fixing her with a steady gaze. At last she gave her shoulders
an awkward lift, took a clumsy step forward and held out
her hand.

"Sorry, kiddo. No moss?"

"No moss, Vicky. I don't blame you an atom. It looked
like a bit of damned cheek. My eye, I was in a mortal funk
up the road there! If Uncle Tom hadn't chanced to come
along I doubt if I could have faced you."

Accounts settled over two glasses of the best port, Uncle
Tom took himself off, leaving the girls together. To Vicky
Lottie confided more of her story than had seemed prudent
at the first moment of renewed contact with the Cabin and
its inhabitants. She mentioned no names, but said she had
lived for several months with a rich man who had treated
her generously and well. But a third party had made trouble;
she had skipped, and now wanted to drop out of sight.

"And to keep straight, too" she added. "I want somewhere to live. I want a job—a real job—and I've come to
you for help. I'm a good fancy cook—cakes and jellies and
pastry and so on; I can sew—"

"You wouldn't consider a dance-act, I suppose?" interrupted Vicky mischievously.

341

"Now, now! Bygones are bygones. And don't be silly. I tell you I want to disappear. So *not* a dance-act nor a thing-ummy-bob plastique nor any sort of an act which sticks me up to be looked at. There's the problem; and while you're thinking it over, I'll take you up West and buy you a new bonnet."

As they emerged from the shop in Wigmore Street which, after prolonged strolling and window-gazing, had finally claimed their custom, Vicky said:

"I've got it!"

She was resplendent in a prismatic headpiece of considerable size which (despite its unsuitability to the time of year) her massive build and high colouring carried off better than one might have expected. Lottie glanced at it amusedly.

"Indeed you have" she said "and do it credit."

The other grinned.

"I don't mean that—though it's a stunner and I feel like the Queen of Sheba. I mean about you. We'll go and see Redge."

"Redge?"

"Me sister Regina. Twins we are, born in thirty-seven and named accordin. Me leadin the procession was Victoria, and then Redge, see?"

Lottie laughed aloud.

"Oh, Vicky, you'll be the death of me! That's prime! And where does the twin hang out?"

"She lives with Ma in Portobello Road and works in the millinery at Whiteley's in Westbun Grove. We'll take the Metropolitan to Bishop's Road and find er in the shop."

Redge was absurdly like her sister in face, but physically less abounding and much quieter in voice and manner. When, after waiting a few minutes while she served a customer, the visitors embarked on greetings and an introduction, she waved her hands.

"For Gawd's sake, Vicky, pipe down a bit! This is an emporium I'd ave you know, not a stall in Petticoat Lane.

Howdydo, Miss Eape; pleasure I'm sure. You know, Vicky, that bonnet of yours—"

"Mind yer step, lovey. It's a present from me lady-friend and very andsome of er too."

"You chose it, though—now didn't you?"

"'Course I chose it, you silly thing! It's me wearin it, isn't it? Not everyone could" she went on complacently. "You need somethin to carry this much, and I've got it. Jealous, that's what you are; plumb jealous."

"I dessay" rejoined Redge good-humouredly. "So long as *you* like it, and don't mind the mashers lightin their cigars at it as yer go by. And now, mem" (in the mincing manner of behind-the-counter convention) "to what do we owe the honour of this visit? Allow me to show you—"

"Stow it, Redge. This is serious." And she proceeded to explain their errand.

A fortnight later Lottie entered the employment of a catering firm in Queen's Road, which had a connection for weddings, receptions, soirées and so forth among the well-to-do inhabitants of the squares and terraces along the north side of Bayswater Road.

(ii) NOVEMBER 1869–SPRING 1873

She remained with Landsell and Spenlow, Caterers and Ball-furnishers, for about three and a half years. Having started as a kitchen-maid, her skill with jellies and preserves and macaroons and charlottes-russes and salads and ices and all the other tantalising fal-lals, which express in terms of elegant appearance and delicious taste the glitter of great chandeliers and the soothing charm of music, soon attracted attention. First the rulers of the kitchen, then the proprietors themselves became aware that here was someone with a natural genius for confectionery, someone who possessed what might (by a gardening analogy) be termed "sweet fingers". Being enterprising folk, with no obstinate respect for conventions of seniority, they removed Lottie from dish-washing, from fetching and carrying, from the multifarious

343

odd-jobs which fell to a kitchen assistant, and told her to invent. She became something of a specialist—a designer of new allurements for the palate, a laboratory expert rather than an ordinary member of the staff.

In these altered circumstances she conducted herself with tact and correctness. Unassuming, amiable, always ready to help a colleague in a difficulty, she contrived, while keeping herself to herself out of hours, to create no jealousies beyond (in the hearts of one or two of her female fellow-workers) that melancholy and half-admiring jealousy which the near-slattern cannot help feeling toward the soignée.

For soignée Lottie emphatically was. She dressed invariably in black—even the overalls she wore at work were black—and her lovely skin seemed almost luminous, it was so white and clear. She still wore her hair like a cap of short curls, which clung to her head and rippled over her tiny ears. Though virtually free from jealousy, the other girls could not fail to wonder how, on the wages paid, she managed to look as she did; and there was a period when uncharitable speculation played with the idea that her rapid promotion and the civility with which she was treated by Mr Spenlow were indications of earnings over and above those entered in the books of the firm.

An episode (fortunately witnessed by a member of the staff) dispelled this suspicion. It was after hours, but Lottie was experimenting with some new sweetmeat, and remained behind after the rest had gone. Mr Spenlow found her at work, and led off with a joke on which he had been expending great industry and now regarded as a winner.

"Bless my soul!" he cried. "Our little Interior Decorator still hard at it?"

She continued her stirring and merely said:

"Good evening, Mr Spenlow. I am anxious to finish this."

"Did you get that? 'Interior Decorator'? Rather good, eh? Think we'll call the firm 'Interior Decorators', and pull in other sorts of business. Ha! Ha!"

She smiled politely, dipped a finger into her confection and tasted it. Then, nodding to herself:

344

"That's good. That's all right."

"By Jove, I don't wonder! Off a dainty little finger like that! Let's try my great paw."

He also dipped and tasted, smacked his lips and patted her on the shoulder.

"Delicious! Never liked anything better in me life. You're a genius, Miss Heape, that's what you are. Which reminds me. I've been thinkin you should be paid more, and I'd like to talk it over with you."

Lottie looked puzzled.

"Talk it over?"

He winked prodigiously.

"Yes. Somewhere quiet. Just you and me, eh? How about a little jaunt to Brighton one day?"

She tightened her lips.

"I don't go on little jaunts with strange men, Mr Spenlow, and I refuse their invitations like this—"

The slap rang out across the kitchen; and the man whose job it was to make up the fires and who had been lurking in the passage and listening with interest to this conversation, stuffed a very dirty apron into his mouth to smother the guffaws of delight which shook him. "Lawks" he thought "what'll the guvnor do now?"

The guvnor was in a quandary. His face hurt: and any man slapped by a woman, however much he deserves it, feels a momentary resentment. Then there was discipline. If girls in catering establishments were to go round boxing their employers' ears, where should we all be? On the other hand he was no practised gallant, but a clumsy good-natured oaf, excited by his own joke and the idea of being alone with this stunning girl, whom he had long admired from a discreet distance. As soon as he had spoken, he had regretted it; he now realised that regret would be no word for what he would feel if Miss Heape gave notice, and the severe Mr Landsell learnt the reason why. So he stammered an apology, and feared (rightly) that he was looking an utter fool. When he fumbled into silence, Lottie said:

"Very well. About my rise. When do I get it?"

NINE YEARS RUIN AND REND

His morale broke finally.

"At once, Miss Heape—I mean next week, Miss Heape. I assure you it shall not be overlooked. Let me say again how deeply I regret—" He had begun to back as he spoke, and was now close to the open door. With a gasped "Good night, Miss Heape" he plunged out of the room. The stoker flattened himself in the angle of the wall and a fixed cupboard. When the disorganised Spenlow had fled upstairs, he cautiously emerged and tiptoed away. No one had seen him; but next day several people heard the story.

This occurred when Lottie had been with the firm for more than a year, by which time curiosity as to whence an extra income could derive had become endemic. The elimination of Spenlow left this curiosity finally in the air, where for lack of alternative satisfaction it remained, floating happily about and harming no one.

No alternative satisfaction was possible, because no visible explanation existed. Lottie, as we know, had gone to ground. In flight from everything connected with Fleischmann—including the self who had been Fleischmann's girl—she had determined to create a new existence which should be in every respect the opposite of the old. Instead of selling her body, selling her fingers and her brain; instead of those arenas of the West End allotted by tradition to the competitive displays of pretty-horse-breakers, the suburban tedium of far Bayswater.

But two features of the old life she took with her into the new—one because she could not help herself, the other because to court squalor when one could have modest comfort was sheer folly. These features were her memories and her savings. The former she must live down; the latter she must eke out with care and realism. About the distant future she had no anxiety. She was young, self-confident and unafraid of ordinary contacts with the world. Something would turn up when it was time for her to go and look for it. She was, in consequence, prepared to spend over a period the money she had set by during the months in Alpha Place, using it to secure just that much cosier a lodging, clothes of just that much better quality, than she would be able to command if she lived on what she earned. No wonder, therefore, that on the rare occasions when she invited a fellow-worker to take tea with her or, on a Sunday evening in summer, to return to her room for supper after a walk in Kensington Gardens, the visitor was conscious that a tributary of some sort must swell Miss Heape's exchequer, yet saw no sign of the obvious source whence tributaries flow.

It should be added that from all her calculations Lottie excluded two fifty-pound notes, sealed in an envelope and locked carefully away. They were still objects of horror, and their use as money was inconceivable. Indeed she hardly realised they *were* money. They were her brand of shame, and she felt that if she were so much as to touch them they would burn her hands. Yet, in a sense, they were her most treasured possession. They must never be lost or destroyed. One day, in conjunction with her recognition of his father, they might help her to repay to Evan Slode the debt of fury and self-loathing which she owed him.

Time went by, and Lottie subsisted in a mood of uncritical content. She had indeed reversed her way of life, and that in itself brought satisfaction. She enjoyed her work; and gradually over the bruised and smarting skin of Lottie, the love-girl of a murdered man, grew the new unlacerated skin of Miss Heape, the expert pastry-cook. Perhaps it was rather a layer of insensitivity than a skin; for although it was thick enough for the time being to stifle the inclinations of the girl it enfolded, it was not sufficiently a part of her to create new inclinations suited to itself.

Nor could it ever be. So long as she was in hiding from everybody and everything connected with the Fleischmann tragedy, she had no inclinations other than a desire to keep out of sight and be forgotten. But as the months passed and then the years, as the danger of chance encounters and the pangs of conscience seemed to fade and weaken, the real and permanent Lottie began to fidget, to regard as a place of irksome captivity the refuge into which fear and remorse had driven her.

Slowly she became conscious that her life was dull and lonely. She wanted people, gaiety, a chance to use her wits and to wear pretty clothes; and here she was, cooped up in a suburban cook-shop with nothing to look forward to as the day drew on but a couple of hours alone in a single room, bed and intermittent sleep, and then the whole thing over again.

Her restlessness increased and was brought to a pitch of desperation by the receipt of a letter from Jackie Sanderson, to whom she had written with the address of her lodgings but whom, for fear of undesired encounters, she had not visited.

This letter contained two startling pieces of news. The first was that the major's wife, who had been ailing for months, had died not long ago, and that Jackie would shortly step into her shoes and, in the eyes of God and man, become Mrs Bulwinkle. The second was that poor Freddie Boreham, before the scandal broke which drove him to the Continent, had told Jackie in confidence that he was arranging to secure for Lottie a legacy of one thousand pounds from the Fleischmann estate, but that nothing must be said to her until the estate was finally settled. Jackie wrote:

It has taken those damned lawyers all this time to close matters up. You bet, if Freddie had been here to push them along, it would have been a different story. With him away they've had a high old time, and charged up six and eight every time they yawned. I suspect Freddie has paid it out of his own pocket, for he said Flashy's will had been made before he knew you, and that the puzzle was where to squeeze out the dibs. Still, better late than never, no matter how it's been done; and a couple of monkeys are sitting in a cage at the bank waiting for little Lottie to let them out. I am so very glad, my dear, and I'm sure Flashy would be glad too.

The letter concluded:

How's the straight and narrow? Don't get too pure for

anything. You shall have my new address when there is one, and *perhaps*—I only say "perhaps"—you will risk a visit to your at long last *respectable* old friend

JUMBO JACKIE.

No more lureful vision of the old life could be imagined than that called up by this sensational letter. Lottie read it over and over, and each time the contrast between the dowdy bondage of the present and the glitter and freedom now within her reach became less tolerable. One thousand pounds! And Jackie married and rich, with a smart home of her own to which only the people she liked would be invited, from which could be excluded the promiscuous acquaintanceships inescapable by a kept woman, even though she be of the elect.

How sweet Jackie was, with her "straight and narrow" and her cheerful self-ridicule! Lottie sat down the very next evening to write her answer, feeling in higher spirits than at any time since the heyday of her affair with Mervyn Crocker.

"Darling Cow-winkle" she began, and poured out congratulations and excited plans for using her new money and gross exaggerations of the dreariness and solitude of her present existence. "I can't bear it much longer" she ended up. "If something doesn't happen soon, I shall have to make it happen. But I'd much prefer not to do that. A girl on her own can't get very far; she must have something behind her—either a position of some sort or a job or, of course, a man. Pray that something happens to me, dear old Jackie, and heaps of love from LONESOME LOTTIE."

(iii) JUNE 1873-MAY 1875

In the early part of June 1873—that is to say virtually at the end of the Season, which started and finished earlier in those days than in more modern times—one of the best customers of Messrs Landsell and Spenlow, the Hon. Mrs Tarbutt, who lived in Hyde Park Gardens, gave a large evening party. She naturally put the entire management of the refreshments into the hands of her usual caterers, and this important commission set the establishment in a flutter for a fortnight before the event.

It was the firm's custom on such an occasion as this to provide maids to help with the waiting, and to send with them as overseer a trustworthy and dignified person of middle age, who presided behind the buffet, controlled the serving-girls and was generally responsible for the adequacy and smooth distribution of the refreshments supplied. Imagine, then, the consternation of Landsell and Spenlow, when this important and experienced female fell sick on the very morning of the Tarbutt soirée and was unable to come to business.

After much agitated discussion, in the course of which a series of possible substitutes were one by one brought up for consideration and knocked down again, Spenlow suddenly said:

"What about Miss Heape?"

Landsell, a lanky stooping man with a long disillusioned face and austere whiskers, gazed at his junior over his glasses.

"Don't be absurd. She is much too young."

"I was thinking of appearance. She looks smart, and she's certainly got her wits about her."

"Miss Heape is a natural confectioner. I should be the last to deny her gifts within her own sphere. But whoever is in charge of the catering for the Honourable Mrs Tarbutt must be a woman with a head for organisation, a disciplinarian, if need be a termagant. Is Miss Heape a termagant?"

"I've no idea" replied Spenlow in some embarrassment. Then added ruefully "But I dare say she could manage it."

The argument dragged on; but as Landsell could make no better suggestion, it was finally decided to take the risk and to send Lottie to Hyde Park Gardens, in charge of the provisions and the personnel.

The girl was on her mettle. Here at last was a break in the monotony of a job she had begun to hate. Also it gave her a chance to wear the sort of dress she would like to be seen wearing, instead of putting on day after day the sensible but dreary things which serve their purpose while there is no one to look at you. Certainly, when she presented herself to the partners at the appointed hour, she looked extremely elegant. The effect was very sober, very dignified, but at the same time very smart. She received her final instructions and the cortège departed.

Everything went smoothly. Mrs Tarbutt liked things done well and no expense spared; and as Landsell and Spenlow had set out to excel themselves, the foods and drinks were exquisite and plentiful.

During the afternoon, and on her own initiative, Lottie had called at the house and ingratiated herself with the butler. This was important. His home-staff had to collaborate with the hirelings under Lottie's command, and it lay in his power to disrupt the whole proceedings, if he inclined to do so. He had not been on the best of terms with the regular lady-superintendent from Landsell and Spenlow, so that Lottie started with the advantage of being a welcome change. When, after a few minutes, the butler realised that this was a very attractive young woman, who used her eyes to good effect and had a remarkable appreciation of the difficulties and responsibilities of a butler's work, he opened up, and became so friendly that Lottie pleaded the urgency of settling their plans at once, so that she could rush back and get ready for the evening. The butler yielded tactfully. They agreed on their respective spheres of influence; and, as she left, he remarked jocularly that there would be no harm in her taking a walk one day soon with someone old enough to be her father. She flashed him a smile, told him not to talk nonsense, and escaped.

The result of this successful reconnaissance was that Lottie was in full charge of the jellies, ices, salads, sandwiches, aspics and eatables generally, as well as the lemonade and the mild claret-cup designed for ladies, while the butler presided over the wines proper, the spirits and the cigars. Two footmen were seconded to help the imported waitresses, and the butler kept the third as his personal assistant.

From her position behind the main buffet Lottie directed operations with unobtrusive dexterity. Her maids and the two footmen came and went, carrying loaded trays into the crowded rooms, returning with empty glasses, used cutlery and plates, which were spirited out of sight, washed and put again into circulation. The guests themselves were not encouraged to attend the buffet in person, because couples or small groups of people hedging the refreshment-counter hampered the service. Nevertheless on more than one occasion Mrs Tarbutt herself or one of her daughters had to request lingering clusters of revellers to move away into one of the reception rooms. The formula was each time the same. As she politely shepherded the trespassers on their way, the hostess or her deputy would murmur: "The servants will bring you anything you fancy", and then, as she herself departed, would exchange with Lottie a glance of humorous pessimism, with perhaps a slight shrug or a twinkling of the lips in deprecation, as between woman and woman, of the obstinacy and greed of grown-up folk who ought to know better. And Lottie would twinkle back, but with respectful moderation as became her status. "That's a pretty girl Landsell has put in charge tonight" remarked one Miss Tarbutt to another. Her sister nodded. "An improvement on Aunt Bombazine" she said. "But the men hang about the buffet more than usual, so it cuts both ways."

After one such clearance of unwelcome guests, the alcove in which she was stationed being for the moment empty, Lottie underwent a curious repetition of an experience of long ago. It seemed to her that she had withdrawn inside herself and, ceasing to be a personality, became merely a watching and a listening post. Through the archway, between the heavy folds of the looped-back curtains, she could see the shimmer of lights in the big ground-floor saloon. She could see the creamy arms and shoulders and the coloured gowns of the women who—sitting, standing or strolling—constituted a slow-moving, ever-changing kaleidoscope, flecked yet knit into a pattern by the sombre strokes of masculine full-dress. She could hear the faint wailing of distant violins, as the orchestra on the floor above played soft background music to the chatter and rustle of the crowded rooms; she could hear the rise and fall of murmured conversation, an occasional trill of happy laughter, the clink of glasses, the small sharp impact of spoon on plate. She seemed for the time being to hover like a disembodied spirit on the edge of a gulf of lights and shadows and softly blended sounds, and slowly there crept over her the conviction that she had done this once before, though with a difference.

It now came back to her with a rush. On her first night out in London, when Leo had taken her to the Crown and Anchor, she had for a few moments enjoyed just this severance of sight and sound from any consciousness of her whereabouts. The colouring had been garish and the noise raucous, but the experience was the same. And when she had slipped back into normal awareness, and the lights and the uproar and the crowded tavern had fused once again into familiar actuality, what had happened? Slode had happened.

She had just reached this point in her strange, involuntary retrospect, and with a shudder of repulsion at the thought of Slode come finally to earth again, when a party of three, two girls and a man, paused just outside the archway of her alcove. They were talking gaily, and Lottie glanced at them in idle curiosity. The man had his back to her; but with a surge of alarm and excitement she realised who he was. Were they coming to the buffet? Her hands were shaking. With a supreme effort she took control of herself, struggling to keep her breathing even, enjoining her heart to beat more slowly. No; they were moving away. The girls had turned from the alcove and, laughing together, were rejoining the crowd in the saloon. The man was about to follow them, when at the last moment—who can say on what impulse?— he looked over his shoulder.

The gasolier, which hung from the ceiling over the buffet, threw a bright light on both their faces. He looked straight at Lottie and she forced herself to meet his eyes, which gleamed suddenly, while the carefully arched eyebrows twitched perceptibly. Otherwise he made no sign, but turned away and strolled out of sight.

The party was over by two o'clock. When the last guests.

had gone, Mrs Tarbutt and her daughters bade Lottie good night, and thanked her for her help. Then they retired to bed, leaving their own servants and Landsell's staff to do the necessary clearing up. The butler came up to Lottie.

"You must be very tired" he said. "I know *I* am. Come and take a glass of wine in my room. We can leave these others to do the work."

She was glad to accept. The reappearance of Dudley Frensham in her life, if only for a few seconds, had thrown her into a state of agitation, of dread and of longing which had only subsided from sheer weariness. She sat, sipping champagne in the comfortable room of Mrs Tarbutt's butler, and replying abstractedly to remarks she hardly heard. Gradually the wine lessened her fatigue and revived the nervous excitement provoked by this amazing rencounter. When she finally rose to go, she felt restored and, for no reason, eager and expectant. She collected her wits sufficiently to thank the butler for his kindness; agreed to meet him at the Victoria Gate on the following Sunday afternoon, and, having climbed the area steps into the moonlit silence of a mild summer night, started to walk home to her not-so-distant lodging.

She had reached the angle of the private carriage-sweep, looping inward from Bayswater Road and dividing the huge terrace of Hyde Park Gardens from the railed-in belt of shrubs and grass to which the terrace owed its name, when he stepped out from the shadow of an overhanging tree. Raising his hat, he greeted her with polite composure.

"Good morning, Miss Heape. A lovely morning too. It is a great pleasure to see you again. I have often thought of our last meeting, and wondered if it really were to be the last. You will forgive my not recalling myself to your memory within doors there. I was afraid of causing you embarrassment."

Lottie was too breathless to reply immediately. The sight of his face, the sound of his voice set her limbs trembling and threw her mind into a turmoil of confusion and delight. The carefully parted moustache over the cleanly-cut cynical lips recalled so vividly his kisses during that mad hour of early evening heat in Alpha Place—how many years ago?—that she felt a sudden dizziness, and swayed against the railings. He stood quite still, hat in hand, and watched her steadily with those bright relentless eyes. She felt self-control returning to the extent of finding her voice; but her defences were finally down, and when she spoke she as good as told him so.

"And you have been waiting for me?" she whispered. "For how long?"

He smiled gently; and the dimples in either cheek and the flash of white even teeth set her quivering once again with delicious memory.

"Silly goose! If you had lost a treasured jewel and, years later, found it again, but were told you could only have it back by waiting an hour or so in midsummer moonlight, would you not wait?"

She seized his hand, kissed it and rubbed it against her cheek.

"How sweet you are!" she murmured. "And what a lovely night. The loveliest night I ever remember."

He took her arm and began walking her slowly toward the main road.

"Let us go back now" he said. "It is very late, or very early, and the night will soon be gone."

"Back? Back where?"

"To wherever you live, sweetness. You know where that is better than I."

"But, darling, I can't take you there! It is a lodging-house which only admits women, and the landlady is the last word in respectability. Besides, even if we could go there, I wouldn't want to—not tonight. I am too excited to be tired, but too tired to stand more excitement. Let me go now. I want to think over this marvellous evening. Tell me when I can see you again."

He neither protested nor showed any sign of pique or disappointment.

"When are you free?"

"Only Sundays, at present."

"Then come to my rooms on Sunday afternoon. Thirty Clarges Street. The second bell from the top."

She nodded, but could not speak for the tears of happiness which choked her. The Tarbutt butler was forgotten. Everything was forgotten, except the sweet enslavement into which she had so joyfully re-entered. He took both her hands, and raising them one by one to his lips, kissed the little circle of bare palm above the buttons of each glove. She could feel the firm smooth hairs of his moustache brush against her skin. When he let the hands drop, she turned and almost ran toward home.

* * * * *

Dudley Frensham was the son of an Englishwoman of noble family by an Adonis from the south of France who acted as valet de chambre to the lady's elderly husband. Proud, masterful and accustomed to being obeyed, her ardent Ladyship looked favourably on the clear olive skin, the bright brown eyes and the powerful yet graceful figure of the manservant, and decided to enjoy them. That this sudden whim should have landed her with a baby was provoking; but she was not one to whine against a fate she had herself challenged, and undertook the suitable disposal of the child with the same imperious thoroughness as had been used in arranging his preliminaries. The birth took place in France, and a reliable foster-mother was found to whose care the infant could safely be entrusted. He was to be known as Dudley Frensham (a name designed to indicate the secret of his origin, and at the same time to suggest forebears of quality) and, as he grew older, was to receive a good education —partly in France and partly in England. When he emerged from babyhood, he would become the ward of an English lawyer practising in Paris and a man in whom the mother had full confidence. The boy was to think himself an orphan

and the true story of his birth was never to be divulged.
Ample funds were put at the disposal of the guardian for
carrying out the lady's instructions. She herself never wished
to see the child again. The father was returned to the
obscurity from which, docile and a little bewildered, he had
been so agreeably drawn.

In consequence, when Dudley Frensham grew up and
entered the adult world, he was modestly provided for, had
the manners and mental equipment of a gentleman, but no
background whatsoever, save that creatable by his individual
qualities. These qualities were the direct product of his
origin, of which he knew nothing.

He was merciless, selfish and sensual; but because he
lacked the social position which would have enabled him to
impose his egotism on others, he was constrained to develop
two distinct manners which, in time, became two aspects of
a second nature. To those he regarded as superior to him,
or at least as beyond his control, he could be sycophantic—
though in a jaunty nonchalant way, as between almost-equals;
but he was arrogant and cruel to inferiors and to anyone
unlucky enough to be in his power. The fine-drawn caressing
good looks of his Provençal father had descended to him,
but were exaggerated and obscurely vulgarised by the hauteur
of a domineering English mother. Seeing that, for the purposes of self-assertion, he was driven to heighten both
amiability and malevolence, his features and his expression
were over-coloured, like those of an actor wearing his make-
up in broad daylight. His smile flashed too whitely; his
frown and his sneer were stage-gestures, reminiscent of the
handsome villain of melodrama.

The majority of the men with whom he would naturally
have aspired to mix distrusted him and, though on nodding
terms, kept him at arm's length. He, therefore, found his
level in that pseudo-aristocratic semi-bohemian world whose
doyen (and by far its most brilliant citizen) was Eustace
Clare Grenville Murray, natural son of the Duke of Buck-
ingham and the inventor of Society Gossip as a department
of journalism. In this cheerful, often talented, always raffish

milieu Frensham was popular and at ease. Bi-lingual, combining a Gallic taste for literature and the arts with the sporting and gambling proclivities of a normal Englishman, he was equally at home in Paris and London, in the studio and on the race-course, in the coulisses of the theatre and at the gaming-table. But a proficiency as various as this requires money, and to obtain money adequate to his needs was Frensham's lasting problem. He solved it with the help of women, to whom he was as generally attractive as to men he was suspect.

To a point this was natural enough. He had the kind of good looks which appealed to feminine romanticism. Further he united virility and elegance in a way detrimental to the effectiveness of neither, and one better suited to Latin than to Anglo-Saxon manhood. His manner toward women was at once fervent, deferential and unabashed. He could appear wholly absorbed in the personality and opinions of the lady of the moment, while boldly appraising her physical attractions. She was flattered to be the subject of this concentrated attention; and although the accompanying scrutiny might bring its moments of embarrassment, it could bring also a twinge of excitement and the pleasurable thrill of feeling that she was more frightened of him than he of her. Should the acquaintanceship develop, she found herself courted by one who regarded even a flirtation as a thing to be handled with solicitude and delicacy. He took infinite pains over his love-making—forestalling the lady's wishes, careful of her comfort, never relaxing for one moment the attitude of one engrossed in her and her concerns. Yet all the time, beneath the gallantry and the ingratiating homage, she was conscious of his ruthless self-sufficiency, and that when he made up his mind precisely what he wanted from her, the odds were that he would get it.

And in addition to these recommendations to women's favour, Frensham was endowed with a mysterious quality which can only be termed an innate sexual fascination. Usually the possessor of this dangerous magnetism is but vaguely aware of the dark power with which he is invested. But now and again the gift—or should one say the curse?—is bestowed on a being who realises its existence and values it as a means to an end. Such a being was Frensham; and with cold detachment he watched it do its work, whether in the exploitation of a rich woman to his own profit, or in the subjugation of some girl he fancied for his own pleasure, or in contriving vengeance on a man who, in one way or another, had appeared to slight him.

Of a successful venture along the lines of the first of these three experiments we have earlier heard a rumour. When Fleischmann, in an expansive moment, had mentioned to Lottie a certain Lady Pridgeon, he had been careful to qualify the indiscretion as a mere repetition of gossip. But he knew well that in this case gossip spoke truth. The second and third directions in which Frensham found it useful to exercise his sinister magnetism have been exemplified—and simultaneously—in episodes already described. Fully conscious that Fleischmann hated and despised him, he had determined, even before their supper-party was over, that he would give the fellow good reason for his hatred. The girl herself had not at that stage greatly interested him. She seemed a nicely made, succulent little thing; but beyond subjecting her to his customary survey of any strange woman, he had not considered her as anything but a joint in Fleischmann's harness. Some weeks later he learnt that the financier had gone abroad, leaving his mistress alone in Alpha Place. Frensham had his connections in the demi-monde of fashion (as in most other spheres abutting on the world of an adventurer), and intimated to a special friend that he was anxious to renew acquaintance with the charming young lady whom he had met in the company of his old crony Fleischmann. If she were to see an opportunity . . . An invitation to meet Miss Heape at Jackie Sanderson's party seemed to the girl the opportunity required; and, having reported to Frensham the time and the place, she stood at the window when he came into sight, ready to announce his coming.

What happened afterwards has been told—except that Frensham (who had set out on a mission of vengeance, which might or might not offer a little incidental pleasure) encountered a personal ecstasy of a kind unsurpassed even in his experience. Lottie, trained in the refinements of love-making at the skilful hands of her middle-aged protector, only needed the stimulus of passion to achieve genius. Frensham inspired the passion, and had his reward.

Then had occurred Fleischmann's murder. Instantly the at-one-time marauder determined, if nerve and fascination could contrive it, to capture Lottie for himself. But this time his luck was out. His intention had been to call at Alpha Place during the brief interval which was sure to elapse between the reporting of the murder in the Press and the appearance at Fleischmann's house of relatives or friends concerned with his affairs. In this interval the girl would likely be alone, and stricken with horror, if not with grief, at the awful fate of her protector. He, Frensham, would be restrained, deeply sympathetic, but masterful. She must not on any account stay alone in this house of tragic memories; he would conduct her to comfortable and respectable lodgings where she could remain in decent retirement, until the dust raised by the abominable crime had settled. Then she would be able to consider the future calmly, and with a full knowledge of her position.

It is probable that, if he had managed to carry this plan into effect, it would have succeeded. But at the last moment, as he was preparing to set out for St John's Wood, a man belonging to a gaming-club at which both played regularly, and one to whom Frensham had owed a considerable sum of money for over three weeks, had called with a friend to say that a sudden crisis had arisen, and that he must have four or five hundred, immediately and in cash. Frensham was cornered. He had not the necessary money in his lodgings. He dared not even seem to default on a gambling debt, for the merest hint of evasion would shut the club doors against him and, in time, other doors as well. To plead an urgent appointment and promise the money on the following day might provoke unwelcome questions and, further, would create an obligation which circumstances might prevent him from fulfilling. Who could say where his raid on Alpha Place—especially if it achieved its object and captured the girl—might land the pair of them? No; there was nothing for it. He must accompany the urgent creditor to the bank, coax the manager into a temporary accommodation, and when he was free again, take his chance in St John's Wood. The business occupied precisely the period of Lottie's solitary brooding after Jackie Sanderson had left. As Frensham turned the corner of Alpha Place, he saw Boreham and three companions entering the front door of Number Four.

Thereafter he lost sight of Lottie altogether, and it is doubtful whether he even gave her another thought. But he did not forget her (he never forgot the face of anyone who had pleased or displeased him), and the moment he saw her through the alcove-arch behind the buffet in Hyde Park Gardens, he recognised her and remembered every incident of their brief acquaintancy.

Flushed and eager, with shining eyes and a song in her heart, Lottie, on that Sunday afternoon, while the Tarbutt butler waited vainly at Victoria Gate, gave herself into bondage.

After the first transports were over and she lay in delicious lassitude on the divan in Frensham's sitting-room, sipping Rhine wine and smoking cigarettes, she chattered of everything which had happened since they parted, seeking desperately for details which might interest him and keep him at her side. She told him of her savings; of her thousand pounds from Fleischmann; of her jewels packed away and in Jackie's charge; of her recent longing to return to a life of gay irregularity and pretty clothes; of her wild excitement when at the soirée she realised he was really he; of her deep contentment at having found her true love again.

Frensham played his part to perfection. He was caressing, tender, pleading, exigent, brutal and soothing. He listened to her prattle, taking mental note of things which might matter, acknowledging the rest with suitable endearments and forthwith forgetting them.

M*   361

As the afternoon drew on, he turned from love to business. The girl was becoming once more urgent in her fondling; but he knew that to send her away hungry would bind her the more closely to him, that his own appetite was slaked for the time being, that he had a dinner engagement and—most important of all—that there were plans to be made. Aloof and practical, he outlined her instructions. She would give notice both to her employers and her landlady, and leave Bayswater as soon as was permissible. He knew of excellent lodgings in Park Row, a cul-de-sac off Knightsbridge and a locality at once retired and conveniently central, with windows overlooking the Park to northward, little noise of traffic, and no questions asked. The rooms were well furnished and the landlady an excellent cook. There he could visit her as often as she wished, which (with a sudden uprush of loverly yearning) could not but be less often than he wished himself. On this note of fervent anticipation he brought the duet to a close, and shortly afterward sent her home.

The next year of Lottie's life was one of sheer enchantment. Wholly infatuated with her lover, she surrendered with rapture to the extremism of her temperament. Frensham's visits (and he was as zealous, as attentive and as passionate as a man could be) constituted of course the framework of her existence. But she soon came to relish her intervals of solitude nearly as keenly as the precious hours of love-making. After the Spartan discipline and long hours of hard work sustained during her three and a half years of "going straight", the enervating idleness of her new life was delicious. She lay late in the morning, pottered along the shop-windows appraising dresses and hats or purchasing flowers and ornaments for her rooms, walked in the Park on fine days with the little poodle-dog which her darling had given her, or in bad weather lolled in an arm-chair reading a novel, nibbling bon-bons or doing desultory needlework. Frensham paid the rent, and she joyfully undertook the trouble and cost of buying food and drink.

Living this different life, her outward appearance began

to change. Gradually the gamine was superseded by the odalisque. She had always moved with exquisite grace, but now, as the curves of her body grew rich and sleek, her taut and restless elegance became a deliberate and languid symmetry. Her eyelids had always drooped; but whereas formerly the eyes beneath had been the bright suspicious eyes of a waif ready to give battle to the world, they now shone luscious and enticing—the eyes of voluptuous beauty in love with love.

Early in her Park Row period occurred the only serious unpleasantness which marred this halcyon year. She went by arrangement to visit the new Mrs Bulwinkle, in order to renew their friendship and to remove the trunks and packages which had been left in Jackie's care. As bad luck would have it, Merlette had chanced to call the same afternoon and was there when Lottie arrived. After joyful greetings had been exchanged all round, the two older women naturally demanded to know what Lottie was doing, where she was living and all about her. In her mood of enslavement to the man she adored Lottie, not surprisingly, forgot what had been said about him at Jackie's party all those years ago. So she declared frankly, her cheeks aglow with pride, that she was now with Dudley Frensham, living in rooms he had found for her in Park Row, and the happiest girl in London.

There was a moment of silence. Jackie gave a little gasp and cried faintly "Oh Lottie!" Then Merlette went into battle.

If she had set out to turn a delicate situation into a catastrophe, she could hardly have handled it more effectively. This was a case where nothing which could possibly be avoided should be said at the outset. Turn the subject; let the child down gently; later on, if you must, insinuate the need for vigilance. Jackie realised all this; but the impetuous Frenchwoman had neither sympathy nor capacity for Anglo-Saxon reticence, and was in full spate before anyone could stop her. As a genuine Parisienne, Merlette knew bogus frenchification when she saw it; as a woman with a wide experience of men, she knew a bounder from a gentleman

363

and a blackguard from both. She had liked Lottie, who for all her youthful inexperience showed signs of possessing both wit and realism. And now the silly little idiot had been caught by this flash bouncer, ce sacré marlou, and could sit there pleased as Punch, as though she were sleeping with the Prince of Wales! So Merlette proceeded to give her views on Dudley Frensham (with anecdotes of his career) and her views on kidlet fly-by-nights who should not be allowed out without a nursemaid. She would doubtless have gone on to give her views on other cognate subjects, if Lottie had not leapt to her feet with a scream of fury, darted across the room and given her a swinging box on the ear. The girl had just broken out into shrill vituperation, using words with which she hardly knew she was familiar, when Jackie took her by the shoulders and removed her forcibly from the room and across the passage.

"Now, now, my dear" she said. "Cool off a bit. Lie down on my bed for awhile and I'll bring you a cup of tea. There! Take your hat off and those boots and get your breath again."

When she returned to the boudoir, the Frenchwoman was still sitting on the sofa, calm, pensive, with not a hair out of place and looking as though nothing whatsoever had happened.

"Merlette" began Jackie. "I am dreadfully sorry—"

The other waved a hand.

"For me it is nothing. But for her—la petite Lottie . . ." She shrugged. "C'est qu'elle est perdue, celle-là. Dommage; parce que dans le temps elle avait de quoi. Perhaps I was too strong, yes? In that case I ask your pardon, Jackie dear, for making a brawl in your house. But I cannot think of that man sans que j'éclate!"

The result of this unfortunate contretemps was to cut Lottie off from her best friends. She was now alone, except for Frensham; and although at this juncture she did not in the least mind being so, she suffered for it later.

During this first year of her happiness she was too deeply

absorbed in her lover to give more than a very occasional thought to questions of money. It is true that now and again she took fleeting note of the fact that the gifts he brought her from time to time, though often amusing and cleverly chosen, were in themselves of little or no value. It is true that he spoke more than once (yet so far had gone no further) of rewarding in the obvious manner the devotion of his darling beautiful little Lottie, and of putting a substantial sum to her account to enable her to go to the great shops and buy any pretty things she fancied. But such trivialities as generosity on the cheap and unfulfilled promises of money were forgotten at the first touch of his lips, at the first murmured endearments in the absurd babylanguage which he had invented for their special and private use. It was unimaginable that she should intrude on their happiness with bleak references to pounds and shillings; and after all she still had money of her own which, to keep the world and its worries away from them, it was a delight and a privilege to spend.

But there came a time, as the first year gave place to the second, when she looked into her affairs and found that the lazy self-indulgence in Park Row—with spirits and cigars for Frensham and a hired carriage for herself and wine and rich food for both of them, over and above the running expenses of laundry and household replacements and clothes and hats and footwear and what not—was proving extremely costly. Indeed her savings and Fleischmann's legacy were melting like snow before the sun; and it was clear that unless something were done, she would before long be penniless.

Accordingly the next evening, when the pair of them had supped, she said:

"By the way, darling, my money is getting low. Can you let me have some?"

He gave her a quick glance, and then, with the famous mocking smile, put his hand in his pocket and pulled out a handful of change.

"There should be a quid or two among all this. Here's

one . . . two . . . four . . . five, by George! Fiver do the trick, honey? More or less cleans me out, but I won't want much before tomorrow."

She thought he was joking, and laughed to please him.

"I wouldn't rob you of it, dearest one" she said. "You may want something for a crossing-sweeper on your way home. Besides it's not needed this very minute. But we are behind on the monthly bills and . . ."

He interrupted her rudely:

"Am I to understand you are nearly broke and expect me to keep as well as lodge you?"

"But, Dudley—darling, don't look at me like that—I have been spending my own money all this time, and more than once you have said . . ."

"Said what? Said I'd pay you to gorge yourself and live in idle luxury for ever? You bet your life! If you want money, you must earn it; and being a good fellow, I'll put you in the way of doing so."

Jumping up, he took his hat and cane, said with a nasty grin "Sleep well!" and flounced out of the room and downstairs. She heard the street door slam behind him.

By next morning she had persuaded herself that he had been acting in order to frighten her, that almost certainly he would pay over a sum of money that very day, and that their meeting in the evening could have all the fervour of a reconciliation, although in fact there had been no quarrel.

But this consoling supposition did not endure for long. When about four o'clock she returned from a walk in the Park, Frensham was in an arm-chair in the sitting-room with his feet on the mantelpiece and a cigar in his mouth.

"Where the hell have you been? I've been waiting nearly half an hour."

"I'm very sorry" she replied submissively. "I'd no idea you were coming this afternoon. If I'd known—"

"Cut all that and listen to me. Chap of the name of Alcester—Lord Alcester—will call tonight about nine o'clock. He's one of the old guard of the crutch-and-toothpicks; but he's good for twenty-five quid if you're nice to him, and you'll be rid of him in a couple of hours. So you see I've kept my word and found some money for you; and I can find you plenty more."

She was too taken aback to speak, but stared at him in horrified silence. He shrugged huffily and got out of his chair.

"I'm damned! Not even a word of thanks. Well, I'll make allowances and admit it *is* all a bit sudden. But you'll settle into it all right—with practice. And practice'll be needed, if you mean to carry on in this style"—and he swept an arm round the pretty and comfortable room. "I must be running. Good cess with Alcester (or 'Fusee', if you get on those terms—big head on a match-stick body, see?—that's what they call him). Not a bad fellow really, and easy to manage as a retired cab-horse. Ta-ta!"

That was how it began.

And that, with variations, was how it went on. She put up no fight. How should she? In the first place she was as much in love with him as ever; and after that sudden outbreak of vulgar rudeness, he had become his former irresistible self—suave, caressing, magnificently virile—just as though everything was as before and there had never been an Alcester nor, in a few days, a Sir This nor, the following week, a Mr That. In the second place, even had she wished to revolt, she could hardly have done so. She had no friends to help her; her money was almost gone. She might, it is true, have found for herself some cheap and miserable lodging and there hung on, virtually in hiding, gradually selling her jewels and other possessions while looking for some sort of work. But good food and comfort and nice clothes had become necessities to her now; and she was just not capable of facing the simultaneous misery of losing her lover and enduring the squalor of pinching and scraping in a slum.

Once and once only she ventured a desperate appeal to the man she idolised. Weeping bitterly she went on her knees to Frensham, and implored him to set her free from her present life of luxurious degradation; to release them both from the vile relationship of bully and prostitute which was, in fact, the shameful thing to which their mutual happiness had been reduced. Protesting her enduring love she begged him to find some humble little lodging where they could still be lovers, where she could cook and work for him, to which no other men should come. She would ask to go back to Landsell and Spenlow on a half-time basis; or she would find scope for her talents with another caterer. She would work herself to the bone to earn enough to keep the modest home going, in order that she might also keep for him alone the beauties he was wont to praise so highly.

He received her pitiful appeal with an amused indifference even more wounding than his previous brutality. Brusquely freeing his knees from the arms tightly clasped about them, he strolled to the window and stood looking out, whistling softly between his teeth.

"You flatter me, my dear" he said, lightly ironical. "I ought I suppose to bow my acknowledgment of being cast for the rôle of the one and only. Unfortunately I have no prejudices on that score. Also I much prefer to find you, when I want you, in surroundings of a certain elegance. Indeed I wonder whether, in the well-scrubbed virtuous love-nest you so touchingly describe—with a flock mattress and oil-cloth on the floor—I should want you at all. And then where would you be—with the world well lost and no love to take its place? No, no, my good girl; so long as you and I are together, you'll go on as you're going now. And I ask you to remember that I do half the work and you get the finnips. You'd land yourself with some queer customers, if you hadn't a man of the world to pick them over for you."

She had remained on her knees when he shook her off, and while he was speaking still knelt, her head bowed, her arms hanging loosely at her sides. She was no longer crying, but her face was tear-stained and she made no attempt to wipe it. The spirit had gone out of her, and as she listened to his casual sarcastic voice, uttering under a surface-flippancy the most dreaded threat of all—that he would tire of her—

she gradually collapsed in upon herself, and sliding to the floor lay there in a crumpled heap.

At the slight noise of her fall, he turned and, leaning against the window-sill, stood for a few moments in silence looking down at her. A tiny frown suggested that he was uncertain what next to do or say. When he spoke, it was gently enough:

"I am sorry if I spoke harshly just now. But what I said was true, and there are no two ways about it. We're not the people for love in a cottage, and I have my own life to keep going. And in a way I am trying to get you a life of your own also. Try and look at it like that. Now have a good rest and a bottle of wine for supper. There's no one due tonight, and I'll be round tomorrow."

Stooping, he patted her dishevelled head and went softly away.

Lottie made no further attempt either to persuade or to defy. Her days passed in a sort of apathy, and she tended to receive the callers and ply her trade so abstractedly that complaints began to reach Frensham.

He remonstrated with her, remarking that when he made love to her she was as she had always been. Why then sulk over what was merely a profession like any other? Maybe she *was* bored, and some of the men were admittedly dull dogs. But for God's sake try not to show it!

"It's not boredom" she replied quietly. "It's just that I'm not there—not the real Me. With you it's different. You see, I love you. But I'll try to do better."

When the desultory entertainment of moneyed strangers had lasted for several months, Frensham's private affairs took a turn for the worse. Thereupon he informed Lottie roughly that she would have not only to work harder, but also to pay over a handsome share of her earnings in order to keep him decently afloat.

"You've got off damned lightly up to now" he said "and I'm cutting in."

He seemed genuinely to believe that hitherto the money had been her perquisite only, ignoring the fact that he frequently ate in Park Row, and continually sent her out to buy him cigars and shirts and underclothes.

She was feeling tired and nervous at the moment when he made this announcement, and the insolence of his manner angered her.

"In that case" she snapped "you can find your own eats and drinks and smokes, and make your own diggings in a filthy mess and see to your own laundry."

He answered her back with curses, and they had their first quarrel.

It was followed by others and with increasing frequency. True to his word, he sent more and more clients; but whereas formerly he had been careful to select only men of decent breeding who could be trusted to behave themselves, he now went wherever there was money to be had.

She complained bitterly of this falling off in the quality of the persons introduced, lamenting the increasing disgust with which she faced up to each new day. Frensham merely shrugged his shoulders.

"It takes all sorts to make a world" he said. "Take a couple of neat whiskies beforehand, and you won't worry so much about the other party."

This callousness finally killed the girl's unhappy passion for an irreclaimable cad. For some while it had been ailing, feeding upon itself, persisting by tradition and unrenewed by feeling; now it wilted finally, lost consciousness and died.

Inevitably this death of her love for Frensham (and for all its animalism it had been a genuine devotion, colouring her whole existence, setting a standard of conduct below which, for fear of being unworthy of him, she would not permit herself to fall) had repercussions on her personal habits. He had suggested whisky as a drug to sensibility, and she had found the idea a useful one. Gradually an occasional precaution had become a habit for its own sake; and now, in the mood of reckless despair which seized her when her former idol had become a hated tyrant, she resorted continually to the bottle, as a means of dulling her awareness of the futility and beastliness of her way of life. With a drift into intemperance went a coarsening of the fibres of her mind. Once long ago she had broken out at Paul Gladwin with the foul-mouthed virulence of a slum-child; once again, not so long ago, she had railed at Merlette in language which had risen unbidden from the depths of her sub-conscious. But except on these two occasions when anger had broken through her self-control, she had maintained a fastidiousness of talk and manner which seemed to have become ingrained. Now, however, amid the ashes of her self-respect, thought and speech were loosened under the influence of spirits, and she found an outlet for her spleen in grossness and profanity. The increasing deterioration of her behaviour was savagely resented by Frensham, to whom she would return insult for insult, as yet another quarrel dragged to its strident close.

(iv) MAY 1875

Early one afternoon in May 1875 Frensham came to Park Row to say that Lottie was to meet a friend of his with a view to business.

"He's rich as Croesus, and adores a fine girl; and as he can give me a leg up if he's so minded, I'll do a deal with you. If you're nice to him and, in return, he does for me what I want him to do, you shall keep every cooter you can get out of him. That's fair, ain't it?"

"I suppose so" she said ungraciously, "though there's probably a catch in it. Where does Mr Croesus Rutty-guts hang out?"

"None o' that" he said sharply. "You're a lady, mind you, and must behave like one. No swearing, no vulgar words and only wine. Understand?"

"Go to hell!" she replied "and tip us the yarn. What happens next?"

371

"We're to meet him at a pub off Fleet Street. He's got business at the office of some sporting paper, and has to get back to Newmarket this evening. I don't fancy the place much, but he insists. If you get on together, he'll let you know when next he's in town. So prink up and we'll get a hansom."

They reached the Marigold about four o'clock. The place was nearly empty. In a corner of the divan an unobtrusive nondescript man, with a coffee-tray in front of him, was turning over a bundle of papers. Behind the bar in the background a barmaid sat on a stool knitting. One wall of the divan was hung with heavy tarpaulin, from the other side of which came muffled sounds of hammering and the gruff voices of workmen, for the Marigold was involved in one of its periodical enlargements. There remained, in the way of human incident, a man of enormous size, facing the door and occupying nearly the whole of a sofa designed for two. He was wearing a suit of sponge-bag checks, and a diamond as large as a pea sparkled across the room from the folds of his exaggerated cravat. When he saw them come in, he moved his hand in greeting, but did not rise.

"Permit me" said Frensham, speaking in a low hurried voice, "Mr Quass, Miss Heape."

"How do, me dear, how do Frensham. Sit ee down and we'll crack a bottle. Hi, miss!" (he roared the words into space, it being no easy task to turn his head and speak over his shoulder) "Magnum of fizz and stir yer stumps."

Lottie, as she took a chair with her back to the light, surveyed the rich man she had come to tempt. Never in her life had she seen anything so repulsive. On a bloated body, like that of a corpse long drowned, lolled a small bald head. The face was crimson and suffused, the mouth tiny and very moist. The creature's hands, at the end of abnormally long arms, were chubby and hairless. She felt suddenly sick, and had to turn her eyes away to still the queasiness of her stomach. They strayed across the divan, and chanced to light on the face of the quietly occupied man in the corner at a moment when, in order to see more clearly a paper he was trying to decipher, he had turned in his chair toward the window.

Her heart missed a beat, as out of the past that face loomed up—younger, then, and less assured, but the same face beyond a shadow of doubt. She looked quickly away, dropping her head in case he should catch sight of her, waiting for him to resume his earlier position so that she could furtively study him once more. At this moment a stool bearing a tray on which were the bottle of champagne and three glasses, was placed in front of Mr Quass who, sitting motionless with his nasty pallid hands lying like lumps of creamed chicken on the vast bolsters of his thighs, commanded:

"Dollop it out, Frenshie, and we'll drink to all we are allowed to see of this lovely young lady."

The toast honoured (she made no acknowledgment nor even raised her eyes), Lottie was free to drink for herself; and the double shock of realising Mr Quass and recognising Paul Gladwin had left her so much in need of a stimulant that she drained her glass at a gulp.

"Ho-ho!" cried the monster "our little girlie takes kindly to the Widow! Not much danger of her bein a widow for a bit, I'll wager—not while Daddy Quass is around anyway! Fill er up again, Frenshie, and loosen er tongue."

She merely sipped at the second glass, and was leaning forward to replace it on the tray, when Quass stretched out an arm, caught her by the left wrist and with surprising strength pulled her from her chair.

"Come and sit by me, pretty one, all cosy like, and let me have a look at you."

His hand, so smooth and colourless, was like a vice on her wrist; and before she could begin to struggle, she found herself jammed in the corner of the sofa, her left side pressed disgustingly into his hot yielding bulk, her right arm squeezed between her own body and the sofa arm. With an effort she kept her head, and spoke in her normal voice:

"Dudley, tell Mr Quass to let me go. I don't like being mauled about."

Frensham flashed his false and gleaming smile.

"Don't you indeed?" he sneered. "I thought that was what you were for. And why all the fuss? Nobody's hurting you."

At this moment Quass reached across with his other hand and began pawing at her breast. It was a warm sunny day, and she wore only a light dust-coat over a thin summer dress. On her head was a shady hat secured by two stout hat-pins. With a sudden jerk she managed to free her right hand, plucked out a hat-pin, and drove it with all her strength into the upper part of the arm which the gross brute had stretched across her. With a bellow of pain Quass released her wrist, and clapped a hand on the wounded spot into which the hat-pin was firmly and agonisingly stuck. By this time Lottie was on her feet and running across the café.

"Mr Gladwin" she panted. "Mr Gladwin! Please help me! That filthy swine has assaulted me!"

For a moment astonishment at this extraordinary irruption set Gladwin staring bemusedly at her face. But the humble adoration and devotion, which for years he had cherished for little Lottie Heape and which no cruelty could destroy, told him, immediately his wits returned, who she was. He felt a surge of joyous excitement, but wasted no time over exclamations of surprise or pleasure.

"Come with me" he said. "Toby's about."

As they hurried toward the bar, the sofa was still loud with noises of pain and rage. Frensham, bending over the wounded Quass, was trying to get a grip of the tumid mass of the creature's upper arm, in order to give the hat-pin the quick jerk necessary to draw it out. A howl of anguish, denoting that the deed was done, sounded just as Gladwin, loudly calling "Toby!", pushed his way through the curtain of the landlord's sanctum. In a few words he explained what had occurred, and the three of them were out from behind the bar by the time he had finished. Toby gave one look toward the sofa and shouted "George!" at the top of his voice. There was a noise of heavy boots clumping up basement stairs, and a powerful cellarman in a green baize apron and shirt sleeves hurried to join them.

"Servant, guvnor. What's the kick-up?"

"Kick-*out*, more like. Keep yer dooks handy." To Paul "Mr Gladwin, do you take the young lady into the office. I'll come along, when George and I have wiped these babies' noses."

Paul obeyed, and Toby bore down on Quass and Frensham.

When they found themselves alone in Toby's office, both girl and man were stricken with shyness. Lottie, in reaction from her recent painful experience, felt suddenly exhausted and, struggling to key herself up to make some suitable acknowledgment of his help, only succeeded in filling her head with memories of Lashwater and of the wrong she had done him. Paul, now that the moment of crisis was over, was seized by breathless incredulity at this wonderful meeting. He pinched himself to be sure that he was really within a few feet of the being he loved best in the world, the adorable child he had never thought to see again. He also had visions of Lashwater, but they were all of Lottie as he wished to remember her—of her grace and gaiety, of the few blessed occasions when she had been kind and gentle with him. With a start he realised that he was staring fixedly at a real and present-day Lottie, with eyes which saw only the lovely half-grown girl of years ago. She raised her head suddenly and caught him gazing at her. With an effort she found her voice:

"Paul" she said softly. "You don't mind if I call you Paul?—you have saved my reason. If that brute had touched me again, I should have gone stark staring mad! I wish I could thank *you* as easily as I can thank Providence for putting you within reach." And as she spoke, she stretched out both hands.

Mumbling an inaudible protest, he took them and held them tenderly, looking down at her as she sat in the arm-chair and gazed up at him, her eyes bright with tears.

"Lottie" he managed to croak out at last "dear, dear Lottie. The very sight of you had knocked me sideways. I always was a clumsy old stupid—you told me that often enough!—and at this moment I'm more so than ever. But oh, Lottie, it's heaven to see you!"

Her relief at having escaped the abominable Quass was suddenly transformed into an immense gratitude to Gladwin, which flooded her whole being with warmth and compassion. He asked so little, forgave so much, looked at her with such gentle yearning! What a debt she owed him—and a debt she must not leave unpaid.

"I would like to hear everything that has happened since— since—well, since we last met. You look happier, Paul— happier and stronger. Are you happier?"

He smiled.

"I was always happy when I could see you, though sometimes we had differences, hadn't we? Now 'happy' is hardly the word. I just can't believe it's true. But what about you? Married?"

She winced inwardly and shook her head.

"No; not married."

"Happy?"

She held his gaze for a few moments longer, then her lips began to quiver, and turning away she covered her face with both hands. He saw her shoulders shake once or twice, but she choked back the tears. Speaking indistinctly through the barrier of her hands, she murmured:

"Not happy either, Paul. Very, very miserable."

He was about to risk an awkward attempt at consolation, when Toby's step sounded beyond the curtain and the landlord made his appearance.

"Well, they've cleared out" he said "and a good riddance of bad rubbish. I regret, madam, you should have had a disagreeable experience on these premises."

He spoke stiffly, uncertain how to treat a young woman who had come in with a man he knew well by sight and by reputation, in order to meet one of the most nauseating specimens in his experience. Toby had no illusions as to the purpose of the meeting; and traffic of the kind associated with Frensham's name was universally known to be at the top of the list of things forbidden in the Marigold.

Frensham had been nervous with good reason; and when confronted by an infuriated Toby and a silent but menacing George, his usual pert bravado dissolved into craven funk. Retreating backwards in the direction of the door and gesturing with shaking hands, he stammered an assurance that he had only come to keep an appointment with his friend, who was a great power at Newmarket and with whom he had urgent business to transact. Toby listened but made no response to these excuses. He stood where he was, watching the poltroon with undisguised contempt, while George stalked him ominously toward the street, keeping in step and face to face with him. The effect was that of some absurd ritual dance, and the scene would have been comic, had not Frensham's abject cowardice reduced it to a level of cringing ignominy.

Paul was immediately conscious of the landlord's reserve, and realised that Lottie was regarded, if not with hostility, at any rate with suspicion. So he decided not to introduce her nor to speak of their earlier acquaintance, as he would normally have done, lest the manner of Toby's response should disconcert or distress her. Instead he thanked the landlord for acting so promptly, and added: "I am afraid this young lady has had something of a shock. May I" turning politely to Lottie "offer you a stimulant of some kind?"

She gave him a quick look, noting the formality of his manner, and her swift intelligence grasped that for the time being they were strangers.

"Thank you" she smiled shyly. "That is very kind."

Toby suddenly smacked his thigh and chuckled.

"There's two-thirds of a magnum of Clicquot standing out there, and paid for by the lump who made all the trouble."

Paul laughed.

"Poetic justice! Let's see how it tastes. I'll go and get it."

While he was out of the room Lottie, with modest embarrassment, asked Toby to direct her to the ladies' room.

"I feel a little pulled about" she apologised, and when Paul returned the landlord was alone.

"Mr Gladwin" said Toby, talking fast and in an under-tone "I must warn you that the fellow who brought this girl in here is a thorough-paced rogue. He's a man-about-town on the surface and is received in some circles where they are not too particular, or are not yet fly to what's what; but underneath he's a shady gambler and a sponger on women. So watch your step with the young lady."

"Thanks, Toby, I will—though I'm not much of a one for the harpies, even if she is a harpy. Hardly worth the trouble."

At this juncture Lottie returned. The champagne had lost its pristine fervour, but tasted agreeably enough.

"And now, if you will allow me to put you in a cab?" said Paul.

With a little bow to Toby, which was drily returned, she moved toward the outer door. Paul collected his portfolio of papers and followed her. They did not speak until they had turned the corner of the lane into Fleet Street.

It was now something after five, and the sun still shone bright and warm.

"Let's go and sit in the Park" she said. "We can talk there."

He hailed a hansom.

"Your friend Toby didn't like me" she remarked, when they found two chairs near the Achilles statue. "Why was that?"

"It wasn't you he disliked, it was your escort. I hope you didn't mind my pretending we were strangers. I felt at once the atmosphere was a bit murky, and when you were out of the room, he told me that the chap you came with was a bad lot."

"A bad lot!" she repeated bitterly. "A bad lot!" Then added in a low tremulous voice "And I was in love with him once . . . not so long ago either. . . . So now you know the kind of girl I am."

Paul was much moved by the pathos of this little confession. To realise that this drooping self-humbling beauty was the same girl as the pert, tart imperious Lottie he had known six or seven years ago both pained and shamed him. The pain was his own—due to a quite unreasonable feeling that somehow he should have protected her from the bruises she had clearly suffered at the world's hands; the shame was on her behalf—that she should have been driven to humble herself like a penitent Magdalen—and, of all people, to him. Paul's self-abnegation, on this as on all other occasions, was perfectly genuine. One might have expected that, adoring the girl as he did and having chanced on her at a moment when she was prostrate at his feet, he would have seized the opportunity of self-assertion, of declaring his love, of pressing her to take an honourable chance of escape from what, by her own admission, was desperate unhappiness. But he did none of these things. He pitied her from the bottom of his heart, blamed himself for the past, yet never for one moment conceived that her future might be his to ordain.

He reached for her hand and nestled it in his own.

"Poor Lottie! Poor ill-used little Lottie! I am so very sorry. Don't think or speak of it any more. It will distress you too much."

She smiled a sad smile.

"You are too good to me, Paul. You always were. I was loathsome to you as a kid, when I had a home and kind friends; but now that I would like to make up to you for my piggishness, I cannot, because the only way I can do so . . . " and her voice trailed into silence.

A lump in his throat made speech impossible. He merely pressed her hand and sat staring miserably across the Park.

Suddenly, and in a more cheerful tone, she said: "Come with me to my place. It is not far, and as we go you will tell me all your news. I want to change my clothes—these things remind me of that monster from whom you rescued me. And then, if you have the time, I will get you some supper and we can talk some more. I feel better already, Paul, and it is all your doing."

As they walked toward Park Row he chattered of his work for Clegg and of the progress of the house-organ.

"All these papers are stuff for the next number. I often

step into Toby's on my way back from Shoreditch to have a cup of coffee and run over what has happened during the day."

Happiness at being with her, at seeing her smile, at feeling that after all these years he and she were walking in London —just the two of them and at peace—took delectable hold of him. It was a sweet and wholesome intoxication; but, like intoxication of the other kind, it made him garrulous. Speaking of Toby brought Matt to mind.

"And I see Matt Merton very frequently also" he said.

She looked enquiry: "Matt Merton?"

"Why, yes, the chap I was with when we pulled you out of Granby Street and took you to Mr Meadows at St John's. He did most of it. He's a grand fellow. Mr Meadows still sees him quite often. Don't you remember him?"

"You old silly, how should I? A kid of nine, and a man I never set eyes on since. I *have*, however, heard the name. He's newspapers too, isn't he?"

The "too" delighted Paul. To be bracketed with the real Press, and by his darling Lottie, was enchanting.

"He's more than 'newspapers', sweetheart, and I'm far, far less. Matt does the big Special Commissioner stuff for *Diogenes*. Don't you recall the hullabaloo over Homes from Home? That was him."

She caught her breath.

"Homes from Home" she murmured, "Homes from Home". Then evenly: "Oh yes, I remember. I did not read Mr Merton, but I heard about the bust-up. He must be a very clever man."

Paul was about to add "and a very plucky one", when he realised with horror that he had divulged a rigid anonymity. "Oh God" he thought "what a babbling fool I am!" and waited in terror for her next question. But she said nothing further on the subject, and pointed to a flower-bed, brilliant with heads of lupin of all colours.

"Isn't that lovely, Paul? Like a spikey rainbow."

With the collapse of Matt Merton as a subject for conversation an awkward silence fell. Each sought anxiously for some neutral topic; but the field was restricted and there were many taboos. Neither desired to mention the final scenes at Lashwater, nor Mervyn Crocker, nor his father's suicide. Lottie suppressed the whole subject of Fleischmann, and only touched in outline on her disastrous association with Frensham. The sole theme which seemed to her to offer no obstacle was her catering period in Bayswater, and this, as a mine of interest, was soon exhausted. So both parties were rather relieved when they reached her lodgings.

She showed him into the sitting-room, and he exclaimed at its prettiness. His appreciation was wholly sincere, without trace of jealousy or hint of disapproval as to the source of so much comfort.

"Make yourself at home, Paul. I won't be long."

He heard her run upstairs and enter the room over his head. Then her steps stopped short. There was a brief interval of complete silence, which was broken by a cry of horror.

"Paul! Paul! Come up here! Come and see what he's done!"

He hurried up the stairs, and found her clinging to the jamb of an open bedroom door. The place was in chaos. The drawers had been pulled out and their contents strewn everywhere; the wardrobe had been rifled; on and around the washstand lay shattered bottles of scent and other toilet preparations. The bed had been stripped to the mattress and soaked with water. A large mirror was starred in several places, and a scatter of boots and shoes on the carpet in front of it indicated how the damage had been done.

"What—what" he stammered. "What does it mean?"

She was white with fury.

"You devil! You filthy rat!" she muttered between her teeth. Then started forward and ran to her wardrobe. "My jewels!" she cried. "My money!" She groped feverishly in the depths of a drawer. Turning toward Paul she held out, in one hand a leather jewel-box, in the other a purse and wallet. The former appeared to be untouched, the latter flapped limp and empty. "Do you see? Jewels not touched—he didn't dare—he knew I could describe them;

381

money all gone. A sneak-thief as well as a dirty ponce!"
Her voice rose to a wail. "What am I to do? What'll
become of me, with my clothes and furniture ruined and my
money gone? There were fifty pounds in here—more—and
the —— has taken them all. . . . Oh my God, my God, what
a poor wretched creature I am!"

She flung herself face downward on the sodden mattress,
and burst into a storm of weeping.

Paul hovered in flustered perplexity. Some of the words
she had used jarred on him; but her misery was so evident,
and the hooligan spite of this silly wreckage so heart-breaking,
that he made every allowance and a few over. What, however,
should he do next? Instinct—that species of nervous bungling
peculiar to his innate incompetence—told him to pat her on
the shoulder and say "There, there"; but for once common-
sense put instinct in its place. Ignoring the still tearful
Lottie, he began putting the room to rights. He collected
the shoes; he collected the broken glass; he began to restore
to their wrong drawers the garments strewn about the floor.
The process affected him strangely. Despite himself he felt
a stirring of excitement as he handled her clothing, and there
came a moment when, hardly knowing that he did so, he
stood staring in a daze at a nightgown two-thirds of the finest
cambric, and the balance lace-insertion. A chuckle from the
bed, and he was startled to see a mocking eye fixed on him.

"Left-hand corner of the second from the top" said a
voice. He blushed and, awkwardly enough, stowed the
lavender-scented trifle where bidden. Lottie swung herself
into a sitting position and with a low gurgling laugh said:

"Paul, you are sweet!"

Once more common-sense took charge. Rising from his
knees, he walked across the room and put his hands on her
shoulders.

"Listen, Lottie. I can let you have some money. But
you must eat. Also your mattress must be dried. Is there
food in the house or would you like to go out?"

She stared at him, uncomprehending.

"Try to understand. The money is in my room off the

Strand. I must go and fetch it. If you have food here, you can prepare it while I am gone and get the mattress to a fire and finish clearing up. If there is no food, you must come out with me to find some, and the clearing-up must wait. Which is it?"

She shook herself, and the film vanished from her eyes.

"I'm sorry. There is enough food for you and me. I will see to all that. How long will you be?"

"Only to the Strand and back. Forty minutes perhaps."

Actually he did not return for nearly two hours. Such cash as he found in his room was insufficient, and he made a round of acquaintances, borrowing until the following day. When at last he regained Park Row, the front door was locked. He rang and in due course heavy steps from the basement announced the approach of the landlady. She was a lethargic uncensorious person, who overcharged for toler-ance. "Miss Heape?" he enquired. "First door on the right" she replied, "but you might give an and with some beddin." He followed her to her basement, and from the front of the kitchen fire they lugged to the first floor the now dry centrepiece of Lottie's bed. Panting a little, they regained the entrance hall. The landlady jerked a thumb. "Door on the right" she said "and I opes as you ain't one o' them tempriss blokes."

Lottie was very drunk. Except for a loose dressing-gown, she was also naked. As Paul closed the door behind him, she wove her way in and out of the furniture, and plumped into a chair directly opposite to where he stood.

"You bin the helluva time" she said thickly. "Got the dibs?"

He was shocked and horrified by her voice and appearance, and one more worldly wise would have ignored the question until the situation had been clarified.

But Paul was too honourable and too timid an innocent to temporise. He produced a little canvas bag, bulging with money.

"There's fifty or sixty pounds, Lottie. All I could get.

I hope it will be enough. Sorry to be so long, but I had to hunt up one or two fellows."

He was holding the little bag out to her, when he realised that, with neither pocket nor reticule, she had nowhere to put it. He became suddenly embarrassed, and turning away laid the money on a side-table.

"Sixty quid? Prime! Don't often net a real swell like my lil Paullie! Have a drink, Paullie? No? Well, I will, thank-ee-very-much."

She walked unsteadily toward the sideboard on which stood bottles and glasses, and, leaning against it with her back to Paul, began to ruminate aloud.

"Whish'll it be? Whisky or brandy? Whish I have last? Doan remember. Never mind. A drop of whisky makes me frisky, a sip of brandy makes me randy. Poem. Dye hear that, Paullie? Didn't know I was a poet, did you? Mustn't tell jolly old Tennyson . . . might upset him. Nor Mr Bloody Browning either."

There was a rattle of glass on glass, and she turned round, holding a tumbler half-full of neat whisky. Paul felt paralysed with pity and disgust, and could only stand there in miserable immobility.

"Siddown, Paullie!" she ordered. "Sidover there."

Hardly knowing he did so, he obeyed.

"Good Lord! I haven't shown you me birthday suit! 'Member I went upstairs to change—when we found what that —— had done? Well, you went off, and I cleared the place up and you didn come back so I got the hump an had a lil drink and sunly real—realeye . . . sunly found I hadn't changed after all. So I went through me things and chose this one. Like it?"

With a noisy giggle she slipped off her wrapper and stood stark naked in front of him. Despite himself he had to look at her, and a magnificent sight she was. Her perfect proportions, her flawless skin, and the range of colouring from the rich brown of her hair through blush-rose and delicate coral pink to a dark cream shading into white, united to produce a consummate blend of tint and symmetry.

She began to pirouette slowly round—shakily at first, so that some of the spirit from her glass splashed over her arm and on to the carpet. But soon the circling motion gave place to a little gliding dance, into which she seemed gradually to become absorbed. She moved as in a trance, and her steps no longer stumbled nor faltered. As he watched her, still repelled but conscious of a warming of the blood, there rose before him a vision of a young girl in a cloak and bonnet, alone in a misty garden among snow-laden shrubs, improvising just such a dance on grass spongey with a sudden thaw. That child, that entrancing half-woman of sixteen, was now this lovely, shameless tipsy creature, who should by rights be terrible, who *was* terrible, yet was his queen and the mistress of his heart. She ceased dancing and stepped meticulously to the sideboard. There she refilled her glass, drained it at a gulp and put it down again with exaggerated care. Then she sidled across the room toward him. The next moment she was standing behind his low-backed chair, bending over him and pressing his head between her breasts. The sensation was delicious, and he closed his eyes.

She began to sway slowly from side to side, crooning softly

> Hush-a-bye baby
> in your soft nest.
> Very soon, maybe,
> you'll ask for the rest.
> Quickly to bed
> and promptly to rise,
> and Lottie will give you
> a lovely surprise.

The last glass of spirits had floated her out of the bemused incoherent stage of drunkenness into another one. This further stage, in her case, was that producing an ephemeral but abnormal sharpening of the wits, which function with extraordinary ingenuity and speed along whatsoever lines come most easily to them, and create in their owner a mood of genial self-complacency. Lottie sober had a mind like quicksilver. It flitted rapidly and apparently at random from subject to subject; it could improvise a story, an excuse, or a lie without an apparent moment of hesitation. In her present state this gift of invention was so stimulated that she had devised impromptu the jingle which accompanied her overwhelming caress. When she released his head and straightened her back, she said (speaking quite clearly, though with cautious deliberation)

"I *am* poetical tonight. I wonder if I'll remember that one. It was good. Don't you think it was good, Paullie?"

Glancing down, she saw that his head had fallen sideways toward his shoulder and that his eyes were still shut. She ran her hand through his hair, and with a sigh and a start he sat up.

"Why did you move away, Lottie?" he murmured. "I was so happy . . . so happy."

"You shall be happy again, poor little man. Let's go upstairs. Damn, there's no mattress!"

"Yes, there is" he replied, still in a dreamy distant voice. "We took it up—the woman downstairs and I."

"Good boy!" she came from behind the chair and, taking his hands, pulled him to his feet. Finding himself standing a few inches from her glorious nudity, his head began to swim. He went down on his knees, his hands slithering the length of her smooth firm flanks. He laid his head against her thighs, and started to cry quietly.

"What in God's name—" she began, but he held her more closely to him and implored in muffled tones:

"Please, please don't move! Let me stay here just a minute. It's paradise . . . and you are so beautiful. . . ."

For a few seconds she humoured him; but the phase of intensified mental quickness and general amiability was already passing, and she felt a craving for another drink. The man, crouching on the floor and pressing against her legs, became an irritation, and she could feel his tears wet upon her skin. Still good humoured but none too gently she pushed him away.

"Get up, you silly! Come on to bed. I'm sick of being a pose plastique with a cry-baby tied round me legs."

He scrambled obediently to his feet and smiled at her mistily. He had surrendered to the call of the flesh, and swung in a delectable coma over a gulf of sensual anticipation. She picked up her wrap and flung it over her shoulders.

"Take the tray" she said "and I'll turn down the gas."

The night was balmy and still, and through the curtains which masked the open window of the bedroom, the soft clean air of the Park crept sweetly in. He set the tray on the dressing-table, and noted with pleasure that the room had been put to rights. Only the damage to the mirror recalled the earlier scene of devastation.

In a few minutes Lottie appeared, carrying the dressing-gown over one arm.

"Lor!" she said. "Ain't you even got ready? You were always one to moon about. Buck up, slow coach, while I have one for the road."

Docile he sat down and began to unlace his boots. When he had taken them off and put them tidily under a chair, he got to his feet and had half-removed his coat, when she came and stood against him and literally engulfed his mouth in a horrible slobbering kiss, which reeked of spirits. His arms were pinioned in his coat sleeves and he could only escape a second assault by turning his head as far as possible to one side. She nibbled at his throat, and her lips were wet and slippery.

A wave of nausea swept over him, and in the moment of its breaking he came back to sanity and to a realisation of the hideous truth. What had seemed a promise of Heaven and the fulfilment of his fondest dream was revealed—now that the fever had abated and left him in the cold sweat of its aftermath—to be a bestial defilement of the only beauty his life had known. His love for Lottie Heape had been a reverential, self-forgetful devotion to an ideal of girlhood which he wished to believe was personified in her; and that enduring, patient love had culminated in what, for a fleeting moment of discernment, he saw to be a squalid debauch between a lecherous good-for-nothing and a drunken harlot.

Yet even in this tragic pass he clung to self-deception, blaming himself, not her. With a desperate wrench he split the seam of one of his coat sleeves, pulled his arms free and, stepping back a pace, thrust out his hands in supplication.

"Forgive me, my love! I beg you to forgive me! I have treated my beautiful Lottie like a street-woman. I was mad, darling—possessed of a devil; but I am sane now, and can only humbly beg your pardon."

The whisky had now brought her to the last sentient phase of its repertoire. She was in the vicious temper which seeks to wound and always finds a way. She broke into a raucous tirade of filthy insult; then sank suddenly to a dangerous and terrifying undertone, which gradually grew louder.

"Borne with you? You snivelling spunkless little rat, d'you think I'd even give you a glance in the street if you hadn't first paid money to have me? Damn and blast it, you've bought me, havenyou? Here's the boodle, isn't it?" (she shook the canvas bag until the contents chinked like an evil grin) "and here am I. I do my job, I'm not here to be darlinged and begged pardon and all that rot!" Her voice rose to a scream. "If you don't want what you've paid for— or *can't*—then go to —— hell and —— yourself!"

While she was spilling this stream of rabid bile, Paul's heart broke. Shattered his cherished image of the goddess he was proud to worship, vanished the hope that life for him could ever again be tolerable. Without a word he put on his boots and his torn flapping coat, and with head bowed went to the door. On the threshold he turned. Lottie, still clutching a glass, was lurching toward the bed. Suddenly she pitched forward on to the mattress and was violently, prolifically sick. The glass fell to the floor and broke with a sharp crack. The woman rolled over, and lay snoring amid her vomit.

Not long before midnight on this evening in May Paul drifted into a tavern in Catherine Street. He was bareheaded. One sleeve of his coat was torn away at the shoulder, and flapped about his elbow. He bought three bottles of gin and took them upstairs to his high room in the corner house.

At about eleven the next morning he emerged unsteadily into the street again, wove an uncertain way along the crowded pavement of the Strand, climbed on to a City-bound omnibus at the corner of Drury Lane and arrived eventually at Norton Folgate. Here he left the omnibus, taking the deep step to street-level with meticulous care, and stood for a few moments swaying vaguely in the bright sunshine, one hand clutching a convenient lamp-post, the other making the waving movements of a hand holding a cigar. There was no cigar; and several passers-by smiled tolerantly to see this respectably dressed if somewhat dishevelled citizen, happily screwed by noon of a perfect spring day, and grace-fully moving his hand from his lips outward and then inward to his lips again, while with pursed mouth and distended nostrils he exhaled delicious but imaginary smoke.

Paul ignored the smiles (perhaps he did not see them) and continued to oscillate amiably on the edge of the curb. But when an urchin with a rolled-up fragment of brown paper in his mouth swaggered up to him and shrilled "Gi' us a light, mister" he came to, and regarded the child with kindly gravity.

"Pleasure, my dear sir" he said at last. "Pleasure I assure you"; and taking a box of fusees from his pocket, solemnly held one to the end of the home-made "cigar", which sizzled into harsh smelly smoke and set the midget coughing.

"And now if you'll excuse me" Paul resumed "I must— I really *must*—be off."

He swung about with the help of the lamp-post and sur-veyed the buildings behind him. Up to now he had made his journey automatically and as though on his usual way to Clegg's place of business which stood a few hundred yards further on; but the sight of a tavern just across the pavement from where he stood suggested a more agreeable occupation than compiling a price-list of boating and cricketing outfits. He made a steady though faintly diagonal course from the lamp-post to the entrance of the Saloon Bar, and was lost to sight.

Three days later Percy Clegg came into the little room where Paul worked, shut the door firmly behind him and leant against it.

"Now then you drunken swine" he began between clenched teeth. "I want to know whatcher mean by blabbing in pubs and giving my snap away."

Paul had risen to his feet and looked at his employer in uneasy bewilderment.

"I—I don't understand, sir?"

"You shall, my gin-swillin mouth-almighty. Only too well. A day or two ago in the King o Hanover, full to the bung of tape, you told a bunch of stinkers that Clegg and Son were goin up west and would close a deal next day for a prime corner site in New Oxford Street. Remember?"

Paul shook his head.

"No, sir. I'm afraid I remember very little of what happened that morning. I—I—I was not at all well."

Clegg snorted.

"Like ell you weren't! Then you'll probly not remember either oo was listenin to you. I'll tell you. Sol Feinbaum— and e went straight up to New Oxford Street that very afternoon, the dirty ——, offered the chap fifty pun extra and snaffled the shop. I come along next day, cordin to arrangement, and find I'm done in the eye. And for that I ave *you* to thank, which I do ere and now with a kick up the arse and the order of the sack, first-class and cash down. Out you go and doan come ere again."

He slammed a few coins on to the table, opened the door wide, and stood aside for the other to walk out. As the bemused and frightened Gladwin did so, Clegg took a quick step backward to give himself play, and then delivered a violent running kick, which sent the helpless creature hurtling down a short flight of stairs and crashing into the wall at the bottom.

For a moment Paul lay where he had fallen, then struggled to his feet. His shoulder was wrenched, one ankle twisted and the palms of his hands were smeared with blood and dirt. He did not look back or utter a sound; merely picked up his dusty hat and limped painfully away.

When this happened Matt was away in the north, busy over one of his investigations. On his return he looked in on Toby and, incidentally, enquired about Gladwin.

Toby replied:

"Well, that's a queer thing you should ask, for I was just going to tell you that the last time he was in—must be five weeks back or more—there was a bit of a dust-up and he was dragged into it. A fellow came in with a girl, a fellow I've had pointed out to me more than once as a rank bad lot. (Oh no, not in here, Mr Merton! Not on yer life!) They sat down with a great fat brute whom they'd clearly come to meet. (I didn't see any of this; I was in the back, but Gladwin told me.) Suddenly the girl runs to Gladwin for help—the place was empty except for these four—and he runs to me. George and I chuck the men out; and after a drink to help the girl recover, Gladwin takes her off to find her a cab. That's the last I've seen of him."

"D'you know the girl?"

"Not from Eve. As for him" (Toby went on) "I've wondered now and again if he was ill, and whether enquiries should be made. It's not like him to keep away for so long. But then—you know how things are, Mr Merton. I'm busy, and Mr Gladwin's not one that likes to be fussed over. So I did nothing."

"I'll look him up one day" said Matt.

But when he called at Catherine Street, the landlady said

Mr Gladwin had left her house nearly a month ago, after selling off most of his belongings. No, she had no idea where he had gone.

Not a word was heard of Paul for over six months. Then a short note, written from New York and bearing an accommodation address, said he was in America and getting on all right. Nothing more.

(iii) JUNE 1875-SUMMER 1878

Paul spent three years in America. They were years of slow degeneration both mental and physical; years of gradual decline from modest comfort, through anxious poverty to apathetic squalor; years of growing resignation, with less and less of inward struggle or of outward protest, to a descent, rung by rung, of the ladder which slopes from security to indigence.

But they were not unhappy years, for the reason that they passed in a haze of semi-drunkenness. During these years he surrendered once and for all to the habit of dram-drinking, yet contrived within the limits of surrender to keep a certain sense of proportion. Twice he had brought disaster on himself by reaching a stage when he lost control of his tongue. That must not occur again; and to make sure it should not do so, he devised, after careful experiment, a system of alcoholic absorption which kept him agreeably indifferent to personal humiliation and hardship, without destroying his awareness of what he was doing and saying or of the company he kept.

The idea of visiting the United States had been suggested to him, some weeks before his ejection from Clegg & Son, by a casual American client, who had called at Shoreditch to order some clothes. This gentleman, the owner of a jeweller's shop on lower Broadway, had happened on a stray copy of *Jokes and Jackets* (Clegg's winter magazine for 1874) which by some odd chance had found its way to New York.

He was greatly impressed with the ingenuity of this form of publicity, and promised himself, when he took his trip to London in the spring, to reward Messrs Clegg for their enterprise by giving them an order. And not only did he do this; he also impressed on the man who served him that his patronage was directly due to the influence of the firm's advertising methods. He dwelt with such energy on this theme that the assistant, hoping to curry favour with the boss, fetched Percy Clegg to the fitting-room in order that he should personally receive the compliments of this voluble customer.

Percy was much gratified to learn that his magazine's influence extended across the Atlantic, and accepted the American's tributes with modest complacency. When, however, the persistent enthusiast, instead of dropping the subject and ordering another suit, demanded whether Mr Percy Clegg himself got together and edited this stimulating periodical, the junior partner began to lose interest. He tried to disengage; but the jeweller had him by a coat-button, and with emphatic monotony thumped away with his questions and eulogies until Percy in despair sent for Gladwin, introduced him as the employé responsible for the magazine and, on the plea of urgent business, escaped in a sweat of boredom. The American wrung Gladwin's hand, bade him wait right there for five minutes while he tried on an overcoat and, that done, insisted that the pair of them step across the road and sample the Scotch. Over their drinks he repeated all over again what he had said in praise of *Jokes and Jackets* to the wife in New York, to his friends in New York, to acquaintances on shipboard, to the assistant at Cleggs and to Mr Percy Clegg himself. "If ever" he concluded "you tire of this burg, take the first boat to lil old N'York and come and see your obedient servant Glorney J. Bragg at the Cave of Aladdin— that's what I call my emporium—corner of Broadway and Duane Street. I'll fix you up, and here's my card." Paul made to pick the card from the bar, but Bragg stopped him. "Wait a minute, wait a minute. Guess I'll write the hotel where I'm stayin. I'll be here some weeks yet, and it would

N*   393

certainly be a pleasure to have a further talk. There we are— The Albion on Aldersgate."

And to the Albion on Aldersgate, two days after his final interview with Percy Clegg, Paul tentatively went. His ankle still pained him and his shoulder was tightly bound up; but his hands were clean (if a little sore) and his clothes brushed and tidy. He was doubly lucky. Mr Bragg was not only still in London, but actually in the hotel at the moment, and welcomed his caller warmly. The jeweller may have been (indeed was) an outsize in bores; but, although he said it too often and too loudly, what he said he meant. A week later he and his new publicity expert were boarding the Guion steamship *Idaho* at Liverpool, bound for New York.

* * * * *

Paul worked for Glorney J. Bragg for something over a twelve-month. He found it impossible to devise immediately, as the jeweller had hoped, a journal along the lines of Clegg's magazine, because he had not the contacts with minor writing folk and artists which in London, thanks to Matt's connections, had been almost ready-made. But he imagined that, given time, he could create them, and even, in his tentative diffident way, went through some of the motions of getting in among the boys and winning their good-will. He had hopes a year later of achieving the desired production. Meanwhile he turned all his ingenuity to the unconventionalising of Bragg's catalogues, circulars and press copy, and with sufficient success to keep the jeweller happy.

The capacity to be on easy genial terms with a crowd of semi-strangers is a gift, and a gift poor Paul emphatically did not possess. In consequence his sought-for circle of contributors hardly showed a sign of even beginning to form. As in London, he made neither friends nor enemies. He became a familiar but dim figure in the bars around lower Broadway; responded civilly to greetings; stood a drink in return for each one offered. But he never originated a party, and always detached himself, once hospitality accepted had been returned, and drifted away to another saloon, once more to drink alone. He was now nearing forty; his hair was thinning, and his pasty face, with its indeterminate nose and chin and plaintive irresolute mouth, seemed to be stringing out, as will half-rolled pastry when picked up from the board to be bunched and rolled again.

Time went by, and the influx of material for the magazine was barely a trickle. Paul began to panic. Mr Bragg kept asking how things were making out, and each time proved harder to satisfy with evasive optimism. Then something happened which seemed to the harassed editor a boon from the Gods. Mrs Bragg's father, a widower living in Milwaukee died, and left an unexpectedly large sum of money and a handsome house to his only daughter.

The lady decided that shop-keeping on lower Broadway was no career for the consort of an heiress; also that their children could move in better-class society as members of a leisured family with an elegant home in the residential section of Milwaukee, than as the offspring of a New York tradesman however respectable. Accordingly she persuaded (Glorney J. Bragg said "nagged and bullied") her husband into selling the business and retiring into refined indolence in the Middle West.

The unfortunate man foresaw loss of friends, loss of congenial occupation and loss of opportunity to spend most of his day away from home. But he was forced to give in; and Bragg's Cave of Aladdin and Paul's job closed up simultaneously.

Greatly relieved not to have to confess his lack of progress with the magazine, Paul nevertheless retained sufficient common-sense to realise that, if he was out of a quandary, he was also out of work. He ventured to ask Mr Bragg for a recommendation, and the worthy man sent him to a broker friend, who wanted a clerk and engaged Paul out of liking for Bragg without any other than perfunctory examination of his qualifications.

It only needed two months to show their insufficiency. The new clerk, though punctual and anxious to please, was dreamy, inaccurate and unable to grasp the simplest operation in brokerage. He was given a week's pay in lieu of notice, and found himself, quite alone and without a reference, face to face with the New York labour-market.

There followed a long and miserable period of unsuccessful job-hunting. Paul's stock of money began to run low. He tramped the streets and climbed a thousand stairs and pored over the advertisements in the newspapers. Winter came on, and bitter weather. The city was crowded with seekers after work. Many had special capacities, many had good characters from former employers; even those who had neither were at least Americans, and in that respect one up on an Englishman. It was during this time that Paul perfected his technique as a tippler. Although he was never incapacitated or publicly obstreperous, he was in fact never sober; and his acquaintance-ship with the cheaper class of saloon became wide and various.

While with Bragg, he had been accustomed to take his drinks apart, either at a small table or away from the line of bar-loungers who clustered against the rail and got the range of the spittoon so dexterously. Now, however, he propped up the counter with the best of them, and it was while doing so in a dingy saloon near the Tombs that he landed a job. He found himself next to a seedy individual, with a scrubby top-coat buttoned up to his neck and a shave badly overdue. They fell into conversation, and Paul admitted he was out for any game which would bring in a few dollars. His new acquaintance looked furtively round, edged away to a deserted corner of the bar, and in a voice hoarse with gin, sugar and tobacco juice, invited collaboration in his business of diddling the district attorney. Paul, he suggested, as a newcomer not known by sight in the Tombs, could be sure of at least a short run as a straw-bail man.

The straw-bail man, or professional bailer-out, was at this date badly on the decline; and Paul's companion, who had formerly practised as a shyster lawyer and then, when that form of fraud became more dangerous than profitable, had taken up bailing-out, was now a marked man in both capacities. He proposed to watch for opportunities, tip Paul the wink and the two would go shares in whatsoever a grateful client paid for his release.

The operation required an intelligence service and careful timing. Let us suppose that a decently dressed man is run in for assault and battery. He has been out on a party, and swooping noisily home has resented the interference of a cop. At the Tombs a sleepy clerk, anxious to get home to bed, enters the charge and tells the policeman to push the guy into "Bummer's Hall", where he can cool his heels until the Court opens at 6 a.m. next morning. At that moment a respectable stranger steps up and offers politely to go bail for the culprit. He assures the clerk that the prisoner, who has admittedly taken too much to drink, is a gentleman well known to him, and will appear for trial without fail and pay his fine. Everyone concerned is glad to be rid of a tiresome formality so late at night, and the stranger gabbles the oath, signs his name and gives a security for five hundred dollars. Outside, the rescued reveller, quite sober enough by now to realise he has escaped the humiliation and horror of a night in a stifling, evil-smelling hall crowded with vagabonds, pickpockets and drunks, slips his saviour five, ten or even twenty dollars, and both parties go their way. Next day the judge's clerk receives his small percentage.

This bizarre activity kept Paul Gladwin going for a while; but a change of party in the city administration, and a consequent shuffle of personnel in and about the Tombs, brought it abruptly to an end.

His career as straw-bail man did this, at least, for him— it gave him a connection of sorts among the underlings who served what one might call the "lesser intelligentsia of crookdom", and this connection procured for him an offer from an Exchange Office in West Street. His mild and (even though down-at-heel) respectable appearance struck the proprietor of this office as an excellent qualification for the job of "runner". The duty of a runner was to hang about the docks when a new shipload of travellers and emigrants from

Europe was due to arrive in New York. He watched for evidence of bewilderment among the friendless strangers, selected as victims those who looked relatively prosperous, and with every sign of helpful amiability took them under his wing. They needed to change their money into United States currency; they needed a lodging for the night; many of them would need on the following day to buy a ticket for the next stage of their journey, find out train-times and generally be prepared to plunge into the unknown vastness of the New World. Nothing simpler. Let them but accompany the runner to a reliable Exchange and Ticket Office, and everything would be attended to.

A runner who could speak their language was allotted to each race of emigrants; and as the great majority of persons to be cajoled were genuine emigrants—poor frightened folk of many nationalities—they were liable to be suddenly forgetful of caution in the delight of being addressed in their own tongue. But the vessels bringing emigrants brought also saloon passengers of independent means—many of them Englishmen—so that there was always a chance of landing a rich flat. To achieve this was Paul's special duty and the crown of his ambition.

Once he had delivered his single or multiple catch of emigrants to his employer's narrow dark office Paul's work on that particular assignment was over. It was none of his business to change the foreign currency at indefensible rates (charging a large percentage into the bargain) nor to sell a railroad ticket for use on the morrow for half the distance at full price, nor to see the strangers on their way to a dubious overnight hotel, with which the Exchange Office had a suitable understanding. He was a runner and nothing more, who, returning to the docks, started again.

One day he made overtures to an obvious Britisher (and, judging by his clothes and demeanour, a Britisher of means) whom he observed standing alone outside the gate of Castle Garden, looking about him in an uncertain and puzzled way. The man responded readily, remarked at once that Paul spoke like a compatriot, and expressed great pleasure at having fallen in with an Englishman at the outset of his first visit to the American continent. He was staying a few days in New York before travelling to California, and required both to change his money and make reservations for his long journey.

When they reached West Street, the stranger had his arm through Paul's and, still talking, pushed open the door and drew his guide with him into the office. The clerk at the counter greeted the visitor with effusive politeness, and then snapped over his shoulder: "All right, Gladwin. You can go now." But the new arrival held him tightly by the arm, remarking genially to the clerk that Britishers abroad never parted without a good talk about the old country, that he would do his business with as little delay as possible, and then take his fellow-countryman out for a drink and a cigar.

Reluctantly, but with what he conceived to be a good grace, the clerk began the process of money-changing. The stranger put a pile of sovereigns on the counter, and after a few minutes of calculation by the man in charge, received in exchange a bundle of notes. With startling dexterity he flipped these over, strode to the door and blew a whistle. Next moment the place was alive with men; the clerk, Paul, and two ill-favoured individuals discovered in the back room were under arrest; the sovereigns were removed from the drawer into which they had been swept, and the bogus emigrant led the dejected procession in triumph to a police-van now standing at the curb.

Paul got off with a modest fine and a stern warning. But he was no longer a runner; was once again out of work; and, being forthwith marked down as the dumb cluck who had fallen for a spotter in fancy-dress, was out for keeps so far as decoy-jobs were concerned or any others requiring a modicum of common-sense.

His existence now became one of constant improvisation. He became a professional chorus-singer, and hung about Sixth Avenue cafés with a few drifters of his kind, picking up short bookings with second-rate touring companies due for an up-State circuit; or walking-on in a burlesque show; or crowding the back of the stage in a musical comedy dressed as a Turk, a Cossack or a Red Indian. For a time he was an usher at a Concert Saloon or "Gaiety" on Broadway. It had not the splendour of that outstanding Saloon-specimen, the Canterbury, but it was a good-class place according to its lights. There was a long bar in the first room; then a large saloon with a stage at one end of it, and a wide floor-space dotted with tables and chairs. The occupants of these tables were served by "pretty waiter-girls", in costumes purporting to be those of Turkish, Spanish or Italian damsels, and the intimacy to which, after several drinks, they attained with their trousered or short-frocked handmaidens was nobody's business but their own. Round the three walls ran a tier of "French boxes" or "Wine Rooms"—curtained cubicles, the allotment of which was the usher's perquisite. To a likely couple he would make the whispered offer of a box, or two men alone were given one with the assurance that two lovely girls would join them in five minutes. As was only right, suitable acknowledgment was made of the usher's thoughtfulness. In this place Paul doubled the parts of usher-proper and liaison between amorous spectators and girls appearing on the stage or seated alone on wall-benches below the Wine Rooms. Then, however, the police stirred in their sleep and picked on two or three "Gaieties" for disciplinary action. Paul's proprietor was behind with his pay-off, so that his establishment was rightly included among those to be raided, and was temporarily closed.

Paul's next situation was one which the boss was pleased to describe as "steward" at a dance-house or "free and easy" on Houston Street. Few dives in the whole city of New York could claim to be as low; yet the place had its own peculiar status as a minor depot for political jobbery. The proprietor had vote-catching influence; and in consequence his dive was frequented by certain boodlers and ward-heelers, who found it convenient and profitable to transact their private business behind the curtain of noise normally provided by a disreputable dance-house.

In this capacity the place was a combination of crooks'

kitchen, flat-trap and the Pit of the Damned. At peak moments it was sheer pandemonium. The lights glared, the band brayed and clattered. A crowd of sweating drunks, of bullies, of sneak-thieves, of raddled and raucous women milled over the dance-floor. Round the walls, on benches covered with stained red plush, couples sprawled enlaced. At a small table two painted lushers, wheedling a fuddled drummer to buy another bottle, leant deftly against him, pinioning his arms, while an expert operator watched furtively for his cue.

Paul's job was, in fact, that of a janitor, with the added duty of reassuring new and nervous clients, who might well hesitate in the vestibule when they heard the racket beyond the hangings covering the entrance to the dance-hall. He looked squalid and gin-sodden; but he was manifestly not dangerous, and his quiet English voice had an almost mesmeric effect on timorous visitors by virtue of its contrast with the rasping metallic uproar of the revellers within. He had a chair and table in this vestibule, took the nominal entrance money, and hung on wall-pegs such hats and coats as their owners were rash enough to relinquish. He was universally known as "Doc Limey"—a nickname which dated from the Concert Saloon, and had accompanied him to this nadir of amusement dens—and lived up to the soubriquet by spending intervals of time, during which he had nothing to do, in reading a book.

He was thus engaged early one evening, when a shadow fell across the page and a gruff adenoidal voice said

"Readin, huh? Ain't you the guy they call Doc Limey?"

Paul looked up at the man who stood at his side. He saw a medium-sized man, with a shining bald head and a thick bush of dry grey hair, which ran from ear to ear and stuck out behind over his collar like a misplaced ruff. He wore spectacles with very strong lenses and had a cigar in the corner of his mouth. Paul recognised him as an occasional patron of the dance-house, who seemed to take no part either in the rowdy jollifications or the sinister side-shows, but strode about purposefully with hands in pockets or, sitting at a table with one or more companions, talked in a loud trenchant voice about political undercurrents in the State capital.

In reply to the man's question he nodded but did not speak.

"My name" the other continued "is Sidney Isaacs and I'm a printer and publisher in Albany. Nown again I take a trip to this city on business and look in here for a bit of fun and a gossip. I've noticed you—I notice most things—and I've an idea we could team up together to our mutual benefit. I want a guy who can read and write—*really* read and write, I mean; not skim a newspaper and pick out a love-letter with one finger—and if I find the right-un there's dollars for both of us. Innarested at all? Think it over, and if you care to meet me tomorrow morning at Ma Flanagan's gin-mill, I'll be there at noon."

He turned on his heel and pushed his way through the curtains, back into the hall.

Mr Isaacs' proposition was that Paul should accompany him—not to Albany but to the neighbouring township of Castleton, settle there, and spend his time writing stories for the firm to print and publish. Put like that, the offer sounded like angels' wings; but there were strings to it. The stories were to be of so unusual a kind that they could not be handled in the Albany works, but must be composed and printed on a special press worked by Isaacs himself and set up in a very private room of an unobtrusive frame house in a quiet street in Castleton. Also they could not be published in the ordinary way. Indeed they could not be published at all; but had to be brought to New York in a valise, small lots at a time, and handed over to a few broad-minded customers, one of whom was the boss of the joint where Paul was "steward". Doc Limey's job, therefore, was by no means merely one of authorship. He must learn to handle the small printing-press in case the boss was ill and the matter urgent; he must practise composing; he must proof-read; he must, if required, work the machine which folded the sheets and

clamped them into unlettered wrappers; and he must take
the goods to market.

"And don't you let em catch you either" said Mr Isaacs
"or it's up the river for both of us. They're devilish hot
on stuff of the kind nowadays in Albany, the silly buggers;
although why those who want it mayn't have it, seeing that
those that don't needn't, beats me." After a pause: "Well,
are you on?"

Paul finished his third gin-sling and gazed mistily across
Ma Flanagan's cool and shadowy tavern. Although it was
late September the weather was brilliantly fine and hot, and
beyond the sunblinds the street sizzled and glared. He felt
neither distaste nor inclination for the means of livelihood
now within his reach. Social morality was no affair of his.
No community had ever looked after him, so the community
in which he now lived might as well look after itself. Of his
capacity to turn out material of the required kind, he had
considerable doubts. No woman except Lottie had ever
stirred him. His sexual experience was virtually nil. Indeed
one of the main reasons why he had been allowed to remain
an "usher" and a "steward" longer than a fortnight (for his
unfitness to hold down tough jobs of the kind was pheno-
menal) was that he seemed unaware that girls existed, and
hardly looked at—let alone molested—any of the oncoming
young females who swarmed in wine-room and dance-house,
and were always ready to double-cross their regular fellows.
Trouble of this kind was bad for a joint, and it was a trouble
only too frequently encountered. With Doc Limey one was
safe. It wasn't merely that he could be trusted; in that
particular department of life, he just didn't happen.

And this was the author to whom Mr Sidney Isaacs looked
to produce red-hot novelettes, to stimulate the senses of jaded
age or instruct the ardours of green and fumbling youth!
Paul wondered vaguely whether a worse choice could have
been made. But he did not say so. Instead he concentrated
on the aspect of the proffered career which interested him
most. The money was not only considerably better than a
"steward's" starvation-wage (tips hardly existed, seeing that

departing clients were either penniless or forcibly ejected or too drunk to dwell on such trifles), but Mr Isaacs also promised a commission on sales, and was confident that these would be as large as the difficulties of distribution permitted. The danger element in an occupation wholly illegal, and one commanding little sympathy even among amateurs of illegality, did not impress him one way or the other. His powers of imagination were dulled and limp, and he had come to regard himself as a being so null and so negligible that he could not conceive authority even noticing anything he did, still less being moved to action by it.

So he brooded, while his fourth drink sank in the glass and Isaacs turned the pages of a newspaper, masterful, self-sufficient and unhurried. At last came a moment of alcoholic vision. Paul sat up in his chair, drained a last mouthful, replaced the glass with a sharp tap upon the table and said loudly:

"How do the ungodly flourish, and to hell with the righteous! O.K. Mr Isaacs. I'll come."

As matters turned out, Doc Limey's total lack of interest in the subjects about which he had to write proved an asset rather than a handicap. He began by reading through a collection of pornographic booklets of the most degraded kind which his employer had collected from various sources. They neither disgusted nor excited him. They seemed monotonous, boring and execrably written. But if this was the kind of thing Isaacs wanted, why not rewrite them, mixing the episodes a little, and present the boss with something to print which would at least be literate? The job would be very dull; but it would also be so easy that it could be done mechanically, while the doer indulged in whatsoever pipe-dreams were his fancy. So he began; and, having begun, went on and on.

The mechanical side of his work required more attention, and he was several times angrily rebuked by Isaacs, because his unsteady hand had spoilt a sheet, or bungled the wrapping of two or three booklets. It astonished him a little to find that the compositor was a youngish woman, whose relations with the boss were unexplained. She sat on a stool in the room which housed the little press, setting type from the cases, distributing and sorting it again, with unerring and flickering fingers. She could not but have known what sort of stuff was being printed; and Paul, for all that he had worked for months in places infested with abandoned women, was shocked despite himself, especially as the girl seemed an unassuming ordinary person and not a flaunting trollop. However, as they seldom spoke to one another and he spent most of the time in his own little cubicle with his manuscripts and proof-sheets, he did not progress beyond this sensation of vague disquiet nor discover who she was or why she was there.

And then one day she was not there, and Paul was set to do her work. When Isaacs came in again, he enquired whether the young lady was ill and when she would be back.

"She won't" replied the boss tartly. "I fired her. She threatened to split if I didn't pay her more, and you don't come it over Sidney Isaacs that way."

"But won't she split all the more now?"

"Nope. Daren't do it. I had her write out a set of verses on some pretext when she first came, and there in her handwriting is enough to sink any outraged-decency story she may fake up. She knows I've got it too. I reminded her."

"And am I to go on fiddling with these damn types?"

"I hope not, Doc. You're the hammiest dud at it I ever dreamt of. Your hands are like bunches of bananas with the ague. No; I'm bringin a chap over from Albany. I know so much about him, he can safely know a bit about me. Don't forget your trip to N'York tomorrow. Have you packed the stuff? O.K. You can knock off that job now and get back to your proofs."

The ex-employee from the secret Castleton branch of Isaacs' Printing Works in Albany had a better plan than the direct give-away which the boss thought he had scotched. Also her motive was something stronger than a desire for more money. She was a passionate, single-minded creature behind her demure exterior, and two years as Isaacs' mistress had thrown her desperately into love with him. She only lived to serve him in anything he wished to do, and what he wished was right to her because he wished it. Trained from girlhood in a printing works she had the nimble skill of an expert, and agreed unhesitatingly to do her share in her lover's dangerous venture, without a thought of passing judgment on the kind of work involved.

But one day it came to her knowledge that Isaacs was on with a new love, and the loyal lioness became a tigress out to kill. Giving no sign of any change of mood, she put to him in her normal controlled and reasonable way that composition of this kind carried special risks, that money was needed at home, and that she wanted double her present wage. She knew him well enough to be sure that such a demand as this would at any time throw him into an extreme of fury; and now so more than ever, when he had his new girl on his hands and wanted the old one out of the way. As she expected, he abused her with the grossest violence and sacked her on the spot. She went at once to New York, and informed the police that a man, whom she described in detail, would come into town next day by such a train. He would be carrying a valise, stuffed with material of the liveliest interest to the District Attorney's office. When they asked for her name, address and proof that her story was true, she refused to give any information. "This is a wise-up, and you take it or leave it" she said. "It's one of the hottest rackets there is, and no squealer signs his name. I swear what I say is true. If I'm lying, there's no real harm done; if I'm not, you'll cop big and maybe the D.A. will give you a box of candy."

Paul had not gone many yards along the platform of West Thirtieth Street when he was stopped and his bag opened. He was then hustled into a cab and locked up to await examination.

One of the precautions taken by Isaacs to keep his private

press secret was to instruct Paul to change at Tarrytown, and take the local to the downtown terminus, rather than continue in the main Albany train to the Grand Central Station. Another was to provide him, on each occasion when he travelled to New York carrying a stock of books, with an alternative rail-ticket. His orders were, at the least hint of trouble, to hand up this ticket, which showed his starting-point as any one of a dozen places between the city and Troy, and to get rid of the ticket from Castleton by any means possible. On the day of his arrest, his alternative ticket was from Yonkers, and it was not difficult for him, while the dicks were opening his valise and examining some of the contents, to screw the genuine ticket into a ball and, as he was being put into the cab, flick it into the gutter. Since the girl who had betrayed him had for her own sake made no mention of Castleton or Albany, the only evidence in police possession as to the place of origin of these illegal publications was the ticket from Yonkers to New York.

Under examination Paul appeared dull-witted and obstinate. The obstinacy was genuine. He was suffering from lack of alcohol and felt a sullen resentment against these damned Yankee bobbies who had pushed him roughly about and stopped him getting his usual drinks. But the stupidity was assumed, his intelligence being, in fact, abnormally bright owing to his enforced sobriety. He declared that he knew nothing of the books' origin. He was dead broke, and a fellow he met in a bar in Yonkers had asked him to take the things along and given him a couple of dollars. Where was he taking them? To a bar called Dave's Dive. And where was that? He had no notion; all he knew was to meet a man with a red nose and a spotted neckerchief at the narrow end of Paradise Square, who would serve as guide. Yes, he knew the sort of books they were; but that was no affair of his, so what the hell.

He looked such a wretched creature that his story was believed. It was inconceivable that this broken-backed hob-jobber could be concerned with the production of stuff so explosive as this. Illicit printing and publishing was a crime

which at every stage required courage, resource and absolute
secrecy from all concerned, and no one of these qualities
could reasonably be looked for from this down-and-out
Britisher. So they locked him up again, pending further
enquiries.

The Paradise Square clue was, of course, useless; and as
for Dave's Dive, these bars in the Five Points Section came
and went overnight. There remained Yonkers.

The Yonkers ticket was a lucky chance for Isaacs, for the
town was a considerable place, among whose population were
numerous individuals engaged in several dubious activities.
If the clue had pointed to Troy or to Hudson, the search
might well have spread to Albany; and although Isaacs, the
well-known Albany printer and publisher, could probably
have kept the lid on his private branch in Castleton, he
might well have had a worrying and troublesome time. As
it was, the investigation wore out its patience in fine-combing
Yonkers, and the search was finally abandoned as hopeless.
It was, however, thought desirable to cover up this dis-
comfiture by making an example of the alien bagman who,
however meagrely, had assisted in the nefarious traffic, and
at the same time to seize the chance of blowing off a major
head of moral steam.

Accordingly, when Paul came up for trial, the judge
erupted in a torrent of virtuous grandiloquence. "No doubt"
he boomed, addressing the prisoner "the effete and debauched
aristocracy of your own tyrant-ridden country read little else
than these hideous, these loathsome products of diseased and
prurient minds. We will not deprive them of your services
as courier for a day longer than we must. I therefore sentence
you to immediate deportation. You will be placed on board
the first ship sailing from New York City to a British port,
and the men, women and children of the United States shall
breathe once more the pure air which is their birthright,
unsullied by the noxious gases from the sewers of the Old
World."

During the evening after the trial the turnkey flung open
the door of Paul's cell.

"Letter for ee" he said. "Here it is, opened cordin to regulations."

The envelope contained a single sheet of plain paper, on which was written in clumsy capital letters: "HAVE WRITTEN TO JACK BERNSTEIN TWENTY TWO HOLYWELL STREET LONDON ENG." That was all. No address or date or signature. Paul stared at it in mulish silence.

"Well" demanded the jailer. "Who's it from and what does it mean?"

Paul shook his head.

"I haven't the least idea" he said.

The man continued to question him in a threatening way; but the prisoner's incomprehension was so manifest that it finally carried conviction.

"Let it go" he said. "You'll be out of this tomorrow, so it can't help you whatever it means. I'll take the bit of paper. They keep all sorts in the office. One never knows what'll turn up."

The message stuck in Paul's mind; and chewing it over and over during the squalid discomfort of the voyage, he was forced to the conclusion that it must have come from Isaacs. In consequence, when at last he was put ashore at Plymouth, he took train to London with the intention at the first opportunity of visiting Holywell Street and perhaps this Bernstein also. What else could he do? The money he had with him at the time of his arrest (it had been returned with the other contents of his pockets when he was removed from jail) was nearly exhausted. He had neither the nerve nor the desire to look up his old friends. The only possible link in the whole of London between Gladwin the home-coming deportee and Gladwin the three-year drifter along the gutters of New York was this total stranger. If the anonymous message meant anything, it might lead to a chance to make a living; if it meant nothing, matters were what they were already—just as bad as bad could be.

Mr Bernstein was not an attractive man; but he offered a

possibility of livelihood—of a kind. More immediately satisfactory was a letter from Isaacs sent under cover to Bernstein and enclosing a draft for a hundred dollars. The Albany printer was good enough to describe Doc Limey as a real guy who knew when to clam up.

(iv) NOVEMBER 1878

One day in November 1878 Paul's lean stooping figure, wearing a shabby black overcoat and a shapeless slouch hat and carrying a small portfolio under one arm, shuffled along the dirty and crowded pavement of Newcastle Street, Strand. He walked rather unsteadily, his eyes on the pavement, and every now and again bumped into a passer-by. At the crossing of Wych Street he raised his head for a moment in case of traffic, and then meandered on his way. A few yards further he turned sharply to the left and entered the narrow chasm of Holywell Street.

A crazy jumble of houses rose on either side. A few of the old timbered buildings, whose upper storeys so far over-hung that two people could shake hands across the roadway, had survived the Great Fire; a few others, partially destroyed, had been patched and tinkered into some sort of stability. Among these stood more or less modern tenements, drearily ugly with their flat fronts of smoky brick, while here and there a stretch of blank wall marked a portion of the Olympic or Globe Theatres or, to southward, the rear of premises with frontage on the Strand. The general hotchpotch was finally vulgarised by scrawls of hideous lettering, by "To Let" boards, by small hoardings carrying posters—some garish and insistent, others flapping bedraggled strips, by metal advertising plaques, and by shop-signs of every kind, which were spattered along the façades on either side. A rag-bag of a street, in fact, and one whose population was as squalid and promiscuous as its architecture.

No wheeled traffic passed through Holywell Street, and the roadway was given over to the activities common to

London courts of that or any period. At either end a group of children danced to a barrel organ. They were ragged and dirty; but they kept to a simple, not ungraceful rhythm in their dance, for most of them were pantomime fairies for a few weeks after Christmas and retained something of their brief and scrappy training during the intervening ten months, when they swarmed from the miserable courts and alleys of the neighbourhood to play where best they could. More than one huckster made a pitch of Holywell Street. A vendor of comic songs stood and walked and stood again, shouting the titles of his penny sheets, often with humorous gesture or lively comment. A knife-seller had set out his wares on a small square of dirty carpet. Others, with trays slung about their necks, offered studs or glass jewellery or secret nostrums for various and often alarming ailments.

The ground-floors of the buildings (the few blank walls apart) housed a succession of small shops. The majority were bookshops, print-shops or jumbles of old glass, china and second-hand furniture; but there was also a sprinkling of food and clothing shops, two small auction rooms open to the street, a jeweller (so-called), a barber, and quite half a dozen cigar-shops. At either end stood a flaunting public-house.

The newcomer passed abstractedly through the dancing children and vociferous street-sellers until he reached a shop on the north side of the alley over which was painted in fanciful gold letters on a black ground:

BOOKSELLER J·BERNSTEIN PUBLISHER

It was a single-windowed shop, and a sloping stall on trestles was so placed in front of the window that passers-by (save at the corner immediately next to the shop-door) could not approach closely to the window but were con-

strained to examine from a distance of some three feet whatsoever Mr Bernstein chose to display behind glass. Laid
out on the stall were soiled magazines, some cheap music
and, at the back, a row of miscellaneous and dogs-eared
second-hand books. A couple of weedy youths, intensely
conscious of one another, were pretending to pick these over,
leaning as far toward the shop-window as possible and
trying, without seeming to do so, to make out certain hand-
bills, chap-books and pictures, which were either pasted on

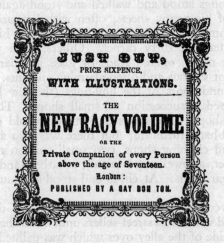

JUST OUT,
PRICE SIXPENCE,
WITH ILLUSTRATIONS.

THE

NEW RACY VOLUME

OR THE

Private Companion of every Person
above the age of Seventeen.

London:

PUBLISHED BY A GAY BON TON.

the inside of the fly-blown panes or propped against carriers
of twisted wire.

Among the first were brightly coloured sheets on which
words in heavy type were easily legible, but others, set small
and lightly inked, could barely be deciphered. Thus the
peering youths could without difficulty make out: "The
Genuine Edition of ARISTOTLE, The famous Philosopher":
also "The something-something of the AWFUL DISCLOSURES OF
MARIA MONK: also "Price Sixpence, with Illustrations. The
New Racy Volume": but strain as they might, the intervening
paragraphs of synopsis or recommendation could only be
guessed at. Even more scrappy was their impression of the

chap-books, set up inside the window. Little song-books like "The Coal Hole Companion", "The Cider Cellar Songster", "The Stunning Chanter" and the "Rum Codger's Collection" were easy enough. But after all a song-book was a song-book, and a fellow had two or three already.

The real teasers were the stories and "revelations." For example: "Just Out" (they read) "Private Secrets . . . Ladies' Man . . . Quack Doctor . . . Examination Room . . . Mysterious Treatment . . . Secret Apartments." Most that lay in between was illegible. Again "Look Here! (they read) Nice Chops for Gentlemen . . . Tender Steaks for

Ladies . . . Maids, Bachelors and Husbands . . . The Art of Wooing" . . . "One Penny!!"

The remarkably low price of this last tantaliser was too much for one of the weedies. Seeing that his neighbour had turned to go, he made a dive for the shop-door and almost collided with the shabby pedestrian who at that moment had put a foot on the step. Feeling, perhaps, that a chap who was now in the market for Nice Chops and Tender Steaks took precedence over a casual stranger in a threadbare coat and broken boots, the young clerk became suddenly aggressive.

"Now then, sir, if *you* please!" he said sharply, and pushing past the older man thrust his way into the shop, letting the door swing to in the other's face. The poor creature showed no resentment, but stepped meekly to one side and stood by the door with bowed head. Although in fact barely forty, he looked well over fifty. His long mild face had the lachrymose red-rimmed eyes of the confirmed alcoholic. Presumably he aspired to be clean-shaven; but a tender skin and a blunt razor had left his face a scatter of grey bristle, while a streak of blood from a nasty scrape beneath his weak dimpled chin had stained his soiled collar and dried into a smear of brown. It was a moist late autumn day, not really cold nor actually raining but raw and damp; and Paul, as he waited, shivered a little in his thin coat and clutched the worn leather port-folio more closely to himself, as though feeling that it at least was his to command or to cherish and that each must share whatsoever warmth the pair of them possessed.

In about five minutes the youth emerged from the shop. His pimples shone a little more redly against his pale face, and a bulging breast-pocket suggested an even heavier invest-ment in "sporty" literature than had been planned. Over-jaunty, to cover his embarrassment, he hurried eastward toward St Clement's.

Paul looked after him, but with such lack-lustre indifference that it was doubtful whether he really saw him. Then he turned, pushed the shop-door half open, crept inside and stood in timid humility before the proprietor.

Mr Jack Bernstein—Bookseller, Publisher, and other things besides—was a heavily-built, fair-complexioned man. He had the soft, rather pleading eyes of his race, but their quality of gentleness was violently belied by a rasping voice, a large cruel mouth full of very white teeth, and a curious roughness of gesture even when (as occasionally was the case) no roughness was meant. He always wore a billycock hat pulled so far down on his head that it rested on his prominent ears, and when he spoke, the traditional lisp and adenoidal blockages were so marked that he was suspected of exaggerating them on purpose. Very possibly he did; for in those days—and in those circles to which Mr Bernstein aspired—Jews were on the crest of the wave; and nature having denied him a dark skin and a fleshy upper lip, he might in casual encounters have passed for a goy and so missed a good thing or two.

On the present occasion he wore a sleeveless cardigan, a pair of what had once been plaid trousers, and of course his hat. When he saw who his caller was, he put his hands in his pockets and thrust his head forward.

"So ith you at latht, ith it? We are oddered to be thure. For three dayth we wait for thtuff we badly wand, but ith lordthip ith too bithy or too stinkid thcrewed to-cub dear uth."

He pulled his hands out of his pockets, and stepping close to the shrinking object before him shook a fist under its nose. His voice went suddenly savage and, with his peculiarities of speech more emphatic than ever (but henceforward to be taken for granted), continued:

"And now listen to me, Mr Bloody Gladwin. You play Charley Wag once more, and you go out of this door as quickly as your —— tile goes into that corner." As he spoke, he struck the other's hat with the edge of his hand, so that it flew across the shop on to the dirty floor.

" —and you won't come back neither" the bookseller went on "but can starve to death in your own time. With trade as it is—and gettin worse—you'll whistle for another job until the cows come ome. Perhaps in the end some kind person will pickle you in spirits so you'll ardly know you *are* dead; but it bloody well won't be me. I wouldn't waste a spoonful of rot-gut on such rubbish. What've you got to say for yourself, you cringin lump of misery?"

Paul Gladwin had not moved during this tirade. Even when the hat was knocked from his head he only blinked. But when the time came for him to speak, he began suddenly to tremble and his voice shook as he replied:

"I'm very sorry Mr Bernstein, very sorry indeed. I have —er—not been well. But I have finished the things you wanted. They are here in—"

"Let's have a look at em, then, for God's sake!" interrupted the other "instead of standin there with the gas on. What are they?"

Gladwin fumbled with his portfolio. His hands were shaking, and as he began to loosen the strap, the thing fell to the floor. He was stooping to pick it up, when Bernstein with a sharp kick sent it crashing against the opposite wall. The worn leather gave way, and a litter of papers scattered right and left.

"God damn you for a clumsy soft! Pick em up, ye fool, and if any are so dirty the comp can't read em, you'll write em out again ere and now."

His deliberate malignity, and the fact that his wretched victim's portfolio was spoiled, restored Bernstein to something approaching good humour. He stood watching with a spiteful grin while Paul painfully collected and set in order his jumbled manuscript. At last he stood upright, a bundle of paper in one hand, his dusty shapeless hat in the other. The ruined portfolio lay cock-eyed against the shelves, just where it had fallen.

With a jerk of the head, Bernstein swung round and led the way into a back room. It was unexpectedly large after the cramped and crowded dinginess of the shop itself, and, although dirty, showed signs of ordered use as office and despatch-counter as well as a certain cosiness, due to a fire which burnt brightly in the open grate and to a kettle which whispered happily on the hob. A large knee-hole desk stood in the centre of the room with a gas-bracket hanging low over it. On the desk, in addition to pens and ink and some soiled sheets of blotting-paper, were half a dozen ledgers, each with a brass lock and standing in a neat row between metal book-ends. Along one wall ran a packing-bench, with shelves above it carrying rows of parcels marked in code. At the bench, dividing large sheets of brown paper with a long straight knife, stood a strange little figure in shirt-sleeves and a leather apron. He was well under five feet in height, very bow-legged and wore a pair of large round spectacles on a very small snub nose.

"Shop, Lockett" said Bernstein "but keep an ear open. I may want you."

The little man wiped his hands on his apron, sniffed damply and tooled out of the room without a word.

Bernstein seated himself in the round-backed chair, pulled open a drawer and took out a long black cheroot, which he stuck firmly in the corner of his mouth.

"Now then, Gladwin. Let's ave a look."

The poor hack had recovered his normal state of remote apathy. Laying the untidy package of paper on the desk, he selected one section and placed it before his employer.

"This" he said, in a low indifferent voice "is virtually harmless and would I think serve as text for 'Tit Bits for the Bed Room.' I think that was one title you wished to use for shop trade, wasn't it, sir? I have had the hand-bill and front wrapper proofed, using the paragraph you drafted."

Bernstein nodded, turning over the handwritten sheets and rapidly skimming them.

"Where are the proofs?"

Gladwin handed him a printed sheet. The paper was a vivid pink, on which the aggressive lettering and ornament made vulgar tracery.

The bookseller nodded approval.

"Looks and reads thunderin well" he said "as I told you it would. Your advert. stuff is too damn lardy-da. Give em

o   417

the long words and the genteel finickins *inside*, outside you've got to it em where they want it!"

JUST OUT.

PRICE ONE SHILLING.

A BOOK ᶠᴼᴿ WICKED,
ᵀᴴᴱ

OR

TIT BITS FOR THE
BED ROOM.

Containing Ninety Pages of racy reading and Ten Coloured Cuts of a nature rather going of it. The reader will be the best judge of the character of the Cuts by the sensations it produces in his own person. This is another of those productions which cannot be sold to the youthful portion of society, any one above the age of Seventeen may possess it.

London :

ISSUED BY A MAID!

"Well, sir, you know your business best. But it's not actually grammatical."

"Grammatical be damned. This is a tickler, man, not an arf hour with the best authors." He screwed himself round in his chair. "Lockett!" he shouted, and the gnome stood in the doorway. "Take this lot over to Bartons and tell em to get on with it. Style of 'Secrets for Young Men'. And it's shop-stuff so they needn't worry who comps. Call in at the Risin Sun on the way back and bring a pint of Old Tom, and a couple of lemons from Swivels."

He threw a coin to the impassive dwarf who vanished as rapidly as he had appeared, and once again turned to business.

"This" said Gladwin, as monotonously as though he were reading aloud "is post-order only. It may be rather strong, but you said there had been one or two complaints that 'The Pretty Girls of London' fell off a bit toward the end."

The bookseller once more ruffled through the bundle of papers.

"It *is* a bit blue" he said finally "but it's good. We'll risk it, especially as title and andbill are all ready waitin. Remember that—?" and rummaging for a moment in a drawer of the desk he threw across to the other a small square of bright-green paper heavily printed in black.

A faint gleam of contempt lit Gladwin's weary eyes; but it faded immediately and he handed the paper back to his employer.

"Very satisfactory to find a use for that after all" he said quietly. "But what exactly is the idea of 'Published by a Gay Lady'?"

Bernstein gave him a suspicious look.

"What dyer mean? What's the idea? Not bein funny by any chance?"

"I meant no offence, Mr Bernstein; but I should have thought 'By a Blushing Newly-Wed' or 'By the Lucky Fellow' would be more—well, more logical."

"There you go again! What the ell has *logic* got to do with this line of trade? And I'll tell you this too. We've got to stir our stumps in this establishment or one of us'll be dead stuck and it won't be me. Slump apart, the competition is gettin otter. That bugger down in Bristol—look ere" (and he pulled one of the ledgers from the rack, unlocked it and took a couple of letters from the inside cover). "Read these and you'll see there's work ahead. E's got three of my customers in the last month."

While Gladwin was reading, Lockett shot into the room at his half-run, dumped a bottle, two lemons and some small change at his master's elbow and shot out again.

"Yes" said Gladwin handing the letters back. "Mr Cook is clearly an ingenious person. But he has the advantage of lax supervision, compared to London; and if business by post is to become the main source of profit, the provinces will get ahead even of Booksellers Row."

Bernstein was now in a good temper. He always felt better at his desk and doing business than in any other circumstances, and the prospect of working off "Two Between the Sheets" had cheered him still more.

"Get two glasses and a knife from the cupboard" he said "and bring the kettle to the boil."

In a few moments both bully and drudge had their noses in hot gin and lemon; and it was curious to observe that, as the minutes passed, the bully became almost genial and the drudge took on a certain wistful dignity.

They discussed their common interests in a desultory manner, Bernstein inveighing against an increasingly dishonest competition and the invasion of the London curiosa-

NEW CATALOGUE

OF

PARISIAN NOVELTIES, &c.

420

market by French and German dealers. He threw over on the desk a small catalogue in a yellow cover, with a wood-engraving of a naked and somewhat dispiriting nymph lying on a bed and waving a banner inscribed: "Bachelor's Gallery of Choice Facetiæ."

"Look at that!" he said. "Icks Catalogue of Parisian Novelties. Icks Catalogue of fancy bunkum, plain and simple. That flat-catcher asn't a book or print in the world, and as for is precious address—it's a mask for a slop-shop in Oval Lane. I know. I've been there. But e sends this thing about and damn fools send im stamps and post-office orders and get devil a thing in return. Get the kettle again, Gladwin."

The glasses refilled, the bookseller was giving his views of foreign dealers, when Lockett came in with half a dozen letters just delivered. Bernstein opened them quickly, extracted the money enclosed in four of them, and handed the letters to the gnome.

"There we are—one Woman Disrobed, two Adventures of a Bedstead and a Fanny Ill. Not so bad. Get em off, Lockett."

The other two letters he put in his pocket. They seem to have reminded him of a remark made by Gladwin some while before.

"The provinces . . ." he said suddenly, as though taking up a conversation just dropped. "No doubt in a good provincial town—Birmingham or Liverpool, or Bristol or Plymouth—the book and print business could be worked as well as in London and cheaper. But there are other lines besides books and prints, y'know, and it's London for them."

He looked at his watch.

"Huh! I must be movin. And you want your rhino I suppose. If I wasn't a kind-earted fool I'd dock you alf of it for bein so dam late with the stuff. But there—I always was me own worst enemy and the things read well, so ere you are."

He pushed a couple of sovereigns over to Gladwin, corked the bottle with firm finality, threw his cigar stump into the grate, pushed back in his chair and put his feet on the desk.

"And what next, sir?" Paul enquired.

The bookseller pursed his lips and looked solemnly at his boots.

"Come in tomorrow mornin, and I'll tell you" he said at last. "I think it will be a prospectus. At the same time you can get on with that whippin thing about the girls' school. It needs doin extra specially well as I'm goin to ask ten bob for it. Don't rush it—and don't spare the orses either."

The other bowed and went quietly away. For a few moments Bernstein continued to study his boots. Then he pulled the two letters from his pocket and began to read.

Paul Gladwin felt light-headed as he left Holywell Street. Lack of food and two glasses of hot gin were playing their part, but more potent still was the knowledge that not for another twenty-four hours need he see that hateful Yid and (though in a way he dreaded it) the prospect, that very evening, of seeing Toby again and perhaps Matt also, and feeling that he was not totally alone.

He had left the wrecked portfolio on the shop floor, and held what remained of his papers inside his threadbare coat under one arm. The raw mist had now turned to heavy rain; and as he rounded the church and shambled quickly toward Temple Bar, his head was so sunk into his collar, his shoulders so hunched and his lamentable hat pulled so low on to his ears, that he looked more like a moving scarecrow than a human being. Up Chancery Lane toward High Holborn went the forlorn huddled figure, no longer bumping into passers-by but slipping unnoticed in and out of the crowds. Sometimes to avoid a knot of people he would step into the gutter, regardless of his split and squelching boots and of the mud and water which sprayed knee-high from under the wheels of drays and omnibuses. Gradually—drab, damp and miserable—he was absorbed into the dun background of November London.

FORLORN SUNSET

IN THE MID-FORTIES a naval officer, Lieutenant John Blackmore R.N., who had been compelled to leave the Service as the result of serious injuries sustained in an explosion of a powder-magazine on board his ship, was looking about for some occupation which might benefit his fellow-men and yet not overtax the strength of an enfeebled body. He was a very religious man; and it happened that while he was anxiously considering how he could best serve the community, two friends spoke to him with horror and pity of the tragic army of women who walked the streets of London.

At that period virtually no effort was made to help such women to escape from their life of bondage. There were Homes for Fallen Women, Penitentiaries for individuals charged by the police, charitable institutions supported by private citizens which, within their limited radius, did good by giving sanctuary. But in most of these organisations the inmates were subject to harsh rules and punishments, wore compulsory and ugly uniforms, and were even condemned to have their hair forcibly cut off. Further, it hardly occurred to the worthy folk in charge of these forbidding asylums to go in search of the unhappy outcasts and urge them to give a virtuous life a trial; nor, when they had themselves had asked for admission to a Home, were arrangements made, save with spasmodic timidity, to train them usefully for a new and different existence.

Blackmore determined to inaugurate a system of quite a different kind. With half a dozen or more devoted friends he formed a little band of missioners, and night after night four of them would go out into the London streets. At a fixed point they would part, and in pairs pursue two appointed routes. An hour or two later, again at an agreed spot, the couples would meet again and report on their experiences. This was the beginning of what soon became known over a wide area of the Metropolis as the Moonlight Mission.

The basis of the undertaking was wholly and assertively religious, but avoided both Torchbearer dreariness and Salvation Army rhetoric. The missioners carried tracts, each headed by Blackmore's name and address and enclosed in a plain envelope so that it had the appearance of a letter. The paper inside begged the reader in simple language and in the name of Jesus Christ, if she desired to turn away from sin and follow the commandments of God, to call on Blackmore himself at the address given. One of the pair of evangelists, when they met on their wanderings girls of the kind to whom they wished to appeal, would give a polite good evening, hand over an envelope, ask as a favour that it be read the next morning, and then try to draw the new acquaintance into conversation. The talk would be couched in terms of pietism, but be neither a call to repentance nor a threatening prediction of hell-fire. It was rather a cheerful invitation to visit the address given, and there to make some new friends, and hear their plans for pointing the way to a different and a happier life.

A more difficult task, or one requiring a higher degree of courage, selflessness and capacity to adapt oneself to strangers, can hardly be imagined. But Blackmore and his helpers so far lived down the suspicion and hostility with which they were at first received, that in a few years' time they could accost almost any girl they met without risk of insult and, once recognised as Moonlight Missioners, were more often implored to help than compelled to plead.

By the time this satisfactory stage had been reached, Blackmore had founded The London Female Dormitory in Abbey Road, St John's Wood, and The Female Temporary Home in Marylebone Road. Both houses, conducted on the lines of a family home whose inmates divide responsibility for the duties of the establishment and between times are kept occupied training themselves for service or business or emigration, soon had waiting lists. No livery was worn; there was no period of probation; all doors were unlocked during the day-time. The length of stay of each inmate was entirely voluntary and averaged eight or nine months.

In cases where a girl was brought once more in touch with her parents (and such renewals of family connection were more than anything desired and worked for by the organisers) her sojourn might well be considerably shorter. As time went on, other similar houses of refuge were opened, including an Infants' Temporary Home in Ealing, where tiny children were cared for, until their mothers, prepared for and put to honest work of various kinds, were in a position to support them. Taken all in all, the story of the Moonlight Mission and of the half-crippled man who created it constitutes a striking page in Victorian London's record of well-doing.

Blackmore died about 1870; but his work went on, and about eleven o'clock of a warm September night in the year 1878, one of the Moonlight Missioners was making his way along Holborn. He was alone (for his appointed companion was ailing and house-bound) and as he wore an ordinary dark suit of decent cut and quality and walked slowly, keeping an unobtrusive look-out for persons of the type he sought to help, he seemed to the keen eye of a burly ruffian lingering with a young girl in the darkness of an archway, a likely customer for what she had to sell.

"That cove over there" he nudged her roughly. "Sharp's the word!"

She was a very young girl, not more than fifteen, and smartly dressed in gay colours and a saucy bonnet. Obediently she tripped across the street and, meeting the solitary stroller face to face, stood in his path with a timid attempt at a professional smile.

"Hullo, darling" she said in a small brittle voice. "Why in such a hurry?"

He stopped and looked at her kindly. He was a big man, largely—almost ruggedly—featured, but handsome in a crude way and with gentle eyes.

"I am in no hurry, my dear" he replied. "Can I help you?"

She snuggled against him, looking up with a pathetic blend of enticement and apprehension.

"Won't you come and love me a little? My room is close by and I will give you a good time, I promise I will."

He took her arm and let her guide him into a side-street. There he paused, released her arm, and said quietly

"My poor child, why are you living this wretched life? A young pretty thing like you should be gay and happy, with companions of your own age and watched over by loving parents. Will you read this letter as soon as you can, and come to the address given there? You will find kind friends, who only wish to help you."

She took the envelope, staring at him suspiciously. No one had ever spoken to her thus. Was this some new thing to which she must lend herself? Even in her short life she had met with demands for strange and alarming satisfactions; and perhaps there were men who made their approach with a pretence of fatherly concern and piety.

He read her thoughts.

"Do not be afraid of me. God has put it into the hearts of a group of men and women to offer a way of escape to any girl caught in the toils of this miserable life. See; I will leave you now, and trust that His infinite mercy will bring you tomorrow or the next day to the refuge whose address you have."

Her anxious little mouth suddenly crumpled, and she began to cry.

"I cannot!" she sobbed. "I cannot get away! I am in a flash-house [1] and every stitch I wear belongs to the madam.

---

[1] The " flash " or " dress " house was a place where several prostitutes lived, but plied their trade in furnished rooms elsewhere. Each was dressed for the street entirely in clothes belonging to the house-owner and, when sent out in search of clients, was accompanied by a " keeper ". The keeper's business was to compel his victim to make full use of her time, to wait for her during each assignation, to take charge of the money earned, and to hustle her back into circulation. He was also naturally concerned to prevent his girl making her escape.

Inasmuch as no men were brought to the dress-house itself and no scandal was caused, the building could barely be described as a " disorderly house ", and there was no risk of the two necessary burgesses lodging a complaint and giving security in order to achieve prosecution. Consequently dress-houses were very numerous during those mid-Victorian years which preceded the strengthening of the law against traffic in women, so as to make it a misdemeanour distinct from the commission of a public nuisance.

My keeper is watching us even now, and if you walk away and do not come to the room hired for me, he will beat me for letting you go."

"Which way is the room?"

"Up this street and a bit along to the left."

"Very well, let us walk on, as though we were going there."

The girl's keeper was slipping through the shadows in their wake. While they were standing still and talking, he assumed that she was making sure of her quarry and that terms were being arranged. When they resumed their walk, he decided with satisfaction that the deal was on, and that he would shortly be spending a pleasant hour in a public-house across the way from her room, waiting for her to rejoin him.

He was only a few yards behind them; but although the gentleman seemed to have a lot to say ("Reglar blatherskite" thought the keeper), he spoke in such a low tone that no words were audible. The next moment, however, came the clear childish voice of the girl, and all the keeper's suspicions sprang to life. From the game-pocket of his coat he pulled out a bludgeon.

"If only I dared!" he heard her say. "Oh, sir, cannot I come with you now? Take me with you now!"

They turned to the left, stopping so suddenly after rounding the corner that the man on their trail had barely time to draw back behind the angle of the brick-work.

"Run for it!" he heard the gentleman say. "Wait for me in Red Lion Square."

The keeper sprang from his hiding-place, knobstick in hand. At that instant a woman's voice rang out sharply from a recessed doorway immediately opposite:

"Look out, sir! Behind you!"

The missioner swung round just in time. With his left hand he caught the bully by the arm already raised to strike, gave a vicious twist and the bludgeon clattered on to the road. Then with his right fist he let go at the corner of the other's jaw, and laid him flat. The young girl, who had already scudded some distance up the street, had stopped at the noise of the scrimmage and now stood panting, hugging herself in fear and excitement. When she saw the keeper crash to the ground, she began edging nervously back toward her rescuer. He was speaking to someone whom she could not see. As she got nearer, she heard a woman answering from a dark entry. Then he said:

"No, I insist. You saved me from a nasty knock, and I must show my gratitude. Come, please; a little refreshment will be good for all of us. Where is that poor little thing? Oh, here she comes. Our friend we will let lie. He'll come round in time and be no worse for his licking than he deserves. I know to a T where and how hard to hit."

Returning to Holborn they entered a good-class tavern, and for the first time the missioner and the strange woman could see one another clearly. She was of medium height, dark and buxom, carelessly and rather vulgarly dressed, though in sober colours which contrasted strongly with the vivid plumage of the young girl. She might have been any age from thirty to forty, but was in fact only twenty-six. Her figure was admirable, but her complexion hinted at an addiction to hard liquor and her face, in an elusive way, was dissipated. Looking at her covertly, the man was struck by her expression. The eyes were cold and watchful, but had the gleam of an intelligence rarely seen in the faces of the unfortunate. Her movements were graceful; and when she took a seat or had occasion to use her hands, she showed an instinctive sense of demeanour and *savoir-faire*. Not the regulation street-walker, he told himself, not by any means.

She asked for whisky; and when he had procured this, a glass of port for the child and a tankard of beer for himself, he sought to draw her into conversation, hoping that talk might do something to resolve the contradiction between her appearance and her manner.

"It was a fortunate chance for me that you were in that doorway at that precise moment."

"Fortunate, perhaps, but not much chance about it. I happen to live there at present and was just coming out."

Her way of speech strengthened his conviction that here

430

was a woman with a history, one who may well have sunk deep into the mire, but had dragged herself free again.

"Oh, I see" he said, and there was something in his voice suggestive of raised eyebrows, which annoyed her.

"Yes" she repeated sharply, "just coming out—*and* at half-past eleven at night. To buy a bottle of whisky, if you want to know."

She was looking him defiantly in the face, and he dropped his eyes in some confusion.

"I beg your pardon" he said. "It was no business of mine. At any rate I can thank you for being there."

"Funny the way it happened" she went on, as though her narrative had never been interrupted. "I'd just turned the corner toward Holborn when I saw the kid here coming up the street with a man. I've seen her pass my window several times lately—suppose you've got a room further along, haven't you, ducky?—and always with that monkey tagging a few yards behind. So not wanting to put the child out of countenance—she's new to it, poor little devil, as anyone can see—I stepped back into the entry to wait till she had gone by. But then you both stopped short; and when I heard you say 'Run for it' I twigged it was what the girls call a 'Moonlight snatch', and thought 'good luck to it', and watched out for the keeper."

The young girl, who had been glancing nervously about her while she sipped her port, now said timidly:

"Please, sir, do you think they will be hunting for me and see me here?"

He smiled reassuringly.

"I doubt it. Even if they do, I'll take care of you. And don't be afraid about the clothes. They shall be returned to the owner tomorrow. In a few minutes we'll be off west and fix you up safely for the night."

Turning back toward the older woman, he found that she was scrutinising him attentively, a little puzzled frown forming above her handsome eyebrows.

"You know" she said suddenly "I've seen you before."

He smiled politely and shook his head.

"I'm afraid not. At least I have no recollection."

431

She continued to stare at him.

"Yes I have. Long ago and I don't remember where. But somewhere. My memory for faces is very good. I have known as many men as most women of my age—indeed a damn sight more, if we are being candid; and up to a year or two ago (when I saw so many I stopped looking at them) I believe I should recognise every one. I don't mean that I could tell you who each one was, or in what circumstances I had met him; but that I *had* met him I should know for certain. And I have met you."

He gave a little shrug and laughed.

"Then I must apologise for my forgetfulness. To me you are a perfect stranger who has done me a first-class turn and whose acquaintance I am glad to have made."

A brief perfunctory smile acknowledged the civility. She took a big gulp of her whisky with the competence and despatch of one inured.

"Often down this way?" she asked.

"It depends. I go wherever I am bidden or where I think the need is greatest. We are Our Master's servants, and He speaks to us through the mouth of the Leader of the Mission or in the voice of our own conscience."

"You couldn't tip Him the wink to send you Holborn way one evening soon?"

The flippancy and disrespect were plainly deliberate, and her eyes derided him.

"Please" he replied gently "do not be unworthy of yourself. If you seek to hurt me by mocking at my faith, you succeed only in hurting yourself."

The look of impudent challenge faded from her eyes, but she did not turn them away.

"I'm sorry. I shouldn't have said that. But I've had my fill of God-botherers, and my tongue's a devil. I'll put it this way. I'd like to talk to you because I think I might be able to help this—would you call it a crusade?—this work of yours anyway. I've seen my share of the seamy side."

"Your help will be most welcome" he said, rising to his

feet. "I will be here on Tuesday at ten o'clock. Now I must take this young lady to where she will be suitably cared for."

"Buy me another drink before you go."

He obeyed: and as he returned from the bar-counter and placed the glass on the table in front of her, she asked in a low voice:

"Would you mind telling me your name?"

"Merrick" he said. "Tom Merrick."

As he left the tavern, with the child like a wilted butterfly clinging to his arm, he glanced over his shoulder. The woman was sitting staring into space and sipping mechanically at her glass of spirit.

When he entered the Holborn tavern at ten o'clock the following Tuesday, she was already seated at a small table and greeted him with aloof composure. Save for white ruffles at throat and wrists, she was dressed in black; and with a care and neatness in striking contrast to the slovenly in-difference of her previous costume. Merrick noted the change, and his wariness increased. He had thought of her several times since their chance encounter, and determined to take no initiative when they met again but to leave her to declare herself. Mysterious lone women, who drank spirits in public-houses at night-time and yet were not out on a prostitute's business, were more likely to be against his work than for it. She had, it was true, helped him once. But that may have been a kindly impulse on behalf of the young girl, or possibly a bid to get acquainted with him and worm something out of him about the plans and contacts of the Moonlight Mission.

When, therefore, he had fetched drinks from the bar, he merely raised his glass politely, and sat silent. She gave him a quick glance, responded to his greeting with a nod of the head, but neither drank nor spoke. For a few seconds she sat with downcast eyes, absently turning the glass this way and that on the table-top. Then, without looking up, she said:

"When I asked you to meet me again, I said that I might be able to help you. I have since come to see that it is you who may be able to help me. Does that make you any less suspicious?"

He shook his head.

"Why should it?"

A fleeting smile and a shrug of the shoulders.

"Why, indeed?—Except that appeals from women are more in your line than offers of help. Did you get the kid tucked away all right?"

He nodded.

"Yes; quite all right." His enthusiasm for his work and his indignant sympathy with the waifs for whose sake it was carried on, swept him beyond the barrier of his reserve. "Poor frightened little thing! The black wickedness of sending these children into the horrors of such a life! It makes my blood boil, and I believe if I could lay my hands on one of the brutes responsible I'd choke him."

Suddenly aware of his own warmth, he became confused, and looked across at his companion with uncertain embarrassment. She was still twisting her glass to and fro in a gloved hand and staring at it. The next moment she raised her head sharply, leant forward with elbows on the table and spoke to him face to face.

"Mr Merrick. I have remembered where I saw you first, and realise why I remember. But you will not. This gave me the idea of asking you for help. You will understand it all in a minute, but first answer me one question. Did you ever, long ago, meet a Mr Meadows, a clergyman, who was at one time vicar of a parish near Waterloo?"

He looked at her, first in blank astonishment, then with uneasy misgiving.

"What on earth—" he began.

She interrupted.

"No, please. Answer me! Everything, for me, depends on the answer."

He was still alarmed and distrustful, but obeyed.

"Yes; I met him more than once."

434

"And, if you found out that he is still alive, could you go and see him?"

"I should not care to do so" he mumbled "but I suppose I *could*."

She sat back in her chair with a sigh of relief.

"Ah! Now I'll explain—myself and other things."

Briefly she told the story of her visit to St John's vicarage in the bitter twilight of a wintry April day, all those years ago. He neither moved nor took his eyes off her face while she was speaking, and, whatever his thoughts, they were veiled behind an expression of sullen concentration.

"Of course you would not remember" she concluded. "You were crazy with your own troubles. You frightened me at the time, but afterwards—when I had heard your name and what was said to have happened—I was desperately sorry for you. And now we meet again—this time, I hope, as allies. My name, by the way, is Lottie Heape."

He found his voice with difficulty.

"Most extraordinary" he muttered. "Most extraordinary."

"Not really, Mr Merrick, when you come to think of it. You walk London on a Mission to street-girls; I am not a street-girl now, though I have been; but I am accustomed to going about after dark, and in just the quarters you would be likely to visit. Narrow the chances down like that, and it seems we should almost be bound to cross one another's path sooner or later." After a pause: "Would it hurt too much to tell me about St John's?"

He thought for a few moments.

"I hardly know. I have put it out of my mind for so long. Why do you want to know?"

"Because even at that time, kid though I was, I thought the story a bit thin. Now that I've seen you again, I'm sure it wasn't true."

"Of course it wasn't true! As if I should ever . . . No; it was a lie, trumped-up to ruin me. And it did ruin me, in a sense. I was defenceless, with no one to help me. I went to jail, and lost the Orders I was so proud to have won. When I came out—well, never mind that for now. Perhaps another time, if you care to hear, I will tell you my story. What had happened when you saw me was a result of what had happened earlier.

"One more thing before I go. You say that when you were in the vicarage I frightened you? In what way?"

"You turned on me; and your eyes went red, like men's eyes do when they think there's a girl for the taking."

He gave an exclamation of horrified disgust.

"How dreadful! It shows what evil power lies in suggestion. They charged me with a crime which, in my right mind, I could not possibly have committed. I would have sworn that sort of thing was not in me. And yet by false accusation they drove me mad; and madness released the very abomination their minds imputed to me! It is I who am frightened now. I must pray for strength and for God's help against myself."

He lumbered awkwardly to his feet and, like a man half-blind, groped his way slowly to the door.

*   *   *   *   *

At their next meeting he told his story.

Country born and bred, and of humble parentage, he had attracted the notice of the Rector of the parish by his studious habits and ambition to learn. This Rector was a rich and enlightened man, who doubled the parts of Squire and Parson and had great local influence. He realised that young Merrick, if he could surmount the several obstacles to taking Orders, would be an ideal curate in a large country parish, being of the people and aware of their needs and problems. He set himself, therefore, to override all the social objections provoked by his unconventional proposal to get a labourer's son ordained as a clergyman of the Church of England. A small theological college in the neighbourhood, whose landlord the Rector was, accepted the boy and put him through his training. In due course he became one of his patron's curates; and for a few years, while he lived and worked in his own country-side and among the folk he knew and understood, all went well.

Then suddenly the wise and powerful Rector died, having previously recommended his protégé to the consideration of the Bishop. The Bishop was also an aristocrat, but his interpretation of *noblesse oblige* was not that of the dead man. He set duty to his caste above duty to his flock. It was distasteful to him to have, even among his junior clergy, anyone as "common" as Merrick; and he lost no time in getting the young man transferred from his diocese to London, and appointed to a curacy in a newly built-up and predominantly middle-class parish. So Merrick left his homeland and came to London, and the great loneliness began.

It was rare that among the clergy with whom he came in contact one was found who treated him as a fellow-worker in a noble cause. To the majority he was a base interloper, unworthy to be the colleague of men of family and education, only fit to do the dirty work and, when he had done it, to be left to enjoy his own company.

Solitary and unhappy, he dragged through a year or two of wretched isolation. His faith was fierce, but inarticulate. In personal contacts with the few really poor people living in the parish he attained to a rough intimacy, although he never made such friends as among the country-folk whose minds he knew intuitively. But he was awkward and clumsy as celebrant and preacher, and in company with his superiors and parishioners of the semi-genteel class, gauche and diffident.

It seemed, therefore, a release when he was instructed to take temporary charge of St John's, Waterloo Road, whose vicar was resigning and whose new incumbent had fallen ill at the moment of his succession. He had been received by Mr Meadows with forthright kindness and good sense, informed in outline of the policy adopted in the parish during the last fourteen years, warned against beggars in guise of genuinely deserving poor, and urged to resist any attempt by the minority of better-class parishioners to deputise for the vicar in the reclamation of the near-slum areas, of which several still survived.

"They will try to get you to themselves" said Mr Meadows. "Conditions are wonderfully better than they were; but the

penalty a parson pays for raising the living-standard of a
parish is that he also raises a class of pious busybodies in
modestly comfortable circumstances, who think it their duty
to discipline their poorer fellows, and seek to divide the cure
into 'ups' and 'downs', with the clergyman as a sort of
figurehead on top of the 'ups'. Set your face against this.
In your eyes, as before the Almighty, every human soul is
equal, with an equal claim on your compassion and your
prayers, an equal right of access to God's House or to the
sanctum of God's Steward here on earth."

Fortified by two or three such talks with the ex-vicar,
Merrick took up his new work. Immediately he was attacked
from two directions. Like locusts the cadgers after charity,
whom Meadows had kept relentlessly at arm's-length for so
many years, swarmed round the vicarage of the new and
inexperienced incumbent. The fact that he was only a curate,
and temporary at that, encouraged their importunities. By
sheer clamour and persistence they hoped to force him to
buy them off with doles. At the same time deputations of
tradesmen and their wives descended on him with plans for
district visiting, for Sunday Schools as compulsory as might
be, for removing to reformatories children from bad homes,
for hounding out of the parish loose women and men suspected of theft or receiving.

Merrick was driven to distraction by this plague of inter-
ruptions; but he was an obstinate man and held doggedly
to Meadows' recommendations. Unfortunately his social
ignorance and inability to manage other people led him to
oppose his persecutors in such a way as to turn importunity
into malevolence. Where Meadows had disciplined by calm
and forcefulness, Merrick, like a savage but nervous dog
which rushes at its tormentors and sets them throwing stones
from a safe distance, only won momentary relief at the price
of vengeful enmity. News of the curate's humble birth soon
reached the self-appointed "classes" of the parish from ill-
natured persons in his previous district; and to his ill-
mannered rejection of their offers of advice and help was
added the further offence of his base origin. Themselves no

more than half-and-half, they resented with all the bitter snobbery of the insecure that a Hodge—even for only a few months—should be set in authority over them. As for the "masses"—the whining mendicants who hoped to work St John's and All Saints, Lower Marsh, on alternate days—they swore that to be sent about their business by someone dressed up as a parson but in fact no better than they were, was an insult not to be borne. Gradually the two hostilities hardened; then coalesced. Merrick must be destroyed.

The simple plot worked easily and well. Rumours went round that the curate-in-charge eyed the girls oddly in class. Those whom Vicky called the "oly Jemimas", who ran the schools and girls' classes, whispered together and pursed their lips and shook their heads. Then two ten-year-olds from among the children of the disgruntled mumpers were coached to make a complaint. The thing was done. Merrick was annihilated.

"And when you came out?" she asked.

"I nearly starved for a while. The jobs I did for a few pence! And then one evening, tramping the streets to find a doss-house, I came across a group of women—real dregs *they* were—screaming and mocking at two men, who stood there, patiently and without flinching, trying to talk to them. I could see that there was going to be trouble. The women were mostly drunk, and it would be only one move from foul abuse to throwing filth. The neighbourhood was a bad one; no police to be seen. So I jumped in and talked the language they understood. They were so astonished to be cursed by a bundle of rags like me, that they made off at once. And that was how I first met with the Moonlight Mission, and the truly Christian folk who had made it their life's work."

Another time he said "May I know your history in return for mine? You have let fall a hint or two here and there . . . but as between friends . . ."

"You are welcome to the whole story. Indeed I should

439

wish to tell it you. But I do not want to do so twice over; and if all goes well, you will hear it soon enough."

"How—if all goes well?"

"If you can persuade Mr Meadows to listen to me."

"I dread going to see him. I had put that wretched business out of my mind. To have to bring it all up again! Besides, what does he know of *you*? How shall I explain you, knowing nothing myself?"

"I am a fool! Of course you must know enough to remind him! Here goes, then—very briefly. I never knew my father. I was taken away from my mother when I was eight or nine and put with bad people; I was rescued by two young men, who left me in Mr Meadows' charge, he being the nearest parson. By the good offices of Mr Meadows, I was sent to the country where I stayed till I was sixteen. Then I made trouble and ran away to London (that was when I first saw you in St John's vicarage) and before long was being kept by a city gent. I made more trouble, and ran away again. For three or four years I went straight and worked hard, until I fell madly in love and went to live with a man who was a blackguard and made a tart of me. We quarrelled and he deserted me, and I began to drink and ceased to care about anything. I passed from hand to hand, having bad times and good, until I met an old fellow who treated me well and whom I nursed in his last illness. He left me a little money—enough to give up the game and set me free to plan a revenge for which I have waited several years. It is that revenge you are to help me to get."

Something in this bald summary of a tempestuous and sinful life—offered without evasion or self-excuse—stirred Merrick's sympathy.

"Poor Lottie" he said gently. "You have had a cruel time. Is revenge necessary? Can you not forgive your enemies?"

"Wait! You will not ask me that when you know more. Do you remember, on that evening when for the first time you came to meet me and thought I was out to catch you or was a spy or a madam or something, saying you could choke a man with your hands who drove young girls on to the streets to his own profit?"

He nodded.

"Well, I can tell you of a man who does worse than that. I can put you on the track of a place where he and his father debauch little children deliberately, groom them for the streets. Shall *I*—could *you*—forgive such a man, for it is on him I want my revenge."

"Steady!" he cried. "You do not know what you are saying!"

"I know it very well; and it is quite true. But we need helpers and careful preparation. Mr Meadows can, if he will, get us help of a very important kind—the help of a newspaper man called Merton. Remember that—*Merton*. He was one of the two young men who took me to St John's vicarage, and Meadows has kept in touch with him. When I stand up and accuse myself—for that is what I shall have to do, so as to get these swine their deserts—I want you to be there, and Mr Meadows, and this chap Merton. Just you three. I think that *you* now believe what I say. You have got to make Meadows listen, for without him we cannot rope in Merton, and Merton is essential. But you can only persuade Meadows if he trusts *you*. He certainly would not trust *me*, thanks to my own folly. I met him once in the street, just after running to London from the country, and thought it clever to accost him and show I remembered his kindness to a child. But then I told him a lot of lies, and he suddenly knew I was lying. You will have a job to live that down. But you must manage it somehow."

He shook his head dubiously.

"He may even refuse to see me. He must have heard of the scandal and of my conviction. Why should he trust me any more than you?"

"That, my dear old fellow, is your problem. But he'll believe you once he sees you. And you can give your word that I can and will betray these ruffians, and shall make a clean breast of the whole business from start to finish. I shan't lie any more, even to save my own face!"

"I must speak to the Leader of the Mission."

"Certainly not, until after you have tried Meadows."

"Certainly yes. I am under orders all and every day, and into the bargain under the deepest obligation one man can owe to others. The Mission saved me. The Leader heard my story and decided to admit me to the community. I have tried to deserve his trust and shall not abuse it now."

She realised the uselessness of argument, that his mind was made up, that this was the fundamental Merrick, speaking from the heart.

"Very well" she said. "You must do what you think right."

Lottie sat in her rather dingy room on an evening in November 1878, brooding at the fire. A tumbler of hot whisky with a slice of lemon steamed on the hearthstone. The arm-chair in which she sat was covered in faded crimson rep, matching the curtains and the mantel-drape. One end of the table was covered with a soiled white cloth, on which a dirty plate and glass, the lower part of a cottage-loaf and a tarnished three-piece cruet, commemorated a supper eaten a while since but not yet cleared away.

Tomorrow she was to attend the vicarage of All Saints, Margaret Street, and there, in front of Mr Meadows, Matt Merton and Tom Merrick, make her confession. A fortnight earlier she had met Merrick at their usual rendezvous, and he announced that he had seen the clergyman.

"The Leader persuaded him to receive me" he said. "So you see I was right to consult my commanding officer."

After a long talk—concerned mainly with the old scandal at St John's, as to the injustice of which Merrick thought Mr Meadows was now convinced—the question had been raised of Lottie Heape and the revelation she wished to make. At first the clergyman had reacted vigorously against the very thought of her. With a grim smile Merrick reported him more or less verbatim. "She was bad as a young girl" Meadows had said "a liar and a wanton. I have heard scraps of her story. As a woman she is probably utterly depraved.

442

I am an old man, and would hesitate to go to war with the forces of evil in this city, even if I were urged to do so by honourable folk in whose word I could trust. But this strumpet! What vengeance can there be for the likes of her, to concern decent people? She is laying a trap or making a fool of us. No, no, Merrick. I must beg to be excused; and you, if you take my advice, will keep out of any scheme from that quarter."

The younger man had stuck to his guns.

"She has been all you say, sir, and would be the first to admit it. But she is speaking the truth about this training-school for prostitutes—this vile Dothegirls Hall; of that I am convinced. I, at any rate, am seeing the thing through. To seize any chance to destroy a source of supply to the hideous market of the streets is my duty; and if the attempt succeeds it might at one blow achieve more than could be achieved by six months of exhortation."

And he had continued to plead, until finally the elderly clergyman had agreed to see Matt Merton and, if a meeting could be arranged, to let Merrick know.

In due course the message came. Date and time had been fixed; and now she who had called the meeting sat, oppressed by foreboding, nervous yet controlled, on the eve of her ordeal.

443

OF THE FOUR PEOPLE gathered in Dr Meadows' study in Margaret Street, only Matt Merton was wholly at ease. The clergyman greeted Lottie with abrupt constraint; Merrick, though reassured as to his own record by his previous conversation with the Doctor, could not help asking himself how convincing the woman's narrative would prove; while she, determined to appear self-possessed, was a shade too unabashed in her anxiety to control the dread with which she faced the task of telling her story.

Meadows, gruffly aloof, made no introductions nor sign that he proposed to conduct the meeting; and an already awkward pause would have been dangerously prolonged, had not Matt taken a skilful initiative.

"I am very glad to meet you again, Miss Heape" he said with easy friendliness, crossing the room to Lottie's side. "My name is Merton and it is a very long time since I had the privilege of helping you to escape a walloping and come under the protection of the good Doctor here. You will not remember me, and I should certainly not have recognised you. Dear me, it must be the best part of twenty years ago! And now" (his manner altered and, in preparation for what he foresaw would be his job of chairmanship, became more formal and resonant) "I understand you have bravely volunteered to lift the veil which hides yet another dark and dreadful corner of our wicked London, and that we are to take counsel as to what we ought to do." He turned to Merrick. "To you, Mr Merrick, I must introduce myself wholly ab initio, for though Miss Heape and I would have met as strangers had chance thrown us together, we are in fact old acquaintances."

The two men shook hands, and Matt addressed the Doctor:

444

"Will you call the meeting together, sir, or would you prefer me to do so?"

"You do it, Merton, by all means you do it!"

The clergyman had greatly aged since our last glimpse of him in Crocker's Bloomsbury lodging. His heavy moustache and such hair as still grew about his ears and above the nape of his neck was iron-grey with flecks of white. His cheeks were hollow, and the projecting chin, formerly a firm and rounded cornice, was now bony and almost fleshless. His fighting life was over; and a tired warrior lingered on, waiting for peace, yet at times embittered by the knowledge that his battles were done. Of his angers and prejudices, formerly ephemeral and quickly forgotten once they had served as spurs to action, a few, denied appeasement, had hardened into permanence. Among them was the resentment he had felt against Lottie for first deceiving and then laughing at him; and this resentment had been deepened, during the long interval since their chance meeting, by what Matt Merton had told him of the incidents at Lashwater and of her association with Fleischmann. She was pitch and her touch defiled. So he set his grim jaws, and prepared to listen to what was probably a farrago of invention.

When all were seated, Matt called on Lottie to begin her tale.

"Take your time, Miss Heape, and do not be embarrassed. We are not here to pass judgment—even silently—on the manner in which up to now you have lived your life. Try to imagine you are telling us about someone else, and we shall listen as to a case-history which is giving us valuable information and preparing the destruction of an evil thing."

She smiled at him gratefully, and began to speak in a low nervous voice which steadied and grew stronger as she proceeded.

The previous evening, sitting for a long while in her musty little room, she had rehearsed the statement to be made on the morrow. How much could be omitted? The sole purpose of her confession was the destruction of Evan Slode and his father. Which incidents in her life were essential to this purpose, and which irrelevant? Very briefly—as would befit a childish memory—she must tell of her kidnapping from Aldershott, of the time spent in the establishment managed by William Slode, of the assault on Evan which had sent her, trussed like a fowl, to Long Meg's hovel in Grove Place. Of the beating, the rescue, the convalescence in the vicarage, the removal to the country, two-thirds of her audience were already aware. One sentence enough for these, and name no names. How about the seduction of Mervyn, and the part played by her treachery toward Gladwin in the break-up at Lashwater? Maybe the facts were known already; if not, so much the better. Surely these could be passed over? Unless, of course, this Mr Merton, who had been Gladwin's friend, introduced his name and asked what she knew of him. What then? She would cross that bridge when she came to it.

Next, the encounter with Merrick, Uncle Tom's Cabin, the few weeks in Foley Street—they were unnecessary. The real story should begin with her meeting—but of course not recognising—Evan Slode in a pub (any need to mention Boreham at this stage? Better not) and his proposal on the following evening to find her a "protector".

From now on, until after Fleischmann's death, she must stick closely to the truth—or at least to most of it. The strange circle of houses somewhere in Islington; Fleischmann; the glimpse of the little man with the pink cheeks (also unrecognised at the time, even though Fleischmann had mentioned his name); Alpha Place; Freddie Boreham and Jack Bulwinkle. Frensham? No, not Frensham; if in any way possible, not a word of Frensham—at this moment or ever again.

Nearing the end now. Evan's bribe to persuade her to eavesdrop. Homes from Home (Merton would sit up when she said those words, and even interrupt with might-be-awkward questions. All right; another bridge to cross, as and when). Her betrayal of Fleischmann; his murder. The two fifty-pound notes.

This would be the worst moment of her ordeal. The very thought of those notes, sealed in their envelope under the false bottom of her jewel-case, was enough to set her trembling. Tomorrow she must handle them; display them to her hearers; live again those terrible hours in Alpha Place when her fingers, which had merely drawn the two crisp brittle-sounding sheets from their cover and thrust them back again, had seemed warm and sticky with Fleischmann's blood. She closed her eyes and sat rigid in the frowsy arm-chair. "You've got to do it" she told herself. "Don't stall. It's no use funking what can't be skipped."

And so to the climax—the vision, as she sat in torment in the drawing-room of the empty house whose kindly owner she had helped to kill, of her first meeting with her dead lover, and the till-now-delayed recognition of the short middle-aged man who had interrupted them, followed inevitably by the recognition of his son.

As a sort of postscript, she would add that after leaving Alpha Place she had lodged with a friend, as instructed by Lord Frederick, until the news of Crocker's suicide had driven her to fly in panic from everyone connected with Fleischmann and his affairs. There she would stop. Her part would have been done. It was for the three men to decide what further action should be taken.

The recital went smoothly enough. Matt spoke no word of Gladwin; and although at the mention of Homes from Home he looked up quickly from the note-book in which from time to time he jotted down a few words while listening, he said nothing. When Lottie stopped talking there was a complete silence, in the midst of which the two bank-notes, lying half-unfolded on the table, crackled sharply.

Matt straightened up in his chair and cleared his throat.

"A remarkable story, Miss Heape, and, if I may say so, admirably told. May I ask a question or two?"

Lottie's heart sank, but she nodded assent.

"I take it that you had no reason to connect Mr Crocker's tragic end with the case of Mr Fleischmann, beyond the fact that you had heard his name mentioned in Alpha Place in conjunction with Homes from Home? Why, then, should the suicide have affected you so strongly that you ran away to hide, whereas after the murder you stayed on the ground?"

Lottie hesitated; and Dr Meadows, in a dry hostile voice, spoke from his corner.

"Possibly I can answer your question as accurately as Miss Heape, and with less embarrassment. When she touched, in passing, on her having been sent to the country from my vicarage, she omitted to state that it was to Mr Crocker's home in Surrey that she was sent. She might have added that, after a sojourn of several years in and about the Crocker household, she returned suddenly to London. With the reasons for this return I am unfamiliar; but is it not natural that the murder of her lover, followed in a few weeks by the suicide of her benefactor, should have combined to frighten her badly?"

Matt grew uncomfortable while the Vicar was speaking. He had no particular desire to champion an obviously disreputable young woman; but he guessed that her confession had cost her a severe effort, and, convinced that she had put them on the track of a major social enormity, was anxious to keep on terms with her so long as her further help might be needed. He glanced uneasily at Lottie, who sat with bowed head, biting her lower lip.

"Thank you, sir" he said politely to Meadows. "That no doubt was the explanation." Then hurried on: "And now, Miss Heape, if you please. Is it a fact that since you gave young Slode the information he wanted as to Mr Fleischmann's business—eight, nine years ago—you have neither seen nor heard of him or his father?"

"That is so."

"Did you, during this considerable interval, make any attempt to track them down?"

She shook her head.

"May I ask why not?"

Still looking down at her hands which lay clasped on her lap, she replied faintly:

"What was the use? I had no one to help me, even if I found them. Besides I was earning my living and had no time."

There was a brief pause. Matt changed the subject.

"This "Circle" in Islington—could you find the place again?"

"It would be mere luck, if I could. All I know is that the cab in which Evan Slode took me to meet Mr Fleischmann turned to the left at the Angel. I saw the name as we went by."

"Well, that should be enough as a basis for enquiry. One more question, if I may. . . . I understand that it was the possibility of approaching Dr Meadows, with a view to getting in touch with me, that decided you to tell Mr Merrick what you had told no one else. Could you not, any time these nine years, have communicated direct with the Doctor?"

She raised her head and replied with a gleam of anger:

"It was only by chance—and not all that time ago—that I knew you were the man who wrote those things in that weekly paper. It is pretty obvious the sort of reception I should have had from Dr Meadows, if I had called on or written to him. I told him a fairy-tale once, when I was very young and foolish, and he has not forgotten it. He wouldn't have believed a word of my story." Swinging round in her chair "Would you, sir?" she snapped.

The clergyman got up and crossed slowly to where she sat.

"Young woman" he said gravely "if I have been over-harsh with you, I am sorry. You now admit having lied to me, but do not say why. There may have been good reason. If so, let us have it. But until I hear it, I must continue to suspect one who, even as a young girl, tried pertly to deceive a man old enough to be her father, and one, into the bargain, who had thought to save her—*temporarily at least*—from a life of sin and degradation."

She did not look at him, but stared straight in front of her, with lips set and obstinate.

"Well?" he queried.

Her eyes flickered toward Matt, who gave her a tiny smile of encouragement. With an effort she spoke:

"I will say this much and no more. There was trouble at Mr Crocker's—trouble of my making—and I was frightened and ran away. What impelled me to speak to you in Regent Street I have never since understood. A sort of silly bravado, I suppose. When you were kind to me and asked me back here for tea, I saw I had got myself into a corner. My only thought was to cover my tracks, and I invented a stupid story about being a lady's maid or some such thing. And then—" She stopped abruptly, pressed her lips tightly together again and shook her head.

Meadows waited a moment. As she remained silent, he shrugged his shoulders and with a sigh went back to his chair.

Matt closed his note-book with deliberate emphasis and rose to his feet.

"I think, sir" addressing Meadows "that we have got as far as we can today, and will not cumber your study any longer. With Miss Heape's permission I will take charge of these bank-notes, and start a few enquiries into this whole business through such channels as are open to me. It may be some time before we are in a position to know for certain whether this abominable institution is still active; but I will communicate with you all when there is any news. The Moonlight Mission headquarters will find you, Mr Merrick, and you will be able to get in touch with Miss Heape if necessary? Good! Then we will take our leave, Doctor, and thank you for putting this room at our disposal."

Outside in Margaret Street, the trio paused on the pavement:

"I go west to Marylebone" said Merrick.

Matt looked at Lottie.

"Holborn" she said.

"Then perhaps you will allow me to go along with you some of the way. I must get back to Fleet Street."

They walked a little distance in silence. Then Lottie said suddenly:

"*You* believe me, I hope, Mr Merton."

"Oh, yes. I believe you. I am distressed that there should be this—this barrier—between you and the Doctor. He is one of the finest men alive, and the world will never know of the good he has done and the dogged courage with which he has fought against misery and wrongdoing. But he feels his years, broods over certain unpleasant memories which time has magnified, and having the stubborn temper of a fearless but now powerless man, has to pity before he can forgive."

A few yards further, and Matt spoke again:

"Miss Heape, I am going to risk offending you because, if we are to achieve anything in this matter, there should be complete confidence at any rate between you and me. You are the source of information; I am the one who has to act on it. We must understand one another. If you are angry and refuse to answer what I am going to ask, so much the worse; but I hope it may be otherwise."

He threw her a sidelong glance. Her face was expressionless, not receptive, or wary, or hostile.

"You have known Paul Gladwin. I also know him—well. He has been my friend for many years. He was as much responsible as I for snatching you from that awful hag near Waterloo. He was at—wasn't the place called Lashwater where Crocker lived?—at Lashwater for nearly all the time you were there. He was dismissed by Crocker, came to me in London and I was lucky enough to find him a job. Never could I get him to tell me, except in very general terms, why he had been dismissed. He was shielding a young girl; that much was obvious, though he made out it was Crocker's son that he wished to protect. But who the girl was and what exactly she had done, he refused to say. Were you that girl?"

She now showed signs of agitation, and her cheeks were flushed. She nodded her head and he heard her swallow with an effort.

"Thank you. Then I will venture further. Paul was in love with you, wasn't he?"

Again she nodded.

"Did you ever see him again, after he was sacked by Crocker?"

"Yes" she said, but so low he could hardly hear her. "I saw him again once."

"And what happened?"

She shuddered.

"Something horrible."

"Horrible for whom? For Paul?"

She turned toward him and he saw with surprise that her eyes were full of tears. But when she spoke, her voice was bitter.

"Why do you plague me like this, Mr Merton? I am only a poor whore and one expects beastliness from whores. Do you want me to say I was beastly to your friend? I will —freely. Ever since I was a kid I treated him foully, and the last time I saw him I insulted him in a way which a *real* man would have killed me for."

"A *real* man?" he repeated. "But, my dear, he loved you." After a pause: "This last meeting was about three years ago?"

"I dare say!" defiantly.

"Then" said Matt, suddenly stern "it may interest you to know that your insult, whatever it may have been, shattered his life and sent him in despair to America, from where he returned a few months ago, penniless, a toper and not far from being dead of unhappiness, dram-drinking and starvation. Indeed, if another friend had not by the merest chance come across him less than a fortnight since, he might well have been a goner at this moment."

She stopped short, and stood with the back of her hand pressed against her mouth. Tears flowed from her eyes which stared at him wide with horror. At last, struggling to control her sobs, she quavered:

"You have seen him, then? Did he mention me?"

"He has not mentioned you for a long long time, and I have for some while suspected why. Paul is a gentle confiding guileless creature, who will talk readily of anything near his heart. For the first years of his time with Crocker his letters were full of you—of your quick wits and pretty ways. Then, as I now realise, they suddenly changed. Not a word. When he came back to London and refused to tell me what had happened, I did not connect you with the trouble. As a matter of fact I had forgotten all about you. But I had dealings with Lord Frederick Boreham after Fleischmann was killed, and your name cropped up and I began to put two and two together. Gradually I came to understand that Paul loved you; and if he never spoke of a girl he loved, it was because she had dealt badly by him. You have been cruel to Paul, Miss Heape—how cruel I do not know—and it is right you should know it." Altering his tone to one of ordinary conversation, he continued: "Here I must leave you. Allow me to give you my card. The address will be useful in case you wish to see me about this Slode affair—or any other matter."

He raised his hat, and was turning away, when he checked and addressed her once more.

"By the way, did *he* tell you I was *Diogenes'* Commissioner? You see he is fond of me; and likes, when he can, to praise those he is fond of—sometimes indiscreetly."

This time he left her, and strode rapidly southward.

Paul Gladwin had kept his promise and gone to the Marigold to meet Matt and Toby. From Holywell Street he had sought his attic off Red Lion Square, and there remained until eight o'clock. Some glimmering of prudence deterred him from converting more than a small fraction of Bernstein's money into gin before he was due to appear, with the result that, though dim and lugubrious, he was sober. In a resigned and dreary way he described briefly his final catastrophic experience in New York, and made no secret of Holywell Street or of how, since the summer, he had kept body and soul together. As previously agreed between them, his two friends took him firmly in hand. They were deeply shocked by his appearance. Not so much the squalor of his wretched clothing moved them —though that was heartrending enough—as his emaciated physique, dirty yellow complexion with patches of dull blue, and shaking clawlike hands. After a warm bath he was to go straight to bed in a small room in Toby's quarters upstairs. When he had been fed and rested and kept warm for a few days, they would decide what to do with him.

He slumped listlessly in a chair while they gave these instructions, and then, as though they had been talking about somebody else, demanded hot gin and water. After swallowing a few mouthfuls, he perked up.

"I can't do that" he said, reverting to a plan he seemed not to have heard. "I have to turn in some stuff tomorrow. I daren't be behindhand again. Bernstein would throw me out."

"He won't have a chance, old man, as he won't see you. He can throw me out instead. There now, drink that up and off you go upstairs with Toby. Give me these papers. It will be a privilege to instruct His Nosiness in the Law and the Prophets."

Gladwin obeyed.

On the evening of the meeting in Dr Meadows' study Matt demanded Toby's exclusive attention.

"Important, Toby; and very much on the q. t. But first of all, how is the old chap?"

Gladwin had now been at the Marigold for ten days or more. He had been dragged into safety from the brink of the precipice, but was still a very sick man. Years of a broken spirit and months of under-feeding and over-drinking spell slow recovery; and he spent most of his days either in a plaintive coma or in restless hankering after the rosy indifference only gin could bring.

"He's mending a bit, Mr Merton; but it's a weary business, and pitiful to watch. The girls are wonderfully good to him, with all they have to do, and Mrs Trotter comes in nights."

"I'll go up and see him in a few minutes; but first I want you fly to the latest job on hand. Now take this slowly."

Toby listened stolidly to the account of the morning's conference and of the events which had brought it about. When Matt had finished, he whistled under his breath, but said nothing until he had refilled their glasses.

"And this judy was the kid from Granby Street, and Fleischmann's piece of muslin, and is now coming it strong as an Angel of Vengeance! Saucy, Mr Merton, very saucy indeed! Do you remember us saying she was the sort to crop up in almost any connection and the rummier the better? Well, this is rum enough for anyone, ain't it?

"And now" he went on "for this ring of houses in Islington. If such a place exists, there's one cove who'll know, and that's an old chap who keeps a little public called the Jolly Bargee near the New River. Box is his name—Joe Box—and I've met him at the Oddfellows. An A1 fellow, straight as they make em and no nonsense. I'll sound him out, casual-like, when I next see him. Better than going up there on purpose; for if there is a hang-out of the kind in the neighbourhood and these beauties are still at their games, you may be sure they keep their eyes skinned for strangers."

Not until early in the New Year could Toby send word to Matt that he had seen Joe Box and obtained certain information. Meantime Matt had been joyfully busy. His journalist's instincts were in full cry, for it seemed he was on a trail after his own heart, with prospect of danger and excitement and, at the end, a smashing revelation to the greater glory of *Diogenes*.

He had acquaintances in most walks of life, who were glad to help with specialised information or inside influence when invited to assist in preparing the dossier of some scandal marked down for exposure. One such acquaintance undertook to trace the latest issue-record of the two fifty-pound notes. Another, conversant with the by-ways of the City, set out to pick up the broken threads of the Burdock sensation of nine years ago, with a view if possible to establishing the subsequent activities of those minor members of the gang who had escaped the hand of justice. A third, to whom the sprawl of London was a fascinating pattern of all sorts and conditions of queer trades, was commissioned to chart the map of prostitution as it existed at this present time, and in terms of the establishments which fed or sheltered the traffic in women. There was a faint hope that from such a chart Larne Circle might emerge as a recognised source of recruits, and so corroborate Lottie's otherwise unsupported story. On the whole, results were disappointing; but fragments of news trickled in, and these—in the intervals of his own researches —Matt indexed and analysed.

One day he had a note from Lottie Heape, asking to see him. She came by appointment to his rooms in Norfolk Street, wearing her black frock with white ruffles, neat, unobtrusive and clearly nerved to a difficult request.

"I want to know how Paul Gladwin is" she said in a tight, controlled voice "and whether it would be possible for me to see him."

"As to how he is" replied Matt "I am glad to say he is slowly improving. He is still very weak and looks a wreck; but he's mending. He'll never be as strong as he should be at his age, and the shadow of such a life as he has led these last few years will never wholly pass away. But he'll pull through, which is more than at one time I dared to hope."

He paused, and she waited in silence.

"The other question" he resumed "I cannot answer right off. Would he wish to see you? That is one point. Even if he were willing, might it mean a set-back—the recollection of the past and all that? You must let me consider and consult—"

"Where is he?" she demanded. Then, realising that her tone had been abrupt and almost imperious, added: "I am sorry. I only wanted to know. I shan't force my way in or anything."

"I think I had better not answer that until—"

She rose from her chair and finished his sentence for him:

"Until I am allowed to come—if I am allowed. Very well, Mr Merton. Thank you for seeing me, and please do your best for me."

Matt saw Tom Merrick on several occasions during this interval of waiting. He had found the organisers of the

Moonlight Mission helpful and friendly. Their records were especially useful in the matter of locating dress-houses. One of the anomalies of the law was that the owner of a dress-house could prosecute for theft (and win the case) not only a girl-inmate who failed to turn in any one of the articles of clothing in which, under a keeper's eye, she was sent into the streets, but also any individual or agency who persuaded her to leave her miserable profession and not return to her prison. Very early in its career the Mission had been forced most scrupulously to return to the house whence she came every stitch worn by a penitent dress-lodger, with the result that a curious relationship had grown up between the controllers of dress-houses and the missioners. The former could not take action to get back their girls; the latter must safeguard themselves from prosecution by obtaining a full receipt for the property which the reclamation of a prostitute had brought into their hands. Naturally the Mission kept a list of the addresses to which returns of clothing had been made; and although those of early date were of doubtful validity, Matt was glad to add them to his dossier, for one never knew what connection might not exist between persons engaged in any sort of underground traffic.

He was dining with Merrick at the Marigold on the evening after Lottie's visit to Norfolk Street and prior to the missioner setting out on one of his professional tours. Matt said:

"I'd like your advice on a matter concerning Miss Heape —your advice and that of Toby Langrish here. Do you mind if we take a glass of port, the three of us, before you start out?"

Dinner over, Toby joined them by request, and Matt briefly outlined the history of the relationship between Lottie Heape and Paul Gladwin, indicated the wretched condition of the latter when recently found, explained that he was bed-ridden upstairs in this very building, and concluded with the girl's plea to be allowed to see him.

"Now you know the woman" he said to Merrick "better than Toby or I; and we know Paul. We tell you frankly—

and I am sure I can speak for Toby without consulting him
first—that our poor friend is in a very delicate state, physically
and mentally. Any shock, any distressing reminder of the
past, any unpleasant scene might undo all the good weeks
of care and nursing have done for him. It might even finish
him altogether. What do you think? Can we believe that
she is genuinely ashamed, genuinely anxious to try to repair
the harm she did him, whatever that may have been? And
if so, has she the intuition to see how frail he is, and the
nous to be quiet and gentle, and to watch for any sign of
fatigue or agitation which should be her cue to stop talking
and leave him?"

Merrick thought carefully before he replied.

"She has never spoken one word to me about this Mr
Gladwin, nor indeed given any account of her earlier life.
Until she told her story in Dr Meadows' study I was totally
ignorant of her past. That she had been an unfortunate I
knew as soon as I saw her, and she herself said—with a
defiance in which I have noticed she is apt to take refuge—
that she had walked the streets. But that I should guess
was in comparatively recent years—during the time she said
she was busy earning her living—you remember? And now,
of course, I realise that she never even mentioned Gladwin's
name. Clearly he represents a section of her memories which
she either treasures or wishes to forget—maybe both. Do
we agree? Well, that being so, I should judge that a request
to see him—*coming from her*—was a request from the heart
and should be granted if possible.

"She is hard—or wears a mask of hardness—and is often
bitter and sometimes deliberately provocative. I recall that
on one occasion she mocked at my religion—suddenly and
without cause. But when I answered her restrainedly, she
changed her tone at once. She was asserting her right to be
low, challenging me to treat her as I am forced to treat the
poor creatures I meet at night, because I have no other
language in which to appeal to them. If I had preached at
her, she would have quarrelled and perhaps insulted me—
feeling a queer inverted pride in degrading herself below her

458

real level. From these facts, also, I should argue that she is not one to ask a favour lightly—especially one liable to betray an emotional side in her character which normally she would be concerned to deny—and that such a favour should be considered with sympathy."

"And she'll behave herself if we let her come?"

"Of that I have little doubt. Her manners are instinctively good. When they are bad, she makes them bad on purpose."

"What do you say, Toby? And should we ask Paul?"

"I say let her come—if only so I can have a look at her meself! She's popped in and out of Mr Merton's and Mr Gladwin's lives for the best part of twenty years and I've never even seen her! As for asking Mr Gladwin—I say don't. If we are fairly sure she means well by him this time, he'll not come to harm; but if we mention her while his last memory of her is—as you tell me it is, Mr Merton— a dirty one, he'll get the collywobbles before the race even starts."

Once again Lottie was in Matt's sitting-room in Norfolk Street. With impassive face she received the news that she was to be permitted to see Paul Gladwin, merely nodding an acknowledgment and waiting for him to continue.

"About five o'clock would be the best time, when he has had his sleep and a cup of tea. You will not be able to stay long, you know. He tires very easily."

Again she nodded; then asked:

"Where?"

"Paul is with a very old friend of his and mine, who keeps a first-class divan called the Marigold in a narrow lane off Fleet Street—"

He broke off in astonishment, as she gave a sharp exclamation and, leaning well forward in her chair, fixed him with wide and apprehensive eyes.

"Not" she stammered "not . . . not . . . the Marigold?"

"Why yes! Miss Heape, what in the world—?"

She sat for a moment without moving, still staring at him as at an apparition; then covered her face with her hands, and began gently whimpering to herself. The sheer bad luck, the cruelty of this eleventh-hour mischance overwhelmed her. Frensham; that loathsome mountain of fat; the suspicious, hostile landlord; Paul, gay and garrulous in the Park; the devastation at her lodgings; and finally the mounting horror of the hours after Paul came back with the money—all that she had so carefully hidden and striven to forget must now be dragged into the open. This was the end. She would never see him again now. Neither Merton nor the man at the tavern would dream for one moment of admitting to the bedside of a sick man a woman whose presence—in that place of all places—could not fail to rouse hideous memories, to throw the unhappy creature back into the pit of misery from which his friends were struggling to rescue him.

Matt hovered uneasily at the elbow of the faintly moaning woman. Totally mystified by her sudden breakdown, he was at a loss whether to attempt general consolation or to apologise for some unwitting blunder of his own.

"Please" he murmured. "Please—what is the matter—have I said anything—?"

She braced her shoulders, let her hands fall on the arms of the chair and with an obvious effort looked up at him. Her eyes were dry, but her mouth was twisted with distress. With difficulty she forced a half-whisper.

"Mr Merton, you must go to your friend who keeps this divan and ask him if he remembers an afternoon—all of three years ago—when a girl, accompanied by a bad character, came to the Marigold to meet a very fat man and, because she was molested, appealed to the only other person in the place for help. That other person was Paul Gladwin and the girl was I. The landlord, if he recalls the incident at all, will recall the sequel. He ejected the two men who had caused the trouble, and in due course Paul Gladwin and the girl left together. The landlord never knew the girl's name —Paul" (her voice trembled) "with the thoughtfulness which is so like him, did not mention it, seeing that in the landlord's eyes she was tarred with the same brush as her company;

OUT OF THE SILENCE AND THE SHADE

but he must know it now. When he knows it—and when
I tell you that the evening of that day was the evening on
which I behaved to Paul like a drunken hell-cat and (as you
yourself said) broke up his life and all but killed him—there
can be no question of my being allowed near him. I am
going now. Good-bye, Mr Merton. You have been kind
to me; and if I could have kept this damnable story to myself,
I should have shown you that I am truly repentant for a
wrong-doing of which you need have known no details. But
that's been impossible, and I must just take my beating."

Matt listened in silence to this painful avowal which, like
a speech from the scaffold, both embarrassed and moved
him. He gave no sign of having heard part of it from any
other source and, when she had finished, merely expressed a
few words of sympathy and showed her to the door.

But the next time he went round to see Paul and Toby, he
was looking forward to joking the latter for having entertained this notorious young lady unawares. He sat with the
sick man for an hour or so, reading the newspaper aloud and
retailing the small adventures of the day, until the patient
dozed. His watch told him the landlord should now be
more or less disengaged; so he tiptoed from the room,
closing the door behind him. On the landing outside he
met Toby, who had crept upstairs to see how things were
going.

"He's dropped off" said Matt. "I've been reading to
him. And by the way I've got the laugh of you. I believe
you said you'd never seen Lottie Heape? Well you have!"

In his anxiety to make no noise he had failed to latch the
door of Gladwin's room, and while he had been speaking it
had swung silently open. A voice called to him.

"Matt! Come back please!" Gladwin was propped on
one elbow, and his drawn, usually bloodless face was flushed
on forehead and cheeks. "What were you saying about
Lottie Heape? What do *you* know about her?"

Poor Matt was taken totally unawares.

"I—I—" he stammered. "I just happened to say that
Toby had never seen her—"

The invalid fixed him with a steady eye.

"He has, as a matter of fact—though he doesn't know it. But *you* haven't, nor to my knowledge ever heard her name. Yet you have seen her—you *must* have—and lately. Now then, out with it!"

Cornered, Matt improvised a confused and clumsy tale about a friend called Merrick, engaged in rescue work, who had chanced to meet Lottie and, through her, got on the track of some bad people and had enlisted Matt's help. At the end he confessed that he had indeed seen Lottie more than once during recent weeks.

Paul seemed indifferent to the story for which he himself had asked. He was interested only in the girl.

"How is she?" he demanded eagerly. "Tell me how she looks, whether she is happy, what she said. . . ."

He was feeling the strain of his own excitement, and fell back on the pillows. But his eyes remained bright and determined, and dwelt without flinching on the other's face. Matt gave a brief and reassuring account of Lottie's appearance and demeanour, feeling more uncomfortable every moment and conscious that Toby was just outside the door, listening with all his ears. The damned joke has boomeranged on me, he thought, bad cess to it! Paul lay without sound or movement when Matt had finished speaking. At last he said wistfully:

"Do you think she could bear to come and see me?"

Relief swept his friend from head to toe.

"It is what she wants to do more than anything in the world!" he cried.

The muscles of Paul's neck relaxed and his head dropped gently sideways, until it lay comfortably cushioned against a bulge of pillow.

"Thank you Matt" he murmured. "You are a good chap. I shall soon be better now."

His eyes closed and he fell into a deep sleep.

MRS ST MAUR's letter went on:

And now for news of a very old friend. You'll recollect
that the Park, after a few years' occupancy by those funny
people one never saw and whose name I can't even remember, was sold for a boys' school, and that the school
started last September. Who do you think is a junior
master there? Mervyn Crocker and no other! He came
to call on Sunday—rather shy, very tall and bony, but
exactly the small boy we used to know on an elongated
scale. He asked after you, and hopes to see you when
you are next at home. Poor boy! he has had a sad time.
Mrs Crocker did not for long survive her husband; John
enlisted and is now soldiering in India; little Georgie is a
governess somewhere in Yorkshire. What a break-up of
a once happy and prosperous family! There is no home
for the children, scattered as they are, and of course
practically no money except what they earn. Mervyn
stayed on at the Park during last holidays in charge of
the two or three boys whose parents are abroad or who
have nowhere to go. He was actually there while we were
all at Temple Vesey. All last term he tried to screw up
courage to look us up, but couldn't face it until January.

He told me that he got the mastership partly on account
of his earlier association with the house and grounds. I
gather there were half a dozen candidates, all more or less
equal as to qualifications; and that Mervyn's familiarity
with the place and neighbourhood—plus, I dare say, a
touch of kindly sentiment—tipped the scale in his favour.
I urged him to come and see us whenever he wanted a
change of scene or company.

463

And now, darling, I hope you are not overworking or taking more risks than you need—.

Hetty read no further, but folded the letter and put it back in its envelope.

Mervyn Crocker! Well, of all the surprises! She tried to imagine a grown-up edition of the schoolboy of nine years ago, and with the oddest results. The plain businesslike schoolmaster suit was easy; and the bowler hat; and the boots; and the stiff collar with the folds of tie neatly filling the V of the waistcoat. But from the collar upwards and from the sleeves outwards projected a snub-nosed freckled laughing face, with hair of a nondescript colour rebelliously on end, and two large erratic hands, not over-clean and liable to chilblains in winter. Hetty smiled to herself at this comic but nevertheless engaging vision, which to her surprise was succeeded by one of Arthur Vesey, comfortably stylish in his shooting-jacket and leggings, a secure and finished specimen of young manhood, set gracefully against the polished intricacy of a towering Jacobean overmantel. With a little frown she put her mother's letter in her writing-desk, shook herself and hurried to find Mrs Barnett and the morning's work.

When the Bishop of London spoke of St Jude's, Whitechapel as "the worst parish in my diocese" he was thinking specifically rather than generally, and by "worst" meant the "most baffling" rather than, from every point of view, the last thing in vice and misery. The parish, for example, could claim two advantages over its neighbour Christ Church, Spitalfields. It was small; and it contained no such ineradicable patch of degradation as that centring on Dorset Street or as the district from Wentworth Street northward to Flower and Dean Street. On the other hand, it had (as his Lordship said) been so thoroughly demoralised by indiscriminate charity, that the church in the eyes of the people

was a milch-cow and nothing more. Further, among its
wretched courts and alleys were an undue proportion consisting of houses let out room by room at eightpence a night
and inhabited by a vagrant, everchanging population of the
lowest and least approachable kind.

The task of Mr and Mrs Barnett, when they took over
St Jude's in March 1873, had been, in fact, one to dismay the
stoutest heart. The parish was like a desolate and uncharted
shore. Here, as you set down a foot in order to take a step
forward, the ground dissolved into watery pulp and oozed
away; here, like a quicksand, it made as if to draw you down
into an insatiable gulf of mendicity. With infinite pains a
contact would be made with one or two families, and promises
given that the growing children should attend a night-
class or a club; but overnight the squalid rooms, with their
peeling verminous walls and few sticks of cobbled furniture,
would have been vacated, and a new lot of tenants—apathetic,
suspicious or openly hostile—installed in their place. The
demand for doles, on the other hand, worked in reverse—
drawing the slums to the church and vicarage, and often in
an ugly mood. Under the previous régime five hundred
pounds, contributed by a West End parish, had annually
been paid out in cash or in tickets for food and coal to those
attending service or begging at the vicarage door. Applicants
came at all hours, demanding assistance as their right; and
during the first year or two of the new incumbency there were
small riots and window-breaking and threats of violence when
the expected largess was refused.

However, by the time that Hetty came to Whitechapel in
the autumn of 1878, the situation in these respects had been
improved. Beggars no longer hung about the parson's
door; several of the worst "overnight" courts had been
reconditioned and now, though still poverty-stricken and
ramshackle, were at least rented by the week or month. But
the way still led uphill, and in surroundings grim and drab
and miserable. The site due to become Toynbee Hall and its
tennis court and open spaces was a maze of alleys, in which
sagging timbered cottages were jumbled with three-storey

horrors of peeling brick and plaster. The church itself, though cleaned and stripped of the hideous galleries which had originally blocked the windows and made the main floor gloomy as a basement, remained a mean and shoddy affair, poorly designed and built of cheap materials. The vicarage, a tall narrow strip of half-hearted gothic carried out in grimy brick, stood sheer on the street. It had an underground kitchen, but no area steps; there was neither pantry nor bathroom; and the only out-of-doors was a cramped back-yard.

Internally, by the zeal of Mrs Barnett and thanks to her having money to command, the house had been transformed. The rooms were cheerfully and comfortably furnished according to the taste of the period; the walls light coloured and hung with pictures. Visitors were frequent; and all the time, in the adjoining schools, classes and lectures and organised music or games attracted, in slowly increasing numbers, the wild young people of the parish.

Hetty's work was largely secretarial, for a branch of the Metropolitan Association for Befriending Young Servants had recently been opened in the vicarage, and this involved much keeping of records, following up of girls placed in situations, canvassing of new applicants. Hetty helped Mrs Barnett with her correspondence, accompanied her to the Local Government Board's District Schools at Forest Gate of which she was manager, taught herself after pain and tribulation how to control classes of rough and rowdy children. She was soon her principal's devoted slave; and, having come to St Jude's as a result of a passionate admiration for Octavia Hill, never tired of reminiscences of the days when Mrs Barnett, as a girl of eighteen, had collected rents for Octavia in Barrett's Court and elsewhere.

She was, of course, not permitted to go alone to most of the surrounding courts; but Mr Barnett, knowing that the meaning of utter poverty and hopelessness can only be grasped by one who has seen them, took her with him occasionally on his constant wanderings. Such excursions called for all the self-control the girl could summon. The sights and the smells at first turned her stomach; but gradually she managed to grow a shell of custom over her natural squeamishness. It was impossible to be in Barnett's company without marvelling at the nobility of spirit which inspired so puny a body, and wishing, so far as might be, to emulate it. So she forced herself to endure the ordeal of these walks in such a way as not to disgrace herself in front of him.

The clergyman was indeed of puny stature, and, owing to his complete indifference to clothes, comic as to appearance. Yet the quaintness of his aspect accentuated the courage he brought to his tremendous task. On his bald head he always wore a tall silk hat, which, having been ordered by post or bought second-hand, never fitted but either tilted forward over his eyes or sat jauntily askew. A long overcoat, made by some out-of-work tailor in the parish, flapped about his ankles. He carried a badly wrapped umbrella in hands covered by black cotton gloves several sizes too large.

Such was Samuel Barnett — an insignificant, almost a grotesque, but nevertheless an impressive figure. From under the hat-brim shone eyes both wise and gentle; the soft brown beard framed a full compassionate mouth, and the stumbling walk and clumsy gestures made the more remarkable the fearless simplicity with which he would penetrate some noisome hovel, from which had come the sound of a blow or of a woman weeping or of a children's brawl.

About the end of February Hetty went home for a week's holiday, and, opening the front door at a quarter to one on the Sunday after her arrival, set eyes on Mervyn Crocker for the first time for nearly ten years. They stood looking at one another in silent curiosity. Then she held out both hands.

"Mervyn! How nice! I should have known you anywhere."

"I can't say the same" he replied. "And I'm glad I can't —for now I have the pleasure of getting to know you all over again."

"Tra-la! The gallantry! Come on in. It's nearly dinner-time."

After the meal they went for a walk. There was a cold

467

FORLORN SUNSET

east wind, but the weather was clear and the paths over the
meadows dry and clean. For a while neither spoke. They
were not shy; but their consciousness of one another needed
adjustment, so long was it since they had met and so changed
their circumstances. At last she said mischievously:

"Well, Mervyn, what do you think of me? Have I worn
well?"

He surveyed her solemnly.

"Admirably; but I am a little frightened of you."

She laughed.

"Good! That gives me an advantage, because I'm not a
bit frightened of you, great big thing though you are. But
it's lovely to see you again. You know, I tried to imagine
you the other day—when mamma wrote you were here—
but I couldn't picture you grown-up. I kept seeing that
funny schoolboy grin and the freckles and arms and legs all
over the place. . . ."

"We can still supply all that" he smiled "except the
freckles, which are out of stock. Bad freckling weather, this.
But you are not the little girl I knew—dimples apart, you
are earnest and self-possessed and—well, as I say, I'm scared
of you."

She was suddenly serious.

"Please" slipping her arm through his "now tell me all
that has happened to you."

His story was simple. The college authorities had most
generously granted him a special Bursary after the Delilah
catastrophe, thanks to his school record and to enable him
to take a degree. At the end of his time at Oxford he had
put his name on the books of a Scholastic Agency and in due
course had gone as an usher to an obscure school in the
north. He did not conceal the dreariness and hardship of the
life in that bleak unfriendly place—a life which had to be
lived on the little he earned, seeing that his widowed mother
was very poor and his sister still at school. When Mrs
Crocker died and John went for a soldier, he and Georgie
were in slightly easier circumstances; but both had to work,
and by good luck she was engaged as a governess by a

468

family living not far from the school at which he was still employed.

Then a college friend wrote to him to say that a well-to-do acquaintance of his father's wanted a tutor to accompany a boy of eighteen on a long trip abroad. Mervyn was reluctant to leave his sister; but his own job was so prospectless, so uncongenial and so badly paid, that he decided to accept the offer, and for a twelve-month travelled the world with his charge. On his return, by the influence of the boy's father who was well pleased with the results of the tour, he got a teaching post in a much larger and more prosperous institution. There he remained until he chanced to read an announcement of the opening of Lashwater Park as a school for Sons of Gentlemen, together with a request for applications from candidates desiring to fill certain staff vacancies. One of these vacancies was for a Sports and Natural History master; and games, athletics and boxing being activities for which Mervyn had a talent, while Botany and Natural History were subjects to his liking, he decided to send in his name.

The interview with the headmaster was impersonal and according to formula. Three weeks later Mervyn heard that the appointment was his, and that he was to start work at the beginning of the school-year in September 1878.

"I learnt later" he concluded "that the old man had found out my connection with the place and given me preference. Decent of him, wasn't it? A queer feeling to be back again, and I was too shy for weeks to venture beyond the gates. Then I plucked up courage to go and call on your people, and very sweet they were to me. Well, that's the whole story and a dull one too, I fear."

She squeezed his arm, but could not trust her voice sufficiently to speak. The thought of those years of drab and pinching drudgery, and now of the strange experience of returning as a salaried subordinate to what had at one time been home and a future inheritance, brought her very near to tears. At last, with an effort, she forced a return to cheerfulness.

"Quite the whole story, Mervyn? No love affairs?"

"My dear Hett" he said "love affairs need a collaborator and pocket-money to keep her going. So far I've had neither. How about you?"

"Oh *me*" she laughed. "I've had dozens. At least I'm sure dozens of men adored me, but unfortunately they neglected to say so. Accordingly, true to tradition, I have hidden my diminished head in social work and become a professional spinster."

He glanced at her quickly, for her rapid nonsense was a thought over-pitched. She was looking straight ahead, with her chin up and her cheeks faintly flushed. "There is some-one—or has been" he said to himself. She heard him sigh and turned her head.

"What—" she began, then checked herself and deftly changed the subject. "What will you do in the school holidays? You can't stay at the Park year in year out. Even coming to Mount Felix would be no change to speak of."

"Oh, I'll get away in the summer, I expect. Go up to see Georgie, or perhaps do a fortnight's scrambling in the Lakes with one of the fellows."

"Poor Mervyn! It's beastly for you. I wish I could—"

She stopped short, in sudden realisation of her more than inability to help. The only place she knew where he might find amusement and change was Temple Vesey, and Temple Vesey—with Arthur in possession—was the last place in the world to which she could introduce him. As she fought down her confusion, an idea crept timidly into her mind:

"Mervyn" she said hesitantly "I suppose you wouldn't care to come to Whitechapel—for the Easter holidays, I mean? It's asking you to be uncomfortable and to work hard—but at least it would be different. . . ."

"What use would I be there?"

"Oh, *use*—plenty of use! Mr Barnett would be delighted. You'd take on the boys' club and run the charades and a dozen things. Help of that kind is terribly badly needed. You'd lodge somewhere near by and—and—well, I should like it too—very much."

They were now back at the garden gate of Mount Felix,

and the gravel of the gently sloping drive crunched under their feet.

"Sounds a good idea" he said, with the deliberation of one turning a suggestion carefully in his mind "provided your Mr and Mrs Barnett are agreeable. I've often wanted to see the East End from the inside—" He broke off abruptly, and with a chuckle pointed to a piece of level lawn lying to their right. "You proposed to me once—on that lawn. Do you remember?"

Hetty looked at his broad ingenuous face, with its high cheek-bones and cheerful uncomplaining smile, and her heart was filled with pity. Throughout the afternoon there had been no self-commiseration, no half-laments for what he had lost, no hint of the weary monotony which his life must have become. And now came this first reference to their youthful friendship—with all the memories it must have brought of cloudless irresponsible days—and deliberately he had chosen one free from melancholy, one at which they could laugh without regrets. Did she remember? Dimly perhaps; no more than that. Better for his sake to say "no", and let him pursue the childish absurdity which it had amused him to revive.

"I proposed to you, Mervyn? How very forward! It looks as though you refused me, which is depressing for a girl. Did I propose with fervour?"

"I wouldn't exactly say 'fervour'; but with much precision. Paying calls, as I recollect, was to be our principal occupation—oh, yes, and buying crackers."

She laughed gaily.

"What a prospect! I don't blame you for hesitating. Was it not a little rash to remind me at this juncture? In almost exactly twelve months from now we shall be on the eve of February 29, and goodness knows what might happen then. I warn you I shall be a much more formidable proposition than I was at the time of your first escape."

"I'm sure of that, Hetty dear" he said. "I must keep out of danger."

Both were conscious of a sudden constraint, and as they walked the short distance to the house, neither spoke.

AT THE BACK OF the Marigold premises, beyond the bar and to the right of the main dining-room, was a room of small-medium size, available for private parties of ten or twelve persons. Near the fireplace in this room, one evening in March 1879, Toby Langrish, Matt Merton and Tom Merrick were standing in a desultory group, sipping whisky and water. The two first were smoking.

Matt looked at his watch.

"Patient and nurse behind time."

Toby cocked an ear.

"They're coming now."

Slow dragging footsteps paused outside; the door was pushed open and Paul Gladwin, in a dressing-gown with a shawl round his shoulders and leaning heavily on the arm of Lottie Heape, shuffled into the room. He moved with the uncertainty and feebleness of one long bed-ridden, to whom the first stages of convalescence are exhausting. But his expression was serene and his eyes happy. Smiling round:

"How's this for an achievement?" he demanded. "First time downstairs! Medal for Miss Lottie Nightingale!"

The three men murmured congratulations and stepped aside as he was led to a wicker-chair piled with cushions which stood at one corner of the hearth. Lottie helped him to sit down and tucked a rug about his knees. She wore a plain print frock and apron, and her hair was hidden under a close-fitting white coif. As she straightened up, after settling her patient in comfort, he gave a little cough. She looked from Matt to Toby and said with a touch of asperity:

"Please no smoking. It catches his throat."

Slightly abashed, yet with a twinkle at being thus professionally disciplined, they threw their cigars into the fire.

"And now to business" said Matt. "Sit down, all of you and Toby will make his report."

The landlord cleared his throat and began:

"Well, a few days ago I had the chance I'd been waiting for to see this chap Joe Box who keeps a pub in Islington, and he was very ready to spill what little he knew. The place Miss Heape told us about—with a circle of houses round an open space—is called Larne Circle. It lies less than half a mile from Box's place, and is by all accounts as murky a hang-out as you could wish to find. There is a sort of outer ring of smaller houses which acts like a stockade, protecting the Circle itself, and everyone gives the place as wide a berth as possible. It's not on the way anywhere, unless you choose to make it so; and if you do, you're fairly safe to be casually challenged and more or less shepherded through and out the other side. No one seems to know exactly what goes on there; but it's locally regarded as a thieves' kitchen on a large scale and the monkeys in charge as dangerous brutes who'd stop at nothing if interfered with. On the other hand, Box says, if you leave *them* alone, they'll return the compliment—from which I gather that whatever cribs they may be cracking are not in that part of the town.

"Then Box went on about the Slodes. It seems he came across the old man (who's dead now, by the way—died two or three months back, Box says) years ago at Newmarket or somewhere, and later—when first he took this Islington pub —met the son. He made no bones about admitting that he was careful to keep out of their way, but at the same time to be on nodding terms if they should happen to meet. The only time he was forced to risk getting across them was when young Slode had the cheek to come to the Bargee one afternoon and annoy a girl who helped behind the bar there and was alone in the place at the time. Box caught him at it, and warned him off quick-sharp. But, as I say, he prefers to have no truck with them or their bunch of scallywags."

While Toby was speaking, Lottie sat motionless on a hard chair at Paul's side. One of her hands lay on the rug en-

veloping his knees and was partially covered by his long
emaciated fingers.

"Is it certain old Slode is dead?" she asked abruptly.

"According to Box. He seemed sure enough."

She nodded, and said nothing further. Matt spoke:

"Well done, Toby. We've spotted the place anyway. My
contribution is, I'm afraid, short, and not even sweet.
Nothing at all came to light about Larne Circle during the
Burdock investigation. The few subsidiaries of Burdock's
which were known to exist but escaped suppression, seem to
have wound-up or so changed their spots as to be un-
recognisable. But of Larne Circle not a word, not a scrap
of evidence that Burdock had ever heard of it. Over Miss
Heape's two bank-notes we have been no luckier. They
were paid out to someone we never heard of, twelve months
or more before they were received in Alpha Place. They *may*
have passed to Burdock and from him to Slode—or they
may not. It is very disappointing. I wanted to tie him up
with the Fleischmann murder, to prove he had bought the
squeak—"

A half-suppressed sob brought him up short. Lottie had
her free hand at her throat, seeking to choke back an uprush
of distress. Almost in so many words he had charged her
with a share in her benefactor's death, and his only regret
was that he could not prove it! This brusque and public
formulation of a dread which had long haunted her in secret
turned the knife in the old wound. The sick man folded
his fingers tightly round her other hand and turned to look
at her.

"Lottie dear, don't!" he pleaded. "Please don't make
yourself miserable all over again. That's finished—part of
the past we have agreed to forget. . . ."

At the sound of his voice she relaxed immediately, bent
towards him and kissed him on the forehead.

"My dear, I am sorry" she murmured. "I've hurt you.
For a moment I thought I was back—" She stopped dead,
swallowed hard, and sitting upright once more addressed Matt.
Her voice was now colourless and almost under control:

"Excuse me, Mr Merton, for interrupting you. I—I—was out of hand for the moment. I just want to say that this thing has two parts. One is the—the Fleischmann case; the other is the house in Larne Circle where kids are ruined for life. The *second* is my business. I know you only have my word for the sort of house it is; but I swear to you that all I have said about it was gospel truth. The place must be wiped out and I must pay Slode what I owe him. I beg you, therefore, to tackle this job first. When that is done, I shall not care what happens to me and they can use my treachery how they like. But I must deal with Slode first."

Merrick, more perceptive than Matt or Toby of the stab of memory which had caused her to cry out, hastened to her support.

"And further, Merton" he urged "Slode will be an important witness if it be decided to re-open the other matter. I think Miss Heape is right. Clean up this devil's cauldron in Islington, collar Slode and then the authorities can twist his arm in any direction they want."

Paul spoke from his arm-chair. His voice was weak but clear.

"Matt, old fellow, is it really necessary to revive the murder problem at all? The poor chap is dead; the people responsible (though maybe not the actual assassin) have mostly been severely dealt with on other counts. If you could pin the crime on to Burdock personally or one of his powerful partners, there would be a certain satisfaction in seeing the man hang; but you can't hope to make him more than an accessory—and is it worth torturing Lottie all over again, just to send some blackguard down for a further term of years?"

Matt frowned as he considered this appeal. It went against his grain to leave a mystery unsolved so long as any possibility of solution remained. His practical persevering mind, like that of a police-officer, liked to regard any case to which it applied itself as perpetually open until neatly and indisputably closed. But he saw the force of Merrick's argument, felt a little ashamed of his clumsiness toward Lottie, and was unwilling to oppose poor old Paul, who was thinking only of the woman he loved and, in his quixotic way, cared more for her happiness than for their joint duty to the community.

"Very well" he said, "our first objective is Larne Circle. Suggestions invited as to how best to proceed."

Lottie stood up.

"Paul has been downstairs long enough and is getting tired. I shall take him up to bed again. You start on ways and means and I'll be with you in twenty minutes."

She got the invalid to his feet, and led him slowly and solicitously away. When they had gone, Merrick said:

"A remarkable woman, that! She confronts the world as though her soul were dead and there was not a soft spot in her whole make-up. We know what her life has been, and she knows we know. Yet she gives no sign of contrition, and, except just now, I have never seen her relax her guard. She just meets us face to face, standing firm on the present as though the past had never been. Yet with Gladwin she is as tender as a wife."

Matt nodded.

"If she has not in so many words saved his life, she has most certainly given him the wish to live. That is a great deal to do for any one. All the same, I can't like her. She has once before lost control in my presence—*really* lost it, and cried as though her heart would break. But even shedding tears her eyes were cold—harlot's eyes."

"Except for *him*" rejoined Merrick. "But that, though to me it is always pathetic, is not uncommon. I have known other cases of the kind. All a girl has of devotion and self-sacrifice goes to the one; to the rest, merely the carcase they pay for. But that is not what I mean, as between Lottie Heape and ourselves. After all we are not her clients. I suppose, if one must put a name to it, we are her comrades— her friends, so far as she has any. But she is no nearer to us now than before she told her story in Dr Meadows' room."

"Scared of something she hasn't told, I wouldn't wonder" Toby put in. He had never wholly revised his first impression of the young woman, brought by a scoundrel to a repulsive rendezvous.

Merrick shook his head.

"Not fear. Remorse. That sudden outbreak when the murder was mentioned came from excess of feeling, not from fright. I think there were two sores on her conscience— Gladwin and Fleischmann. One has healed, or is healing fast; the other is still an open wound and she means Slode to answer for it."

They fell to discussing strategy. The problem was not an easy one. Assuming the police would take their word as to what went on in Larne Circle (and that was barely conceivable) any regulation raid would at once be reported by the watch-out men who, according to Joe Box, let no one— however harmless in appearance—pass through the area unchallenged or unaccompanied. The first glimpse of a posse of unmistakable policemen would mean an urgent word to headquarters; and it might happen that, when at last entrance had been forced, nothing incriminating would be found. The police would appreciate this possibility from the first. They dreaded using a warrant to no purpose, for a mistake of the kind could lead to retaliation, with results both shaming to the prestige of the force and disastrous to the individuals concerned.

Further, as Matt pointed out, their only evidence of the existence of captive children in one of the houses in the Circle was far from up to date; and now that old Slode was dead, they had no grounds beyond those of general probability for supposing that the traffic persisted.

"I am sure Miss Heape is telling the truth about what went on there at one time" he said. "But it is years ago, and we must have something definite and actual to go on before the authorities will move."

At this juncture Lottie returned and was briefly informed of the dilemma.

"I know all that" she said calmly. "There is only one thing to be done; and now that Paul is over the worst and on the mend, I am going to do it—if I can."

The members of the Marigold Committee for the Suppression of Larne Circle (among whom, in this particular connection, Paul Gladwin was not included) made several united efforts to dissuade Lottie from what she was determined to do.

"It's too dangerous." "It's worse than dangerous, it's madness." "Once in you'll never get out. He'll see to that." But to no purpose.

"It's my quarrel and I'm going to fight it out. Besides, what other plan do you suggest?"

Here the discussion always ended. They had no other plan. Reluctantly, therefore, they accepted the situation and turned to consider, assuming that she gained entry, how action should be organised. They came to one important decision. Police assistance was essential. Useless to fight illegality with illegality. But, with a view to delaying—and perhaps modifying—the alarm-signal, the uniformed men should be screened behind an advance party of ordinary citizens. This party should include, in addition to the three leaders, Toby's cellarman George, a brawny waiter from the Marigold dining-room, and three or four bargees whom Joe Box undertook to collect, whose good faith he guaranteed and whose usefulness in a rough-and-tumble was beyond doubt. In a moment of retrospect, when he was thinking back over the whole bizarre history of Homes from Home and its offshoots, Matt remembered the Crocker boy, and the promise to let him know if ever a chance seemed to offer of renewing hostilities with the men who had wronged his father. He had no other address than the Scholastic Agency; but to that he wrote a guarded letter, asking the young man to come and see him at the first opportunity.

Lottie, at this period, was still dogging the footsteps of Evan Slode, charting his places of resort, primed, when the moment came, to take the final chance. She was careful to spread and vary her times of absence so as not to rouse Paul's suspicions. He knew in general terms that there was something in the wind. But of her personal share in the venture he must be told nothing—beyond (when the time came) that she might have to leave London for a few days in the immediate future, and that he must take every care of himself and get stronger in readiness for her return.

Evan Slode slouched in his usual chair in the innermost room of Mariotti's. He was stouter than when we saw him last, but less florid. Indeed his face, once round and rosy-cheeked, was almost haggard. The blue-black hair, still crimped and waved, showed flecks of grey at the temples, although the man was only in his middle thirties. These signs of age and worry were of very recent appearance, and betrayed the troubles which had come upon him since his father, a few months earlier, had caught a bad cold which turned to pleurisy and pneumonia, and died after an illness of ten days.

Evan, with the bland self-confidence typical of him, had entered undismayed on his inheritance. But he was not long in finding out that the conduct of the business on which his father's livelihood and his own had mainly depended, required qualities more subtle than he had conceived.

William Slode had pliability, quickness in reading the minds of others, an instinctive sense of when to browbeat or override and when to seem to yield. His amiability was not all of it assumed. Certainly he cultivated an avuncular jollity he did not always feel; certainly he relished, when conditions were favourable, striking like a viper at an opponent with whom a moment before he had been genial or ingratiating. But there was in his make-up a natural cheerfulness, which expressed itself in little giggling jokes or set him whistling and humming as he went about the house.

Evan had none of these characteristics, and even if he had, would have been too crass and bumptious to use them. When he was acting as procurer for a wealthy man, he treated his patron with knowing heartiness. To a point the client was in his power—they had at any rate one secret in common —and Evan (provided he did the job he was paid for to the other's satisfaction) saw no reason for servility. Two men of the world doing a business deal—that was his idea of the relationship. When, however, he was concerned with persons weaker than himself, the bully took command. It was nothing

to him what the other was thinking or wanting; and as for
there being at any time a moment when it might be better
policy to concede than to domineer, the very idea was beyond
his scope.

Compelled at a moment's notice to take over his father's
practice, he naturally applied to its management the principles which had served him adequately in the simpler and
less dangerous occupation by which he had been used to
supplement the parental allowance. To him the kidnappers,
the decoys, the pedlars of destitute children, the madams
and the various export-agents were subordinates—employees
of the central bureau of which he was now the head. And
as subordinates he treated them; only to find in a very
short time that they had no intention of kow-towing to
one who depended on them for the working and—more
important still—for the secrecy of his business. The discreet bonhomie which had ruled between them and William
Slode—the assumption that they were a band of jolly outlaws working together in mutual confidence to exploit the
vices of society — totally disappeared. In its place came
brusque formality, orderings-about and sometimes harsh re-
buke. The victims of this change of method were at first
dismayed, then offended and finally outspokenly resentful.
Quarrels multiplied, returns suffered, and Evan became distraught, trying to fix the blame in every quarter but the
right one.

This evening in Mariotti's he brooded confusedly over his
worries. He had been drinking steadily, and was now in a
mood of hazy melancholy. The latest vexation was a threat
of trouble with the matron in charge of the young boarders
(their number was now so far reduced that one supervisor
was sufficient) who showed signs of insubordination and had
even told her employer to his face that she "had never been
accustomed to be spoken to like that and was not going to
start now." "Damn the old bitch!" Evan muttered to himself, his head lolling on his shirt front and rolling slowly
from side to side. "Damn the whole boiling of them. I'll
show em who's master."

At this moment "Good evening, Slode" said a brisk, close-clipped female voice. "I half-wondered if I'd run across you here. I don't expect you remember me."

He raised bleary eyes, and saw standing in front of him a handsome young woman, smartly but not loudly dressed and heavily made-up. She was regarding him with a half-smile, and before he could respond to her greeting, crossed quickly to the other side of the small table and sat down.

"Get me a drink, there's a good chap. Whisky, and plenty of it."

As she spoke she rapped sharply on the table, and when the pot-boy came ordered her own drink and jerked her head at Slode. "He's paying" she added.

He had now pulled himself up in his seat and collected sufficient wits to enable the real Evan to show himself.

"Look here" he began roughly. "What the devil is all this and what the hell do you mean by—"

"Pipe down, old fellow!" she said with easy assurance. "No need to bust your braces. I'm an old friend and you ought to be damned glad to see me. Does Lottie Heape mean anything to you after all these years?"

He studied her carefully and an ugly sneering grin spread over his face.

"I'll tell you just what Lottie Heape means to me—a sneaking little draggle-tail, who lost her head over an unlucky accident, welshed on her best friend and vamoosed. That's what. She owed me everything, did Lottie Heape, from the shift she stood up in to the bottles of cham her jew-boy gave her. I put her on the town, and it was my preserve to keep her there. So she skips, and does me out of my lawful takings. And now perhaps you'll tell me who gave you leave to call me Slode?"

"Oh, stow it, you bloody fool" she retorted. "What d'you want to be called? Your Majesty or something? And don't come the big bully over me. I'm no longer the kid you used to pull about. We can be useful to one another, if you'll behave like a human being and cut the imitation of a gorilla."

Q   481

His brief period of clarity and aggressiveness had passed and he was slipping back into confused self-pity. Her tart retaliation abashed him and he changed his tone.

"All right, all right" he mumbled. "No offence! Useful to one another, you say? I could do with something useful, but I'm damned if I know what. Where have you been all this time?"

She took an ivory case from her bag and extracted a cigarette.

"Light?" she queried.

Obediently he struck a fusee and stretched unsteadily across the table.

"Mind my glass. Thanks. Where have I been? Paris mostly. After poor Fleischmann died, I stayed with a girl I knew for a bit, until I hitched up with a decent sort of chap—scent-maker with a factory at Rouen. We were together a couple of years, living out there. Then we both thought we'd like a change, and I went to Paris."

"On the game?"

"More or less. But my idea was to go into management —chuck up the nun in favour of the abbess—and Paris is the place to learn the ropes. I learnt them."

"Why back to the Smoke?"

"Why d'you go to bed? 'Cause you're tired of sitting up. I got tired of Paris. Besides I want to do a good turn to one or two of my friends—you, for example."

He snorted and called for the pot-boy.

"Quite right" she said quickly. "I *will* have another."

With a scowl he gave the double order.

"And what kind of a good turn can you do me?" he demanded sulkily.

"About a dozen, by the look of you. I never saw such a dismal jimmy in all my born days. What's the trouble? Daddy's job too much for you?"

He almost bounced in his chair, and in the way she well remembered thrust his face as near to hers as the width of the table allowed. But instead of being truculent, his expression was one of astonishment, almost of alarm.

"What—what—" he spluttered. "What do you know of my guvnor or his business?"

She waited till the boy had served the drinks, took a slow mouthful of neat whisky, wiped her lips with a lace-edged handkerchief, drew at her cigarette and exhaled the smoke with leisurely satisfaction. At last, with the little secret smile —half-malicious, half-tantalising—with which she had first greeted him, she spoke.

"Sit back and take it easy. It's all quite simple. I know your old man's kicked the bucket. Never mind how I know; it's part of my job to keep track of people in the same line of trade. As to what I know of his business—that's first-hand. Does it surprise you to hear that I'm an 'old girl' of that delightful little Academy? Takes one back, doesn't it? Well, though I says it as shouldn't, I think I do Slode Senior credit, and I am sorry he is not alive to see it."

Evan had slumped back into his chair as instructed, and, while she was speaking, had stared at her in muddy amazement. His glassy eyes were wide open, his lower lip hung loose, and he was dribbling on to his cravat.

"I'll be ——" he gasped. "You were one of the guvnor's pullets? Then I must have seen you as a kid."

She nodded composedly.

"Oh yes, you saw me—or rather set your eyes on me, for you wouldn't notice one kid any more than another. I saw you anyway—once or twice. But we were never introduced, if you understand what I mean. I took damned good care of that."

"And after you went away, did you ever see the old man again?"

She lied serenely.

"Never."

"Then the day I took you to meet Fleischmann you knew the place already?"

"I recognised it, if that's what you're getting at. But I didn't know where it was, and I'd never been in that particular house before."

"Why the hell didn't you say so?"

"Why the hell should I? It was my affair, wasn't it?"

Again the flash of pugnacity faded, and he crumpled inward on himself. She half-turned toward him, put her elbows on the table, and said in a quiet friendly voice :

"Come on, Slode. Don't let's quarrel. Tell me what's your worry and see if we can't do something about it."

Her sympathetic and conciliatory tone so deepened his sense of ill-usage at the hands of fate that he became maudlin. At first disjointedly, then in a spate of stumbling words, he poured out his troubles. Much of what he said was incoherent; and as he gulped spirits all the while he was talking, he was not long in becoming wholly incomprehensible. But she let him maunder on, making condoling noises at intervals, and only when he dithered into comatose silence, did she attempt to speak.

"Poor old fellow. What a time you are having! Now you are going to drink a cup of really hot strong coffee and take a cab home."

The coffee partially sobered him, so that he became temporarily clear-headed but very sleepy. A hansom was fetched and she accompanied him downstairs to where the cab was waiting.

"Now remember! We meet here tomorrow" she said "and I'll have thought over what you've told me. I could make one or two suggestions right away, but you must get to bed and they can wait. It's understood then—tomorrow about the same time? Good night."

Two days after she had accosted Slode in the corner of Mariotti's, Lottie summoned the committee and announced that, so far, she had succeeded. She was severely practical, and showed no sign of misgiving. Indeed she seemed to be enjoying herself. After summarising their first talk she went on:

"I thought he might not turn up the next evening, and if he had not done so, it would have been necessary to start all over again. But I know from experience that however tight a fellow may be—short of being under the table—if you can jerk him sober for a few minutes at the end, he will remember next morning what was said at that moment, though likely as not he'll have forgotten most of what went before. As in this case. Slode remembered we were to meet and that I, in my capacity as a madam of Parisian experience, was to give him advice. He's in a nice mess, trying to run that place, and as he told me more of his difficulties than he realises, I can understand that advice might be very welcome.

"The upshot is that I go to Larne Circle by special invitation in three days' time. To put it further away might have made him suspicious, so you must look sharp with your final arrangements. I am supposed to have business of my own to attend to during the three days.

"Slode's worst problem at the moment is his matron—so there *are* kids there still. I talked to him like an elder sister last night, telling him that women get attacks of nerves and feel so wretched they hardly know what they are saying. I said the poor woman was probably run down and over-tired, and that if he spoke to her kindly and told her to take a week off, she'd probably come back a different person. I said that I would take her place while she was away, as well as help him with his other worries.

"Now listen carefully. The big house in the Circle—the one we want—backs on to the canal. The men Box sent along by boat the other day to get their bearings confirm that the little wharf is still there. The public way to the wharf is down steps at the side of the house; but there is a door at the very bottom of the house which opens straight on to the wharf. The old man used it sometimes to get inconvenient pupils away by water. At an agreed hour— or as near to it as I can—I shall unlock and unbolt that door. Then I shall hurry to the top of the building, at the back of which there used to be—and it can hardly have been moved —a roof-playground for the children. A wall shuts in this playground from the canal side, but it is not so high that a grown person can't reach the top. Over that wall I shall fling a table-cloth or something white, and that will be the signal that Slode is carrying on the business and that the door below is open. Whoever you decide are to be hidden ready in the barge must then make hell-for-leather for the wharf, in at the door, up the stairs and deal with whatever gets in their way as they think fit. Meantime the peelers will close in on the Circle and, I suppose, beat on the main door in the name of the law. That's for them to work out; but they *must* be on the tick, and you'll need some scheme for getting the news of the signal to them without a moment's delay." She paused. "And that, I think, is about all—except that I'm as dry as a dusty floor. D'you think you could spring a slosh of whisky, Mr Langrish?"

"That I can!" cried Toby, jumping to his feet. "And, if I may say so, it's a pleasure to serve such a well-plucked un!"

TOWARDS THE END OF March Mrs Barnett broke down under the strain of years of overwork, and within a few days was seriously ill. The vicar was beside himself; and the few helpers in the parish—men and women, of whom Hetty was the youngest and most recent—were confronted with a sudden and alarming increase of toil and responsibility. It would have been impossible for Mervyn to have chosen a more welcome moment to arrive for his holiday-weeks of social work; and almost overnight he was up to the eyes in duties of diverse kinds. No one had time to instruct him; he was given an assignment, and left to get such results as he could.

And then one morning, when he came to the vicarage for his orders for the day, he was handed Matt Merton's letter, forwarded by the Agency to Lashwater and thence sent on again. Throughout a twelve-hour day of multifarious activity, he kept the strange summons at the back of his mind. It must be concerned with the mystery of his father's death. He clearly recalled Merton's promise; but during the years since it had been given had resigned himself to the fact that nothing more would ever be known. Now the tragedy had suddenly loomed up again, and he felt simultaneously a devouring curiosity to hear what Merton had to say and a strong reluctance to be dragged back into the sinister shadows of the past. Also he was needed in Whitechapel. Amateur though he was, unqualified—save by enthusiasm, natural common-sense, good humour and a powerful body —for the manifold and baffling labours to which he was being set, he was another pair of arms and legs, another self-reliant being to be given charge of unruly boys or to discipline a rowdy drunk. If he went elsewhere now, he would be badly missed by others and shamed in his own conscience. Also he was near Hetty, caught glimpses of her several times a day, and usually managed to have half an hour's quiet talk with her over a cup of tea, late in the evening when finally the work was done. This last reason for his reluctance to become involved elsewhere in a problem of any kind seemed to him the best reason of all.

On this evening—the evening of Matt's letter—he broached the subject immediately the two of them were seated, giving her the letter to read and, while she read, preparing what he should say.

She handed him back the sheet of paper with a puzzled frown.

"I don't understand what it means. Who is this Merton?"

Briefly he outlined the facts of the matter, and continued:

"I have never spoken to you about my father since we met again. It is not your trouble and I did not wish to make you sad. But now I have to decide what to do. This chap gives no hint of what he wants to tell me, but he writes urgently and he didn't strike me as a man who'd get excited over nothing. I feel I *ought* to go; but, oh Hetty, I don't want to leave here! I might never have got the letter, doubly sent on like this. I want to stay here as long as I can and do what I can for these poor devils. And I want to be with you. What do you say?"

"That you must go instantly—tomorrow morning first thing—to see Mr Merton. When you know what's up, there'll be time to consider the next move. Of course you must go, Mervyn; and I'll be here when you come back— that I promise you—and gladder than ever to see you."

She was out at Forest Gate all the next afternoon, deputising as best she might for her absent chief, and did not see Mervyn till he came in from taking a boxing-class at about nine o'clock. He was smiling all over his face and hailed her with schoolboy jubilation.

"Oh, Hett, you've no idea! Such a jamboree! I saw Mr Merton and there's a party of stalwarts going to storm a

488

kind of crooks' castle somewhere in north London and give
the ruffians the biggest walloping ever and I can go with
them!"

"For mercy's sake" pleaded Hetty "begin at the beginning
and stop for breath just now and again. I haven't a notion
what you're talking about."

He burst out laughing.

"I'm awfully sorry. How should you? But I'm so on
tiptoe I hardly know what I'm saying. Now I'll get a firm hold
of myself and go through it slowly from beginning to end."
When the account of the morning's interview was finished
he said: "And the grand thing about it is that the whole
spree won't take more than half a day, so I shan't miss much
time here and can give you a hair-raising first-hand report
the moment I get back."

She had watched and listened to him with delight in his
delight and with fond amusement at his boyish exuberance.
He was so sweet when he threw himself about in his chair
and waved his hands and grinned and twinkled with sheer
excess of vitality. But her prudent feminine mind had
reservations.

"You'll be careful, Mervyn? Won't it be dangerous?"

"Rather! I should jolly well hope so. What's the fun in
giving a cad a hiding if he doesn't fight back?"

"And it's all connected with—with what you said yesterday?"

He nodded, suddenly sobered.

"I can't tell you exactly how; but these bouncers belong
to the same crowd that drove the guvnor over the edge, and
it's prime of Mr Merton to let me help settle their hash."

"Oh Mervyn, do take care! Suppose you got hurt. . . .
You'll carry a weapon of some sort I hope?"

"The nattiest little knobstick you ever saw, my dear—
perfect balance and a hard round blob on the end. Swish,
swish, ping! Thank you, sir. Next please. Oh, there I go
again, like a fly in a glue-pot! Hetty, you adorable little
bundle of caution, I'm so excited I could hug you!"

"Well" she said "you don't seem to be controlling yourself

489

in most respects at the moment, so why make an exception of that?"

He did not immediately take her meaning; then, with a long "oh-h", pulled her to her feet and folded her tightly in his arms. A few seconds later he was kissing her mouth with long slow tender kisses, which ceased abruptly when he realised what he was doing. He released her and stood staring, a picture of contrite bewilderment.

"I say" he stuttered "I'm terribly sorry. . . . I don't know what came over me. . . . Please, Hetty, forgive me. . . . That wasn't the kind of hug you meant. . . ."

"Oh, yes it was" said Hetty softly, her eyes shining and full of laughter. "Exactly the kind."

Matt's connections among the police, and his reputation as a man whose nose for hidden crime had never yet betrayed him, made it possible for the assault on Larne Circle to be fully prepared within the short time available. Officialdom demurred at the advance-guard of volunteers, but yielded when confronted with Box of the Jolly Bargee and his experiences of the sentinel system which kept the Circle informed of the approach of strangers.

"But we can take no responsibility, Mr Merton, for anything which may happen to your friends. And no fire-arms, mind you, of any kind! If there's shooting to be done, we do it."

To a regulation canal-barge was attached a covered row-boat, large enough to accommodate half a dozen persons, and with oars shipped. Barge and trailer would be towed to an agreed point just short of Larne wharf, where the row-boat would cast off and would lie under the bank until the signal was given. The horse and barge would plod on their way, and to anyone who might chance to see them pass, appear a normal specimen of canal traffic. Opposite the place chosen for the dropping of the row-boat was a timber-yard, with neat stacks of sawn timber, one of them of considerable height. This tower of timber was easily climbed, and commanded, not only the back of Slode's house, but also an entry to the southward just clear of the outer perimeter of the Circle, in which a police-sentry would be stationed. A signal from the timber-yard to this sentry that the white cloth was showing would be passed on from sentry to sentry, and set the police-cordon rapidly converging on the Circle from every direction.

The row-boat, when it started on its journey from the neighbourhood of Box's tavern, would carry, crouched under its tarpaulin roof, Merrick, Mervyn Crocker, George the cellarman and two bargees. Two other professionals would man the main barge, contrive the cast-off and proceed imperturbably in the direction of Kingsland Basin. Matt undertook to climb the timber-stack and, lying full length in an interstice between two rafters of the topmost layer, to await the coming of the boat and the moment for handing on the signal. "I am too old" he said "to storm redoubts, even if they are only a basement door. I should slow down the whole adventure." Toby and the waiter from the Marigold undertook the nerve-racking job of strolling, in the manner of ordinary citizens gone astray, through the approaches to the Circle and, if possible, right across it and out at the other side. It was hoped that this manœuvre would draw the attention of the enemy sentinels and focus it inward, while the police were taking up their positions and the raiding-party preparing to make their dash for the wharf.

The operation was timed for half-past five, when dusk would be at hand, but there would still be sufficient daylight for inter-communication between the attackers. The morning of the appointed day brought traditional early-April weather —a fresh breeze, intervals of sunshine and sudden drenching showers; but as time wore on, the wind strengthened and heavier cloud piled over London from the west. The conspirators wished one another luck, and sought their various stations.

It was the second day of Lottie's installation in the house

491

of Evan Slode. She had chosen the second day for the all-important venture, because she needed to be familiar with the geography of the building and also in order to lull any suspicions Slode and his henchmen might still have. She wished to show her readiness to tackle forthwith some of the problems of re-organisation which were the ostensible reasons for her presence. On the other hand, she had advised against delaying action beyond the second day, on the ground that, while she felt fairly confident of keeping Slode himself on the premises while they were discussing preliminaries of reform, she feared that, once she had convinced him of her capacity to clear up his most urgent muddles, he would gladly leave her to it and go west on more congenial business.

She needed all her nerve to go through the twenty-four hours before the crisis came. She found half a dozen youngsters, of various ages between eight and fifteen, cooped in a much more restricted section of the building than that in which she and her twenty-odd companions had passed their time of schooling. This closer confinement was in part a natural consequence of the fall in the number of pupils; but partly also it exemplified the extent to which Evan had thought fit to depart from his father's methods. Lottie had an hour, immediately on her arrival, in which to make the acquaintance and ask questions of the Matron proper. This woman, who now that she was off for a week's rest and change was amiability itself, told her *locum* that Mr Slode disliked the noise the children made, and would no longer give them the run of most of the house, as his father had done. He made no attempt to know them or to distinguish them as individuals. Indeed he hardly saw them until the moment came for launching one or another on her career, when he handed her over as one hands a parcel over a counter, interested in nothing but the settlement of his account. "I could've cried sometimes" the Matron said "to think of the pains the old guvnor took to put the kid at ease with er new mistress and suit the one to the other. After all, you're dealing with flesh and blood, ain't you? And it stands to reason that uman beings ain't all alike." Lottie was careful to make no comments, but inwardly she relished this glimpse of the greedy stupidity of the creature now doomed to destruction.

The children's quarters were at the top of the house, and their only playground now was that on the roof. One of her first tasks was to secure this playground against interruption. This she did by re-opening, as a great treat, the central courtyard on the ground-floor, extorting Slode's consent by pointing out that this courtyard was partially roofed, and that in showery weather the girls could have air and exercise without getting wet and catching cold. He grumbled a little; but when she reminded him that health and looks were a large part of his victims' market value, he sullenly agreed.

Lottie had no difficulty in surveying the roof-area from which her signal must be given. No one except the youngsters and their keeper ever went up there; and now that the former could excitedly enjoy the unfamiliar spaces of the courtyard below, Lottie could choose her own time to explore and to prepare. She found on the inside of the wall above the canal two iron brackets which had at one time carried a short ladder, kept up there for the convenience of access to the gabled portion of the roof and, when not in use, slung below the parapet. To one of those the table-cloth could be hitched.

The afternoon dragged intolerably. Closeted with Evan on the first floor, and forced to concentrate on plans and personalities each one of which recalled some incident of the past and set her raging, she had to maintain an air of hard efficiency. He had a clock on the mantelpiece. Now the hands crept round with infuriating slowness; now—if she forgot to watch them—they jumped five minutes, and set her heart beating lest she miss the vital hour. Outside the wind was whistling round the desolate curves of Larne Circle, and the boughs of the big plane-tree creaked and rattled.

Suddenly, at about five-twenty, a bell rang. There came a noise of footsteps, and a man put his head round the door.

"Strangers" he barked, and disappeared. Here and there about the house could be heard the noise of shutters being released and made ready for instant closing.

Lottie felt as though her heart had turned to water. She could have no knowledge of her friends' detailed time-table, only the moment for her signal. What had happened? Were they ahead of time or was the clock wrong? In fact this first alarm had been provoked by the ambling appearance in the outer Circle of Toby and his companion, who were not destined to get further than the archway through which they had hoped to pass. There they were challenged with gruff civility, and compelled to ask the way to some imaginary destination. The questioner feared they must re-trace their steps. Their way lay in the other direction.

Slode's attention had been for a moment distracted by the intrusion of the lock-up man, and she managed to glance at the little watch pinned to her breast. There was no mistake about the time. The moment was at hand.

Affecting dismay at the disturbance, she jumped to her feet.

"I must go and fetch those kids in" she said hurriedly. "They may be scared and the weather is getting wild."

He nodded absently, for he was listening for further sounds or indications of danger. She ran down to the ground-floor and along the passage leading to the basement stairs. One of the servants was in the hall; but he knew this strange woman was in charge of the children and that they were playing in the yard. He guessed she was hurrying to collect them. The door into the yard faced down the passage from the far end, the top of the basement stairs was round a corner to the right. The first risk—would the man see the way she went? In that instant a second bell rang out and the servant had more important things to think of. Behind and above her the house was loud with the clang of shutters thrown violently to and barred, with the rasp of the front-door bolts roughly shot, with the trampling of feet on the upper floors. She darted to the right and down the stairs to the wharf door. Back with the bolts, double-turn back with the key— all oiled in preparation and tolerably quiet. Up the stairs again; into the yard; summon the children and shepherd them upstairs, keeping in their midst so as to be unmistakably busy with her job; hurry them with reassuring words into their own quarters, bidding them stay quietly till she came to them; lock them in; up one more flight and on to the deserted playground.

The table-cloth, thrust out of sight in a corner, was quickly knotted to the bracket. Bunching the rest of it into a ball, she flung it over the parapet and fled back toward the door giving access to the house. The job was done. She felt a great sob of relief rising in her throat.

But suddenly, with a sharp clap like a bellying sail, the table-cloth, caught by a swirl of wind round the house-corner, came cracking back at full-speed, hovered a moment over the flats and then flopped in a crumpled heap in the angle of the wall. For a second, as she watched it fall, Lottie hesitated. Surely it had hung down long enough to be seen? Surely it had uncoiled as she threw it from her and, in un-coiling, spoken its message? But probability was not enough: she must make certain. Everything depended on the complete and accurate fulfilment of her mission. She ran to where the cloth lay, snatched it up and, this time to secure display beyond a doubt, put one foot on the bracket and hoisted herself so that she could lie along the wall and, after dropping the cloth, hold it against the outer brickwork with her hands. "I will hold it while I count ten" she told herself. "Then they *must* see it."

The second alarm bell, which meant serious danger, had called the garrison of Larne Circle to their battle-posts. Crouching in a gulley, on the roof of the house separated from Slode's headquarters only by the steps leading down to the wharf, was an armed man. His alert eye was caught by a figure bunched on the wall which enclosed the flat space of the Big House. He could not do more than glimpse the figure, nor see clearly what it was doing, for owing to the curve of the Circle the gulley in which he was hiding ran diagonally and had been chosen because it commanded the

fortress' central space. But he could not mistake the white
flash of the table-cloth as it whipped to and fro in the wind,
and instinct told him this was no moment for flying white
or indeed any other colour. Shots from below confirmed
that something serious was afoot. Better be on the safe side.
His rifle cracked.

The bullet struck Lottie in the groin. She was lying
astride the wall, face downwards, holding the cloth with both
hands tightly against the ramp. The stab of searing pain
jerked her sideways. Her balance went, she rolled outwards,
and crashed on to the wharf sixty feet below. As she fell
she clutched desperately at the table-cloth, which came apart
at the knot and fell with her.

Even in that brief moment before the wind had first caught
the cloth and flung it back on to the roof, the signal had
been seen. Matt, from his place in the timber, had set the
force of the law in motion; from the row-boat the four
watchers, headed by Mervyn, had scrambled on to the wharf
and dashed for the basement door. Merrick came last, and
had just followed the others into the darkness of the house
when he heard a rifle-shot and, immediately afterward, a
horrible crunching thud. He stopped short, looked back
and for an instant stood paralysed with horror. Then,
oblivious of the sounds of conflict which came confusedly
from the other side of the building, ran to where the body
lay. She was stone dead, with a broken neck and limbs
unbearably twisted and shattered. Merrick set his teeth.
Having gently released the torn sheet from her fingers and
spread it over the poor mangled corpse, he knelt bareheaded
on the rough boards by her side and covered his face in
anguished prayer.

Inside the house matters moved quickly to a climax. As
the attackers from the wharf reached the top of the basement
steps, the police were battering down the front door. At
the foot of the main stairs, with his back to the passage
leading toward the courtyard, stood the bulky figure of
Evan Slode. He had a revolver in his hand, and was watching

the timbers and hinges of the big door as they strained and cracked under the blows from without. Slode meant nothing to Mervyn. He knew only that a big man with a gun was waiting to shoot, would in all likelihood shoot any second, and must be stopped. No chance for his precious knobstick; he would never get near enough to use it without being heard. There was only one way. Gathering himself together, he launched himself into the flying tackle for which he was renowned on a dozen football fields. Slode received a violent blow just above the back of the knees, and fifteen stone of good living—plus all the bone and muscle his assailant possessed—hurtled violently to the floor. Slode's head struck a corner of the skirting, and he lay like a log. Mervyn snatched the revolver which had slithered across the hall and, with the bargees at his heels, sprinted up the stairs. George the cellarman was busy with a man who attempted a flank attack from a side room and soon regretted it. Upstairs there were only two men to be found. One threw up his hands, and was frog-marched downstairs by an ungentle barge-hand. The other showed fight, and there followed a brief shooting-match round the corners of a corridor before Mervyn's remaining ally, sent to explore, found the back-staircase and took the enemy in the rear.

Out in the Circle resistance was at an end, although one or two snipers, their ammunition exhausted, still hid among the roofs. Two policemen had been wounded, one severely. Of other casualties there were none more serious than scratches and bruises. A police-van removed the prisoners and the still unconscious Slode.

At this juncture Matt, very much out of breath, came hastening through the dusk.

"I got over the canal as quick as I could" he gasped. "Something terrible has happened—on the wharf. But first we must find the kids. They must be somewhere in the house."

He spoke rapidly to the police chief, who nodded and detailed two men to search the premises from top to bottom. Matt then turned to his friends.

"Merrick is with her" he said unsteadily. "Which way do we go?"

Mystified but awed by his manner, Mervyn, George and the two bargemen led the way back through the deserted house, down the basement stairs and on to the wharf. At the sound of their approach, Merrick stood up, hat in hand. Instinctively the newcomers bared their heads.

"She must have been killed instantly" said Merrick. "Poor, tragic, gallant creature! God rest her soul."

They stood in a desultory group, stunned by the sudden horror, abashed in the presence of the pitiful shrouded heap of what had been living flesh. For a minute or two there was no sound but the wail of the wind and the gentle plopping of water among the piles on which the wharf was built. Then Merrick pulled himself together.

"We must get her away. Shall we go for a conveyance or ourselves be pall-bearers and take her in the boat?"

Matt fought down tears of shame for his own lack of charity. 'She has cold eyes' he had said, 'harlot's eyes.' Cold eyes indeed!

"In the boat" he muttered, "with only friends about her. She never had any friends—until now."

"Please, sir" asked Mervyn timidly. "Who was she?"

"Her name" Merrick replied "was Lottie Heape."

The young man repeated the name in an undertone, and stood for a moment with bowed head. Then he looked up and turned in vague bewilderment from one man to the other. "Lottie Heape?" he whispered. "Lottie Heape? . . . I knew a girl called that . . . years ago . . . when I was a boy. . . ." Matt had a sudden impulse to tie the final knot. "Yes" he nearly said, "as a young girl she was in service with the late Mr Crocker of Lashwater in Surrey." But he checked himself. A vision of Paul Gladwin rose before his eyes. Paul, who had once sacrificed himself to save this lad, must be told of Lottie's greater sacrifice. Save by the merest chance the two episodes were wholly unconnected. Let them remain so. The boy had almost forgotten, and must quite forget. Spare him the knowledge, as Paul would wish.

"If so, she was someone else" Matt said indifferently. "It's probably not an uncommon name."

Then, with a deep sigh, he braced himself for the ordeal of the homeward journey.

It was now nearly dark. On the little wharf, under a crumpled sheet which gleamed pale in the dusk, lay the mortal remains of Lottie Heape. Away to the west, through gaps in the cloud-wrack as it raced before the wind, glowed the forlorn and tattered remnants of a stormy sunset.

THE END

499

P   O   S   T   S   C   R   I   P   T

APART FROM A FEW deliberate embellishments (for example
Larne Circle and its creator are inventions) the London
topography of this story is as correct as I can make it.

The reader is asked to bear in mind that at the latest date
to which the tale runs—that is to say the year 1879—although
the area of London under the supervision of the Metropolitan
Police was about 120 square miles and the population one of
$3\frac{1}{2}$ millions, the amenities of the city and the chances of
interaction between the various classes, occupations and ways
of living which constituted it, were proportionately far more
restricted than in our own day.

The Metropolitan Inner Circle, with its few outward
extensions, was the only means of urban travel by rail, while
surface communications (private and hackney carriages apart)
were limited to certain tramways in the suburban fringe and
in the central region to some sixty lines of horse-omnibus,
privately operated and frequently in competition over the
same routes.

London's street-plan was in most districts haphazard, complex and unsuited to through traffic. One consequence of this
was that the several quarters of the town were isolated from
one another, and that a community of one kind might live
within a half-mile of another very different community, yet
remain unfamiliar with, and almost unaware of it. A second
consequence was that the areas of popular resort—whether
fashionable, social, official, professional, commercial, pleasure-
seeking or dissolute—were few and circumscribed, so that
chance encounters between folk of a similar sort were much
more frequent than is the case nowadays. Outside these
crowded areas, life and manners were left more or less to

their own devices, the strict surveillance of a maze of streets, mostly poorly lighted, being virtually impossible.

Such real episodes as form part of the background of the story have been slightly adapted to meet its requirements. Thus, no second man of title was involved in the case of Boulton and Park, and I am very doubtful whether the Moonlight Mission was carried on as late as 1878. But where historical fact *is* introduced, it is basically correct and properly dated. Certain details of legal and financial procedure may be queried by purist experts; but I am advised that what is made to happen could conceivably have happened at the date in question, and my story demanded such liberties as have been taken with technical probability.

I am indebted to friends and acquaintances for specialist help at several points in the narrative. Their assistance need not be particularised, but I must express my grateful thanks to: Mr C. P. L. Anderson of Barclays Bank, Mr J. R. Brown of the Ecclesiastical Commissioners, Mr Edward Last-Smith, Messrs Stanley and Harold Rubinstein, Mr Robert H. Shelton, Mr E. Fletcher Trew, Mr Carroll A. Wilson of New York City, and Mr William T. Gaynor of the New York Central Railroad System.

M. S.

Printed in Great Britain
at Hopetoun Street, Edinburgh,
by T. and A. Constable Ltd.
Printers to the University of Edinburgh